KT-394-943

PRIVILEGE

MARY ADKINS

HODDER

First published in Great Britain in 2020 by Hodder & Stoughton
An Hachette UK company

This paperback edition published in 2020

1

Copyright © Mary Adkins 2020

The right of Mary Adkins to be identified as the Author
of the Work has been asserted by her in accordance with
the Copyright, Designs and Patents Act 1988.

All rights reserved. No part of this publication may be reproduced, stored
in a retrieval system, or transmitted, in any form or by any means without
the prior written permission of the publisher, nor be otherwise circulated
in any form of binding or cover other than that in which it is published and
without a similar condition being imposed on the subsequent purchaser.

All characters in this publication are fictitious and any resemblance
to real persons, living or dead, is purely coincidental.

A CIP catalogue record for this title is available from the British Library

Paperback ISBN 978 1 473 67337 3
eBook ISBN 978 1 473 67340 3

Printed and bound in Great Britain by Clays Ltd, Elcograf S.p.A.

Hodder & Stoughton policy is to use papers that are natural, renewable
and recyclable products and made from wood grown in sustainable
forests. The logging and manufacturing processes are expected to
conform to the environmental regulations of the country of origin.

Hodder & Stoughton Ltd
Carmelite House
50 Victoria Embankment
London EC4Y 0DZ

www.hodder.co.uk

For my parents, who loved us enough to want the world for us

CARTER COLLEGE

Academic buildings and hospital

The Student Center

The Rooster

Wiggins Library

NORTH CAMPUS

ΠΚΑ

ΑΤΟ

"FRAT ROW"

MAIN QUAD

The Bridge

First-Year Dorms

SOUTH CAMPUS

Copyright © 2019 Springer Cartographics LLC

PRIVILEGE

Y033001

PRIVILEGE

ALSO BY MARY ADKINS

When You Read This

That Girl

BY P. K. FOX

If you blew her up and shared her,
she'd disappoint.
Pixels and haze.
She won't survive an email
with the word "res."
You'd open her, agonize, wonder
how to clean up her fuzziness.
You know what's funny? How often
I see a sunrise and think it's a sunset.
Like I forgot what time of day it is, or maybe
the time of day forgets to bug me
for a minute and I see
the beginning and the end
of light.
Even she, reduced to a thumbnail,
has her side to tell.
For all that time she was awake,
she was a woman.

PART I

Hope

Thursday, August 24

Welcome to Carter! 10 Pieces of Advice for First-years

by the Irreverent Rooster

Cock-a-doodle-doo! It's O-week[a] in these parts, and campus is filled with brand spankin' new Roosters arriving en masse, unloading Teslas,[b] Priuses,[c] and Dodges.[d]

Allow me to introduce myself. I'm the Irreverent Rooster.

Today on tap: my top 10 pieces of advice to make the most out of your first year at this wondrous institution.

1. Read my column.
2. Don't bother trying to figure out who I am. I am all of us and none of us.
3. Really, anything to do with me is probably a good idea.
4. The Rooster serves decent coffee, but stay away from the croissants.[e]
5. As we know, this campus is adorned with many gargoyles. Be sure to look up next time you pass the entrance to Stoling.[f] When you do, you will notice a set of gargoyles perched above it. These are—*unmistakably*—recent additions.
6. Scream in horror.
7. Nope, you are not hallucinating. These are real, and, yes, they are gargoyles *with real human faces*.
8. Who are these people/gargoyles? These sapien-goyles? These garg-hominums?
9. Why on earth are they in modern clothing? What are they doing hanging over the entrance to a building? What was this column about again?

10. Mojito, at the intersection of Beech and Smith streets off South Campus, has the best tacos—and you're only likely to get trampled by a Big Boss[9] if it's after 1 a.m.

Welcome to Carter, where the fraternities still rule, the gargoyles still mutate, and I'll be here every week to make fun of all of it.[h]

Cock-a-doodle-doo!

Signing off,
Your Anonymous Humor Columnist

Glossary

a. O-WEEK: Orientation week; get your mind out of the gutter.

b. TESLA: Driven by your parents, who are more successful than you will ever be.

c. PRIUS: Driven by your parents, who, wishing they were more successful than you will ever be, have settled for dumping epic pressure on you.

d. DODGE: Driven by your parents, who filled out a FAFSA.

e. CROISSANTS FROM THE ROOSTER: Stale as Professor Henrick's adherence to the rational choice theory of economics.

f. STOLING: New dorm being constructed on main west quad because Carter loves to find ways to spend rich donors' money.

g. BIG BOSS: Frat guy in boat shoes and madras shorts who grew up in Manhattan and summers with the Kennedy heirs. Pastimes: keg stands and light rape.

h. IT: You. To make fun of you.

Annie

My story of Tyler Brand begins the day I met him, the first week of my second fall at Carter. I have a vivid memory of that day, no doubt in part because my senses were heightened by the fresh air on my legs, the jolt of exposing my scarred flesh for the first time in years.

About my legs—my saving grace, or they were supposed to be. "I prayed for you to get your dad's legs, and you did," my mom told me repeatedly, as if she'd forgotten she'd already said it. I was told I'd be a runner, that I perhaps would be very tall, a basketball player or a supermodel. I was told I'd grow into them, that they'd drive boys crazy, that I would one day be able to pull off *all* kinds of shoes, not just universally flattering styles and heel heights.

And then, just as I was growing into them, they got fried. The summer after eighth grade I was sitting in our backyard when the grill tipped over and the blanket beneath me caught fire. Three square feet of tissue—two and a half from a donor and six inches from my own left butt cheek—were grafted onto my left calf and shin, my right knee and inner thigh.

After the chaos and panic subsided, I was slow to grasp how changed I was in others' eyes. At first, their sadness confused me. Didn't they understand that the bad part was over? I'd survived being on fire.

My toes, hands, breasts—I'd grasped before the accident that these were subpar. Scars, I'd thought, were different—they weren't a part of *me*. They were more like an accessory, only unflattering; you may not like someone's earrings, but you wouldn't call her ugly for wearing them. My scars hadn't been generated by my body; they were acquired from without, my backyard mishap's I WAS HERE.

When they didn't disappear or even fade, however, and when they, in fact, darkened and hardened, their tough and reddened permanence allowing me ample time to observe and learn, I discovered that they were nothing like earrings or stamps. Gasps, grimaces, slack jaws—these were the reactions my legs drew, the ones that were supposed to score baskets and drive boys mad. Jeans became the only bottom I'd wear. Parties, summers at the pool and beach, graduation—I even wore my jeans to church on Sundays after threatening to become an atheist if my mom insisted on a dress.

When I googled "how to live with burn scars," the Internet told me to learn to make burn jokes. Instead, I adopted what would become my strategy for the next seven years: I didn't acknowledge that I had legs. From the waist down, I might as well not have existed.

My hometown of Pineville makes "small" sound like an overstatement. We have a Red Lobster, a desolate shopping mall, and a couple of crumbling churches dubbed historic landmarks by the state of Georgia. My county's nickname—on a sign as you enter on Highway 280—is "Almost gone but not forgotten." There were forty-five people in my graduating high school class, six of them with the last name Cooper.

But even small towns have their social pressures. What I didn't realize as a teenager was that my scars were a mixed blessing. Being so visibly flawed freed me to an extent from believing my looks could be my salvation. Excluded from the category of "pretty girl," I was permitted to make the case for my personhood in other ways. I took up bassoon. I won contests in the city, then in the state. I was flown to Washington, DC, to play for the president with other high school kids as part of the National Youth Orchestra. Annie Stoddard, bassoonist, burn victim, denim obsessed. That my body was invisible at best and hideous at worst spared me in a way. I watched friends starve, purge, cut themselves, cry over low Insta likes. But not me. Why bother when no one is watching? Blessed are the plain.

AND THEN THE impossible happened. I got into Carter.

Carter had been a fantasy ever since National Youth Orchestra camp. The first flute, president of her private school senior class in Michigan, told me she planned to go there like her older sister, whose college friends were so smart even their parents didn't know what they were talking about when they came home and debated around the dinner table. Although it was only two states away, in North Carolina, not a single person from my high school had ever matriculated there, per my guidance counselor, Ms. Flo. When I'd told her I planned to apply, she'd raised an eyebrow.

"Wanna maybe focus on UGA? You could probably get into the honors college," she slurred (we were pretty sure she was always drunk), sipping from the lipstick-stained straw in the bottomless, twenty-four-ounce travel mug she never put down.

But Ms. Flo underestimated the value of being a bassoonist in a world of cellists and violinists. Not only was I admitted to Carter, I was even offered a scholarship—three-quarters tuition. My parents, who had emptied my college fund for an emergency gallbladder operation for my brother a year earlier, both cried.

"But how will we afford the rest of the tuition? And room and board?" I asked, flipping over the letter as if there were more money hiding on the back.

"We'll figure it out," my dad said, reaching proudly for the letter, although he'd already read it. (He would, by Christmas, begin five years of weekends tutoring SAT—six hours on Saturdays and three on Sundays—to cover the remaining eighteen thousand annually so as not to saddle me with student loan debt.)

Word spread quickly through my high school. Younger students I'd only known in passing stopped me in the hall to offer their congratulations.

"That's Annie Stoddard. She got into Carter," my calculus teacher told the new AP Bio teacher in the hall between third and fourth periods.

"Girl, you must be wildly smart!" he said and winked. I repeated it under my breath the rest of the day, liking the way that the word *wildly* felt on my tongue. I'd sailed through high school making easy As, but I'd never entertained the idea of being especially "smart" in any world bigger than Pineville High.

The week before graduation, my twelfth-grade English teacher, Mr. Royles, sheepishly handed me an article he'd clearly printed from the Internet entitled FORTY MUST-READ CLASSICS. "Here's what you should have read in high school," he said. Over the summer I made my way through four of them: *The Great Gatsby, The Remains of the Day, Mrs. Dalloway,* and *Moby-Dick,* the last of which took all of August. Finishing it made me as proud as I'd ever been of anything.

My first year at Carter, my life consisted of classes, orchestra rehearsal, and my work-study job at the campus bookstore. Some of the orchestra kids hung out on weekends, but I didn't join them. When I wasn't studying, I was with my best friend, Matty, and my roommate, Samantha, the first person I ever heard describe herself as being "from the Bay Area." We spent Saturday nights watching documentaries that introduced me to the nuances of white supremacy, the most endangered victims of climate change, and capitalism's dark underbelly. No moment of my time at Carter was unchallenging. By May I felt changed, fundamentally unlike the Annie who'd proudly completed *Moby-Dick* the previous August. I'd joined the Campus Progressives; I'd been to my first protest; I'd swapped my English major for psychology, having realized Mr. Royles had, in fact, understated my ill-preparedness for college lit coursework; I was by far the least read in my lit class, while my Psych 101 professor had drenched my papers in praise. Whether I was particularly interested in the subject didn't seem all that relevant.

I would study endless hours in the dorm's reading room, watching through the window as other students tossed footballs or lay gossiping in the sun. I wanted to be like them but didn't know how. What I knew how to do was hunker down; what I knew how to do was to cover up and stay inside. I was making As, and I was lonely. Even at Carter, just as at Pineville High, I was the smart girl with burns.

Then, one afternoon in late February, my orchestra conductor told me that a local parent was in search of someone to teach her son bassoon, and she was offering sixty-five dollars an hour—an outrageous sum to me. What's more, little Danny Yeager's parents wanted me to meet with him three times a week. The dutiful twelve-year-old didn't miss a single lesson. By late May, when I returned home for the summer after finals, I had made over two thousand dollars.

There was no question what I wanted to do with it.

The dermatologist in Atlanta recommended a series of pulsed-dye laser treatments over the course of the summer, assuring me that we could schedule them so that come fall, my legs would look better. My summer job as a nanny for a newborn meant I spent most of the day sitting around in someone else's house anyway.

"We can't improve the scars 100 percent," he said, "but 70 percent isn't out of the question." Treatment of the magnitude I required cost over ten thousand dollars, but miraculously he offered to write off 80 percent, given that the lasers were a new model, and thus I was going to be a before-and-after model, which terrified me a little, but he promised not to show my face or use my name. I was able to pay the two grand out of pocket from my bassoon money.

I lay on the paper-wrapped table as the lasers pricked their way along the edges of my skin grafts, sounding like the snapping of rubber bands. After a cluster of snaps, an intern in a white jacket would lift a hose and spray my skin with a burst of cold air. You'd think the smell of flesh burning might have raised memories of the accident, but it didn't. This time on the medical cot, I felt like a superhero being outfitted for her uniform.

The total process involved three treatments, spaced three weeks apart. Altogether it took twelve weeks, including the recovery periods, during which time the new wounds created by the lasers evolved from worse to better. With each round my legs were looking more normal than they had in years.

My parents were embarrassingly supportive. The day before I left to return to school, my mom and I were at the mall shopping for fall clothes. I was lighter—peach and gauzy in the places where before I'd been red and ropey; where shades of purple had jutted angrily from my flesh, smoothed patches of pink were stitched with a scarlet I could live with.

Walking along the clearance rack, I picked up things I wouldn't normally choose: a short dress, two pairs of shorts, and, on a lark, a turquoise leather miniskirt. I wasn't yet the girl who would wear a leather miniskirt, but I could see that I might be someday.

When she caught sight of the garments I'd pulled, my mother (a veteran coupon clipper who asked for a doggie bag at a restaurant if she had four green beans left on her plate) took them from my arms with a smile.

"I haven't tried them on yet!" I called after her as she made her way to the register, but she ignored me, handing the cashier her credit card before the woman had even scanned any tags. "You can try them on at home," she said.

We were both so full of hope as that summer drew to a close.

ON THAT FIRST Friday of the year, I stood in the closet of my gothic dorm room on the campus main quad, solely mine now that my first-year roommate, Samantha, had transferred to Stanford in mid-August, taking her violin and gum-chewing addiction and late-night computer glow with her. She'd never liked Carter; for her, a West Coast daughter of filmmakers, Carter was as confining as a straitjacket, and so, before even showing up for sophomore year, she'd abruptly changed plans. Room assignments having already been made, this left me with a coveted single room on Main Campus.

A gold mine.

"The *luck* of this!" my remaining friend, Matty, shrieked, throwing himself onto my bed. "I mean, of course, we'll miss Samantha, blah blah, but *will* we? You have a single. For free."

"Definitely not for free," I said from the closet.

"Fair," he called back.

Before me were mostly jeans and tanks, but under them, just next to my bassoon, was the shelf where I'd laid my new clothes: the sundress, the leather mini, and the pairs of still-tagged shorts.

I stripped off my black jogging pants and pulled on a pair of the shorts, ripping off the tag as I did, which felt like a new tier of commitment even though their return-by date had passed. I wrapped a dry towel around my torso and stepped into the room.

From my bed, leaning against the wall, Matty looked up from his laptop.

"What do you think?" I asked. I never asked Matty for fashion advice—that wasn't our dynamic. He asked *me* for fashion advice sometimes—especially when he would rope me into going with him to gay clubs our first year. But I had my uniform since I'd known him. On my end, there had been nothing to discuss.

"You should probably wear a shirt," he said.

I didn't take the bait. I turned away from him to face my full-length mirror. There were my legs.

"If you mean the shorts," Matty finally said—it was clear in his voice he'd known exactly what I'd meant—"I think it's about time you dressed for the weather. It's August in North Carolina. It only took you a year to figure that out."

I didn't move. He caught my eye in the mirror.

"You can do it," he said.

That was how it began.

Bea

By the fall of her senior year of high school, Bea had made some assumptions about what would happen next in her life. She assumed she would be premed and that after graduating from Miss Porter's, she'd join her closest friend, Lorn, at Vassar or Amherst or Dartmouth or, if they got lucky, maybe Harvard or Yale, where she would go into medicine, following in her mother's footsteps. An OB and surgeon turned hospital administrator, Bea's mom had spent Bea's childhood accumulating small, shiny statuettes with gold scrawl lauding her contribution to women's health. What other career could Bea possibly choose?

But then, in September of senior year, Bea's AP Government teacher, Mr. Canon, assigned a book called *Radical Justice*, by Lou Friedman, a criminal defense attorney and legal scholar whose high-profile work fighting capital punishment, along with his prolific, accessible writing on the topic, had garnered him widespread popularity in liberal circles. His book profiled five generations of men from the same black southern family, starting with the enslaved great-great-grandfather, followed by his descendants through Reconstruction, the Jim Crow era, and, finally, the 1990s, by which time the youngest man, in jail awaiting trial for larceny because he couldn't afford bail, had hung himself after serving two years. The charges were ultimately dropped. The man's imprisonment and suicide, Friedman argued, were emblematic of the deep systemic abuse of his family for over a century.

Friedman proposed a radical notion of justice in light of the country's historical mistreatment of black citizens: that government-sanctioned justice must be intentionally and wholly blind to retribution. To Lou Friedman, an acceptable definition of justice could be about only two things, lest it replicate black subordination: rehabilitating the offender and restoring the victim's sense of dignity. This was achievable through restorative justice. He argued an approach focused on reconciliation that was being adopted in pockets around the world.

Bea read the book in one sitting one October Thursday night, enamored of the author's idealistic tone and probing research. In what she found to be the most moving parts of the book, he told the stories of victims of heinous crimes who'd found, by working with their wrongdoers, a sense of resolution. The family of a woman killed after a break-in was moved to forgive a twenty-one-year-old perpetrator, who'd since become a woodworker and a playwright.

"I'm going to write about how he's Christ-like," Lorn had said after Bea had summarized the book for her—Lorn had not found it as compelling as Bea had and hadn't finished reading, which was causing her some difficulty with her two-page response paper.

"Did Christ write plays?" Bea asked.

"He was a woodworker," Lorn said. "Don't steal that."

Bea had not stolen the Jesus parallel but instead, on a lark, wrote her paper about Friedman himself. This book, along with his other ones that followed, had been a *New York Times* best seller. She'd discovered a feature about the book in which he'd pledged to donate his royalties from it to a nonprofit dedicated to criminal justice reform. But Bea wondered—and wrote her class response essay asking—why, as interested as he was in the ongoing, changing face of black subjugation for white gain, as illustrated by this particular family, hadn't he given *them* the money? Wasn't he himself enacting the dynamic he'd written about: a white man profiting off black experience, one more rung in the ladder? His pledge to donate royalty monies didn't much solve the problem, Bea argued, since it was to a nonprofit *he'd* chosen. A more cynical view might even be that he had ties, financial or otherwise, to the organization or that he'd made the "donation" more to protect his reputation than anything else, to avoid precisely the kind of critique Bea was making. She wrote her paper quickly, pleased with herself and high on her critical insight, and emailed it in a full day before it was due.

A week later, Mr. Canon announced a surprise: Dr. Friedman had been a schoolmate of his growing up and would be paying the class a visit.

Friedman—"Lou," as he introduced himself—looked younger than Bea expected. In his forties with a buzz cut, he opened his hands wide and chopped the air as he regaled the class with stories— of a recent trip to Rome to teach a course about the Italian judicial system to NYU undergrads studying abroad, of his new book in progress, and about a program at Carter University in North Carolina that he ran for students interested in justice.

Bea sat still, fixated. In the presence of this man, she felt as she had around her mother—as if she were bearing witness to a person who mattered. Being in his company made her want to be around him more, as if by staying close enough for long enough, the substance igniting him might rub off on her.

And yet she knew better. She'd discovered the fallacy of this notion upon her mother's passing two years earlier. Phaedra had vanished overnight—cardiac arrest in a seemingly healthy fifty-two-year-old woman—and, in addition to grief, Bea was surprised to encounter something else in the wake of Phaedra's death. An unmooring. An identity void. Scattered—not just her mind, but her selfhood. Stripped of association to her magnetic, larger-than-life mother, Bea felt aimless, a balloon unhinged from its bunch. As the months passed, she came to recognize that this had always been the case; she was always going to have to chart her own future. With a living parent, she had unknowingly viewed the world as a game. It had all felt like play.

She didn't know that Mr. Canon was going to share their papers with Dr. Friedman. She certainly didn't know that she would then have to face him. As she exited the classroom after his presentation, the man with friendly eyes stopped her.

"Bea?"

"Yes?" she said, startled.

"Your paper. Thank you for putting such thought into it." Then he gave her his card, and she hurried back to her dorm.

Later that day, she learned she'd won the National Science Award—only the sixth student from Porter's ever to do so. The headmistress made an announcement at lunch and had her pose for a picture holding a calculator by the fountain.

That night, she checked the school's Facebook page. Scrolling through the comments, she found that in addition to the chorus of "Congratulations!" and "Way to go, Bea!" were almost as many references to her mother.

"Your mother would be proud!"

"Following in her mother's footsteps!"

"Is there any question she's Phaedra's daughter? What a remarkable woman. May she rest in peace."

Irritated for a reason she couldn't identify, she closed the tab and reached for Dr. Friedman's card.

She opened a new email, entered his address into the "to" field, and began to type. That she didn't think he'd see the paper; that if she had known, she'd never have been so rude; that she'd loved hearing about his work, particularly about the Justice Scholars Program at Carter; that she'd googled it, and it looked intriguing, but that didn't look positive enough, so she changed it to "fascinating."

After sending it off, she went to bed.

By the next morning he'd replied, inviting Bea to New York for coffee.

AS THE TRAIN inched its way out of the station in Greenwich, where she was staying with Lorn's parents before taking Metro-North down to New York to meet with Dr. Friedman, Bea compiled a list of questions about the Justice Scholars Program he ran at Carter, mainly because she didn't want to show up with nothing to say. Her cursory online research about the program had provided some details. She knew that only ten to twelve first-years were admitted, that three to four of them were "scholars" and received partial tuition grants, that the program entailed a preset curriculum of first-year courses on the theme of justice, and that Dr. Friedman taught one of these courses.

What kind of time does the program leave for outside activities?
Does it help students obtain summer internships?

She'd closed her eyes. Bea didn't know why she found herself daydreaming about a school she'd never visited, a green campus she'd never laid eyes on. She pictured herself crossing the quad, a stack of books on criminal law in her arms. In the fantasy, no one knew her as Phaedra's daughter. She was a blank slate.

When she arrived at Johnny's, an old New York diner in the West Village, Dr. Friedman was already seated in a booth, his laptop open before him on the table.

"Bea, hi!" He shut it and slid it into a canvas satchel as she slipped into the seat across from him. "How was your trip down?"

"Smooth," she said. The commute from New England to Manhattan was familiar to her. In seventh grade, her mother had briefly worked in the city before they'd missed Boston too much and returned. They'd lived on the Upper East Side, by the park, and Phaedra had allowed Bea to take the train alone on weekends to visit her friends—all by herself, at twelve. She'd felt incredibly mature and had become fond of trains, found their timetables and rumbling and musty smell comforting.

Dr. Friedman ordered grilled chicken and cottage cheese from their aproned server. Bea ordered a blueberry muffin and a coffee.

"I meant to warn you, the coffee here is not good," he said.

Across the aisle, a table of four middle-aged men bickered loudly.

"I fuckin' told her—I—I—I fuckin' told her. . ." One of the men, determined to tell a story, was repeatedly being interrupted by his tablemates.

"Excuse me, miss!" another called to the server's back as she disappeared into the kitchen. "What, is she fucking milking the cow back there?" he said to his buddies.

"About the Justice Scholars Program," Bea said, trying to ignore the men. "I was wondering if it helps students with summer internships."

Dr. Friedman nodded and interlaced his large hands on the table. He leaned forward as he spoke, looking her in the eye. His attentiveness and openness calmed her.

"We encourage all of our students to find internships in criminal justice, but there's only one funded position that we're able to offer at the moment. It's with me in New York. Well, partly with me. You'd be working for the CJRI—that's the Criminal Justice Reform Institute, my organization. Over three months, you'd spend a month working with me on research, a month working with the advocacy group, and a month working with the direct services group. Last year's fellow is actually publishing his paper in the *Journal of Criminal Justice*. That's essentially unheard of for an undergrad. Law students don't even author publishable scholarship often. But Kyle is exceptional. His study on medicinal interventions and juvenile recidivism has already been cited in state law. Colorado. Can you believe it? He's starting at Columbia Law in the fall."

"Like, a judge referenced his paper?" Bea asked, astonished.

"Yes, ma'am."

"Wow," she said. "But that slot's just for one student."

He folded his hands.

"Funding is an eternal battle, my dear. Criminal justice is not the sexiest charity for philanthropists. People want to give to good poor people, not bad poor people." He chuckled. "You and I both know that systemic oppression gives rise to criminal behavior, plus the designation of 'criminal' loses its heft when you consider who defines it. Did you ever hear the saying that when the guy on top makes the rules, the guy on the bottom hasn't got a damn chance? Point is, growing a program like this one takes time. We're building. Slowly. My hope is that one of these days all of the scholars can have funded summers."

As her coffee and muffin arrived, Bea relished his phrasing—*you and I*. He'd included her! She tore her muffin in half and picked off the sugary top while, a few feet away, their neighbors began complaining to the server about their coffees being cold.

"So are you going to apply for the program?" Dr. Friedman asked.

"I'm thinking about it," she said, though she didn't know why she didn't just say yes.

"Why?"

"Would I? Or would I not?"

"Would you?"

Plucking up a blueberry that had rolled onto the table, she realized why she hadn't answered yes: She didn't have a good response to this question. It wasn't as if she had negative personal experience with the law, or any at all for that matter—she'd never even gotten a parking ticket. At fifth-grade graduation, to her embarrassment, she'd been given the Most Likely to Follow Directions award. The one time she'd been pulled over for not wearing a seat belt, while driving Lorn's car to Whole Foods, the cop spotted her wrist brace (from slipping off a horse—the end of all things equestrian for her) and escorted her two miles back to the Birches' house.

But there was one thing. The summer after ninth grade, in the Hamptons with Lorn and her family. She and Lorn had agreed to sneak out at midnight and meet up on the beach with a few boys whose families also had houses in East Hampton. They had been trying unsuccessfully to build a fire, and Hugh, the other black kid in their group that summer, had run back to the car to get some more newspaper. Within twenty minutes, he hadn't come back and wasn't responding to calls or texts. By the time anyone heard from him it was hours later. Someone had seen him rifling through the trunk of a car and had called the police to report a break-in. The cops who had showed up hadn't believed Hugh's story that it was his friend Tom's car. They'd called Tom's dad, who, of course, had thought the car was supposed to be in the driveway. (Also, they were all fifteen and not supposed to be driving in the first place.)

It was a story the group of friends recounted for years—that one crazy night Hugh got taken in, when they were all being stupid. No one talked about the unspoken underbelly of the story, racism. (Bea had brought it up once to Lorn, but not a second time after Lorn had said, "You don't know that's why they called the cops.")

"I have a friend who got arrested once for something he didn't do," she said to Dr. Friedman. "It sort of made me interested in the subject."

"Did you read about the student advocacy piece?" Dr. Friedman asked, and Bea shook her head.

Dr. Friedman explained that at Carter, students who found themselves involved in campus judicial proceedings, either as the complainant or respondent—those were the names for the parties— were assigned "student advocates," peers who supported them through the process. The fellows in the Justice Scholars Program automatically joined the roster of student advocates.

"You mean," Bea said, "be a fellow student's lawyer? As a freshman?"

"Ha, no." He smiled. "You'd be a support person. There's a whole training. You'll learn the details. You don't argue on their behalf or anything. More like a resource. Nonetheless, it's valuable exposure to what it means to be an advocate in an adversarial system." Dr. Friedman's food still hadn't arrived. "Looks like you're enjoying your coffee." He'd nodded at her mug, which she hadn't touched. They laughed.

"About your paper," he said suddenly.

"Oh . . ." she'd stammered. "Like I said in my email, I didn't think you'd ever see it."

He interrupted, "Here's the real story. I couldn't . . . not publicly. Would *you* want everyone to know you were suddenly coming into wealth? With the pressure that brings? The eyeballs? Think of the Powerball winners who go broke within a year, two years—is it because they're financially foolish? They simply can't manage their money?"

By his tone Bea could tell that the answer he was searching for was no, but, in fact, that's exactly what she'd always thought about those people.

"Of course not," he said. "They got the money, Bea."

"What?" Bea asked.

"Of course, the Washingtons got the money. I just got it to them in a way that didn't put them in the spotlight. Through a trust."

"Oh." Bea felt a loosening in her chest. She had not realized she'd been holding it against him.

Suddenly she noticed that one of the men at the next table, who was wearing ripped jeans, sunglasses, and a camo T-shirt, was staring at her. Despite his reflective, fuchsia-tinted shades, she could feel his burning gaze asserting its authority.

Ever since she was a little girl, when people would study her as if trying to determine whether Bea belonged to the woman whose hand she was holding, Bea had been sensitive to stares. She could feel them thinking, *The child isn't white, but the woman is so much darker.* Sometimes they'd outright ask Phaedra if she was the nanny.

"Can I help you?" Bea said to the man's mirrored lenses. The man's eyebrows rose behind them. He grunted.

"You're staring, so I asked if I could help you," Bea said. The man shrugged as his friend snickered. Dr. Friedman watched silently and, after a few seconds, stood. He pulled out his wallet and dropped a twenty on the table. His cottage cheese and chicken still hadn't arrived.

"Let's go," he said to Bea, eyeing the men. She followed him out, embarrassed that she'd allowed her temper to flare in front of him.

On the sidewalk, he turned to her. "What happened?"

"Oh, I just . . ." That he'd expected there had to be more to the story had deepened her embarrassment. "I just have a thing about being stared at."

"Sure," he said after a pause. Looking past her, a mischievous expression came over his face. "Hey, look! Another coffee shop! What're the odds? It's a New York City miracle." Across the street, under a sign that read MOCHA, large windows were lined with warm yellow bulbs. Inside, rows of red bistro tables were empty.

She laughed.

"There's that smile." He put a hand on her back to lead her into the crosswalk. They had the light.

Only eleven days after sending in her application to the JSP (which was concurrently considered an application to Carter), she'd received a congratulatory email from the assistant director telling her she'd been admitted to both. In the spring she'd been awarded one of the program's merit scholarships. At only ten grand a year, it barely covered a fifth of tuition, but with her inheritance and life insurance payout, she didn't *really* need it anyway. Still, it offset the exorbitant cost of Carter. Ten months later, the Friday before classes began, Bea sat in the back of an Uber, traveling from the Greensboro, North Carolina, airport to Cartersboro to begin her first year.

Her phone rattled against her thigh.

YOU IN THE CAR???

Lorn's mother, Audrey—her guardian once her mom died—was far more overprotective than Bea's mother had been. Bea found the constant check-ins via text—invariably in all caps—irritating, and she was often unsure how to respond.

Yes, she typed back, then turned back to the window. The abundant pines in North Carolina were different from the maples and birches of Connecticut, though she couldn't quite pinpoint how. Taller? More dense?

"Ma'am, what dorm are you going to?" the driver asked. In the rearview mirror, she caught his twinkling eye. So this was southern charm. "I can get you to Carter, but that's about as far as I know."

"Sure," she said, pulling her orientation folder from her bag and removing the map with her dorm starred on it. She handed it to him. "It's there."

"Uh oh, am I gonna need my readers?" He chuckled.

"It's that star."

"All right then," he said.

To reach South Campus where the first-year dorms were located, they had to drive under the prominent Carter bridge—known to students as the Bridge, featured in the school brochure. It was a campus icon, a concrete arch and overpass blanketed in colorful graffiti. On this day it was covered in promotions by student groups targeting the arriving first-years:

Love a cappella? Join The Scarlets!

Black Student Union 1st Meeting: Sept 12

CRU: Bible Study, Ev Tues @7, SocSci Fl 4

Bea's phone hummed in her hand. She looked down, expecting another text from Audrey but finding one instead from Early, her new roommate, with whom she'd traded numbers and a few logistical messages over the summer.

See u soon roomie!!!!!!!! ☺ ☺ ☺ ☺ ☺

Stayja

Stayja ran, then walked, then ran across the quad, cup full of pee in hand. Fucking Nicole. She pushed through the building's heavy glass doors and made her way up the stairs to the Carter health clinic, where her cousin was holed up in the bathroom.

where r u?! it's getting obvious!

almost there, Stayja typed back, rounding the corner of the carpeted hallway to pass through another smooth, soundless door. A girl around Stayja's age, presumably a student, sat behind a white, expansive reception desk, her bone-straight hair gleaming in the fluorescent light.

"Can I help you?" she asked Stayja.

"I was wondering—if I need, like, a pregnancy test, do you guys do that?"

"Are you . . . a student?" the receptionist asked, her voice rising an octave.

"I work at the Rooster Roast," Stayja said. The girl's face scrunched in confusion. "The coffee shop in the student center?"

"Oh! Right, I didn't know it had a name. Um . . ."

The girl drummed her fingers on the desk. This was Stayja's plan, and it was working. As Stayja shifted her weight, the pee sloshed a bit in the coffee cup she was holding before her like it contained a hot drink, and she noted again how oddly warm it was, like actual coffee. The fucking things she did for her fucking family. Here she'd managed to get Nicole a job at the Carter Quik-Mart, and then Nicole couldn't pass the goddamn drug test. Of course. Nicole hadn't had clean urine since she turned fourteen. Jesus only knew what combination of pot and what the fuck else was in her bladder.

"Do you have a health plan here then?" The girl looked Indian—not the Native American kind but the kind Stayja had never met until she came to work at Carter, the ones her mother called "dot heads" (as opposed to "woo-woos").

"No," said Stayja.

The girl pressed her lips together and swiveled slightly in her chair. *Yes, go. You have to go ask.*

"I'll have to go check with my supervisor. Give me one second."

Supervisor. It sounded so much classier than boss. Suddenly Nicole appeared, lurching from the hallway, hand outstretched.

"Give it, give it!" Her younger cousin grabbed the cup and lid from Stayja and darted back behind the door as the student with shampoo-commercial hair returned.

"Are you a member of the health plan?"

Stayja wasn't a member of the health plan, because with reduced or nonexistent hours over seasonal breaks, coupled with the fact that the coffee shop was closed over the summer, her annual hours, even with overtime, averaged just under the threshold to qualify for benefits.

"Nope," she said.

"We only serve members of the health plan, unfortunately," the girl said, easing into her high-backed chair. "But there's an urgent care a few miles east on"—glancing down at a small piece of paper she wasn't holding before—"Wythe Avenue?"

"Cool, thanks," Stayja said, turning to go.

"Do you want this?" The student held up the torn scrap.

"No, thanks!" Stayja said over her shoulder as she pushed through the doors.

Hurrying back across the quad, she checked the time. Three minutes left in her break. Just enough time for a cigarette.

She took a deep breath through her nose until her gut was as full as can be, then exhaled. Repeat. Exhale.

This time, unlike the other times, she would stick with it. It didn't make sense, she reminded herself as she crossed the green, sunlit lawn, for a nurse to be a smoker. While for two years she'd justified her habit by distinguishing between being a nurse and being in nursing *school*, telling herself she'd quit before she got an actual job, she knew this was a load of shit. Anyway, now, thanks to Nicole and her uncanny knack for crapping all over Stayja's life plans, Stayja was once again two years away from her degree. And that was assuming no more crises came up, and Nicole didn't fucking do anything else stupid, like getting a DUI and having to be bailed out of jail.

Buzz.

Mom: which way on morehead is hospital

Stayja groaned and called her mother.

"Left or right on Morehead?" Donna answered.

"Mom, take the bus."

"Bus isn't running. I'm walking. Left or right?"

In addition to her diabetes, Donna had now been diagnosed with COPD. Her once-vibrant mother—the woman who, for their entire childhoods, had been an unstoppable force; who had driven Stayja and Nicole across the North Carolina/South Carolina border every July 3 to smuggle in illegal fireworks, the kind that spin and dash and explode; who had secured no fewer than twenty-seven jobs over the course of her lifetime by inventing elaborate work histories in every field imaginable; who had left her husband while pregnant after deciding he wasn't worth the space he took up in the bed; and who once socked a lady in the face at Target for calling her white trash—now sat at home all day, every day, wheezing. At fifty-nine, forty-four years of smoking had finally caught up with her. And last week, Donna's doctor had informed her that she would henceforth require weekly blood transfusions. (To Stayja's shock, these were actually covered by disability insurance.)

Stayja knew her mother was self-conscious about her health problems. When Donna had taken her and Nicole on a trip to Asheville and they'd had to climb a flight of stairs to their motel room, Donna had claimed to be too tired to join them for dinner. Stayja didn't know if it was to save money or to keep from having to go back up the stairs again, but since Donna loved going out to eat more than anything, it had to be one or the other. They'd brought her back calamari, and she'd asked questions about the restaurant, the service, the drinks. Was the ice cubed or crushed? Were the rolls warm?

Technically, Donna could still drive—her license was valid—but Stayja needed the car to get to work. So Donna took the bus when she had to go somewhere.

"Wait at the bus stop, I'm coming," Stayja said.

"I'M WALKING HOME! MEET ME THERE." Donna hung up.

Stayja entered the student center through the main entrance and hurried down the long corridor. There was still a week before classes started, but hundreds of students always returned early for reasons Stayja had gleaned over the years—their performance group had to rehearse, or they were in sorority or fraternity rush.

Undergrads decked out in tan leather flip-flops and oversized shades stood in clusters, clutching their pristine, just-purchased textbooks. Peeking out from their pages, white tops of crisp receipts flickered in the breeze. She passed the bank of bronze student mailboxes and the student government meeting rooms. Ahead of her, the Rooster Roast had no door or wall—the corridor simply terminated in six round wooden tables, three geometrically patterned sofas, and an espresso bar. In spite of the laminated BE BACK IN 5 sign Stayja had placed on the counter, a line three customers deep had formed. The student nearest the register, a pale blonde, was pulling at a hangnail. Her ponytail clung to the sticky skin on the back of her neck.

"Can I help you?" Stayja asked as she texted her manager Frank.

just got super sick, have to leave. sorry.

She looked up.

"A small oat milk latte, please."

Stayja made sure to turn her back before rolling her eyes. She quickly filled their orders and headed home.

WHEN SHE PULLED into their gravel driveway, her mom was waiting outside the house.

"Don't get out!" Donna yelled, heaving herself up off the rusty metal chair she kept by the door for occasions such as this. Donna liked to keep no one waiting. She'd rather sit outside facing the brick wall of her sister's adjacent house than make someone summon her with a horn or have to park and ring the doorbell.

Only two years earlier, Donna had been darting about, cigarette in hand, getting jobs and getting fired from them with impressive turnover rates. She'd been hired by a cleaning company but didn't know how to clean (putting bleach on a wooden dining room table once). Her stint at the 7-Eleven had ended when she'd lent a twenty to a customer. And she'd quit the gig reshelving books at the library because her boss was a "dumb dick." Donna had explained that she did not "believe in bosses."

"At least *most* bosses. All the bosses I've ever had," Donna had clarified. "I don't believe in working for somebody dumber than me, and every boss I've ever had has been dumber than me!"

Donna's knack for circumventing rules as well as ignoring policies and expectations she categorized as useless or inconvenient had been something she had tried hard but unsuccessfully to instill in her daughter.

"You realize you can just make up that stuff," she'd responded when Stayja had told her she wanted to go to bartending school. "You don't need school. Just memorize the drinks. I'll make you a résumé." Donna had found a template online and filled it with fictions. It reported that Stayja had tended bar for seven years, which would have meant since she was fourteen. Stayja had been too afraid to show up with the forged document, so she'd skipped the interview and told her mom she didn't get the job. She hadn't wanted her mom to think she was a wuss.

This was the woman who now hobbled toward the car, rainbow cane in hand, chest rising and falling under her wrinkled cream blouse. Small movements took visible effort. She'd gained forty-five pounds in half as many months.

"Off we go, daughter of mine," Donna groaned as she fell into the passenger seat. "Let's get me some blood."

They drove through the neighborhood past houses like their own, on crooked frames with peeling sidings and overgrown side yards littered with broken appliances that had cost too much to be thrown away but were too useless to keep indoors. She turned onto the road that led to the hospital. They drove in silence.

"What's the matter, teacup?" her mom croaked.

"Nothing," Stayja said. Soon she pulled into the lot for the cardiology building and headed to the building's front double doors. "I'm going to drop you off and study in the car."

Her mom muttered something about texting Stayja when she was done and then lugged herself out, wheezing.

Stayja found a spot as far from the entrance as possible, on the edge of the lot, where she was unlikely to be distracted by people coming and going and where the fierce afternoon sun was blocked by the shadow of another medical building. She reached into the backseat to riffle through the pile of novels shrouded in library plastic in search of the advanced anatomy text she'd bought for the semester before she'd had to drop her class. If she wasn't going to be in class, she might as well learn on her own. She identified the bulky tome by its heft, dug it free, and brought it to rest on the steering wheel as Frank's name lit up her phone.

when are you going to be unsick? need you tonight. Trudy decided her 2 wks notice was no wks notice.

Stayja squealed.

feeling better (not contagious) so I can do night shift tonight. Also can I switch to nights??? she typed, pausing for an instant before pressing SEND to ponder how exhausting it was going to be to work until 10 p.m. five days a week. But it would give her the daytime to study or pick up other work. Or, now, drive her mother to her doctors' appointments.

I can cover day & night shifts for now til you find someone 4 day. . . . She knew Frank wasn't fond of her working overtime—she got time and a half for every hour over forty in a given week—but if he was in a bind, he'd do it.

Dot dot dot. The dots disappeared. He'd started to respond and stopped.

She wrote: feeling better. back by 5.

Dots.

Ok, just till I find someone.

She set her textbook aside and opened her notebook to confirm the calculations she'd done and redone. Six classes completed of the nineteen she needed for her degree meant that she had thirteen left. The program was designed for people to attend full time.

Scheduling her twenty-plus hours of work each week around her degree requirements was like high-stakes Tetris: three courses were only offered during summers, and the pre-reqs for those were only offered in the fall and spring. If she missed a spring pre-req, for example, it rippled into the summer and fall, setting her back an entire year.

At the Rooster she made $16,500 a year. Their household bills were mostly covered by Donna's SSI, thank God. Stayja contributed two hundred dollars or so a month toward other bills and a hundred dollars a week for food for them both in addition to Donna's food stamps. That left roughly fifteen hundred dollars she could save per semester, which would cover the three spring classes, two in summer, and two in the fall. (Her summer job, catering the city's Friday Night Movies in the Park, was barely enough to pay her cell phone bill.)

She and Donna would do what they'd always done when things got especially tight—case the "Nearly Expired" bin at Dollar Savings; take advantage of the pasta special on Wednesdays at 50 percent off/sixty-nine cents a box at Walmart; do the forty-five-minute drive out to Sam's Club to buy the $1.88 frozen chicken breasts in bulk.

In all of her calculations, though, Stayja hadn't factored in her smoking. A pack cost $5.45, over a third of their combined daily food budget. She had to be realistic: she hadn't ever quit successfully. At about half a pack a day, she was spending about eighty bucks a month on fucking cigarettes, a habit she couldn't afford, which made her feel even worse about not having kicked it.

As she gazed into the woodsy distance beyond the hospital lot into the trees that separated it from the highway, a burn rose behind her eyes. She was just tired, she told herself. She only cried when she was tired.

STAYJA AWOKE TO knocking on the window. She reached to turn the latch and shove open the passenger door of her ancient Corolla, which could only be opened from the inside.

"Sorry, Mom. Fell asleep," she said.

"Just glad you didn't leave me here," Donna said, breathing hard from the trek across the lot. Stayja had seven missed texts, three from her mother and four from Nicole. It was 4:29.

"How was it?" Stayja asked, starting the engine.

"Easy," her mom said. "They said I could do it myself at home if I wanted, but that makes me nervous."

"Really?" Stayja must have sounded too hopeful, because Donna lifted her eyebrows.

"Don't let me overburden you, Miss Thing."

Stayja pulled out of the lot. "It would just be good if I didn't have to leave work so I don't fucking get fired."

"Who's going to fire you? No one has ever fired you. You're impossible to fire. You're too good at everything." Donna turned on the radio. Easy listening came on, some eighties love song, and she hummed along.

"Meet any eligible bachelors today?" Donna asked after a few minutes.

"I've hardly seen anyone today, Mom," Stayja said.

"It's afternoon!"

"Classes haven't even started."

"Not just anyone. Someone on your level," Donna said as Stayja turned into their neighborhood.

"Well, it's not that easy to meet people," Stayja said, a mistake. Donna launched into her well-worn diatribe: Stayja worked at a university, for God's sake—she must be surrounded by smart, ambitious men.

"Those guys don't want to date me," Stayja said. "They date

girls who had braces." As soon as she said it, even though her tone had been playful, she regretted it. She sensed Donna's body slump. Disappointing Donna or, rather, seeing Donna's disappointment at Stayja's disappointment had tormented Stayja since second grade, when she'd come home from school thrilled about an upcoming class field trip to the Charlotte zoo. Giraffes! Dolphins! The trip included a two-hour bus drive complete with bag lunches. They wouldn't even return until after dinner.

They couldn't afford it, of course. The day of the trip, Stayja had sat doing enrichment work in the first-grade classroom while the rest of her class had gone to see the giraffes. That part had been hard, but worse had been Donna's face when Stayja had told her the cost. Even at seven, Stayja had understood that her mom was more crushed than she was. From then on, she had faked sick on field trip days, hiding from her mother that more than anything in life Stayja longed to be different than they were, than Donna was. She loathed all the words for "poor," the degrading euphemisms: low-income, high-need, underprivileged. But she loathed *being* poor even more. Ever since first grade, when Stayja would be handed a bright blue ticket each morning by her teacher to exchange for a tray of free food while she was surrounded by kids who brought lunches from home, a single desire had trumped all others: to escape poverty.

"Ridiculous," Donna said defensively. "That's all in your head. You could've gotten in there if you'd wanted!"

Stayja often wondered if it was true—she'd considered applying to Carter but didn't, since even if she'd gotten in, which was a long shot, they could never pay. Then Rhonda Jenkins from her class, who didn't make as good grades as Stayja—Stayja was ranked fifth, and Rhonda was not even in the top ten students, whose names were the only names released—announced in April of their senior year that she had applied and been accepted with a full scholarship for students of color from North Carolina who had attended public school. Stayja had vacillated between jealousy and disappointment at the news and had never really stopped. Rhonda had since graduated and moved to New York, where she walked to work over the Brooklyn Bridge and posted the same photo of that damn bridge over and over on Instagram.

No, Donna didn't understand the clear boundary that distinguished students from staff on campus. It was in their clothes, in the way they spoke to one another versus the way they spoke to Stayja. Stayja wore Goodwill clothes bought on Friday Color Clearance (50 percent off everything a single color on Fridays!) and Nicole's more modest Forever 21 hand-me-downs. She didn't hate her clothes or wish she dressed like Carter kids—many of them were far too preppy for her taste, sporting bright shirts with little alligators on them or patterned dresses that looked to Stayja like children's birthday decorations. But she was astounded by how *many* clothes they had. There were regulars at the coffee shop whom she saw every day for entire semesters, never once in the same shirt. They spoke without accents, as if they were from everywhere and nowhere. Their smiles were perfect.

Annie

That Friday, at the first orchestra rehearsal of the year, I found my spot behind the flutes and next to the trombones.

"Welcome back! To those of you who are new, welcome," Juan-Pablo, the music theory professor and orchestra conductor, said from behind his music stand. "Let's get settled quickly, please."

I moistened my reed and waited. My thighs stuck to the cold metal chair.

I'd picked the bassoon because my high school band director, Mrs. Hays, had begged me to, bribing me with immediate acceptance into the Pineville County Youth Orchestra. She needed a bassoonist, and, having successfully persuaded the school to invest in a bassoon, she needed to justify the expense.

Playing in an orchestra sounded much more interesting and classier than playing solely in high school band, and I liked that I could borrow the school's instrument and wouldn't have to burden my parents with having to buy me something like a French horn. The rest was history.

The bassoon: how I'd gotten into college for free and, now, how I'd afforded to fix my legs. It had turned out to be the best decision I'd ever made. After five years, though, I was tired of bassoon even as I was grateful for all it had gotten me. I was obliged to stay in orchestra to keep my scholarship, but I wouldn't have quit anyway. I wouldn't do that to Juan-Pablo, leave him without a bassoonist.

I'd had a tender spot for khaki-pants-with-ASICS-wearing Juan-Pablo ever since the fall of my first year, when I'd declined to join an orchestra trip to a nearby waterpark (because I had to wear a swimsuit) and he'd called me to his office to ask why I wouldn't be joining. I hadn't told him, of course. I lied and told him I had to work.

Still, at the next rehearsal, he announced that the orchestra would be going to Six Flags instead. I had a feeling it was for me.

We began to sight-read a new piece, the theme from a movie called *October Sky,* which I'd never heard of. As the music swelled, even with the mistaken notes and clunky rhythm of a sight-read, I was glad to be back.

After rehearsal, we trekked as a group to the campus gardens for the orchestra's annual start-of-the-year picnic. Around me, students discussed their summers in regional orchestras, their class schedules, and the luck of their new dorm room sizes and locations, but the breeze on my thighs was alien and distracting, and I struggled to pay attention. If people were aware of what was left of my scars, they weren't showing it.

Then I was lying in the sun, my lower body drenched in invisible zinc that reflected the glare, a decade of obscurity bouncing the light. I closed my eyes. I didn't know what was to come, but I sensed that it was good.

CARTER PROGRESSIVES WAS holding a back-to-school roller-skating party that night, and I'd persuaded Matty to come with me.

Social events with large groups of people weren't Matty's idea of fun, which I learned quickly after he and I had met in my first college class, a seminar titled Introduction to Philosophy.

"Is there an advanced syllabus for those of us who have already read these?" a small, angular boy with a meticulously gelled swoop of hair asked. I surveyed the three-page document: *Three Dialogues between Hylas and Philonous*, *Dialogues concerning Natural Religion*, *On Liberty*. On it went, more titles I'd never heard of.

"I can create a supplemental reading list for you," the professor, an energetic, bow-tied doctoral student who couldn't have been older than thirty, said. The boy thanked him.

As I walked back to my dorm after class, wondering if I should drop the course, the boy appeared next to me.

"Hey. I'm Matty. Where're you from?"

"Pineville. In Georgia," I said, stopping.

"Sounds metropolitan." He grinned. "You hate me," he said, still smiling.

"What?"

"You do *not* have a good poker face."

"It's just that if you have already read everything for Philosophy 101, maybe you don't need to take it," I said.

"Fair," he said, reaching out his hand as if we were adults. We shook.

"I'm Annie," I said.

"So how big is Pineville?" he asked.

I had no clue how many people lived in Pineville. It wasn't as small as Argyle or Jenkinsburg, but it wasn't Augusta. "Medium?" I said.

He howled. "You're hilarious! Medium. Like it's a T-shirt. Want to get coffee?"

And that's how Matty Solomon bullied me into becoming his fast friend.

At the coffee shop, I learned that he'd grown up as an only child in Washington, DC, his father a congressman from New Hampshire and his mother a serial nonprofit president. He didn't believe in government, religion, or really any institutions, including college. He'd been out of the closet since he was thirteen and casually recalled only nontraumatic homophobic teasing at his small, liberal prep school near the capital.

Matty explained to me that first day we met that he was at Carter for one purpose: to write for the school paper. His singular aspiration in life was to become a journalist, and he treated writing for the school daily as a tedious but necessary first step in that direction. He talked about college as if he'd already been to it. Since I found our classmates intimidating and he found them boring, we were perfectly matched in our reclusive leanings.

So getting him to come to a roller-skating party was no small feat, but once we arrived, he refused to skate.

Side by side—Matty in no-show socks and loafers, me in my brown, neatly tied rental roller skates—we sat on a bench. The jovial roster of howling students scrolled past, cycling through.

"Get out there if you want," he said for the third time.

"I don't want to skate by myself," I said for the third time.

"Oh, fine," he finally said, standing. "I'm sick of your sulking. You've sufficiently guilted me." He disappeared and, several moments later, returned with a pair of skates and two pints of beer. "But I need to tell you something. I don't know how to skate. So we're going to have to get drunk for this."

Half an hour later, Matty and I were making idiots of ourselves, giggling uncontrollably on the rink floor. It had turned out that the one thing Matty didn't know how to do he was, indeed, very, very bad at.

"Be brave!" I yelled, pulling him with both hands. His legs widened as he rolled forward, his body hinging forty-five degrees and panic in his eyes, until he slowly regained his balance. We stayed on the rink through the hokey pokey, the limbo, reverse skate, couples skate, and something called "shoot the duck," where you crouch down and roll on one skate while sticking your other leg out straight in front of you. We kept falling over, Matty especially, who, with the flexibility of a ninety-five-year-old, couldn't straighten his leg.

This is what I remember about the first part of that night: having the time of my life.

When Matty had to use the bathroom, I rolled over to our bench, breathless, and plopped onto it.

I had first spotted the boy during the hokey pokey, across the room from me in a circle of people so sprawling it nearly grazed the oval wall. At first I noticed him because he was the only one in the circle who wasn't wearing skates. In bright blue Converse sneakers, he shook one foot and then the other and pranced around as a clownish voice blared on the crackly speaker, "And then you turn yourself around; that's what it's all about!"

He was handsome in that way that a nerdy kid who sprouts into a man is handsome. He had a strawberry blonde mess of unruly hair and was just shy of tall, with calf muscles that bulged when he walked—I could tell this even from a distance. "Shaggy Tyler," I'd later learn he was called by his PiKa brothers, to distinguish him from "Big Tyler" and "Gay Tyler" (who wasn't gay, just slight and therefore the locus of the fraternity's latent homophobia).

As the crowd turned rowdier and the room dimmer, the strobe light casting the only lights apart from the soft glow of the corner rental booth in the distance, I found myself emboldened by the beer I'd consumed. I stood and made my way over to where he was leaning, alone, against the wall. I believe he was wearing those pastel beach shorts that southern college guys wear in warm months, though I forget what color.

"Nice hokey pokey out there," I said.

The corners of his eyes crinkled when he smiled.

"Thanks," he said. "I really should have stretched after. Don't want to cramp." He leaned over and touched his toes.

I laughed.

He rose and pushed his wild hair from his face.

"I'm Tyler," he said. "You are?"

"Annie Stoddard," I said, immediately embarrassed at having offered both names.

"Is the last name so I can stalk you online?" he asked.

"Only if you want," I said, feeling a dreaded red flush crawl up my neck. At least it was dark.

"Annie Stoddard, let's play a game," he said. "Would you rather"—he looked around, contemplating—"have hands for feet or feet for hands?"

"Hands for feet," I said. "Of course. I'm a bassoonist. I need my hands. But also, who would ever choose to have four feet?"

"Good point. Your turn."

The game was familiar to me—my brother and I had played it on road trips for years.

"Would you rather stink the rest of your life or have a really annoying voice?" I asked.

He pondered this.

"How stinky am I?"

"There is no question that it's you who smells."

"Voice then. When you have death fantasies, who do you imagine dying—yourself or other people?"

"Wow," I said.

"Okay, I'll answer first. Myself. Now you answer."

I hesitated.

"You know you do. Everyone has death fantasies," he said.

"Both," I said. Then, seeing that this didn't satisfy him, I continued,

"Other people more. My dad. I'm scared of that most, I guess." A knot of girls rolled by. He high-fived one of them. "You fantasize about your own death?"

He nodded. "I am constantly anticipating how I might die. I have since I was twelve. Somehow I'm still around. It quite honestly shocks me."

"Why?" I asked.

He shrugged.

"I haven't made any real contributions to the world. I've taken more than I've given. I'm a tax on global resources."

This struck me as funny—assuming that one would have done anything meaningful before even finishing school.

"You're in college," I said.

"So?" he said. "By my age, Mark Zuckerberg had already launched Facebook."

"The *one* guy who dropped out of college and did something huge?" I was definitely drunk. I sort of wanted to laugh, but there was something about his earnestness and his grand ambitions that made him seem vulnerable.

"Is that your boyfriend?" he asked, and I followed his gaze to Matty, walking toward us.

"No, my best friend," I said.

"What's he like?" he asked.

A wave of panic passed over me as Matty moved closer. The conversation we were having was not the kind of conversation Matty was willing to entertain. Matty didn't relate to insecurity—he seemed immune to it, somehow already an expert at warding it off. It left me in awe, it made me feel safe, and it was also why being friends with him could be so lonely.

"Witty," I said.

Suddenly a girl with a long braid was careening toward us with great speed, crashing into Tyler and pulling him out onto the floor.

He waved at me as he jogged to keep up with her skilled skating—too skilled, I noted, for the collision to have been an accident.

Seeing that Matty had made a detour to get another beer, I headed to the bathroom, where, stationed safely in a stall, I searched through Instagram until I found his profile. I scrolled through his pictures—of friends at parties, his family dog, a vacation to Cabo. The girls in the photos held nylon Longchamp totes in bright hues, the kind I'd never seen before arriving at Carter and couldn't afford myself, but at least there didn't seem to be one particular girl featured in his feed.

Then I googled him. He was a fourth-year in PiKa and was on the board of the Interfraternity Council. Diversity Chair. He'd been interviewed for the campus daily *The Chronicle* the year before as part of a series called "Getting to Know Campus Leaders." His dream vacation was to sail around South America, having been taught by his father during family vacations in Nantucket as a boy. He was a Pisces but didn't believe in astrology. His parents, both of whom attended Carter in the 1980s, were college sweethearts who lived in Houston. His dad had founded some kind of addiction-treatment company. He was a history major and an art minor. He planned to apply to law school.

AS MATTY AND I meandered back to campus, my phone dinged. Matty groaned, peering over my shoulder. Tyler had found me as well on Instagram and followed and messaged me.

"You *had* to pick the guy too good to skate like everyone else?"

"You weren't going to skate either until I made you!" I said, desperate to read the message but also to hide it.

He ignored this.

"Was he one of the ones who did a keg stand? If you start dating a keg stand guy, I will begin drafting the obit for our friendship."

"He didn't do a keg stand," I said, suddenly irritated by Matty's snobbery, which was how it often happened with us—his smugness would not bother me at all until it did. "He's chair of diversity for the Greeks."

Matty snorted, then shrieked, "Oh yes—a public servant!"

"Shut up," I muttered. It was always better with Matty if you didn't engage. His opinions were to be heard, appreciated, and left alone.

"Don't make this about his leadership qualities," he said. "You just think he's hot."

"Isn't he?" I smiled.

"Not my type. He's far too unkempt."

The only thing unkempt about him was his hair—the opposite of Matty's highly manicured style, which cost so much to maintain that he wouldn't tell me the price of his cuts. (He said only, "I don't trust anyone down here to touch it" and scheduled them during visits home.)

"I like his unkemptness," I said.

"Exactly." Matty was quickly losing interest in the conversation, and I was glad. Soon, he'd change the subject. "But you extoling his role as a champion of tolerance was my favorite thing of the night. The white MLK of Carter, he."

I didn't answer.

"Can we get some food, please?" Matty whined. "I need carbs to sop up the booze."

My phone buzzed. Another DM from Tyler.

I covered my screen with my palm.

"Sure," I said.

As I fell asleep that night, my phone glowed in my palm. I opened, closed, and reopened his two messages, basking.

I like your voice, and you don't stink.

And:

Goodnight, Annie. ☺

Perhaps Matty was right. Perhaps I just thought he was hot. But he was. And he liked me.

Tingling with possibility, drifting into sleep, I felt anything could happen. Nothing, I recall, felt out of reach.

Bea

In leopard-print leggings, purple fuzzy slippers, and a light gray sweatshirt that fell off one shoulder, the girl sat cross-legged on a bedspread covered in bright red poppies. Her yellow hair zigzagged to her waist. She was weeping.

Bea stood in the doorway, one hand on the handle of her rolling carry-on.

"Are you okay?" she asked.

"Oh, God, oh, God. Hi, hi. I'm Early. Obvi." Her new roommate pressed sparkly, manicured hands onto her eyelids. "I didn't know when you said you were close you meant this close. I promise I'm not crazy." She hopped to her feet and opened her arms for a hug, then noticed that her palms were streaked with mascara. "Oh, God. Let me go wash my hands," she said, hurrying past Bea into the hall.

In the little correspondence Bea had had with her new roommate over the summer, she'd found the girl to be a completely foreign concept. Excitable, rambling, overeager to be friends—these were terms that had come to mind during the single phone conversation they'd had in July. Early's latest email, which had been about color-coordinating the room, Bea had ignored. Was everyone in the South like this?

Bea looked around. On Early's side of the room, bright plastic tubs were stacked on wall shelves that also held books organized by spine color: *Tuesdays with Morrie, Gone with the Wind,* and *The Workings of the Brain* were flanked by large Tupperware bins marked "Winter Sweaters" and "Travel Appliances." Bea's side was bare apart from a university-issued mattress, desk, and chair.

Early returned.

"Long story short," she said as they hugged awkwardly, "I was cut first round of rush. Not a single sorority invited me back." She sniffled.

Coming from an all-girls boarding school, Bea was well acquainted with tears. But the tears she was familiar with were of a different kind. Her classmates at Porter's aspired to direct indie films, to disrupt industries, to run companies and nonprofits and governments. They measured intelligence by the presence of a proper sense of irony. Their families and thus they, too, valued decorum. Bea's friends cried over boys, over girls, over expectations, over abstractions of failure, but Bea could not imagine any of her Porter's classmates weeping so openly over a sorority. Well, maybe a couple of them.

"I'm just devastated," Early continued. "But I sound selfish; listen to me. Hungry? I have snacks in here." Early pulled a clear container out from under her bed, which she'd lifted onto stilts for yet more storage space. "Or can I get you a Coke? There's vending down the hall. I always need one after a flight to settle my stomach."

"That's okay, thanks." Bea felt Early studying her as she unzipped her bag. "Did any boxes come for me?"

"Oh, is *that* what's in the study room?" Early gestured for Bea to follow. As they walked down the hall, Early chattered without pause. "I grabbed some brochures for you at student group speed dating this morning. And I saved space for you in the closet, but if you need more, just say the word. I have extra hangers, too."

The enclave at the end of the hall, the size of a master bathroom, was crammed full of Bea's things.

"Holy crap," Bea whispered. She didn't remember her stuff taking up so much space when the men showed up to her dorm at Porter's to pack her things and move them. She'd had the opposite reaction when a different set of men had packed up her and her mother's house to send their belongings off to storage ("in case she wants them someday," Audrey had insisted). That their entire lives could be consolidated into a few neat stacks of boxes in a handful of hours—it was fast and easy, much faster and easier than it should have been.

"Did you think you had a bigger room?" Early chuckled. "It's okay. I have extra bed stilts." She wrapped her arms around a wardrobe box and eased it through the doorway on its corners. "Welcome to college!"

OVER THE NEXT several hours, Early helped Bea organize her things. While they worked, she rattled off a million questions—what other schools had Bea applied to? Where did she get in? What was her SAT score? GPA?

"I got a 1520," Early said, "which was the highest in my school, but I only had a 3.87 GPA, which put me third in my class, which sucked because I always wanted to beat out Lisa Gardener for salutatorian. But Ross Hughes was always going to be valedictorian because he *literally* did nothing but study. He got into Yale. Did you get in there?"

Bea answered truthfully: 1550, 3.9, ranked fifth, and, yes, she was admitted to Yale, Harvard, and Princeton. No, her mom didn't still live in Connecticut because her mom was dead. It's okay. No, she doesn't have a relationship with her father. Yes, she has other family (Audrey would have been thrilled that she said this). No, she didn't know anyone who had gotten a full ride to Carter, but she'd gotten a small scholarship as part of the Justice Scholars Program.

"My brother was in that," Early said. "You got into *Princeton*? I'd go to Princeton over Carter any second of any day."

"What's your major?" Bea asked to change the subject. To Bea's surprise, Early was a coder. She was going to major in computer science and was considering a double major with math. Her brother was a fourth-year in a fraternity. Early winced as she said the word. Her undereyes were still smudged black.

"Are you going to rush?"

Her mouth full of one of Early's granola bars, Bea shook her head and furrowed her brow in confusion. Rush was over.

"I meant, if you want to rush a black sorority. Since those rush later." Early looked nervous that she'd said something wrong. "In January, I think." Bea already knew the sororities at Carter were essentially segregated by race. The photographs in the brochure had made that apparent.

"I'm not interested in Greek life," she said.

BY 10 P.M., Bea's side of the room looked as if it belonged to her, thanks to the tangerine bedspread with the blue trim she'd used throughout high school. Lorn had been shocked that Bea didn't want a new comforter for college, but Bea liked this one that she and her mom had chosen together in eighth grade.

Hours alone with Early, coupled with the fatigue of travel, had eased her inhibitions, and she suddenly spoke frankly.

"Since you didn't get into a sorority, does our room have to look like you did?" she asked. Early's face fell, and Bea felt bad. "Just kidding?" she joked. "I, uh, love paisley."

"You're a bad liar," Early said.

"I'm not lying. I'm kidding."

"Well, *I* like paisley."

"Good. If *you* like it, fine. I just don't want some sorority you're not even in as our third roommate."

"Ha. Meet our third roommate, Kappa," Early said. A moment passed before she added, "Fuck Kappa."

"That's the spirit!" Bea said.

Soon, as they lay in their beds in the dark, Lorn began to blow up Bea's phone with texts.

WHERE ARE U ANSWER PLZ SO I KNOW YOU AREN'T DANGLING FROM YOUR CLOSET ROD.

Suicide is not a joke! I'm alive . . . for now.

Oh, good. How is Late, the roomie?

Early, on her bed, was also occupied on her phone.

A lot, Bea typed back. Lorn responded with an emoji storm of exasperated expressions.

"Can I ask you a question?" Early said, dropping her phone. "I hope you won't be offended."

Bea knew what was coming. She'd attended private and boarding schools in New York and Massachusetts since she could walk. When she'd started Porter's in ninth grade, there were only two other students of color in her class—Tina from LA and Sujita from Nepal. She'd been the brownest person in classrooms her whole life and had felt this in small and big ways—being picked last for the math showdown in middle school, being the only one of her friends without a date to the eighth-grade dance, being accused outright of stealing Sloan Peterson's parka out of her room based on nothing other than the fact that Bea owned the same jacket. Then there was the question Early was about to ask.

"My mom is black, and my dad is white," Bea said.

"I was going to ask why you don't want to be in a sorority."

"Oh," Bea said. How to answer sensitively? Sororities struck her

as something that interested women who lacked real ambition—
the kind of people who would grow up to be like the mothers of
her friends from high school, including Audrey. She loved Audrey,
but she didn't want to be her. With degrees from Ivy League colleges
and law schools and medical schools, they'd abandoned the professional world to run households, which as far as Bea could tell
meant bossing around hired staff, doing Pilates, and becoming
overly invested in their children's academic and social lives. Bea
half-pitied, half-disdained these women for giving up so casually,
for wearing their coveted pedigrees like accessories.

"Just want to have time to focus on school, I guess," said Bea.

"It's just really hard to have a social life here if you aren't in one.
I mean my brother says the frat houses are where all the parties
are. And they have mixers with the sororities. So if you aren't in a
sorority . . . I guess you *can* go to parties on frat row, but can you
really?" Early said.

"We'll be okay, I think," Bea said.

"So what are you in besides your justice classes or whatever?"
Early asked, yawning.

"Physics," Bea said, wondering if every night was going to be
like this—interminable chatter after the light was out.

Of Bea's four fall courses, two were required as part of the Justice
Scholars Program, "JSP": the seminar that Dr. Friedman flew in
once a week to teach on Friday mornings, simply called Justice,
and the writing course all Carter first-years were required to take,
which for her was a JSP-only section: Notions of Justice Around
the World. Her other two courses were electives. She'd picked
Abnormal Psychology because it sounded interesting—and because
she'd knocked out the Psych 101 pre-req as an AP. For her fourth,
while perusing the course catalogue she'd come across Writing
Crime Fiction, which sounded impossibly fun, and she'd clicked
ENROLL.

But then, three days before flying down to North Carolina, she'd gotten nervous. What if she changed her mind back to pursuing medicine? At midnight she swapped the fiction class for physics. She'd done well in physics in high school and liked talking about torques and velocity.

"You know my brother's class of Justice Scholars was the first?" Early said.

"Oh, yeah?" Bea mumbled.

"Three years ago. No one from his year is going into anything related to law, though. They're all econ majors now and already being recruited for consulting jobs."

"Mmm."

"He says you get disenchanted pretty quickly. Or disabused. I can't remember what word he used. Basically it convinced them all that criminal justice reform is a waste of time. But, like I told him, it saved him basically a hundred thousand dollars instead of going to law school to find that out, you know?"

Bea was glad it was dark so she could roll her eyes. It was like when you're excited to go on a trip and someone tells you all the reasons why your destination is shitty.

"Cool," she said, then yawned loudly.

In seconds, Early was snoring, and the glow of Bea's phone was the only light in the room. She scrolled through Instagram, then signed into Facebook and typed a name into the search bar: Lester Bertrand. Her secret.

BEA AWOKE EARLY, tied on her sneakers, pulled on her headband, and set out. The sky was overcast as she jogged toward the six-mile trail that encircled campus, which she'd read about on the school's website, navigating on her phone to her running mix. As she always did when she turned on her music at the start of a run, she thought about the guy who'd inspired her to take up running. Noah had gone to Avon Old Farms ("AOF"), Porter's brother school. At AOF-Porter's prom, they'd made out behind the music building, then had hooked up a few more times after that. He was into long-distance running but didn't believe in listening to music while he ran. He said it got in the way of his focus.

Apart from Noah, Bea's only other romantic experience was with a guy named Demetri. In East Hampton the summer after sophomore year of high school, she'd met Demetri at the ice cream shop where the high school kids gathered in the afternoon. He was from Massachusetts, a rising senior at a country day school she wasn't familiar with. He'd known Lorn from summers in the Hamptons and had gotten Bea's number right away. They'd spent two evenings together, one alone and another with everyone on the beach, before he'd stopped responding to her texts.

Long after Lorn and their other friend, Isabel, had believed Bea to be asleep in her upstairs bedroom of the family beach home, she'd come down for a glass of water and had overheard them talking on the porch.

"He said she's too clamped up," Lorn was saying. "He felt like he was with a mannequin: she didn't react to anything. I told him she is actually hilarious once she's comfortable around you."

Bea had wanted to scream at them: *My mother just died! I'm doing my best!*

He hadn't known. But lying in bed that night, she thought that even if he *had* known about her mom, it wouldn't have been surprising for that to freak him out and turn him off. People acted as if grief were contagious.

I'm totally hilarious once you know me, she reminded herself as she jogged to the beat. In eighth grade, at slumber parties, they would play spin the bottle. Meredith Welcher would make girls go into a closet and kiss, saying you can tell if someone is a lesbian by how warm her lips are. She was very into outing lesbians. Everyone was scared of Meredith, so they complied, until one night, Bea had wound up in the closet with her and pressed a cold jalapeño swiped from the pizza onto Meredith's lips. Meredith had screamed, and the closet coercion had eased up after that.

Despite being a rule follower, Bea had gotten detention a couple of times in high school for being unable to resist an opportunity to make the class laugh: Once, in Mrs. Wood's Latin class, she'd spotted the detached, freshly glued, sticky, papier-mâché scrotum sack of Pegasus. The horse was being created collaboratively by the Latin students as a contribution to the school arts fair, but he wasn't supposed to have balls, of course. Earlier that day Mrs. Wood had ripped off the balls and placed them on her desk, where they now sat within Bea's reach. As Mrs. Wood turned to offer a lengthy lecture to a student on the other side of the room, her long blonde hair pooled on her desk. Bea had simply given the balls a nudge, and the testicles had wound themselves into the woman's hair without any further provocation. "What the . . . ?" she said when she felt them dangling. She stood and pulled at them, worsening the tangle, while screaming, "Get the horse genitalia out of my hair!"

Again, it had just been too easy.

Mannequin. Please. She had merely been vacant for a bit. As if she were moving through quicksand. She was a Justice Fellow now!

Three miles into her run, she had to pee. She sped up until she reached the student center, slowing to dab the slick sheen of sweat off her face with her shirt before going inside. As she walked the long corridor in search of a restroom, she recalled from her visit to campus earlier in the year that there was a coffee shop at the far end of the student center. Surely it had a bathroom. She made her way past the mailboxes, past a long row of darkened offices, to the café. Finally, a door with two stick figures on it, locked.

Her phone vibrated.

Want me to wait on you for breakfast? It'll be Lord of the Flies in there soon, Early texted.

Bea was about to reply that Early should go on ahead when a flyer on the wall caught her eye. C.U.N.T., it read, and in fine print beneath the large letters: CARTER UNIVERSITY'S NIMBLEST TURTLES, THE MOST CELEBRATED IMPROV TEAM IN THE SOUTHEAST! Underneath was a cartoon drawing of a sea turtle with excessively long limbs in Warrior II pose. The flyer announced a performance that evening.

Want to go see the improv group's show tonight? she wrote to Early.

Ok!!! Early responded as the bathroom door opened and a bleached-blonde woman in a green apron emerged.

"Toilet paper's out so I'd grab a napkin if I was you," the woman said.

Isn't that your job? Bea thought, following her into the café to retrieve one.

THE DOORS OPENED, and a student in a Carter sweatshirt appeared, yelling orders at the sea of milling students in line for the show.

"House is open! Fill every seat! Keep moving! Fill every seat!"

Bea felt as if she were boarding a plane as a hundred-plus people shuffled forward into a space that appeared too small to hold them.

"Once all the seats are taken, make rows on the floor!" the sweatshirted student yelled.

Early and Bea found spots on the ground in front, and Bea pulled in her knees, surprised by the size of the crowd.

At 7:05, the room sank into darkness, and the chatter quieted. A cheer rose to the familiar bars of Drake:

You used to call me on my cell phone
Late night when you need my love

Then the lights flew back on to deafening cheers as the members of the team—eight guys and one girl—ran out onto the stage.

A chubby fellow with shiny, cherry-red hair stepped forward.

"Welcome to the first C.U.N.T. show of the year!" He paused for whooping and applause. "If this is your first show, raise your hand!" Bea and Early timidly lifted theirs. "Fantastic to see all of you first-years here tonight. For those of you who are new to us, I want to be clear that our name, C.U.N.T., is just that—an *acronym*. It is not a *word*. We're vulgar, but not *that* vulgar."

Laughter.

"Quick origin story. . . . In the early days of the group, before it had a name, before we were even an official group, we would meet up on Tuesdays to do improv for fun. One afternoon a group member—someone says his name was Stephen, but this was long before my time, so I don't have any clue if that's right—said, "See you next Tuesday!" without realizing that he was using a euphemism for"—he paused and then whispered, "cunt."

He continued, "From then on, C.U.N.T. was our name. Of course, when parents visit, we are Carter University's Nimblest Turtles, spelled out. They're confused, but they aren't so offended that they withdraw their children from the university, at least as far as we know."

He explained that the group would be coming up with a performance on the spot, based on a single suggestion from the audience. The show would be improvised from start to finish; nothing had been planned, practiced, or decided in advance. It would begin with a monologue—a true story—told by one of the group members, to give the team more ideas to play with.

"Could I have a suggestion of a personal characteristic of a human?" he asked.

Shouts peppered the air. From just behind Bea, "Narcissism!" From somewhere, "Psychopathy!" "Altruism!" When Early timidly shouted, "Kindness!" Bea found herself giggling. The ginger-haired improviser had heard "altruism" first.

"Altruism is our word," he announced. The crowd howled as he backed off the stage.

A tall boy with a bushy brown beard stepped forward.

"When I was in secondary school—or high school as you call it over here"—he had a British accent, and Bea found herself leaning forward to get a better look at him—"I was terrified of girls. Utterly terrified. And I know what you're thinking—that all boys are terrified of girls. Um, not this terrified. Despite being from a very secular family and having no interest in religion whatsoever, I started going to a Christian youth group with my mate Fritz just so I could meet a very devout girl in the hope that, well, being Christian, she wouldn't pressure me to have sex."

Laughter rippled through the crowd.

"It wasn't that I didn't *want* to have sex. I just didn't like the expectation that I was supposed to be immediately, totally DTF the second any girl decided she was feeling a bit randy. And I know this isn't how guys are supposed to be, so I was a little bit ashamed. Well, it worked. I started dating someone who was saving herself until marriage, and this was great because I could also save myself but do so without having my masculinity called into question.

"Until things took a turn. On my seventeenth birthday, I walked into her parents' house to find that her parents weren't home and she was totally naked. 'It's your birthday present,' she said. *My birthday present.*

"I had no choice but to come clean. I said, 'You know, Sally,

I don't know if I'm ready for this,' and she was sort of offended, naturally, and I told her it wasn't anything about how she looked, and she put her clothes back on and we watched *Skins*, which you all don't know because it's a British show but it's this teen drama. And lying there I was feeling actually very liberated, you know? Very relieved. I had been honest with her, and I felt understood and accepted. And I started to think, maybe I *do* want to go for it. Now that the pressure was off, I could experience my own sincere desire.

"And just as I'm thinking these things, she says, 'Russell, I'm really glad that didn't happen today.' And I'm like, 'Yeah, I agree.' And she says, very serious and tenderly, like she's telling me something delicate, 'Do you realize you're gay?'"

"My next girlfriend found that story hilarious," he said, pivoting to an eruption of laughter. The one girl in the group dashed to the front of the stage in his place. As the laughs subsided, she clasped her hands behind her back and lifted her chin, assuming the position of a child in a spelling bee.

"Altruism! A! L! T!"

Two more of her teammates scurried forward and crouched in front of her.

"Mr. Nettles," one said, facing the other, "I know you're chair of the bee this year, so I don't mean to be out of line here, but do you think you're being totally fair?"

"Mr. Watts," the other said, "I have no idea what you're talking about. Are you suggesting that because Delilah is my niece, I'm showing her favor of some sort?"

"Well, perhaps. . . I mean. . . ."

By this point, three other teammates had lined up behind the girl, playing students who were also competing in the spelling bee.

"Scarlett!" the student playing Mr. Watts called to one of them.

"Can you remind us of the words you've spelled so far today in this bee?"

"Certainly!" she said. "Pugnacious, supercilious, divergence, anemone, and supercalifragilisticexpialidocious."

"Marcus, how about you?"

"I've spelled wanton, aghast, jeopardize, pyrrhic, and skullduggery."

"Thank you," Mr. Watts said. "And now, sweet niece Delilah, what words have you spelled so far?"

"Cat! Dog! Rat! Me! I! And I was about to spell *altruism*!"

Mr. Nettles shrugged. "Seems pretty fair to me!"

"I would like to ask a question for clarification on a definition," the girl as Delilah said. "Is *altruism* a synonym for *favoritism*? Or is that just a misunderstanding, Mr. Watts?"

She broke into a laugh, and the audience joined her as Mr. Nettles sprang to his feet and ran across the front of the stage, signaling the end of the scene.

Bea couldn't peel her eyes from the girl. In one scene, she played a bicyclist who could only pedal backward. Everywhere she went, she went backward, with one hand on the "bike handles" and the other balancing herself on her "seat." In order to create this character, she'd had to flee the stage to procure a stool from the far back corner of the room behind the audience. While everyone waited, she'd tromped through the mass of people, stepping over laps, holding a stool above her head. The boldness of this choice!

After the first half of the show came a ten-minute intermission. Bea's butt was numb from sitting on the cool tiles, and her cheeks ached from laughing.

"Bea, look! You should try out." Early handed Bea a sheet of teal printer paper on which was typed: AUDITIONS: WED, 8/30, 6–10 P.M. WE ENCOURAGE WOMEN, TRANS FOLK, AND PEOPLE OF COLOR TO APPLY, BECAUSE . . . LOOK AT US OTHER THAN LESLEY AND RAJ.

"Why don't *you*?" Bea said.

Early shook her head confidently.

"I'm funny enough, but I lack the self-assurance."

"*I'm* not funny enough," Bea said. "Though I guess what's funny is the spontaneity. You don't have to be funny, you just have to be spontaneous."

"Right! You just have to be smart. I could be your groupie. I'll come to all your shows, and you can set me up with that redhead." The lights flickered, and people began to settle back into their seats.

"Just try it," Early said as the room grew quiet. "What do you have to lose?"

Stayja

LA was waiting for Stayja when she arrived at the Rooster.

"Thought you might want some company," he said as she entered the shop.

"I have work to do." She swung her bag into the cabinet under the sink and noted that campus catering had delivered a new supply of ready-made meals for the students too busy to pause for an actual meal in one of the dining halls. Carter students: always hurrying toward something Stayja couldn't see.

"Boo," he said and made a pouty face.

They called him LA because two years earlier, a production company had come to campus to film a season of the network miniseries *Carolina Crimespree*. LA had gone in for the extras casting call and then had been given an actual speaking role, appearing in no fewer than four episodes as himself: Grounds Guy Number Two. He'd made three grand, with which he'd bought a flat-screen TV and a used Honda, selling his old tangerine Corolla to Stayja for ten bucks. (It had once been a driver's ed car, but he'd taken out the passenger-side brake after he'd bought it seven years earlier. It had logged nearly 240,000 miles yet somehow still ran. On both front doors, you could still see the faint ghost of a phone number for the old driving school.)

Rugged as usual, he wore his standard pair of work jeans, tattered and smeared with mud stains, and a cotton button-up shirt with rolled-up sleeves. This image of him coupled with a subtle grassy, outdoorsy scent was why, Stayja assumed, he'd made it to prime time as himself. LA was sweet—unbearably so—and had been since he was the kid who lived next door, always coming over and asking to play with her and Nicole.

After Nicole's dad was killed on a worksite seven years ago, when Stayja was sixteen and Nicole fourteen, they'd used his life-insurance money to transform his machine shop in the backyard into a house for Donna and Stayja so they could stop renting an apartment a few streets over. When they'd run out of money before the roof was complete, LA had climbed up a shaky ladder with a bundle of shingles and spent a week in the July sun finishing the job. He made Stayja and Donna homemade cards on their birthdays—actually cut the goddamn letters out of construction paper like some kind of scrapbook-crazed middle-aged woman. And yet Stayja couldn't imagine kissing him, a fact that he'd never fully accepted.

The plastic ready-made meal trays were filled with mayonnaisey sushi rolls, plump clumps of tuna salad, nearly indistinguishable lumps of chicken salad, and some "spicy" vegan version of the same. Stayja tied on her apron and began moving the containers into the refrigerator.

Nicole walked in, beaming.

"I got the job!" She held up her hand for a high five from Stayja.

"That was lucky," Stayja said.

"Thanks for the urine, cuz."

"What's she talking about?" LA asked.

"What's up?" Nicole said, looking at Stayja and ignoring LA. Nicole and LA liked to pretend that they didn't get along. They each thought the other demanded too much of Stayja's time.

"Nothing," Stayja said with a sigh. "Oh, I'm working a double tonight. So maybe LA can take you home."

"I stole you these." Nicole chucked a pack of Marlboro Lights onto the counter.

"Nicole!" Stayja said.

"No, listen, it's not traceable. People pay in cash for coffee, you don't log it, and once you have enough cash to cover a pack, you log a cigarette purchase. Brill, right?"

Stayja rolled her eyes. "It doesn't work like that. The coffee is inventory, too."

Nicole shrugged. "Doubt it."

"I thought you weren't smoking anymore," LA said to Stayja.

"What are you, her keeper?" Nicole said.

"You can do it, Stayja. Some of the greatest feats in history were accomplished by people who didn't know they were feats."

"Where did you hear that, LA? That's too smart for you," said Nicole.

"It's also not true," Stayja said. "Guys, I need to work."

Nicole raised her eyebrows at Stayja, then clucked her tongue. "Fine, can I get the keys? When should I come back for you, ten? Eleven?"

"No," Stayja snapped, her voice rising. "You can't drive right now, remember? You got a *DUI*. You can take the bus home, or walk, or make him give you a ride."

"I'm only good for favors now?" said LA. He turned to Nicole. "Hey, I have one for you. Ready?" Nicole's favorite ongoing game was to come up with two names, the first of which sounded normal until you heard the second. She was the sole arbiter of who reigned champion at any given time, and Stayja had held the lead for months now after coming up with "Phillip and Flathead," followed by Donna in second place with "Jean and Denim."

Nicole had never allowed LA to move above second-to-last place because his spot there drove him crazy, providing Stayja and Nicole endless amusement.

"Frank and hotdog," he said. "Good, right?"

"You did not come up with that, LA."

"I did!"

"You heard it somewhere."

"Motherfucker! I didn't!"

"Stayja? I just feel like I've heard that one before." Stayja and Nicole laughed as LA sulked. A pair of professors entered the coffee shop.

"Dudes, time to go." Stayja shooed them.

"If I give you a ride, will you trust me that I came up with that one?" LA said as he and Nicole walked out.

When the dinner traffic slowed, Stayja popped an Aleve Cold and Sinus—her drug of choice when she needed to stay awake and alert—and grabbed the stolen cigarettes Nicole had left her, then exited through the side door to the parking lot. She took a seat on the curb and batted the box against her palm before ripping off the plastic encasement. Some asshole had decided cigarette packs should be plastered with photographs of decimated lungs and bloody gums, and this one featured a grotesque tracheotomy. She tore the glossy wound from the box and let it fall onto the pavement next to her sneaker.

"Like we don't fucking know," she muttered. As she drew a long, precious inhale, a guy she took to be a student stepped out from the shadow of a tree into the glow of the orange lamps that lit up in synchrony on Carter's campus each evening well before dusk.

"Can I bum one?" he asked.

Not many students at Carter smoked out in the open, although Stayja knew many *did* smoke, because she'd spent her first year of employment at the university selling them cigarettes at the Quik-Mart. She took her smoke breaks in a relatively secluded location behind the Rooster, in the lot hardly anyone used other than she herself and the few guys with cars in the adjacent frat house. It was rare for a student to ask to bum one, and it always miffed her when they did. *Give me a dollar, then*, she dreamed of saying. *Since you have about a million more than me.* But she always handed one over.

Tonight, she didn't care. He could take the whole fucking pack. Flicking a cigarette to life, he plopped down on the curb next to her.

"How's your day going?" he asked.

He was blond, preppy in the way that Carter boys were—he wore a quilted vest over a crisp white T-shirt and pastel yellow shorts. His voice was deeper than he looked like it should be, though, and there was a lived-in air about him, as if he'd been through something.

"Fine," she said.

He let the smoke float from his mouth in a slow cloud. "You want to start, or you want me to?"

She turned to face him.

"Just a long day," she said. "I made a lot of oat milk lattés."

He laughed. It caught her by surprise. "You mean you don't love being a barista to the women at an elite university?" His sarcasm was evident, but she couldn't tell if he was flirting with her.

"Believe it or not," she said, feeling herself soften a little.

"Listen, I'm not perfect. But when I got here, I couldn't believe some of the entitlement, especially with the girls. One night a year or so ago I was out, and walking back to my dorm I passed this girl dancing on the quad buck naked. She was tanked. Her friends were, like, not even trying to stop her because they were wrecked, too. By the time I got there I guess someone had called campus police. I watched this cop walk up to her and try to get her to put her clothes on, and she yelled, 'Do you know who my dad is?'"

Stayja chuckled. "Who was her dad?"

"I mean, I'm sure some donor or something. But talk about things you never say aloud."

Stayja took a drag. "I don't know. I'd say it if it helped me not get arrested or some shit. Whatever they do to you. Suspend you."

"She wasn't going to be suspended, please."

"How come?"

"Do you know who her father is?"

They both laughed.

"I can't talk. I'm a legacy kid myself."

"What does that mean?"

"Legacy kid? Means I got in because my parents went here."

"Ah." Stayja looked at the ground.

"Do people confide in you a lot?" he asked after a moment.

Stayja snorted. "All the time," she said. "Apparently I have that air about me."

He took a drag.

"You need to unload? Go ahead," she said.

"What do you want to hear about first—my substance-abuse issues or my daddy issues?"

"How can I possibly choose when they're presented that way?" He laughed.

"Daddy issues," she said.

"You ever hear of New Start Treatment Centers?"

"As in call 800-NEW-START? Kill your painkiller addiction without the pain?"

"That's my dad."

"He owns a drug-recovery center?"

"He owns a *fleet* of drug-recovery centers. Like two hundred something."

"Okay, and?" she said. Whenever someone made a comment meant to stress how wealthy a person was, Stayja's reaction was to feign indifference. Just because people got a lucky draw in life didn't mean she had to give them the satisfaction of thinking that impressed her.

"I don't know how much you know about opiate addiction."

"I'm not addicted to opiates, if that's what you mean."

"You're lucky, because if you are, you don't get un-addicted. It's a life sentence. You treat the addiction with drugs that don't fix it. They just relieve it, and then you have to come back for more. His centers make money off the same people for years. *Decades*. It's a revolving door. There *is* no end to treatment. Do you know what 'recovery is a lifelong process' means? It means the guy who's profiting off your lifelong process? He's very rich."

He spat onto the pavement, then continued. "Meanwhile, he's glorified as this hero. Everyone loves him. Like he's doing good. Such a lie."

"How so?"

"The new wing of Wiggins Library is gonna be named after him, for one. A gallery at Dallas Art Museum. I mean that's because he donates to those places, of course. He's a real do-gooder on paper."

"What're your substance-abuse issues?"

"She cuts to the chase." He was playful, not defensive. "Just alcohol and weed. I got my wisdom teeth out last year, and I wouldn't let them give me any painkiller but ibuprofen. I won't give my father the satisfaction."

"You think your dad *wants* you to be addicted to painkillers?"

He dropped his cigarette on the ground.

"I think my dad likes to be in control of everything. I think part of him wants me to succeed because I'm his kid and it makes him look good, but part of him likes when I fuck up because he gets to feel like he's better than me."

"So, maybe stating the obvious, but your dad sounds like a jerk."

He chuckled. "You should hear how happily self-righteous he sounds when he tells people how long it's taken me to finish college."

"How long?"

"I'm a senior. I'm already twenty-three. I took what we call a gap year when people ask, but it was a gap year I spent at rehab."

"So? Who cares if you're twenty-three?"

"Twenty-three is old to still be in college."

Stayja let out a loud laugh. "I'm twenty-three and have two years left to go for my associate's in nursing, so you get no sympathy here."

Suddenly sheepish, he said, "Well, I'm not saying it's something that bothers me. I'm saying it makes my dad gleeful and smug." He paused and then said, "You're gonna be a nurse?"

"If I can ever finish school," said Stayja. "I'm two years in, but I keep having to drop classes. . . . It's a long story."

He raised his eyebrows and waited.

She took a breath. "I've been working at Carter since I graduated high school, first at the QuikMart, then at the coffee shop. Three years ago I decided to go into nursing and started saving— I have seventy-six credits to get through at WCC—um, that's Wake Community College. Those are $490—but every time I manage to save up a chunk, something goes wrong. The roof on the carport caved in. Then one time I had to go to the ER when a cyst on my ovary burst and I thought it was my appendix. There was nothing to be done but wait for it to heal itself, but it still cost me $1,700. So I had to drop anatomy three weeks into the semester and never got the tuition back."

Donna had encouraged her to just not pay the bill, but Donna didn't mind creditors calling all the time. Stayja would rather pay a debt every time than have to live with the barrage of calls about it that left her feeling like a failure, full of shame.

"So I'll take the three classes I need in the spring to knock out the two classes I need in the summer, which will keep me on track to graduate two years from now."

When she was done, he said, "And I thought I had it rough."

"It's okay," she said, suddenly self-conscious. "I wasn't telling you to get sympathy."

"Hey," he said, bemused. "Smile for me."

Caught off guard, she offered a closed-lip smile.

"No, like this." He demonstrated.

Shyly she parted her lips.

"Your teeth are cute," he said.

"Shut up," she said. "I get it. They're crooked. Asshole."

"I'm serious. I'm not making fun. I like them."

She smiled. A real one.

CHETSON "CHET" BLUM, Esquire, as he was called on the billboard, looked to be around forty-five years old. The hair on his crown was slicked back, the sides cut short. He hardly looked at Nicole and Stayja before turning to his computer screen and typing something on his keyboard.

"Last name," he said.

"Rankin—" Nicole answered.

"Spelling," he interrupted.

"What?" Nicole asked.

"Spell it," he said. Stayja couldn't see the screen, but she could tell something new had flashed onto it. Chet Blum, DUI attorney, studied it for a moment.

"Twelve hundred."

"What?" Nicole said.

"Up-front as a retainer. I'll take it from there."

Stayja asked if that meant the whole bill was twelve hundred or if that was only the first part.

"Should be it, minus costs and fees," he said distractedly.

"How much are those?" Stayja asked.

"Depends. If I can get it dismissed before a hearing and we just have one filing fee, thirty bucks."

"I may not have to go to court?" Nicole asked hopefully.

"Depends. Maybe not," said Chet.

"Do we need to pay it now?" Stayja asked.

"Yes, ma'am," said Chet, checking his email. "Money order or debit only. Or cash, of course."

Stayja and Nicole looked at each other.

"We don't have the cash right now," Nicole said in her most girlish voice. "Would you be willing to do us a big one and let us owe you? I can't even tell you how grateful I'd be."

Her tone caught his attention. For the first time since they walked in, Chet Blum looked hard at Nicole, who was now leaning against his desk, her hips pressing into it.

"No," said Chet after a long pause. "Cash or debit only." He turned back to his monitor.

"We'll be back soon," Stayja said. "Thanks."

As they walked back to the car, Nicole fumbled in her purse and pulled out a hot pink Post-it pad speckled with crumbs and fuzz.

"Pen?" she said.

Stayja reached into her own bag and pulled out a green highlighter. "Just this," she said, then watched as her cousin wrote *Nicole*, followed by her number and a heart. She approached a BMW parked in the reserved spot closest to the entrance and slid it under the front-door handle.

"Nicole! What the . . . ?"

"Don't worry, it's his! Check the plate," said Nicole. The car's front license plate read: CB ESQ.

"No," Stayja said. She marched over to the door and yanked the Post-it from where Nicole had lodged it beneath the handle.

She balled it up and began walking toward their car. "You cannot be serious."

"Stayja! What the fuck?" Nicole followed her cousin across the parking lot to the Corolla, which was now hidden by a monster truck that had arrived while they were inside. "He totally wants me, and this way we don't have to pay him, because he's not allowed to sleep with his clients. So after we sleep together, I'll just say that I'm going to report him unless he gives back the twelve hundred dollars. Plus fees."

Stayja spun around. LA was waiting for them in the car, and she didn't want to continue this conversation in front of him.

"You're not his client yet, Nicole. Are you retarded?"

Nicole crossed her arms. "No. I'm not. But thanks for being so mean. And you're not allowed to use that word anymore."

"I'm the one who told you that!"

"I know! So *you* can't use it, especially!"

Stayja took a deep breath. "What you are describing, I believe, is blackmail. Or extortion or something. I'm pretty sure it's illegal."

"I don't know why you feel so free to judge *me*," said Nicole, trying to dump a cigarette into her palm and accidentally releasing four. Three rolled across the pavement, one hitting Stayja's toe. She picked it up and gestured to her cousin for a light. Nicole lit her own, then handed back the lighter. "You're the one who thinks you're going to date some Carter guy."

"What are you talking about?" It had been three days since Stayja and the blond guy, whose name she hadn't gotten, had spent almost an hour on the curb talking. (Thank God this hadn't gotten back to Frank, at least not yet.)

LA had gotten out of the car and was listening. "Who?" he said.

"No one," Stayja said.

"Some guy Stayja met whom she almost got fired for so they could canoodle in the parking lot."

"He goes to Carter?"

"This has nothing to do with you, LA," Stayja said.

"Is he Jewish?" LA asked.

"What on earth?" Stayja said.

"You can't say that word," Nicole said.

"You can say the word *Jewish*, Nicole!" Stayja said.

"You really want to be with some Carter loser? Who can't even change a fucking tire?"

Stayja shushed him.

"Stop shushing me. It's not that Muslim guy, is it?"

The last time LA had professed his love—a biannual event—had been in the spring, while she was at work at the coffee shop. Stayja had made a mistake. Thinking that if she gave LA a concrete foe, he would finally drop his bid for her love, she'd told him the name of her crush-from-afar: Eric Gourdazi.

Eric was olive-skinned and lanky. He parted his thick, straight black hair on the side and wore khaki pants, even to class, a habit Stayja knew was dorky even by Carter standards but that she found inexplicably endearing. He seemed, to her, ideal: sophisticated, nerdy, and respectful. He ordered a black coffee every time he came in and always smiled and thanked her while looking her in the eye, something few students bothered to do. He'd never asked her name, but she knew his from his student ID. Over the summer, she'd looked forward to seeing him once school was in session, but since her encounter with the blond guy three days earlier, she hadn't thought about Eric once.

She'd realized her error immediately when LA, raising his voice, had said, "Since when do you like ethnic types?"

"Stop it," she'd mouthed and, thinking quickly, poured milk into a canister to steam, desperate to drown him out.

"I hate Jews," said LA now. "Everyone at that school is Jewish."

"You don't even *know* any Jews, LA," said Stayja, walking toward the car. "Can we just go?"

"Hell yeah, I do. Guy who fucked over my dad was a Jew." Stayja struggled for a moment to remember what he was referencing—his father had worked at a tobacco plant outside town until it closed down a few years earlier. Now he worked at Lowe's in the gardening department. "Remember? Some big-wig Jew from Charlotte. Moved the plant overseas and fucked everybody over. Greedy son of a bitch."

"That didn't happen because the guy is Jewish," Stayja said. "Jesus."

"Oh, there's one, Nicole!" LA said. "Twins: Jesus and Jewish."

Nicole was staring at Stayja. "You know he is never going to date you," she said.

"Did I say I wanted to date him?" Stayja asked. "Did I say that? Because I don't think I said that."

Nicole's face softened, almost as if she pitied Stayja.

"You don't have to," she said and put out her cigarette even though she'd only smoked a third of it. "Jesus and Jewish isn't bad, LA. You're in second place now."

Annie

I have a date with Tyler Brand. The sentence played over and over in my mind as I struggled to focus on the piece of music before me, a Halloween medley we would be performing over Parents' Weekend in October. *I have a date with Tyler Brand.*

Okay, maybe it wasn't a date-date, but it wasn't *not* one either. He'd invited me to PiKa's first party of the year, the Blue Party—everyone was to wear blue—featuring a popular local band called Something McGee. I'd never heard of Something McGee, and when Tyler texted me that they'd be performing, I hurriedly looked them up on YouTube so I wouldn't be lying when I texted back cheering hands.

Saturday arrived, forecast to be the city's hottest September 2 in a half century. Becoming increasingly anxious with each hour, I ate a mini lemon poppy muffin and churned out a four-page paper for Poli Sci on the impact of voter turnout on elections. Then I went to the gym, where I forced myself to stay on the elliptical until I'd finished my Abnormal Psych reading.

Rehearsal was from noon to three. As the trumpets sounded the end of "Monster Mash," my reed snapped against my tooth. I fumbled for my spare, wondering if I had time for a mani-pedi before the evening.

"All right, 'October Sky,' everyone. 'October Sky' from the top."
Juan-Pablo lifted his baton.

I moistened the new reed with my tongue. For the first time
since rehearsal began, I found myself present in the room, eager
not to miss anything. In the week since I'd first heard the theme
to *October Sky*, I'd fallen in love with it. I'd been in orchestras for
four years, played hundreds of pieces in dozens of styles, and few
pieces of music had moved me as much as this song.

Like Bach's prelude to Suite no. 1 in G Major for cello, which
I first heard as a nine-year-old at my cousin's wedding. At nine I
hadn't yet experienced any real trauma—three more years would
pass before the fire, and my acquaintance with death was limited
to my grandma's, the saddest part of which had been witnessing
my mother's tears. But that prelude on cello summoned in me,
out of nowhere, a consuming grief, a sense of melancholy with no
origin. After the ceremony I'd approached the organist and asked
for the name of the piece. How was it that music could stir such
emotion?

It turned out that the prelude moved a lot of people. I'd come
to hear it at every wedding and funeral I attended over the next
decade, alongside Pachelbel's Canon and *Jesu, Joy of Man's Desiring*.
Gradually, I stopped hearing it in the same way. Rather than a
symbol of the power of music to transport, it became for me a
symbol of how a magical work of art can be corrupted by overuse.

Still, that first experience of the prelude, that taste, was the bite
that turned me into a musician. From then on, I lived in search of
music that trembled in the pit of my being, encountering it only
occasionally, relishing it when I did—"Nessun dorma," some of
Max Richter's compositions, the theme to *October Sky*.

As I followed along, measure by measure, my reed not quite wet
enough, the feeling the piece evoked was unexpected: hope. I felt
an opening in my rib cage, a prying.

Energized from practice and tingly with anticipation, I arrived at Beauty Snail around 3:20 to discover there was a forty-five-minute wait. The only salon within walking distance of campus, the Snail was perpetually packed, particularly on weekends. I scribbled my name and "mani-pedi," and then, because the day had turned out *not* to be unbearably hot, only beautiful, I decided to go for a stroll and give my mom a call. She'd been fighting bronchitis the last time we'd spoken three days earlier.

"Yo." My younger brother, Cory, picked up when I dialed her cell. I was surprised to hear his voice.

"Hey! You don't have football today?" I took my sunglasses out of my bag and put them on, taking long strides in the sun. If I walked briskly, I could make a full loop around South Campus before they reached my name at Beauty Snail.

"Mom made me quit," he grumbled. "She saw some documentary about how it causes brain damage."

"Oh, no," I said, trying to disguise my satisfaction. I wasn't about to tell Cory that I'd been the one to recommend the documentary to our mother. "How do you feel about that?"

"Fine." It made little sense that he actually did sound fine with it until he said, "She said she'd buy me an Xbox One."

"She bribed you to quit football with video games?"

"Pretty much."

I could hear my mother in the background ordering him to tell me something but couldn't make out what she was saying.

"What're you guys doing?" I asked.

"She's driving. We're going to Target. I will! I am right now! She says to ask you if you're wearing your new shorts."

"Tell her I am."

"Mom, does it matter? Which ones?"

"The jean ones. Is she feeling better?" The track team sped by in matching Carter shirts.

"She says she is. She says have you worn the skirt?"

"Let me talk to her!" I could hear my mom pleading.

"No!" Cory snapped. Then to me he said, "Since I'm not allowed to play football, she's not allowed to talk *or text* while she drives." Every now and then, my brother exhibited exceptional maturity. "Mom, the light! Dammit!" he cried.

"Don't curse!" she yelled.

Then she was mumbling something, and Cory said, "Mom says to ask if you're going to be careful on your date tonight."

Not only was it a date in my head, but I'd also told my mother it was one. Parents needed terms like that.

"Tell her I'll try as hard as I can *not* to be careful."

"She says she saw a *20/20* show about alcohol poisoning on college campuses that you should watch. Also remember you have to work tomorrow."

My mother treated my afternoon Sunday shift at the campus bookstore as sacrosanct and as if I were always on the verge of being fired. She'd text me during it How is work going?, to check that I was there—as if I'd just not show up for work.

"Bye, Cory," I said, aware of my mother still talking in the background.

"Later," he said.

Looking back, I can't help but see us as a family that sought to save one another from ourselves. We aspired to be safer than we were.

I'D DECIDED TO wear a blue tube top and my turquoise leather skirt. Worried about bloat, I served myself a bowl of miso soup in the dining hall and took a hundred-calorie pack of Cheez-Its from the snack stash in my dorm kitchen before heading over to PiKa.

The dorm that housed PiKa, like my own dorm, was on the main quad but on the opposite side of the yard. There were no concrete paths connecting our buildings, so to cross the grass in heels, I had to teeter on the balls of my feet, lest I arrive in mud-coated stilettos. By the time I reached his building, my shoes were unsoiled but my calves burned. I followed a group of girls through the door, which was propped open with concrete bricks. Since he hadn't told me the exact location of his room, I set about finding it. The girls before me were giddy and slumped, and I inferred that they must be first-years given how nervous they seemed. Like an amoeba, all flat-ironed and high-heeled and clean-shaven, we moved down the first-floor hall, peeking into rooms in search of our respective hosts. After they found theirs amid a whirl of squeals, I was alone in the hallway. It was dark, lit only by the squares of light from bedroom doors left ajar. Inside them, groups of people sat and stood under sloppily hung blue streamers, sipping cans of beer. None of them was Tyler. Finally, behind the second-to-last door at the hall's distant end, I spotted him seated on a brown leather sofa behind a coffee table, where playing cards were scattered. Three other guys, who looked like PiKa members, along with a rail-thin girl in a gold tank and jeans, sat in chairs facing the couch.

"Annie," he said, standing. "This is Blake. Andrew. Sam. And Ellen."

"Hi," I said to their flurry of greetings as Tyler sat back down on the sofa, slightly farther to the right, which I interpreted as an invitation to sit next to him. I slid past Blake and lowered myself onto the couch, careful to keep my knees together in my skirt, which suddenly felt shorter and tighter than it had in my room. I was grateful for the dim light, conscious of my legs.

"Have you played Kings before?" Tyler asked, cracking open a PBR and placing it in front of me.

Ellen leaned forward. "Do you want the punch? It's Everclear and Crystal Light." She smiled. I smiled back.

"That'd be great, thanks," I said.

Tyler slid the beer toward himself as Ellen walked gracefully to the corner of the room, where a bowl of yellowish liquid sat on the university-issued wooden desk. I wondered what her legs looked like under her jeans. In them, they were, like those of an impossible number of girls on campus, perfect.

As she poured, for the first time I noticed that there was only one twin bed in the room. So Tyler had a single. That was pretty common for the fourth-years who remained on campus.

"I had a feeling," said Ellen as she handed me a red Solo cup of punch, "that you are also a punch girl, not a beer girl." She was calling me skinny. At once my confidence lifted.

Sam or Andrew—I'd already forgotten who was who—held up an ace.

"Waterfall!" he yelled. Everyone's cups flew upward, and the group began to chug. I followed suit, holding my cup to my lips, my head tilted back like theirs, taking gulps, but small ones, apportioning my intake. Finally Sam or Andrew, whoever had drawn the ace, crinkled his can in his hand.

"You're done, Annie!" he said, then belched. I lowered my drink. So did Tyler, then Ellen, then the other boys.

We played for an hour or so. The rules of Kings: a two card meant two people of your choice drink; a three card meant you take three drinks yourself; the four card through the queen meant various iterations of the same. When the first three king cards were drawn, the person who drew the hand dumped a splash of his or her drink no matter what it was—beer or liquor or watered-down backwash—into a dreaded red Solo cup in the middle of the table, which slowly was being filled with a revolting liquid. Whoever drew the last king had to drink it.

By the time I flipped a king of clubs—the fourth and final king—the cup in the middle of the table contained a mixture of punch, beer, and whatever Sam was drinking, some kind of brown liquor.

"You don't have to chug the whole thing," said Tyler. "Guys, are we okay with her not chugging the whole thing?" Then to me, "Annie, you can just take a sip."

But then the others started chanting, "Down it! Down it!" And so I took as many gulps as I could of the foul mixture before handing it to Tyler, who grabbed my hand and finished it off in a sort of collegiate act of chivalry. He shuddered as he brought down the cup, then looked at me. I wiped my lips, then his, tipsy. We both laughed.

"Fucking nasty," he said, and I said, "brutal" so loudly that it took me aback.

"When is the band starting?" asked Ellen, checking the time on her phone.

"They can't without me!" Tyler said. To our quizzical looks, he explained, "I'm introducing them." He was looking at Ellen but stole a quick glance at me as he said it, and that I could tell he hoped it impressed me endeared him to me further.

"Well, you guys want to go on outside?" said Ellen. We agreed and stood, refilling our drinks before exiting the room. As we made our way down the hallway, now packed with people, I noticed that my vision wasn't keeping up with my movement. I had been really, truly drunk—not just tipsy, but drunk—twice in my life, and I recognized the sensation.

Tyler held my hand, leading me through the swarm of bodies. His palm was warm and neither dry nor damp, and I tried to enjoy the contact of our skin as the nausea hit. I swallowed and took a deep breath, then puckered my lips and blew it out, as my dad had taught me to do when I was a kid. I did it again, failing to notice that Tyler had turned and was studying me.

"Are you okay?" he asked, his face so close to mine that I could smell his breath, beer with a tinge of mint. He was hyped up, his eyes jumpy, his body emanating a kind of ferocious energy. He seemed ready to either dance or take off into a sprint.

I nodded and swallowed as the taste of bile flooded my throat. I needed to sit. I closed my eyes. Closing my eyes was a bad idea. I opened them, swaying.

"Whoa," Tyler said. "Come on." He escorted me back to his room, where he helped me lie down on the couch. "Breathe," he said. I followed his instruction.

"I'll come back and check on you in a bit," he said. Then he filled a fresh Solo cup with water from a Brita in his mini fridge and placed it on the floor next to me.

The last thing I remember is feeling embarrassed at getting so drunk before the night had even begun, before he'd even introduced Something McGee, before they'd even played our song that he didn't yet know was our song. I remember thinking that Tyler had handled my humiliating behavior magnanimously, with understanding and kindness. I remember hoping that I hadn't ruined my chances with him. I remember feeling dizzy with gratitude.

When I awoke, the room was dark, and I was making myself vomit; my fingers were in my throat, like the one time we all tried it in the girls' bathroom in middle school.

No—no, they weren't.

"Yeah, girl. Eat it, girl." A low, gravelly voice with a slur was giving orders. It took me several moments to recognize whom it belonged to. His hands gripped my head, pressing against my ears, my earrings digging into my cheeks.

"You like that?" he kept asking. "You like that," he answered his own question.

With each thrust I gagged, and just as I felt the rise in my stomach, I was freed. Then there was warmth on my face, in my eyes. Through the wet, the blur, I was becoming more aware, more alert, my eyes adjusting to the moonlit room, to my body's position-ing, to my skin touching the sticky leather. Before me, Tyler was silently pulling on a pair of basketball shorts. He walked over to his closet door, disappeared behind it, and then reappeared with a T-shirt, which he handed to me. It was white and folded neatly in thirds.

Back in his normal voice, he said, "Did you get cum in your eyes? Sorry."

I dabbed my face without unfolding the shirt, then placed it on the sofa next to me as I adjusted my skirt, which was hitched high, exposing me completely—my underwear was gone. It was nowhere to be seen. No, there it was, on the floor. Dread folded into me.

"That was hot," he said, crossing his arms and yawning. "You want to crash?"

I was still squinting hazily at my underwear on the floor, fo-cusing all of my energy on trying to remember the last thing I remembered.

You like that? You like that.

"No," I said, picking up my underwear and balling it in my fist.

"Cool," he said indifferently. "Hey, get back safe."

And then, while I stood there, my arms dangling at my sides, one hand holding my underwear, he kissed me on the lips. It wasn't a long kiss. There was no tongue. But it was soft and lingering, as if he wanted to leave me with something good. And though I hated myself for it, though my mind recoiled at the idea of it, my body accepted it with relief.

I AWOKE FEELING as if my head were being packed with sandbags. I reached for my phone to check the time and found it dead. Parched, my eyes dry and burning, I dragged myself to my desk, where I opened my computer. 11:22 a.m.

I was supposed to meet Matty for brunch at 11:30 before my bookstore shift at 2. Four emails from him flashed into bold at the top of my in-box—

meet where?

WHERE TO EAT

your phone is dead. can we do 11? Starving

omg Annie for real I hate you

There was a knock at the door, then the knob rattled.

"It's me," Matty said from the other side, annoyance in his voice.

So I'd made it home, and I'd locked my door. Flecks of recollection came in no particular order.

I was alive.

I hadn't dreamt it.

My underwear in a ball, the gagging, the semen, the T-shirt. Had we had sex? Surely, I would feel something—a soreness, an awareness. But then, the only time I'd had sex before, it hadn't hurt or left me sore. And then: they were on the floor.

"I knew it," Matty said as I opened the door. "How late did you stay out? Who *are* you?" I never slept past eight. He found my dead phone and began looking for the charger.

"Does Converse have something to do with this?"

I reached into my bag, pulled out my charger and handed it to him. He plugged in my phone, then turned to me and put his hands on his hips.

"What?" I said.

"Are you going to insist on showering, or can we go eat? God, maybe you should. You smell like a sink drain."

I remembered washing my face, but I didn't remember showering. My clothes—skirt and top—were crumpled in a pile by my desk. I picked up my purse and looked at him. "Fine, let's go."

He scrunched up his face.

"Aren't you going to change? Or at least put on a bra?"

I looked down. I was wearing the Carter T-shirt my dad had bought me two years earlier, before I even started, the one I still slept in. I had on yoga pants, and the strapless bra I'd worn the night before. I must have forgotten or lacked the energy to take it off.

"I have on a bra," I said.

"Your face . . ." He narrowed his eyes, studying me. "Did you sleep on top of something? You have these weird marks."

For the first time I looked in the mirror to find red scratches on my cheeks where my earrings had been smashed into them. Clouds of mascara encircled my eyes. Maybe I hadn't washed my face.

"I fell asleep in my earrings," I lied.

"Maybe let's at least towel off last night's smoky eye?"

"What the fuck, Matty?" My voice cracked. "I'm not your girl-friend. You don't get to be embarrassed about how I look when I'm with you."

"Okay," he said, holding up his hands. "You just look a *little* bit like, you know."

"Like what?" I said, unable to believe what was happening, what I thought he meant.

"Like you're auditioning for the role of a victim on *SVU* or something."

I felt my eyes well up.

"It was a stupid joke, sorry. I'm hungry because I've been up since seven. Can we just go eat please?"

I had dropped my purse on the ground while he was talking.

"I don't want to go anymore," I said.

"Because of a dumb joke?" Matty said. "I'm sorry. Rape culture is not a joke. I'm a feminist. Blah blah. Now let's eat. You look fine."

"I'm not available to you all the time!" I yelled. "God. Can't you go two hours without stuffing your face?" I threw myself onto my bed facing the wall, aware of how out of character this was—surprising even myself. A few seconds later, I heard the door shut and his footsteps fade.

I texted Frank that I had food poisoning and couldn't make my shift. Then I fell asleep and slept until the ding of my recharged phone woke me up.

Hey. How are you today?

What the . . . ? I sat up and grabbed the phone with both hands, which were shaking. Whether it was due to fear or alcohol withdrawal or low blood sugar, I didn't know.

Been better, I typed back. As soon as I'd sent it, I wondered if I should have written something else, something honest. *Other than waking up last night with your dick in my mouth and now feeling a lot of things, including rage at you and shame at myself and guilt that I just picked a fight with my best friend, I'm okay.*

He wrote back: Can we talk? I can come to you.

I froze, conflicted. The last thing I wanted was Tyler in my room. But I also did want to talk, and not in public. I needed to understand what had happened. So many questions—what had gone on from his perspective? Why had my underwear been on the floor? Why hadn't I woken up before I did?

I'll come to you, I wrote back. I would shower first.

HIS DOOR WAS cracked. I nudged it open to find him seated at his desk barefoot, in a fresh long-sleeved T-shirt—army green—and jeans. The shirt still had two creases down the front from where it had been folded by someone else, not a college boy, and I remembered the white T-shirt suddenly, the one he'd handed to me. He must send his laundry off to be done, like some of the wealthier students did. His hair was still half wet, and his room smelled like men's shampoo. I noticed he'd cleaned—there were no signs of the party, no signs of me.

"Come in," he said, and I saw that he was working on a Power-Point, a detail that struck me as funny. I laughed.

"What?" He frowned, as if I were making fun of him.

"PowerPoint?" I groaned, lifting my hands to my face and covering my eyes. More to myself than to him, I asked again. "*Power-Point?*"

"What do you mean?"

Should I show him my cheeks? Or let him notice for himself? I'd wound up showering but hesitated before putting on makeup, ultimately opting not to. I didn't want to care how I looked for Tyler, not now. The least I could do to salvage what dignity I retained was not to stoop to applying concealer.

"Have a seat," he said formally.

"No, thanks," I said sharply, sick at the sight of the couch. My tone was unfamiliar—it had much more edge than I'd heard in it before. Tyler also seemed alarmed by it, which gave me a dash of satisfaction.

"Okay." He put his hands in his pockets. It occurred to me that he was performing sheepish, as if he were about to admit his carefully curated most embarrassing moment.

Please. Please don't apologize, I thought.

"I was just hoping you could tell me," he said, "what happened last night?"

I held my breath. What *happened*? Was it a trick, a ploy? Did he fear I was going to report him and therefore had decided to feign cluelessness? I searched his face and found it unreadable.

"What do you mean?" I said carefully. "Which . . . part?"

"You passed out," he said, glancing at the sofa. I braced myself as he continued, "and I partied for a while and then came back here, but I don't remember what happened after that. This morning when I woke up, I felt like . . . I thought I remembered—did we fight?" When I didn't respond, he went on, "because I woke up feeling like you were mad at me."

"You thought you remembered what?" My voice quivered.

"A fight. You left because you were mad at me. Did we hook up?"

Still he appeared mystified. His expression gave away nothing, not the tiniest clue.

"Here's what happened, Tyler. Since you don't remember. I woke up with your dick in my mouth." I spat the words. "And my underwear was on the floor, but I don't remember taking it off. Because I'm pretty sure I didn't." I should have put the emphasis on *I*: pretty sure *I* didn't take it off, but that was too much for my own ears.

The silence that ensued was the strangest few seconds of my life. Tyler seemed to take this in, to process it, and to decide that it wasn't plausible.

"No," he said, shaking his head. "Impossible. I came in, and you woke up when I turned on the light. You asked me how the band was and kept saying how sorry you were for being drunk. We had a whole conversation. Then I got myself another drink and you some water, but you didn't want it." Another pause. "You don't remember any of this?"

I shook my head, doubt seeping into the back of my neck.

"We both fell asleep on the couch," he said, suddenly more confident in his recollection of events. "And I don't remember anything after that, apart from at some point we hooked up. I definitely don't remember what you just said."

"Well, I don't remember any of what *you* just said," I said. How was this happening? We sounded like a couple of schoolchildren. Was what he was describing possible? I *was* very drunk. I'd passed out. No, no, no. He wasn't going to confuse me like this.

"Okay, but I promise you it's true," he said. "I swear. And I swear, if we hooked up, you must have been into it, or I at least thought you were. I would never . . . while a girl is unconscious? Are you kidding? That's fucking gross."

"Did we have sex?" I asked, forcing myself to ask the question that had been haunting me.

"I don't think so."

"Are you sure?"

"Um, are you asking if I *raped* you? No."

I was baffled, flailing in a haze of bewilderment and shame and anger. Once I'd awoken, it was true I hadn't fought him off. Coming to, I'd cooperated. Why? If it had been against my will, why hadn't I resisted? And anyway, if it was only a blow job, was it rape? If my underwear was off, but we hadn't had sex . . . The questions swirled.

"I thought you'd raped me," I said quietly. *I still think you might have*, I didn't say.

"I knew something was wrong when I woke up." He sighed with relief, like clarity had finally been reached. He came over to me and tenderly placed his hands on my elbows. "Annie, I was shit-faced. We both were. We were two bombed people having a sloppy hookup. I would never *rape* you. I really like you. I think you're beautiful and smart. And I thought you looked insanely hot last night in that skirt, so no wonder I couldn't keep my hands off you."

I smiled involuntarily. Why was I smiling?

Suddenly I had the urge to cry.

"No, don't. Don't cry." He pulled me into a hug, and I let him. His scent was reassuring in some way my ragged body craved. I let my face sink into his collarbone. "This week, can we have a real date? Like one where we aren't drinking, at least not as much? We can get to know each other for real, and I'll keep my hands to myself. It'll be PG. Maybe PG-13 if we're, you know, feeling handsy."

Looking back, I am unable to diagnose myself in this moment. I recall being afraid—not of the future but of the past. I recall hope so vicious that it sliced through me, disguising itself as belief. Because while I don't think I did believe him, I wanted to believe him more than I'd ever wanted anything. I had never more wholly, more unequivocally hoped for something as I did that Tyler Brand had not raped me.

"Okay," I said, lifting my head to look him in the eye.

Bea

WEDNESDAY, AUGUST 30—SATURDAY, SEPTEMBER 2

"Cooking product!"

Bea's audition group consisted of her and six other hopefuls—all guys. They were to strike poses based on whatever Chris, the mustached guy who'd MC'd the show she'd seen, called out from a folding chair. Along both sides of the fluorescent-lit room, the rest of the team members observed the audition.

Bea hurried to the center of the room and raised her arms above her head with her palms touching.

"Hello, what are you?" asked Chris.

"Olive oil. As long as I'm displayed *somewhere* on the counter, I'm fine," she said, aware of a few snickers behind her, "but I should under no circumstances be relegated to a cabinet. I'm far too lovely for that." She returned to the line of hopefuls milling near the back wall while the others took their turns.

The next two rounds unfolded in similar fashion—they did not have to improvise *with* one another; they only had to step out and individually improvise a single idea based on whatever word Chris hollered. For "sea animal," Bea chose an agoraphobic conch, wrapping her arms and legs around herself. For "circus performer," she chose a stuttering mime with jerking gestures. While miming, she heard the girl from the team—whose name she'd learned was Lesley—laughing, and this filled Bea with pride.

"For the next scene, we're going to partner you up," said Chris. When he spoke, his mustache bounced the tiniest bit, as if it were riding on his words. "Two of you will take a seat"—he pulled two folding chairs out to the center of the room and placed them side by side facing the same direction. "Together, you'll tell us about yourselves and your relationship. As if the two of you are being interviewed for a documentary or on a talk show, minus the interviewer."

He went on to explain that the point of the exercise was to learn to say, "yes, and."

"There are two cardinal rules of improv," Chris shouted, holding up two fingers. "One, you do not *negate* your partner. If your partner calls you an elephant, you're an elephant. If your partner decides you're a clown, what are you?"

"A clown!" everyone yelled.

"We call this 'Yes, anding': whatever your scene partners do, you say *yes* to it, and then you *add* something. Yes, and. Rule number two is that you have to step out. You can't stand back. This isn't an art form where holding back works. When people are hesitant to step out, it leaves your scene partners with blue balls and saps the energy from the room. Got it?"

Everyone nodded.

"Got it?" he asked.

"Got it!" they shouted.

"Who's up?"

Bea was in one of the two centered chairs before she even had time to notice who else was moving. She turned to face her partner: the guy who'd posed as a kumquat in response to "tropical."

"Hi," he said. "Paul."

"Bea," Bea said and smiled.

"Let's hear it for Paul and Bea!" Everyone clapped. "Ready when you are, guys."

Paul spoke first.

"We met about . . . what was it, four years ago?" he said, placing a hand on Bea's knee. She put her hand on top of his.

"That sounds about right, babe," Bea said. "Four years ago, you asked me out before you even knew my name. And the rest is history."

"Should I tell them *where* we met? Because that part of the story is pretty hilarious," said Paul.

"It'd be silly to keep it a secret," Bea said. "Tell them. Oh, shucks, I will. We met in his bathroom. In his house."

Titter.

"It's very unusual," said Paul. "That we met in my own house. In my . . . own bathroom. But she was there for . . ."

He appeared stuck, and so Bea said, "I was there for this party."

"She was there because I'd had a party the night before, and the place was a total mess. I don't usually use cleaning ladies, but there was no way I was going to clean all that up alone."

"Annnd scene," said Chris, his words for wrapping us up. "Okay, guys, I want to try that again, but this time, Paul, be careful not to negate Bea."

"Did I negate Bea?" Paul appeared shocked.

"She said she was there for a party, and you said she was there to clean your house."

"Oh, right. But isn't that a form of being there for a party? She was there *because* of the party, just not attending it. I thought it would be a more interesting dynamic if we got together because she was my cleaning lady. I felt like that's way richer than just, like, two people meeting at a party, you know?"

"Your choices are your choices. Just be careful not to negate is all I'm saying," said Chris.

They started over. This time, Bea was still the cleaning lady, and they hit it off because Paul's character was such a gentleman that he insisted on helping her clean. By the end of the scene, he had asked her out.

"And, like she said, the rest is history," said Paul, squeezing her thigh.

"I think you're leaving out one little piece, aren't you, love?" Bea said. Was she cooing? She was cooing.

"Oh?" said Paul, nervously. He appeared to have decided the scene was done. "What's that?"

"I said no."

"She said . . . right, she said no . . . at first. She wanted to think about it."

"I said no because I felt like he was so self-congratulatory for helping me clean that there was no way he was going to be anything but an entitled little shit. And even one date with him sounded so boring that I couldn't stomach the idea of spending a single hour across from him. I was sure he'd just talk about himself the whole time and expect me to be impressed. So I said no."

Paul said nothing.

"But then he wouldn't stop stalking me, and eventually he told me that if I didn't come to this interview, he'd kill me. So, here we are. HELP!" Bea cried, aware of guffaws erupting from the cluster of fellow auditioners as she threw her arms in the air dramatically and rushed offstage.

"That took a turn," Paul mumbled, openly irritated.

"And scene," said Chris, grinning. "Thanks, guys. Next pair!"

As the audition moved to scene work, Bea's doubt grew, bottlenecking in her gut. Why had she done that? Sure, she'd drawn a few laughs, but Chris hadn't looked amused, and Paul was downright pissed. She'd definitely negated Paul, and knowingly. She'd done so because he'd made her into the goddamn housekeeper. *So hilarious, the idea of him, the white man, helping out and then hitting on his own brown housekeeper!*

But, dammit, Bea, she scolded herself. *It was an audition. And the only rule once you were out there was not to negate.*

Bea smiled and applauded along with everyone else while deciding that if she didn't get called back for the second round, she would know why. She'd let personal offense get the better of her.

When the audition hit the ninety-minute mark, Chris stepped aside so that another guy, Mike, could offer a parting spiel. Those who were selected to return for the second and final round would be contacted; they'd all been great; improvising was about bravery and taking risks and merely for showing up they should be proud.

As Bea walked to the shuttle stop to catch the bus back to South Campus, despite lingering regret over that one choice, she nonetheless felt alive, electric. It had been the most energizing two hours of her life.

Her phone buzzed with a number she didn't recognize, a 305 area code.

"Hi, this is Bea," she answered.

"Bea! It's Chris. From C.U.N.T."

"Hi, Chris," she said, surprised.

"Congratulations. You're one of us."

She stopped walking. "Wait—isn't there . . ."

"A second audition? We let some people skip it. Today, actually, you were the only one everyone agreed was a definite yes. So, yay! Good job. Congratulations."

"But I negated Paul. I don't know why I did that." She did know why she did that. Why did she just say she didn't?

"Listen," said Chris. Bea was pacing next to a blue emergency phone—*those are everywhere*, she distractedly registered—with her own phone against one ear and her finger in the other so that she could hear Chris against the whir of a mower on the lawn and the chatter of students passing by. "You were shitty to Paul. Sure. We also saw you in plenty of scenes where you *weren't* a shitty teammate. Do you have stuff to learn? Of course. And you're right to pick up on what happened, because he's still your scene partner, even if he's being a dick. Even dicks can be your scene partners, and you have to treat them like your team members. So, yeah, you took that a little far. But at least it was intentional, and, frankly, you bring a much-needed perspective."

When she didn't respond for a moment, he said, "Hello?"

"I'm here," Bea said. "It's all good. But what do you mean by 'much-needed perspective'? . . ." She trailed off. She'd not only been chosen; she was being allowed to skip the normal process. Before she stepped out to perform in front of the whole school, she needed to know that she was actually funny. People weren't going to laugh to be politically correct.

"Bea, honestly, that was my way of saying you were the strongest one at the audition today. You elevated the entire group's performance. That was the first thing Lesley said after everyone left." He just continues. "Lesley. Who also isn't a token, by the way, if you haven't noticed. She's fucking brilliant."

Lesley!

"But for fuck's sake," Chris said, "don't let it go to your head. I hope you'll join us. We have a blast, obviously. That's why we do it. But it's a huge time commitment. We're also under some pressure this year, because . . ." He chuckled. "I guess because of me. I'm putting pressure on us. Four years ago, the year before I started at Carter, the team won the National College Improv Championship. It's my last year, and I want a championship. But first we have to win regionals at UVA in December. So you in?"

"Oh, obviously," Bea said.

"Fantastic. Let's talk schedule. Rehearsal is Sunday, and I thought your first show could be next Saturday night. September 9. We have shows a few nights a week this time of year. It's pretty busy. But that'll give you time to get two rehearsals under your belt first. Sound good?"

"Yes," she said. *Yes, and; yes, and; yes.*

IF MAKING THE improv team her first Wednesday at Carter had heightened Bea's excitement about her first year, Thursday's events hoisted it to a feverish peak.

Dr. Friedman came down from New York to teach Justice on Fridays. Thursday evening he'd invited Bea and the other three scholarship students to Ovolini, an Italian restaurant within walking distance of campus.

On the last day of August, a balmy evening, Bea made her way to the restaurant. She wore a cotton tank dress she'd borrowed from Lorn over the summer and then never returned because she liked how it fell over her hips, giving them the illusion of shape. She'd pulled her hair back in anticipation of the humidity and swapped her platforms out for well-worn flats at the last minute, unsure about the walk down the stony, sloped path that led from campus to Main Street.

She arrived at Ovolini, which glowed in the dusk, and pushed open the door to a blast of cold air. The restaurant still smelled faintly of fresh paint, and its dark hardwood floors shone. At the center table in the back, she spotted Dr. Friedman seated across from two scholars—Mark and Dionne. Dr. Friedman was sampling wine, swirling it about as the waiter hovered over him, bottle poised.

"Bea! Hello!" He stood and gave her a hug, which sent an ache through her chest, a longing she couldn't place, except that it was for something tender and present in his touch. She reluctantly pulled away. "Now we're just waiting on Veronique."

The waiter poured white wine into Dr. Friedman's glass as he ordered a burrata appetizer for the table.

"I was just telling Mark that this semester I'll be trying to come in early enough on Thursdays to get dinner with you all, whoever can join. I'm in and out of town pretty fast—I leave class and head straight to the airport to get back for Friday afternoon dad duty." Dr. Friedman had two boys, Irish twins he'd called them. Bea had assumed this referred to Irish heritage until she came across the term in a novel and realized it referred to children born fewer than twelve months apart. She was relieved she hadn't embarrassed herself by saying something to reveal her misunderstanding. He'd called her "special" after reading her essay the previous fall, and she didn't want to let him down, even in such a small way.

His wife was a high school Spanish teacher, which is all that Bea knew about her. She felt confident that the woman did not teach at the kind of high school Bea had attended; Dr. Friedman would have a wife who taught in public school, given his unflinching commitment to social justice and equality issues.

Veronique arrived minutes after Bea, wearing a silk scarf loosely looped around her neck and a linen jumper. Bea wondered if the messy bun on the top of her head was as effortless as it looked.

Dr. Friedman asked them to go around the table and introduce themselves, beginning with Bea.

"I'm Bea," she said. "I grew up in New York and Boston and went to school in Connecticut." She always left out the "boarding" part.

"Hello, friends. I am Veronique. I spent my first eight years in France," their newest addition said. She had only the slightest French accent. "I've been here in America since, in Los Angeles, where I acted and was homeschooled." Bea didn't recognize her from anything—but then she'd never watched much TV, even before Porter's. Veronique told them they could call her "V."

Mark, an ROTC student from Houston, came from a third-generation military family, and Dionne hailed "from down the road" and was a graduate of the local arts charter school. Dionne had a charming southern twang, similar to Early's in saturation but with different round vowels.

"Seeing all these disparities in resources on and off the campus of my high school," Dionne said, "I was really bothered. So I decided to stay local and come to Carter just for this program."

"Great to see you all," Dr. Friedman said. "Tomorrow you'll meet your classmates. There are fifteen of you." Bea was feeling inadequate following the others' intros. Had there been nothing else she could have shared? Besides the fact that she'd just made the improv team the *night before*, which felt too recent and frivolous in this context. "And did you get your invitations for the student advocacy training?"

They all nodded as the waiter topped off Dr. Friedman's glass.

"Dr. Friedman," said Mark.

"Lou," said Dr. Friedman.

"Lou," said Mark happily. "What's the hardest case you've ever tried?"

And then Dr. Friedman—Lou—was telling them about the time when, while working as a young public defender in California, he was assigned the case of Walden Summers, also known as the Merrell College shooter, who'd slaughtered eleven students and injured seventeen more before, in a sick twist, surviving his own gun blast as well as police fire. He was left to stand trial.

"Walden was universally loathed, of course, for this monstrous act." It was strange, even unnerving, to hear Dr. Friedman refer to the shooter by his first name. "He'd wrecked the lives of hundreds of people. He had no remorse. He understood what he'd done. He said it was to avenge his rejection by the women on Merrell's campus. You may recall this. He was a maniacal misogynist."

They listened, rapt. A plate of seared scallops wrapped in bacon arrived and was placed, steaming, in the center of the table.

Bea only vaguely recalled the shooting—there had been so many over her lifetime, too many to remember the details of them all, and, honestly, they were so depressing and frightening that she'd stopped reading about them. At Porter's she'd felt safer than her peers at co-ed schools across the nation. She was cognizant that an elite girls' school was unlikely to be the target of a massacre, for while motivation had apparently varied across the spectrum of deranged teenage shooters, what linked them was the glaring fact that they were almost exclusively male.

"How was I to defend this guy? I mean ethically speaking?" Dr. Friedman asked, his eyes flickering in the soft candlelight. "People were livid, and understandably so. They *hated* me. Not just me—they hated my role, that it even existed. Why did this guy get an attorney? My car was egged. Someone left a squirrel carcass on my porch. I got so many threatening calls I had to change my number at home and at work. The refrain was 'How *could* you?' And it wasn't like I wasn't asking myself the same question. Only, my own questioning wasn't rhetorical. *How could I?* How was I going to bring myself to perform this task I was professionally obligated to do? When I graduated law school and went into public defense, I knew I'd have to represent people I knew were guilty, okay? Of bad stuff. I wasn't under any illusions about that. It was going to be a huge part of the job. But I believed deeply enough in the sanctity of the Sixth Amendment, that critical sliver of American justice, to accept this."

He paused. Mark chewed ferociously on a scallop.

"I was in a new realm, one I hadn't braced myself for. And to be honest I didn't know if I could do it. I believed he had a right to representation, but I didn't know if that representation could be from me. It wasn't the public pressure—that was its own challenge, but one I could stand. Don't go into criminal defense unless you're able to give no fucks what people think of you. No, the harder part—it was my own soul that wasn't sure anymore. *My* gut was at odds with itself for the first time. I thought I was going to have to quit."

The waiter emptied the bottle into Dr. Friedman's glass. Bea and the others waited, alert. They knew how the story ended, how it had to end because of where they were and who he was, but even Mark had stopped chewing.

"And that was a pivotal point in my career. I realized that what I was experiencing—a gut at odds with itself—wasn't going to be the exception. It was going to be the norm. It was going to be my life. An occupational hazard, so to speak. Like a construction worker learns to wear earplugs, I was going to have to learn to hold two colliding values in my head and heart. That, or I wasn't going to survive in this work. And if I *was* going to stick with it, I only could if I was going to give it my best, my all, *every* time. Every case, including this one. There was no middle ground."

Veronique was nodding knowingly, and Bea tried to ignore her.

"There I was, sitting on my bed drinking a Diet Coke. It was 8 p.m. I told myself that if I went to work the next day, it meant I'd made my choice. And the next morning, I got up, I put on my suit, and I went. I'd made my choice. I haven't looked back."

"What happened?" Dionne asked. "To the guy?"

"He got life. Not the death penalty. I don't know how much credit I get for that." He paused to sip his wine. "But that notion— that you have to be able to hold two conflicting values, embrace the paradox—it's been what's sustained me ever since. We'll talk a lot more about it over the course of the semester."

Bea blinked for the first time in what must have been minutes. The room had filled with more diners and grown warm; her forearms stuck to the glass tabletop. The burrata had arrived at some point and sat, untouched, oozing, and the scent of truffle oil and garlic wafted through the air as she caught herself releasing her breath, settling into the moment. The world was so big, so complicated, and over the previous forty-eight hours, she felt she was barreling into the heart of it. There was no part of her that resisted, not the smallest ligament held back. She wanted what Dr. Friedman was offering, what Carter was offering. She wanted it all: the yes ands, the gut-wrenching conflict, the two competing ideas.

ON SATURDAY BEA'S first improv rehearsal passed in a whirlwind, a frenzy of delight, of play—a blaze of more joy than she could recall experiencing in ages or maybe ever. It had felt as if the weight of growing up had been lifted for a few precious hours. It was startling, to remember how to play, to realize that she could, that it was still in her. "Play" to Bea meant "toward no purpose." She wasn't working toward yet another feather in her cap, no check mark, notch, or milestone. Improv didn't earn her a grade or improve her candidacy for grad school; it didn't qualify her for any coveted internship or status. It just made her body come alive, her right brain dance. In the rehearsal room, just as at the audition, Bea the scholar stepped aside, and out came the child she'd been all along.

First, Bea learned the fundamentals of a "Harold," the standard improv show format for the team. A Harold was basically a collection of improvised scenes strung together in a way that gave the show a loose theme. It always began with an opening monologue from a team member, one inspired by a word plucked from the audience. The ensuing series of scenes was then based on that monologue. In the show Bea had seen, Russell, the scruffy Brit with big green eyes who'd she'd since learned was a second-year, had delivered the opening monologue.

The Harold format was explained to Bea in much more detail by Bart, the most self-serious improviser in the group. Unlike the rest of her teammates, he rarely laughed while watching others perform. His humor was primarily intellectual; it wasn't uncommon for him to bring up Kant or Nietzsche while improvising, and not in a direct way. He'd make an obscure reference and become frustrated when his scene partner didn't pick up on it, irritation that he tried, and frequently failed, to hide.

"Get it? Master-slave morality?" he said to Bea during her first rehearsal following a scene Bea had initiated in which she played a philosophy professor and in which Bart had entered and introduced himself as head of the philosophy department.

"Nope," she said, to his clear disappointment.

At the end of rehearsal, just before they wrapped, Chris informed them that at Bea's first show the following Saturday, she would be delivering the opening monologue of the Harold.

"It's a rite of passage," he said, smiling playfully at her. "To be followed by a series of hazing activities that may end your life, give you hemorrhoids, or turn all of your shoes into boat shoes."

Bart, in boat shoes, groaned, and Lesley laughed, but Bea didn't notice. She was panicking.

IMPROV WAS ONE thing—leaning into absurdity, assuming a character, playing a role. She'd found it surprisingly easy to "moo" her way onstage or scramble into the limelight in imaginary flight from a rabid camel. The monologue was different. A story from her actual life? Of course, there were stories she could tell, but in her experience, solicitations involving her personal life invariably wound up touching on the big hole at the center of it.

"He's just a man" is what her mom would say with a disinterested shrug when Bea asked about her father. Just a man.

Is he nice? Yes.

Successful? Quite.

Did you love him? Once.

Does he know about me? Yes.

And the one question she couldn't ask: Does he want to know me?

Bea had accrued scraps of information over the years. She knew that he had been on staff at the hospital where her mother had been a resident—which meant that he was a doctor living in Boston at the time. She knew he'd funded part, but not all, of her trust fund and that he was white. And hours upon hours of snooping had yielded one, critically valuable find: a tarnished silver necklace crumpled in a navy velvet box stashed in the back of her mother's sock drawer. One side of its pendant contained a date two years prior to her birth and the other a set of initials that did not belong to her mother: *LRB*.

When Bea was seven, Phaedra had explained to her that he'd wanted to marry her both before and after they discovered she was pregnant but that Phaedra refused, knowing they were fundamentally incompatible. A galaxy has only one center, she said, and they were both the kind of people who would never settle for being anything but stars. They split so that he could be the center of his life and she of hers. And that's what she was—president of Boston's Brigham and Women's Hospital system, in charge of over twelve hundred physicians. She and Bea, plus the nannies, tutors, piano and ballet teachers, and boarding schools, formed a constellation with Phaedra at its core. Her father's absence, if anything, was the dark interstitial space.

The last time Bea had asked her mother if she knew where he might be, Bea was fourteen. Her mother had said, "I have no clue."

The question was only half sincere; by then Bea had already found him on her own. The necklace had been her first clue, and, after that, it hadn't been hard. The Internet, specifically Facebook, had narrowed her search within minutes. (Typical of her mother's generation, she'd found, he clearly didn't understand privacy settings.) He lived in Michigan and had a small son named Roland who was often featured in pictures playing outside with him and his wife, a blonde woman who looked kind. He'd been a surgeon at Brigham back when Bea was born, but now he was head of a research institution based in Ann Arbor that conducted genetic research. She'd meticulously analyzed the few videos he'd posted for commonalities between them and noted with satisfaction that he was, like her, left-handed. This, plus the fact that he didn't wear glasses, even to read (there was a photo of him reading to Roland), seemed to confirm their relation. (Her mother had worn corrective lenses since she was a child, but Bea's vision was 20/15—"Better than perfect," the optometrist had said.)

He knew about Bea, too, as far as she understood, but only one thing about her: her existence. She was a dot on his time line.

She'd never truly considered contacting him, as it would have been a betrayal of her mother, although at one point she did change her mother's Facebook profile, which still existed as a memorial page, from private to public, in case he was ever inspired to search for Phaedra's name.

Obviously she wouldn't have to talk about her father in a monologue. So why was she nauseous?

On the shuttle back to South Campus she recalled Russell's monologue the weekend before. Bea loved Russell's Britishness, which was of a less posh variety than that of the few Brits she'd known. She already adored his "have a laugh," his bearded ebullience.

Later, in their room, Early had referred to him as "the English guy who came out," and Bea had had to explain his punch line—that he wasn't gay but that his girl was so self-confident she couldn't imagine another explanation for his rejection.

One thing was certain—she wasn't going to talk about sex or the fact that she hadn't had it yet.

Back in her room, she decided to do a little research, dig up videos of Harold monologues on YouTube. She watched them for over an hour, discovering, to her relief, that they weren't all exclusively personal. Some were hardly stories. Shaky, poorly lit videos taken on phones captured monologues with hardly any coherence—an anecdote strung together with a political opinion and an observation about human behavior. Some veered into diatribes, for comedic effect but still diatribes: taxes, global warming, the Trail of Tears.

The monologue began to feel less daunting. If she didn't have to stick to facts about her own life, well, perhaps it wouldn't be so dreadful.

She would find a way to make it work without giving too much away. Hadn't she always?

Stayja

TUESDAY, AUGUST 22

"This new schedule of yours isn't working for me," Nicole said, thumbing a $4.99 sack of candied almonds cinched with a green ribbon that read *Rooster Roast*. Stayja reached over, plucked it from her cousin's hand, and placed it back into the metal bucket labeled "Impulse Buys." "What am I supposed to do for an hour while I wait for you to get off?"

Nicole's shift at the QuikMart ended at nine, and Stayja's new shift ended at ten. Since Nicole didn't have a car (and couldn't drive anyway owing to her DUI), this meant she had an hour to kill every night while she waited for Stayja to finish.

"Maybe you could learn to read," Stayja said.

"Shut up," Nicole said as LA sauntered in, swinging a half-empty bottle of Sprite.

"Yo. Hey, what's that?" he said, nodding at the pack of cigarettes peeking out from under the register.

"What does it look like?" Stayja said.

"But you quit," said LA.

"Did I?" Stayja slid the pack into her hand, tapped out a cigarette, and put it behind her ear. She was hard enough on herself—she didn't need anyone else, especially LA, guilting her.

The possibility of another chance run-in with the Carter guy had infused the habit with fresh appeal. Perhaps it was an addict's justification, but she told herself that a few more smoke breaks were not that big a deal, just until they ran into each other again and she learned his name, maybe got to know him a little better.

It was 9:18, which left forty-two minutes in her shift.

"Why are you still here?" she asked LA. His shift ended at five.

"I went home and took a nap."

"And you came *back*? Why?"

"Why does LA do anything?" Nicole said absently as she typed on her phone. A coy smile passed over her face.

"To bother you, of course," he said to Stayja.

"Who are you texting?" Stayja asked.

"No one," Nicole said. She slipped her phone into her back pocket.

"How about Mary and Divorce?" LA said to Nicole.

"Divorce isn't a name."

"Stayja did Phillip and Flathead!"

"Someone might actually be called Flathead as a nickname. No one would call someone Divorce."

"Bullshit!"

"Actually, LA, the left side of *your* head looks a little flatter than the right."

"Quit tormenting him," Stayja said.

"Can I have a brownie?" Nicole said.

"Yes, it's $2.50."

"Seriously?"

"It's called inventory. Yes."

Stayja caught the eye of the solemn grad student who spent all day every day at the same table, tapping away at her laptop, who'd just looked up meaningfully. It was a look meant to hush them.

"You guys talk quieter," Stayja said. "You're going to get me in trouble."

"Oh, my God," Nicole said, rolling her eyes. "I'm going to lie down and play Candy Crush until you're ready. I'll be on one of the couches downstairs." She swiveled and strutted out, wagging her hips in the way she did when she thought someone might be watching.

"I have a story for you," LA said. "It's about a bush that full-on attacked me today. I was trimming . . . "

"Hey!" a voice called from the side door. There he was, taller than she remembered, with an energy that drew her in as it had that first night. His keys dangled from one hand, and he held a six-pack of bottled beer in the other. He dropped his keys into his pocket, lifted the beer, raised his eyebrows, and grinned. Stayja glanced at her phone: 9:23.

She untied her apron with one hand while moving the CLOSED sign from the shelf to the counter with the other. She'd clean the machines before she went home or, fuck it, in the morning.

"What are you doing?" LA demanded. "Who's that guy?" When she didn't answer, he hollered at the boy, who'd already disappeared through the door, "She already took her break!" She shook her hair from its elastic band and dug out a tube of Chap-Stick from her purse.

"Should I wait for you?" LA asked.

"What? Of course not." She locked the register and headed for the door. "See you tomorrow, LA."

HE OPENED THE back door of his SUV, which was parked in the far corner adjacent to his dorm, and they let their legs dangle off the edge while he drank the fancy beer he special ordered from a local brewery, one with a navy-and-white-striped label in an ornate font. He opened a bottle using a Carter Bulldogs bottle opener from his key chain and handed it to her, then opened one for himself.

"Cheers," he said, as they tapped the glass necks. He took a long swig, and she followed his lead. It was bitter and surprisingly thick.

"Nurse, huh?" he said, lowering the bottle. A third of it, Stayja could make out through the tinted glass, had been emptied.

"If I can ever finish." She took a gulp.

He uncrossed his legs and adjusted his shorts underneath him. He finished his beer, stuck the empty bottle snugly back into the cardboard carrying case, and popped open a new one.

"Can't you just take out loans? Everyone I know has student loans."

"I don't know," she lied. No, she couldn't. For one, her credit was shot. She'd maxed out her only credit card, a Visa, three summers earlier. She was still paying it off—old, stale debt she chipped away at only to see it rise again over the months she couldn't make payments. Last she checked it was almost a grand.

"The government'll give out loans to anybody." Half another bottle, gone.

"But then I have to pay it back," said Stayja.

"How much will you make as a nurse?"

This, Stayja could answer—it was the primary reason why she'd picked it, in addition to adoring her own nurse when she'd broken her arm at twelve.

"The starting salary is around fifty," she said. "It goes up if you specialize, but I don't know what I'd want to specialize in."

He crawled to the front of the vehicle and fetched a ragged yellow pack of Camels from the glove compartment.

"At this point even doctors are just glorified nurses," he said. "They all just do whatever Big Pharma tells them. Just take out a loan," he said.

"Let's talk about something else."

"Yes, ma'am."

"Where did you grow up?" Stayja asked.

"Born in Jersey, raised in Houston." He explained that his parents moved to Texas shortly after he was born because of income tax. Or, rather, lack of it. He leapt off the car and started doing jumping jacks. As he jumped up and down, lifting and lowering his arms, she shifted her attention toward the trees. His energy was different and beginning to make her nervous.

"How much do you make here? Or is that none of my business?" he asked suddenly, still jumping.

She hesitated.

"Feel free to tell me to fuck off," he said.

"Sixteen thousand," she said.

"A year? Fucking Christ." He stopped jumping and began gesticulating with his bottle. Beer sloshed onto the pavement. "Dude, even in Cartersboro, how do you even live on that?"

My mom's on SSI and food stamps, and we don't always have to pay rent because my aunt is our landlady, and we didn't for a long time, but now we do, and so, yeah, it's not easy.

Stayja loathed everything having to do with money. Money had fucked her over again and again. It had divided her mother and her Aunt Adrienne—despite living on the same property, Donna and her older sister were not currently speaking, a standoff that had now lasted months. Adrienne felt Donna took her for granted, even though Stayja was paying Adrienne $300 a month in rent for the two of them. She'd seen how finances had stressed out Nicole and Adrienne, how Adrienne's health worsened after she was purged from SSI owing to a technical error on her reapplication. One night in the spring, Adrienne had gone to the ER because she'd stopped being able to *see*.

She shrugged.

"We get by," she said, immediately wishing she hadn't told him. "Do they give you insurance here, at least?"

She shook her head. "The Rooster is closed in the summer and winter, so I guess it doesn't average out to enough hours or whatever."

"So you're on Medicaid or something? Do you get a subsidy? Obamacare?"

She did receive a subsidy, one that made her profoundly anxious, because on the phone the woman had told her that if she wound up making over a certain amount by December, she might have to pay it back. *Might have to pay it back* were doomsday words for Stayja.

"Yeah, I had a subsidy," she said, sighing. "But I just need to become a nurse as soon as possible so that I make enough so that my mom can go back to work."

"Huh?" he asked, swaying a little.

Stayja explained that it depressed Donna not to work, but she couldn't if she wanted to remain on disability. Without the disability income, there was no way they could afford both Stayja's school expenses and their living expenses. Basically, Donna made more on disability than she could make working, given her health restrictions—she couldn't stand for longer than two to three hours a day.

"Can't she just work under the table and keep getting SSI?" Tyler asked.

"If she gets caught, it gets terminated."

"Damn," he muttered, flicking his lighter. "And people think the poor don't want to work."

"The *poor*?" She grunted and rolled her eyes. "Jesus. We aren't a species."

"Hey, maybe I could get you a better job or something."

"How would you do that?"

"My dad."

"He's that connected, huh?"

"He's like a Delta hub. He's Atlanta."

She smiled. Was he serious?

He held his bottle up to the light and looked at it.

"I should stop drinking," he said. "I really should stop drinking."

"Why don't you, if you think you need to?" she asked.

He sighed a long, slow sigh, sitting back down beside her.

"Daddy issues? Shame spiraling? Self-sabotage? Rinse and repeat?" He rubbed his eyes. "I don't fucking know, Stayja."

"What's so bad about your dad?" When he didn't answer, she said, "I mean, I know you think he's this monster who profits off drug addicts, but, like, what's that got to do with your drinking?"

After a pause, he said, "I was never great at sports. I, uh, don't have the hand-eye coordination. I had a lazy eye as a kid and had to wear a patch in elementary school to fix it. Like a pirate. Anyway, this impeded my athletic abilities, wearing a patch for two years and then suddenly not wearing one—I never really figured out the spatial orientation thing.

"But my parents signed me up for, like, every sport—softball, basketball, soccer. Until I was a teenager, I didn't know I was bad. You know how it is when you're a kid. . . . The coaches played everybody, so it wasn't like I had any signs that I sucked. I didn't think I was *good* because I never scored, but I figured I was somewhere in the middle. I really just didn't think much about it.

"My dad didn't know I sucked either because he didn't come to my games. He was always traveling for work and whatnot. One night, I was invited by my softball coach to throw the first pitch at the Rangers game. My dad was super excited about it, must've thought it was because I was good or something. He rented a box and invited all his friends, my uncles, my cousins.

"That night, I went out on the field, and I wasn't the only one—there were three of us, all throwing pitches from the mound. The other two were girls from different schools from mine. One of them was in a wheelchair, and the other had a robotic hand. I was still wearing my eye patch then. I didn't think much about the girls. I was proud. I got my T-shirt, I got my photograph made with a couple of the players. I ran off the field where my mom was waiting, and we headed back up to the box.

"I could hear my dad yelling before I even got through the door. 'My kid isn't disabled!' So I walk in, and he's like, 'Tyler, come here!' Everyone is quiet, watching. He says, 'Toss me that ball.' And for the next . . . I don't know how long, half hour? Hour? He makes me play catch with him to 'prove' to all of his friends that I'm not disabled. But I kept missing it. And he'd say, 'Try again.' And then we'd take a break and stop. And then a few minutes later, he'd say, 'Tyler! Toss me that ball!' And we'd have to do it again. I didn't know if he was just forgetting we'd already done it—this was before he got sober—or if he just wasn't giving up. But at some point . . . I mean, I was only seven, but at some point, I remember thinking, *Is he trying to get me to show I can catch, or is he mocking me because I can't?* Eventually I started crying, and my aunt intervened and took me to get popcorn."

"Was it different after he stopped drinking? When did he stop?"

"He got sober when I was in high school. It just made him madder. He didn't choose it. His liver was pickled, and the doctor said he was going to fucking die if he didn't. So for six years he's been sober and pissed off about it."

"How does your mom handle it?"

He shrugged.

"She doesn't really engage. She's sort of in her own world. You know how poets are."

"Your mom is a *poet*?"

"Not a famous poet or anything. She has a couple of chapbooks out."

Stayja had never heard the term *chapbook* and assumed it was a book of poetry but didn't ask.

"So I have a 3.8 GPA, right?" he said.

"Okay."

"That's really good."

"I know how GPAs work."

"When I told my dad my GPA and that I'll probably graduate summa, he said, 'With grade inflation, that's probably like a 3.2 in 1992.' That was the year he graduated from here."

"Why is he so competitive with you?"

He shook his head. "Not competition. There's no fight. It's a bludgeoning. He lives to stomp me out."

Without thinking, she took his hand. His clasped around hers instantly, gripping it as if she were going to save him from something.

Holding his warm hand in that moment, she would do anything he asked.

Annie

Over the following week, our banter over text and Snapchat was constant. He sent me funny videos and screenshots of old political cartoons he was collecting for a paper on the emergence of political satire as what he described as the primary mode of public political discourse in the contemporary United States. (When I asked him what that meant, he said, "Colbert.") He was also working on a paper for his Religion in America class on the rising popularity of mysticism within both the religious population and the secular population.

"Everyone is interested in personal spirituality. Mysticism is the only way that traditional religion is managing to stay relevant." Take Kabbalah—the Jewish brand of mysticism that had become popular among a critical mass of people who, he claimed, would never have subscribed to traditional religion but now studied its ancient wisdom as a means to individual enlightenment.

I didn't know you were Jewish, I texted back. How observant are you?

I'm not, he wrote. Just fascinated by Kabbalah.

I was grasping for every clue that he was a good person, seizing onto them and storing them up as reassurance, filing them away as evidence that he was a decent person.

How could someone devoted to his religion be a rapist?

But then, when it turned out he hadn't meant that he himself was religious:

How could someone interested in personal spirituality be a rapist?

"Kabbalah also embraces the divine feminine, defying, like other popular strands of mysticism in contemporary culture, the misogyny inherent in every major religion."

How could someone who points out the importance of gender equality be a rapist?

He told me about his final project for his art minor—a series of paintings themed on "the gølden ratio." I didn't know what the golden ratio was, and he didn't explain it. He'd collaborated with a dance major, who'd choreographed a dance based on this mysterious ratio. He'd then taken stills from the video of the performance and made watercolors of them.

He paints.

He collaborates with women.

I needed him to be normal so that I could be normal—not his victim or anyone's victim. Just a girl he was interested in.

It was in these seven days that I experienced just how dangerously close belief is to incentive. Both charmed by Tyler Brand and determined to be charmed by Tyler Brand, at the end of our weeklong, post-assault courtship, I felt only a tinge of fear when I stood in my closet, choosing what to wear for our second date—this time an actual one, so that when I had used the term to my mother, it hadn't felt like fudging. (I obviously hadn't mentioned anything about how the previous weekend had gone, other than a vague "it was fun.")

He'd asked what my favorite restaurant was off campus, and I'd answered Pi.

A rapist doesn't ask you what your favorite restaurant is.

AT PI, THE digits of Pi were scrawled in black Sharpie across the walls, trickling off into nothing as it circled the room once, twice, three times. Late on weekend nights, drunk engineering students would take turns reciting as many digits as they could from memory—hit 314 and get a free cheese pizza. (Drunk liberal arts majors couldn't get past the second digit.)

After Pi, he'd said, we could check out the improv show on campus.

I surveyed my hanging clothes in search of an outfit. In reaction to the weekend before, I found that my overwhelming desire was to appear casual, as if I hadn't put in effort. I knew green brought out my eyes. I pulled out a hunter green T-shirt and denim cutoffs— more laid back than the navy ones. I wouldn't resort to jeans, wouldn't let him send me back into hiding.

An hour later, I got to the restaurant before he did and waited outside, finally spotting him walking toward me with a small wave. Watching him, it occurred to me that his gait—its child-like bounce, its slight tilt forward—may have been the root of his attractiveness. There was nothing cool or withholding about it. It was easy to imagine him as a kid with that same toe-walk, the same involuntary lean-in that said, *I'm open, and I won't bother pretending otherwise.*

Pi offered pizzas in varieties like garlic truffle parmesan and chorizo pineapple. "Sausage" appeared nowhere on its menu. Bread sticks were "cheddar spears." He insisted that we share a pear and prosciutto white pie topped with toasted almonds, his favorite.

Growing up, my pizza-eating experience had been limited to the Little Caesars three blocks from my house, where you could play the old-school electronic game Simon to win free bread sticks with your meal. We were there every Friday night like clockwork, my dad pounding his palm on the colorful buttons to save us the $2.99.

"How'd you choose history as your major?" I asked after we put in our order, feeling boring but too nervous to think of a better question. I felt sensitive, maybe fragile. Like using your arm for the first time after you've sprained your wrist and it's supposed to have healed. It doesn't hurt anymore, but you're not quite sure you trust it.

"I decided when my Office of the Presidency class in high school got a private tour of the West Wing."

I choked on my bite and guzzled my water, jarred out of my jitters. He laughed. Over a year in, I was still frequently amazed by how different my high school experience had been from those of my peers. They spent semesters—*of high school*—in Italy, France, and Spain. They had performed theater in Mandarin. They had had alpine skiing as a PE option.

"My school," he said as I wiped my eyes, running with the opportunity to make fun of himself, "had an outdoor swimming pool *and* an indoor one. We had a restaurant for lunch with table service, along with a normal cafeteria, of course. And, yes, we had an entire course called The Office of the Presidency, for seniors. Each of us was assigned a role in the White House, and the whole semester you worked together to run the country—international crises, bills, lobbyists, PR."

"Let me guess . . ." I said.

"Yep," he said, beaming. "Mr. President!" He looked overjoyed. It was so dorky.

A rapist doesn't act like a dork.

After dinner, we walked over to the show, which was in the big auditorium on campus and made me laugh so hard I peed on myself a little and had to rush to the bathroom afterward to make sure I wasn't mistaken about the wetness, that I hadn't started my period. I had not.

I found Tyler outside, chatting with one of the only two girls who had been in the show. I was intimidated by how effortlessly confident she and the other girl seemed. Did Tyler know her?

"Hey, there you are," he said as I approached. "Ready?"

"You were amazing," I said to her.

"Thanks," she said and smiled at me.

As Tyler and I walked in the direction of both of our dorm rooms, he began talking about a film the show had reminded him of—using the word *film*. He said he owned it but hadn't watched it in a long time.

"It's from the nineties. It's just footage," he said as we strolled more slowly than was natural, as if we didn't want the night to end or weren't ready for what was coming next. "Footage from everywhere. There's no story line or commentary. Just visuals of stuff from all over the world. Like, have you ever seen Reggio's *Koyaanisqatsi*?"

"Who?" I asked.

"Like a kaleidoscope, sort of," he said. "I'm telling you, this movie changed my life."

"Wow," I said.

He stopped and faced me.

"What do you think? Want to come over and watch it?" His hands were in his pockets and his wild, messy hair was blowing in the breeze. My stomach tightened, and I took a deep breath in, then let it out. Did I want to? I didn't know what I wanted—but I knew what I didn't want. I didn't want to be afraid.

A rapist doesn't say a movie changed his life.

"Sure," I said.

WHEN WE REACHED his room, he opened it without unlocking it.

"It's a pain to have to unlock it every time," he said, entering. I followed. "I did the same thing in high school with my locker. Never put a lock on it. One morning senior year, I opened it and all my books were gone. It was completely empty. Turned out Derek, the vice principal—we were close—had cleaned it out as a joke. I found all my stuff sitting on his desk in his office and took it right back."

"But that was just a locker," I said.

He shrugged.

"It's all just stuff. Nothing is irreplaceable. Well, except. . . ."

He went to his bookshelf and pulled down from the top of it an oversized black leather folder.

"Can I show you my project?" Carrying the folder with him, he plopped onto his bed to lean against the wall and patted the comforter, gesturing for me to join him. Then he opened it to reveal a watercolor on paper. Even upside down, I could tell it showed a dancer on her toes, reaching skyward.

My body felt as if it were moving against an invisible pull, as if there were a rope around my waist trying to hold me back, as I moved to the bed and took a seat next to him.

He carefully, painstakingly, as if the pages were as delicate as flower petals, flipped through fifteen or so of them, pausing for several long seconds on each one. The paintings were muted but vibrant, in jewel tones that jumped off the page. There was movement and ferocity but also a softness that left me shocked that they'd been made by a man. They were so tender.

"This is the project I told you about," he said. "Of the golden ratio. Also known as the Fibonacci sequence. I have three more to make."

"They're amazing," I said.

He closed the portfolio and hopped off the bed. With both hands, he slid the portfolio out of sight onto the top of the shelf between a stack of reams of printer paper and a small plant I hadn't noticed before.

What college student keeps a plant?

Not a rapist.

"I keep it up here where it's safe," he said.

"Can I ask a dumb question?" I asked. "What's the Fibonacci sequence?"

"Not a dumb question," he said, lifting up his shirt. On his chest, squares of various sizes were inscribed inside one another, forming a sort of angular spiral.

"Recognize it? The golden ratio?" he asked.

"Honestly," I said. "I've never heard of that either."

He grabbed his laptop and climbed back onto the bed. Next to me again, he googled "the golden ratio." Images filled the screen: seashells, orchids, the *Mona Lisa*, a cat curled up sleeping. "The ratio that defines all of nature. The relationship between plants and stems, animal skeletons, crystals. It's the grounding principle of all beautiful forms." He pulled up a photo he'd taken of a brown, sandy beach on which rivulets of water formed tree-shaped divots in the sand, creases branching in stunning formation. "Like here—see how the water recedes and leaves this same form? That looks like hands, or trees? This is in Costa Rica."

"But your tattoo . . ." I said. His tattoo didn't look anything like seashells or trees.

"Well, the actual spiral felt a little too cliché as a tat. The rectangles were more like a puzzle. Plus I didn't want a seashell on my chest." He snickered as he stood again to fetch a spiral notebook and a pen. I watched over his shoulder as he scribbled:

$$^{(a+b)}/_a = ^a/_b$$
$$^a/_a + ^b/_a = ^a/_b$$
$$1 + ^b/_a = ^a/_b$$
$$1 = ^a/_b - ^b/_a = ^{a^2}/_{ab} - ^{b^2}/_{ab} =$$

He stopped, looking frustrated.

"I can't believe I can't remember how to do this."

"It's okay," I said. "We're in college and don't have to remember algebra anymore. That's one of the nice things about it." I laughed at my own joke. He didn't.

"No," he said distantly. "I need to figure this out."

"We can just look it up," I said, reaching for his laptop, still open.

He ignored me. For several more minutes he worked until, finally, he picked up his pen.

"Finally," he said. "That's it." He handed the notebook to me. The page was filled with a manic scribble, ending in the equation $\varphi + 1 = \varphi^2$.

"Congrats?" I said.

He looked embarrassed as he took it back and said, "My seventh-grade algebra teacher, Mr. Getty, showed this to me. When he saw how excited I got, he asked the principal to move me from regular math to advanced math. It was the first time I remember feeling smart."

"What happened to Mr. Getty?"

"Happened to him? I guess he's still teaching, probably."

"You don't keep up with your favorite teacher?"

"From when I was eleven?" He seemed flabbergasted.

"Sure," I said.

He grinned at me.

"Wholesome!" he said. "That's the word I was trying to think of. You're wholesome."

"I'm not wholesome," I said, offended.

"Oh, you're totally all-American."

I scoffed.

"It's not an insult."

"Who wants to be wholesome? I'm not Amish."

"See? That was a wholesome thing to say."

"Fuck off."

"Even your 'fuck off' is wholesome."

I turned away, and when I turned back, he was staring into his computer screen at the tulips, curled-up cats, and snails.

"I just love that it's, like, nature's secret code for beauty," he said. He turned back to face me. "Just because you're wholesome doesn't mean you aren't beautiful," he said.

Beautiful. No one had ever called me beautiful before. A warm sensation rose through my chest and neck.

"You haven't said anything about my legs," I said, glancing down at my bare skin, splayed out on his bed.

"I figured," he said carefully, "you would tell me about them when you're ready."

I had studied his legs, of course, as I did everyone's. They were slender and muscled under a layer of blond fuzz—the illusion of hair, a haze. His skin was sort of translucent, like a shade or two of pigment got left out of his genome by accident.

"Cool," I said and smiled.

I really thought I was going to be okay. I really did.

Bea

"Something you love!" Chris's voice as he called out the prompt sounded small, and Bea wondered if the people in the back of the auditorium could hear him. The space was twice as large, if not larger, than the black box theater where she'd first seen the team perform two weekends earlier. *Doughnuts!* Bea heard. *Harry Potter! Ariana Grande! The Obamas!*

"France!" Chris announced. "France is the word." As he turned, he glanced only briefly at Bea. As promised, she stepped forward. She'd been struck by an idea in the shower that morning—she would tell a story about Lorn's family rather than her own. As luck would have it, "France" immediately summoned a memory. She took the center of the stage and inhaled.

"A few years ago, I was in Paris on vacation with my friend's family. My friend's dad doesn't speak great French—by that I mean he speaks really bad French. My friend and I had both studied French for years, and his wife spoke a little, but he was determined to practice without our help. Every restaurant we'd go to, he'd order, and we weren't allowed to correct him, because he wanted to see if he could—quote—*communicate*.

"'The goal is just to communicate,'" she said, imitating Lorn's father's deep, domineering voice, "'which is much easier than people realize. You don't even need grammar. We make it way too hard on ourselves.' This reasoning led him to conclude that he more or less 'spoke' five languages—because if he gestured enough, eventually someone would figure out what he was trying to say."

Snickers peppered the room.

"One night we were eating, and he decided he wanted more clams. He didn't know the word for clams, so he just kept saying 'beaucoup!' and flailing his arms. The server looked at him kind of funny, which we were used to by this point. We just figured that, yet again, the server was thinking, *Why does this man seem to think that by staring at me so intently that his eyes look ready to pop, I'll eventually understand him?*

"The next night we were joined for dinner by a French acquaintance of his. This time, when he started yelling 'beaucoup!' and flailing his arms, his friend covered her mouth like she was about to spit out her wine and grabbed his arm. Apparently his pronunciation of the word—'beau *cul*'—means 'nice ass.'

"Throughout Paris, he'd been yelling at waiters and waitresses, 'Nice ass! NICE! ASS!'"

A loose applause accompanied Bea's walk back to the line as Lesley dashed past, launching a scene in which she played a clam stuck shut.

THE SHOW WAS a thrill. During the final ovation, Bea felt proud, elated, afire—the sense of possibility that took hold when she did improv! The world felt as if it were waiting, ready for her to spin it into fun, into delight. All she wanted to do was spin from now on.

Standing outside the auditorium and waiting for the others to head over to Russell's dorm room for the after-party, she felt lazy with happiness.

"Hey, there," a voice said. She turned. A boy with puffy hair stood smoking a cigarette.

"Hi," she said.

"You're funny," he said.

"Thanks," she said.

"You're the funniest. You and the other girl."

"Bea!" Early called out, waving as she made her way through the stream of students trickling out of the building. "You were awesome!" Her roommate dove into Bea for a hug.

In the same moment, a girl in a green T-shirt and cutoffs appeared behind the boy, and it took him a moment to notice her.

"You were amazing," the girl said to Bea. As she and the boy turned to go, Bea noticed the girl's legs, which were covered in scars.

How sad, she thought. Not the scars themselves but whatever had caused them—it was obvious that it had been something painful.

THEY STATIONED THEMSELVES around Russell's room, which was located in one of the "independent" upper-class dorm buildings, as they were called to distinguish them from the Greek ones. The twelve of them sprawled across two bunks, a dingy shag rug, a black leather desk chair and a futon Russell said he'd inherited from a previous occupant.

Chris sat next to Bea on the floor, a fact she assumed was coincidental until, three hours in, during a round of Fuck, Marry, Kill, he chose to fuck her and marry Todd. As her beer consumption climbed, Bea became aware that perhaps, possibly, her consonants were slipping out from under her, just as Lesley and Todd stood and announced they were going to a bar if anyone wanted to join.

"I should go home," Bea said, standing, a bit wobbly. It was her first night drinking at Carter, and she could tell it was time to call it a night. Besides, she didn't have a fake ID.

"Me too," said Chris.

The group trickled into the quad, with Todd and Lesley leading the way to the bar and the others scattering in the direction of their rooms. Turning to face her, Chris offered to walk Bea home.

"I'm on South Campus, remember?" she said. "Plus, I'm a feminist."

It was a dumb joke, but she was drunk. Drunk, she tried to forgive herself for it.

"You can walk me home then," Chris said as Bea fumbled in her bag for her phone. Before she found it, he had stepped forward and placed a hand on her hip. His breath was warm on her nose. He asked if he could kiss her.

"Okay," she said quietly.

His lips were muscular, more so than she expected, and his mustache tickled less than she would have thought. She closed her eyes and kissed back as her own hand drifted up to his neck. It was prickly, his skin cold. She pulled back.

"What's wrong?" he asked.

"Nothing. I should go home." She dug again for her phone, found it, and checked the time. "It's almost two."

"All right," he said. "I can at least walk you to the bus stop."

"No," she said quickly. "I'm good."

"Got it," he said, not unkindly but as if he'd received the message. "Goodnight, Bea." He gave her a disappointed half grin before turning and jogging off. She could tell she'd hurt his feelings, but it wasn't as if she'd had a choice; her revulsion had been instant and unequivocal.

Why had she allowed him to kiss her in the first place? Dammit, Bea, she cursed herself as she crossed the dewy quad in the dark, making her way to the bus stop. Now it would be awkward forever.

On the ride across campus, she ceased thinking about Chris

and let her thoughts return to the night's show, how much fun it had been. By the time she reached her room to find Early deep in sleep, snoring loudly, her buzz had lost its edge, and she'd caught a second wind.

As had become her regular routine many nights, she signed into Facebook to pull up Lester Bertrand's profile. This time she didn't just browse through the photos.

Was it the alcohol coursing through her that made her do it? Her pride at having performed—well—for a crowd of her peers? Not just her peers, but her older peers? The puffy-haired boy who had called her the funniest?

Add friend, she clicked. The text in the box disappeared, and "Pending" appeared in its place. To the throaty sounds of Early's snores, she stared at the letters on her screen until they began to blur. Alone, it was too weird, the friend request. Without explanation, without introduction, it wouldn't be strange for him to find this bizarre, even if he did know about her.

She clicked "Message" and began to type.

Dear Lester,

I know that you and my mother, Phaedra, worked together at Brigham in the '90s. I don't know if you are aware, but she passed away three years ago.

For a long time now I have wondered if you and I are related. In other words, if you may be my father. Therefore, I wanted to introduce myself. If not, please disregard this message.

I hope all is well. You have a very cute son.

Sincerely,
Bea Powers

TWO DAYS LATER, on Monday, Bea still hadn't received a response to her late-night message, but she did awake to two emails from Carter faculty—one from her academic adviser, a squirrely man named Dr. Toast (Dr. Toast!) with whom she'd had to meet briefly so that he could approve her course schedule. His email reminded her to schedule at least two "check-ins" with him before the end of the semester. But it was the other email she'd been waiting for. It was from the coordinator of the Justice Scholars Program: she'd been assigned her first case as a student advocate.

At the student advocacy training on the previous Saturday, she and her classmates had been lectured by a woman in her thirties in a coral blouse and cream pencil skirt with sand-colored patent heels, a corporate-looking ensemble that outed her as a Carter outsider. She'd presented via PowerPoint, dwelling interminably on a slide that read, in block letters: ADVOCATE: Both a verb AND a noun! One called to AID. <u>SUPPORT</u>.

Over the course of the three-hour training, the trainer had repeatedly stressed the breadth of the word's application:

"You aren't the support *in* judicial matters," the skirted woman had said over and over. "You are the support *around* judicial matters. Being a party to a case is lonely, even isolating for students. Often they're hesitant to talk to their friends about their case out of embarrassment, shame, or simply wanting to retain privacy. The process itself can also be confusing and disorienting, as clear as we try to be about what they can expect. You are there as an emotional support and a source of information and guidance. Think of it this way—if they don't know whom to talk to or what to do? That's where you come in."

The email directed Bea to report to the student affairs office at her earliest convenience to receive the case file. As she made her way to Dean Arroyo's office on her way to physics lab, she spotted Veronique and Simone, a third-year Justice Scholar, walking toward her.

"Hi, Bea," Veronique said. Bea noted that both were holding manila folders. "Are you going to pick up your case, too?"

"Yeah," Bea said. "Do we all have cases already?" It seemed early in the year for there to be so many.

"The three of us do, at least," Veronique said, "although mine apparently is a carryover from the summer session." Veronique explained that two summer students had removed a temporary gargoyle from the façade of the new dorm going up on the southeast quad. It was found in the gardens in a sun hat next to a cooler of Corona. "I'm not telling you anything that isn't all over social media," she added. "They posted the whole thing in real time."

"What's a temporary gargoyle?" Bea asked.

"A gargoyle that's not permanent? I don't know." Veronique's laugh was raspy. "I think it was made of plaster or something. The weirder part is, these gargoyles are supposed to *look like* the donors who paid for the building. Like making a monster version of your face is a compliment? Talk about a terrible idea."

Bea had found herself wanting Veronique to like her. Veronique reminded her a little bit of Lorn—the nonchalance, the air of not caring what others thought. Bea had wondered if she and Veronique might even become best friends. But if "V" had any interest in a friendship with Bea, she wasn't showing it.

"How about you, what's your case?" Bea asked, turning to Simone, who smiled politely. She'd met Simone only briefly at the program's meet and greet.

"I probably shouldn't talk about it," she said. "Not without permission."

"Of course," Bea said, embarrassed to have asked but also embarrassed for Simone, whose tone was unnecessarily condescending, smacking of sugary self-righteousness.

Moments later, she entered Dean Arroyo's office, where an administrative assistant handed her a folder with her name on it. Bea took it from her and managed to make it just outside the building before she couldn't resist opening it.

After reading some technical exposition about not assigning advocates and students of the same class year in order to avoid conflicts, yada yada, she reached the important part—two allegations of sexual misconduct. She wasn't provided the name of the complainant yet—a female second-year student—only the name of the respondent, her assigned student. He was a fourth-year, and she was to reach out to him as soon as possible.

Bea took in a breath and held it.

Fuck.

These days Bea fell into the camp of believing any woman who said she'd been sexually assaulted. She'd spent enough hours at Porter's— both in class and out—discussing #MeToo to know where she stood.

A sexual assault had to be her first case?

She stood and began to walk in the direction of Science Row, the suite of science buildings that ran along the back side of Main Campus. She was already late for lab, but she wasn't thinking about physics. As she drifted, case file in hand and her bag hanging on her shoulder, Bea found herself thinking about Samantha Pilch, who dropped out of Porter's in eighth grade after telling them all—not the adults, but just her peers—that the soccer coach, Coach Reed, had groped her. He was in his twenties, cute, and occasionally flirty, doing things like patting their butts or pinching their waistlines. They'd enjoyed it, frankly. A bunch of them had crushes on him, including Bea, if only because he was the only male approximating their age within walking distance.

So when Samantha said he'd grabbed her breasts and tried to take off her jersey one Sunday after their game, their fourteen-year-old reactions tended toward suspicion. They wondered aloud about her motives in telling them about it. Was she hoping to make the rest of them envious?

It wasn't until she didn't return for ninth grade that the incident had truly begun to bother Bea, when she started to wonder if she'd responded appropriately by listening but then moving on, changing nothing about her own behavior or treatment of Coach Reed. Coach Reed had remained at Porter's for a couple more years. By Bea's senior year, he was gone, and with the more mature perspective of an eighteen-year-old, she saw him in a different light. He was a faculty member, an adult. He shouldn't even have been flirting with them.

But she also believed in due process.

Two ideas.

She reached the physics building and checked the time—she was now twelve minutes late, but she spotted a bench a short distance away and headed for it. She dropped her bag onto the grass and took a seat. She'd never called Dr. Friedman on his cell before, and she had no idea if he'd pick up.

As the phone rang, she felt pathetic; how quickly her excitement over the two-ideas notion had crumbled. Her first case, and she was already reluctant.

Dr. Friedman picked up after the first ring. She cut to the chase.

"I got my first case. It's a sexual assault," she said.

In the background she could hear horns honking and the wail of a distant siren.

"How do you feel about that?" he asked, as she noticed she could also hear his quick footsteps on the pavement.

"Uncomfortable," she said. "More uncomfortable than I expected."

"One second," he said. For several seconds, she could only hear city noises and shuffling. "Okay, back," he said. "I just texted you a photo. Let me know when you get it."

Just then her phone chimed, and there it was: a photo of a snapshot of a chubby kid taken before the days of digital photography.

"Got it?" he said.

"Yes," she said.

"That's me," he said.

She laughed. "Okay."

"That was *after* I did the Atkins diet for an entire year and spent the summer at fat camp."

She waited for him to say more. What did this have to do with her case?

"I was overweight until I was thirty. It was a huge source of insecurity for me. One of my first clients was a man who thought it was funny to make fun of my weight every time I saw him. He called me the biggest loser. That's just one example. I've had clients call me all kinds of awful names. Tell me I'm worse than the prosecutor. That I'm an idiot and not smart enough to be their lawyer. That they'd rather the devil represent them than me. That I'm worse than Donald Trump."

Bea chuckled. This time, she heard him chuckle too.

"Meanwhile, there I am, working my ass off for them! Late nights, weekends. . . . I'm working for people who don't blink twice before insulting me. One guy fired me four times. Four times!"

"How?" Bea asked.

"Well, usually he'd rehire me about an hour later or the next day. But every time he assured me that it was only out of desperation. What am I getting at here? You have to remove your personal feelings from the case. That includes your personal feelings about its substance. Your biases. Your own fears. Your own triggers. You, Bea Powers, cannot allow what a client throws at you to affect you, because if you do, well, you'd only end up doing your best for people you like. And that wouldn't be very equitable, would it?"

"Okay," she said. It made sense.

"I'm not scolding or correcting you," he said. "So please—no reason to sound dejected. This is hard stuff. You're just starting it. You only learn by doing. I have to head into class. We can chat more next week. Hang in there. And, Bea," Dr. Friedman said, "remember—each of us is more than the worst thing we've done."

"Right," she said. It was a line he'd said at least four times.

"Hey, let's practice. What kind of support are you going to provide to this person?"

". . . emotional?"

"Certainly. But I meant your best," he said. "No less than your best."

SHE SAT, THE campus still and quiet apart from the birds now that classes were in session. She toyed with her phone, which was resting on her lap.

She knew she shouldn't skip lab, but at this point she was over twenty minutes late, and her lab partner was surely already well into the experiment. She'd missed the previous week's lecture as well, after she had decided to sleep in following a late C.U.N.T. rehearsal. It was unlike her to shirk schoolwork, but the more immersed she'd become in Justice and improv, the harder she'd found it to care about physics. She wasn't going to be a doctor. That was becoming more and more clear.

She reopened the case file and located his contact information. She entered his number into her phone, considered saving him as a contact, and then changed her mind and just sent him a text.

Hi, I'm Bea, your student advocate in the pending case against you. Please let me know when you'd like to meet.

She leaned back and squinted in the sunlight, now peeking behind the chapel's steeple. She closed her eyes.

Her dad—or Lester, whether or not he was her dad—still hadn't written back. It had been less than forty-eight hours since she messaged him, but that was an eternity on the Internet. (She hadn't worked up the nerve to open the message to see if there was a tiny check mark indicating that he'd seen it.) Since he hadn't accepted her friend request, he likely hadn't seen the message, as it would be relegated to a separate, buried file of messages from non-friends. But why hadn't he accepted her friend request? Was it because he didn't know who she was? Or because he hadn't signed into Facebook over the weekend? Or because, being his age, he didn't know how to see and accept friend requests?

These more innocuous possibilities fell flat to her. The more time passed, the more foolish she felt for having written to him. It was very likely he was not even her dad. Why would he be? Just because he worked with her mom during the proper time period, had the initials L(?)B, looked a little like Bea, and had fantastic eyesight?

But . . . *yeah*. Those things.

He had to be her dad.

He *could* be her dad.

Was he her dad?

Was he embarrassed of her? Was he racist? Was she a secret he didn't want to face, a Pandora's box he didn't want to open?

As she spiraled, brimming with regret and anxiety, her phone vibrated in her lap—a text from Audrey to both her and Lorn.

HI GIRLS,
2 THINGS: 1) TGIVING HERE??? 2) ARE THESE SANDALS TOO
YOUNG ON ME

Attached was a photo of Audrey in a dressing room wearing heels with straps that climbed up the leg. Bea winced. They weren't cute shoes. She'd let Lorn tackle that one. Before she set her phone down, she noticed she'd received another message—the boy had replied.

Hi. Now is good. I'm in PiKa 112.

So she was expected to go to his room. Sure.

She was the emotional support person, she told herself as she gathered her things. It was only right to meet where he preferred.

SHE LET HERSELF into the PiKa dorm with her key card and wandered down a hallway reminiscent of every other dorm hall she'd ever been in—brutally lit, cold, and uninviting—in search of 112. Behind the doors that stood open, boys in caps sat typing at desks. In one room, there were three lined up on a futon clutching game controllers and shrieking, "Go! Go!" She found his room at the end and knocked.

"Come in," a voice called. He was seated on a sofa, leaning forward, his elbows balanced on his open legs.

"Hey, it's the improv girl," he said.

"Hi," she said, startled to see the bushy-haired guy from Saturday night. When she'd read that he was a fourth-year, she'd assumed he'd be a complete stranger. "I'm Bea."

"Tyler," he said. "Help yourself to some tea if you like." He nodded in the direction of an electronic kettle, a box of packaged tea, and a mug on the corner of his desk.

"I'm okay," she said, wondering where she should sit and deciding to pull over his desk chair. "Is it okay if I . . ."

"Of course," he said, lifting a hand to swipe it aggressively across his face. Only then did she notice he'd been crying, his eyes bloodshot and puffy and his cheeks still glistening.

"How are you doing?" she asked.

And at that, this boy, this fourth-year boy, began to sob. His sobs were irregular, jolting. He covered his face with his hands completely, muffling the sounds jerking from his body. She didn't know whether to touch his shoulder, try to comfort him. She decided to stay put. Finally, he lowered his hands.

"I don't know . . . I don't know what to do. I can't tell my dad. I cannot fucking tell my dad. But I feel like I . . . don't I need a lawyer?"

He covered his eyes again, but this time, he was silent.

"You don't necessarily need a lawyer. Some people get them," Bea said, reciting what she'd learned in the training.

"My dad is going to lose it. He's going to . . . He'll never talk to me again."

"How do you know?" Bea asked.

"He told me. He said if anything like this ever happened again . . ." Bea's breath caught in her throat. He picked up on her stiffening. "Not like that. Not like *this*. I mean, if I got in trouble again, he said I could consider myself no longer his son. I had a DUI once. But this is . . . fucking worse."

Relieved, Bea said, "But you've only been accused. There's no outcome yet."

Tyler shook his head. "Doesn't matter. He won't care."

She raised her eyebrows. "You don't think your dad will believe you?"

"He won't *care*," Tyler said, sighing. "He'll be pissed I let this even happen. He'll find a way that this is my fault no matter what. I shouldn't have gone out with someone I didn't know better. Or I shouldn't have been drinking. Or I shouldn't have let her lie down in my room. Or I shouldn't exist."

He began to weep again. Bea stood and made her way around the coffee table to perch next to him on the couch. She softly placed a hand on his shoulder.

"It'll be okay," she said, because she didn't know what else to say.

"You don't know that," he said.

He was right. She didn't.

At once, he seemed to realize the inevitability of the situation: that his father was going to find out about the accusation. He stopped crying and sat up straight.

"It's going to happen," he said. "He knows everyone in the administration."

"That's a bad thing?" Bea asked.

He looked at her meaningfully, seeming almost irritated.

"You don't know my parents," he said.

"Even if you're found innocent?" The technical terminology wasn't "innocent," but "not responsible" didn't yet feel comfortable on her tongue.

"With my parents," he said, "it's not about what is and isn't. It's about how things look. This looks as bad as it gets." He clasped his hands behind his neck, closed his eyes, and sighed.

"I don't have parents," Bea said.

He looked at her.

"My mom's dead, and I've never met my dad."

After a moment, he said, "I'm sorry."

"I'm not telling you for sympathy. I'm saying . . . if the worst happens and you're right, well, you'll survive. I have."

His gaze flitted across the room, then back to her. He was unmistakably calmer; the panic had drained from his face.

"Okay," he said. "Thank you."

"Let me clarify what my role is as your advocate," she said, following instructions. "I'm here for you as an emotional support and as a reference if you have questions about how it works, that kind of thing. I'm also supposed to remind you that the campus judicial process isn't a legal process. Any possible outcomes are restricted to what the university can do—have you been told this?"

He nodded.

"I'm also available to help you gather witness testimony. We'll have to get names of witnesses in by the end of the week." The trainer had explained that the new judicial process, which included hard deadlines on a tight time line, was all about expediting case outcomes. Under the old system, cases would languish unresolved for months or even semesters, with students walking around campus together, going to class together, all while they had a case pending.

"Can't I just talk to her?" he asked suddenly, urgently.

Bea knew she had to advise him against this idea, but that it was his first instinct disarmed him for her.

"Isn't it weird that you saw us together? At your show?" he said distantly.

Wait, what? Bea thought, then realized: *it was the girl with the scars.* How had she not thought of it as soon as she'd seen him? She'd not only seen *him* before; she'd also seen the girl he was with that night. The night in question. Having a face to associate with the claim, with the story, made Bea's stomach tighten. She shoved the image of the girl from her mind.

"Yeah, that was her. You saw her. She's so *nice*. See? It has to be a misunderstanding, so I think maybe if we just talked . . ."

He let the thought linger unfinished. After a moment, Bea said, "I don't think that's an option for you, given the rule that you aren't supposed to contact each other." But she was relieved he'd suggested it. Maybe she *could* be on his side. Maybe it *was* a misunderstanding. "Can you tell me what happened? Maybe I can help you figure it out."

12

Stayja

FRIDAY, AUGUST 25

"He's got abs. I am not kidding. Actual, rippled, model abs," Nicole said on their drive to work at dawn. Nicole was now sleeping with Chet-the-lawyer, who was indeed representing her for free.

"So those are, like, a perk of trading sex for favors?" asked Stayja. It came out meaner than she intended.

Stayja was now working a double on Fridays. Frank, who ran all the campus eateries and the bookstore, had moved the girl who worked the Rooster morning shift to the coffee shop on the other campus, which opened earlier. And just this Friday, Nicole, too, had offered to cover for her coworker at the QuikMart because she had a date. It surprised Stayja to see Nicole taking on extra work, even for a single instance, and she figured her cousin must have an ulterior motive—it being easier to steal cigarettes on Friday nights or something when Frank was off.

"You talking about you or me?" Nicole asked.

"Tyler doesn't do me favors, and we haven't had sex."

"So you're dating now?" Nicole asked snidely. "He's your boyfriend?"

Stayja didn't answer.

"Does he take you to parties with his friends?"

"Shut up."

Stayja thought about the one party Tyler had mentioned, one that he was planning. It was a mixer (the word he'd used). She hadn't bothered asking—she knew she wouldn't be invited. And wasn't that reasonable? The school was funding it; it was a party for students who paid tuition. It wasn't as if Tyler could just invite the whole damn town of Cartersboro.

They parked and headed their separate ways, Nicole to the Quik-Mart and Stayja to the Rooster, where she discovered that nothing had been delivered—not coffee, not breakfast or lunch platters, not pastries. Apart from the black rubber mats along the floor that remained sticky no matter how hard or often she mopped them, it was barren.

"Excuse me," a voice behind her asked, "are you open? Or not until seven? Could I go ahead and get a coffee?"

"I don't know if I have any coffee," Stayja said, peering over the end of the counter to see if a box was hidden there.

"You don't have coffee? Isn't this a coffee shop?"

"One second," said Stayja, opening cabinets she knew held nothing but supplies she never used. The Rooster had had a few lives before its current iteration—once as a smoothie bar, then as a sushi bar, then as a smoothie bar again. The remnants of these past lives crowded the cabinets, which Stayja continued to open and shut mostly for the sake of the impatient student scrutinizing her every move. Once she'd combed the cupboards, she took her phone from her back pocket. The girl performed an exasperated sigh. Stayja pretended not to hear it as she texted Frank: no coffee or anything . . . where is delivery? She placed her phone on the counter and opened the tall door behind which she hung her apron. As she tied it on and spun back around to see her phone lighting up, she saw the girl was still watching her, eyebrows raised.

Shit ok. Am investigating, Frank responded.

"No coffee yet. Sorry," she said to the girl, who huffed away just as Tyler entered the shop.

"Hi!" Stayja said.

"Hey," he said. "Got a minute?"

"Well, we don't have any coffee, so there's nothing for me to do till it gets here."

"Weird," he said.

"I know." She followed him through the side door. He turned, slid his hands into his pockets, and smiled.

"Idea," he said. "Why don't you try to go to medical school?"

He paused. She gave him her best *are you crazy?* look.

"Why be a nurse when you could be a doctor?" he said.

"Um . . . a million reasons?" she said.

"Like?"

"Like . . . I'm twenty-three? And can't even find the time and money to get an associate's degree? Like med school costs a million dollars, literally, and first you have to have a bachelor's?"

He pulled his phone from his back pocket.

"What if I told you"—he tapped it once and handed it to her—"that all of that didn't matter?"

The screen read Gibson College Linkage Program. She'd never heard of Gibson College. She looked up at him. "I'm confused," she said.

"If you can get in there or somewhere like it, you basically start college now, and it goes right into medical school. It's faster. And I bet it's not that much more than what you're already paying. And I bet you'd get in because you make good grades. I mean, you'd have to move. That one's on the coast, but who doesn't want to live at the beach?"

She skimmed the website.

"How'd you know about this?"

He shrugged.

"I knew there were med-school linkage programs because my cousin did one. So I just googled ones in North Carolina."

She scrolled on his phone, skimming, trying to process it.

Tyler's comment a few days earlier about her being in the category of *the poor* had continued to trouble her. It had left her wondering if she was making the kind of choices poor people made and rich people didn't make. *Should* she have tried to take out student loans to go to college? Should she have applied to Carter? Should she encourage her mom to work under the table? Should she try to get a different job that paid for health insurance? *The poor*, he'd said. She'd been defensive. But in the intervening days she'd found herself wondering—was the way she thought different from the way people like Tyler thought?

"For phase one it's like no work at all. You just have to"—he grabbed the phone from her—"write an essay. One essay. Write an essay and fill out the application. Then, if they invite you for an interview, you can deal with the rest at that point."

Her phone buzzed.

"Just think about it?" he said.

Here with coffee where r u Frank had written.

"Thanks. I'll think about it," she said, turning to go back inside.

"Want to come over tonight after work?" he asked.

How would Nicole get home? Stayja hesitated. She could take the bus. She wouldn't be happy about it, but she would live.

"Yes," Stayja told him.

ALL DAY, SHE found she'd break into a smile at the thought of him and the evening ahead. No more just sitting on the curb or in the lot—she was going over to his room. Even being on her feet for five, seven, nine hours, her heels aching, her lower back beginning to groan, she found her giddiness was impenetrable. As dusk approached, she was filling the milk canisters when Eric Gourdazi, clean-cut, towering, and, as ever, dressed in an ironed collared shirt, entered the café behind a girl who approached already holding out her student ID with one hand while typing on her phone with the other.

"Tuna salad, please," the girl said without looking up. Stayja took the card and swiped it, then fetched a tuna plate from the fridge, her heart pounding. She handed the plate to the girl, who frowned and brought it to her nose without even lifting the lid.

"I think this has, like, gone bad," she said. "I mean I could smell it without even opening it." She held it out to Stayja to sniff. Stayja opened the lid to smell it; it smelled like tuna always smelled: bad. Donna loved when she brought home the uneaten, expired plates; she had come to expect them as her lunch staple many days. But Stayja had never seen the appeal of stinky canned fish.

The plates always arrived chilled, but the day before, she'd been on break when they arrived, placed out of her line of sight left of the counter. Then the café got busy, and she'd forgotten about them. By the time she'd loaded them into the fridge, they were room temperature. But that didn't seem as if it could possibly have made a difference. Tuna was tuna.

"It smells normal to me," Stayja said. The girl, who had scrunched up her face, shook her head. "No, it's bad. It's definitely bad," she said, turning to Eric Gourdazi and lifting the plate to his nose. "I mean, tell me I'm not crazy."

When he shook his head instead of taking a whiff, the girl continued, "This is not safe to be serving people." She shoved the open plate across the counter as Stayja heard Eric Gourdazi say the thing that changed him for her. The thing that made her feel lower than anything anyone had ever said to her at Carter—and she'd been the subject of some truly nasty, truly predatory comments over the years. Sweet Eric Gourdazi, whom she'd once watched push a child in a wheelchair—a relative? a mentee?—into the Rooster and play checkers with her for a full hour, whispered to the girl, as if Stayja didn't have ears: *You'd probably know better than her.*

What did he mean? Because Stayja wasn't rich, she couldn't tell when food had gone rotten? She must not know what fucking tuna salad was supposed to fucking smell like?

She dropped the plate into the trash, then returned to the register to issue the girl a refund.

STAYJA HAD NEVER been inside a Carter dormitory or any college dorm, for that matter. In her imagination, wide, carpeted hallways were adorned with ornamented mahogany furniture, like the campus libraries and art museum. But as Tyler swiped his card and led them into the building, she was surprised to enter a sterile, tiled hallway lit by fluorescent bulbs.

The first person they encountered as they made their way down the hall was a guy Stayja didn't recognize, though he looked like every other white frat guy on campus. He gave Tyler a silent nod. The next, Stayja did recognize from the Rooster. Luke? Loren? As he passed, he whispered, playfully, "Shaggy, is this a good idea?"

Tyler waved him off, and though she couldn't see his face, she could tell he was smiling. Assuming that "this" had meant her, she made a note to spit in Luke/Loren's coffee next time (which she'd never actually done to anyone, to Nicole's disappointment).

They finally reached his door, which he held open for her.

"Why do they call you Shaggy?" she asked, surveying the room. He was clean. Things were in their place, neat—his textbooks lined vertically on his desk, his bag hanging on a single hook on his closet door. His bed was made, and a green hoodie hung on the back of his desk chair. On the windowsill were three glass candles whose wicks had clearly been lit in the past.

"Because they're jealous of my hair," he said, tossing his keys on the coffee table, taking a seat at his desk, and bending over to untie his shoes. "Make yourself at home," he said. "I'm just gonna change."

After he took off his shoes, he disappeared into a walk-in closet as Stayja took a seat on his brown leather couch. It sloped toward the back, the cushions giving way easily under her weight, and she sank into it, her thighs settling at a forty-five-degree angle. He reemerged in shorts and a T-shirt, shutting the closet door behind him to reveal a painting of the American flag on the wall next to it.

"I like that flag. Where'd you get it?" she asked when he reappeared.

"I painted it," he said, falling onto the couch beside her. When she didn't respond—she was remembering the part of the incident where Eric Gourdazi had shaken his head and was wondering why—he asked, "Are you okay? What's wrong?"

And so she told him the story of the girl with the tuna and the comment about Stayja's not knowing how to recognize rotten food.

He listened, his eyes narrowing, and when she was finished, he squeezed her knee.

"Fuck them. You're going to be a great doctor," he said and winked. Then he surprised her—he put his head down in her lap. She set a hand on his coarse, wild hair and stroked it softly. He closed his eyes.

"What's your biggest regret?" he asked, his eyes still shut.

She considered it.

"I kind of wish I'd applied to a real college and taken out loans now. Or maybe I'd have gotten financial aid. Who knows?"

"You still could," he said.

"And you? What's yours?" she asked.

He didn't answer but instead asked, "What's the worst thing you've ever done?"

"I broke my cousin's bong on purpose," she said. "I smashed it onto the tile floor."

"That's it? Something you did out of concern for your cousin?"

"I didn't do it out of concern," Stayja said, her gaze still fastened to the flag. "I did it because she liked it, and I was pissed at her."

He opened one eye just long enough to cast her a mischievous look.

"And you?" she said. "The worst thing?"

He didn't answer for a long moment. When he did, he sat up and began to pull off his shirt.

"A lot worse than breaking a bong," he said from behind the blue fabric. "Come here, Miss Stayja." He tossed his shirt aside, leaning forward to cup her chin in his hand. When he slid his hand under her bra strap, she could think nothing but yes, yes, yes.

"And you—" Una's voice—"no idea?"

He didn't answer, but instead said, "What's she like that you're ever seen?"

"Very," he caught, his eyes puzzled, "a radical, I think," she told him at last, too.

"That's it. It's what you've got plenty of in your country—radical, if it does you any. You," said he sure he stood understand. "That's as it should be," and said, changed a bit. He or more—he was just long enough to catch her a moment or two.

Enderson "So," said. "There we go."

He didn't draw his elbow across her. With his head bowed up and begun to pull off his shirt.

"What—more than breakfast I can, he said it he's behind the bar again. "Come here, I bet Sleep," she tossed his drink, take instructions to empty her drink in the hand. When he shook them under her hot-box shop, she would, but in a minute, yes, please.

PART IA—COMPLAINANT TESTIMONY

Name: Annie Stoddard
Class Year: Second-year
Policy Allegedly Violated: Sexual Assault
Date: 9/2/17, 9/9/17   **Time:** 11:30 p.m., 9:30 p.m., respectively
Location: PiKa fraternity house
Incident Description (add additional sheets if needed):

The first night I was drunk and sleeping on his couch. I woke up with his penis in my mouth. I didn't push him off me at first because I didn't understand what was happening. By the time I figured it out, I sort of pulled back, but he pushed me back and held my head in place.

The next day, he convinced me that I had been confused and that it had been consensual.

The second rape happened a week later. There was no alcohol involved. We were watching a movie in his room. We made out, and I consented to my shirt coming off, but after that I was clear that I was not consenting to intercourse. However, that is what happened.

When I left his room, I went to the hospital to report it and have a rape kit done. I ended up not staying to have the test done, though, because it was overwhelming.

I reported it the next day to the dean.

PART IB—RESPONDENT TESTIMONY

Name: Tyler Brand
Class Year: Fourth-year
Policy Allegedly Violated: Sexual Assault
Date: 9/2/17, 9/9/17   Time: 11:30 p.m., 9:30 p.m., respectively
Location: PiKa fraternity house
Incident Description (add additional sheets if needed):

Annie Stoddard was present in my room on the night of September 2 along with multiple other parties. Everyone was drinking heavily, including her and me. Several hours into the night, we hooked up.

The next morning we discussed the night before and agreed that we were both very drunk and couldn't remember the details. We made out again that morning, so I thought everything was fine and we were cool.

The next weekend we went for pizza and to an improv show. Afterward she came back to my room, where we watched a movie and had sex. At no point did she tell me she wanted to stop, so I was completely under the impression that our actions were consensual. I am honestly shocked and appalled to hear otherwise.

This has been devastating for me. I am a good person. I never meant to hurt anyone. I would never rape anyone.

Investigator's Report

To: Dean Sharon Arroyo, Dean of Student Conduct
CC: Annie Stoddard, Complainant; Tyler Brand, Respondent; Carla
**   Bitman, Assistant Dean of Student Conduct**
From: Lila Wutke, Esq., External Investigator
Re: Investigation into alleged sexual misconduct
Date: Friday, September 22, 2017

A. INVESTIGATION PROCEDURE

Between September 15 and September 18, the investigator interviewed the following parties at the Carter Boathouse hotel:

- Annie Stoddard, Complainant
- Tyler Brand, Respondent
- Joelle Pasha, Witness for the Complainant
- Matty Tuttle, Witness for the Complainant
- Ellen Harris, Witness for the Respondent

All witnesses agreed in writing to audio recording of their interviews with the understanding that the interviews would be used in connection with this investigation.

B. INTERVIEW SUMMARIES

I. Interview of Annie Stoddard, Complainant

The investigator found no material discrepancies between the complainant's version of events as described in her complaint and those presented in the interview. The investigator used the interview to clarify the precise nature of two particular aspects of the complaint that the complaint leaves unclear:

a. How the complainant communicated her lack of consent to the respondent, and
b. Why the complainant left the hospital prior to the rape kit being performed.

In regard to the former question, Ms. Stoddard stated the following:

INVESTIGATOR: How did you know he knew you didn't want to have sex?

MS. STODDARD: I was making it really obvious with my body.

INVESTIGATOR: What do you mean?

MS. STODDARD: It's not hard to tell if someone doesn't want to have sex with you. Just like it isn't hard to tell if someone doesn't want to kiss you or touch you or talk to you.

INVESTIGATOR: Physically and verbally, please describe for me exactly what you did to communicate this. Both times.

MS. STODDARD: Well, on the first night, I gagged and pulled back, but his hands were there, so I just, um, kept going. And on the second night, I was just, like, squirming and trying to get out from under him. But he was on top of me, and I was, like, I'm not sure this is a good idea.

INVESTIGATOR: You said you weren't sure it was a good idea?

MS. STODDARD: Yeah. It was, like, my way of saying no but not saying the word "stop."

INVESTIGATOR: Why didn't you actually want to say the word "stop"?

MS. STODDARD: I don't know. I didn't. I couldn't say it. I didn't . . . I think maybe I didn't want to be raped. And I thought maybe if I didn't actually tell him to stop, I could make it not be a rape, you know? Like, I could pretend to both of us that wasn't what was happening. My friend and I were talking a little bit about this today. . . . We were talking about how, like, if you don't say the actual words, you can try to convince yourself that maybe it isn't what you think it is. But also if you don't say the actual words, you're going to make it harder to prove later that it was what you knew it was. And maybe you need to be able to do that to get, you know, peace. Like I am now. So it's, like, you're lying there, and you have to make a guess of what your future self is going to feel like. But you have no idea what you're going to feel like. And you don't have any time to think about it because it's happening right then. . . . It's just so awful and confusing. So I was . . . I think I was sort of pulled in different directions and ended up kind of, like, going with this middle ground where I didn't say no but I did struggle? I mean I didn't decide, like, "I'm going to struggle." I just did because, I mean, I didn't want to be doing that.

INVESTIGATOR: That meaning . . .

MS. STODDARD: Sex.

INVESTIGATOR: When did you decide it was rape?

MS. STODDARD: I knew it as it was happening.

INVESTIGATOR: Do you think there is any possibility that he thought you were consenting?

MS. STODDARD: Absolutely not. Like I said, my body language was very clear.

In regard to the second question—why she didn't get the rape kit—the complainant stated the following:

INVESTIGATOR: Tell me about what you did after. You left his dorm room and then what?

MS. STODDARD: First I went to student health. There was a nurse there, the weekend nurse, this older lady who gave me a pack of cheese crackers and a bottle of water and asked me if she could call an ambulance for me, which I turned down because I didn't need an ambulance, I mean, I just . . . it was weird. She gave me Advil.

INVESTIGATOR: What do you mean it was weird?

MS. STODDARD: Like, I think it was more serious than cheese crackers and less serious than an ambulance. But those were the two things she offered.

INVESTIGATOR: How'd you get to the ER?

MS. STODDARD: Walked.

INVESTIGATOR: How far is that?

MS. STODDARD: A couple of miles. I don't know. It took a long time. Maybe forty-five minutes.

INVESTIGATOR: Then what happened?

MS. STODDARD: I got to the hospital around 1 a.m. and was given a form to fill out, on a clipboard. I wrote that the reason for my visit was rape. I only waited a few minutes. The nurse—you are interviewing her, right? As a witness?

INVESTIGATOR: I am, yes.

MS. STODDARD: She took my blood pressure and had me tell her what happened. She told me she . . . she commended, I think that was the word she used, me. For seeking medical help, um, right away. Then she asked if I thought I was in immediate danger or if a dangerous person needed to be arrested. I said no. She said in that case, it was okay if I wanted to wait and call the police after the medical exam. I didn't want . . . I told her I didn't want to involve the police. She told me she was obligated to inform them and then asked if I was over eighteen. I said I was, and she said, Okay, well we don't have to use your name, then, if you prefer to remain anonymous. And I did. I don't know why.

Then she told me that a complete medical and forensic exam would take two to three hours. First, I would need to take off my clothes and put on a hospital gown. She left to get me one.

While I waited, I just sort of started to wonder, like, why I was there. To prove that I'd been raped, I guess? But also it hadn't been that kind of rape. Like, I doubted there would be physical evidence of a struggle. So I just started to doubt if there was any point. And I was so tired by that point.

So then she came back with a hospital gown and this big green bin and a clear plastic bag. She told me to put my clothes in the bag and put on the gown. And then when it was time to go home, I could pick out other clothes from the bin to wear home. She said they were all clean, donated items. She said I'd eventually get my clothes back but they had to keep them now for evidence.

So I changed into the gown and put my clothes in the bag. She came in and took the bag and gave me a cup for a urine sample. She left again, and I was sitting there with this cup to pee in, and I was, like, just feeling like a specimen. It was too much. I left.

INVESTIGATOR: In the gown?

MS. STODDARD: No. I got a random sweatshirt and leggings from the bin.

INVESTIGATOR: Then where'd you go? Home?

MS. STODDARD: I was trying to get home, but I sort of collapsed in the quad on a bench before I made it. I was just really tired and overwhelmed. So I texted my friend Matty—you're interviewing him too, right?

INVESTIGATOR: Yes.

MS. STODDARD: I texted him, and he came and got me. We went back to his room. I stayed there on his futon. I mean at that point it was after 2. And, then, you know what happened next. The next day I went to the dean to report it.

II. Interview of Tyler Brand, Respondent

The investigator found no material discrepancies between the respondent's version of events as described in his written testimony and those presented in the interview. The investigator used the interview to clarify the respondent's understanding of the complainant's state of mind and the evidence on which he based his view that she was consenting to sex. The respondent stated the following:

INVESTIGATOR: Ms. Stoddard has said that her body language made it very clear that she wasn't consenting to intercourse with you. How do you respond to that?

MR. BRAND: I do not agree.

INVESTIGATOR: Can you elaborate? What do you remember?

MR. BRAND: I don't remember specifics because to be honest I was pretty drunk both times. I was pretty hammered. And she was, too, the first time. I'm not saying that as an excuse. But it's just why I can't give you really specific information. And, honestly, I think it's probably why this kind of thing happens sometimes, because neither person is making great decisions.

I'm not saying my bad decision was rape. I would never do that, no matter how drunk I was.

I just think . . . I don't know, I can see how people can get confused. Not that I was confused. She didn't tell me no or to stop or whatever, and even if she wasn't that into it, I mean, am I supposed to read her mind? Like, what does she mean she made it clear with body language? Not to be too graphic but people do all kinds of stuff during sex. . . . Sometimes people like doing weird stuff. You can't just assume someone, like, moving their body in a certain way means they want to stop.

INVESTIGATOR: Do you remember her pulling away?

MR. BRAND: I do not.

INVESTIGATOR: Squirming, trying to get out from under you? She said you held her down.

MR. BRAND: I don't remember doing that, no. But, like I said . . . squirming? Sex is a physical act. There's going to be some squirming. [Laughs]

INVESTIGATOR: Okay. Anything else you want to add before we move on?

MR. BRAND: I just want to say that I would definitely know if there were any possibility that I had raped her. That seems really obvious to say. But I feel like I should say it.

Also, I don't know if you want to know my theory of what's going on. But if I can just share it. Annie is very self-conscious of these scars she has on her legs. She just had cosmetic surgery last summer, and now she's more comfortable in her skin and, like, wearing different clothes, really short skirts . . . going out . . . drinking. She was supposed to have a roommate, but that girl transferred last minute. Now she has a single. I know they were good friends. She doesn't really have many friends here now, honestly, that I know of. And I thought it was weird that the roommate just left suddenly.

Anyway, point is her lifestyle dramatically changed this semester. And I wondered if this behavior—the instability, the alcohol, the accusing me of rape because she, like, regrets it and is ashamed . . . it all sort of falls in line if you think about it. I mean, you don't understand how drunk she got at my place. It wasn't normal drunk. She was out of control.

And, like, why did she go out with me again if I'd raped her? It doesn't add up.

One other thing I know is that she is on a bassoon scholarship but is kind of tired of bassoon. She told me that. And that she couldn't afford to go here except for her scholarship. And so part of me wondered—is she trying to, like, set herself up to, you know, sue my family or something? I mean, I know it sounds crazy, but is it actually? It's pretty well known at the university that my parents are big donors. She definitely knew.

So I just wanted to get those possibilities on the record. Because this just doesn't make sense to me unless something else is going on.

III.   Interview of Matty Tuttle, Witness for the Complainant

Mr. Tuttle is a second-year student and friend of Ms. Stoddard's. She sought his help in the early morning hours of September 10 when she "collapsed" of fatigue on a bench on one of the Main Campus lawns. Mr. Tuttle states that he arrived several minutes after receiving her text to find her "distraught, exhausted, and sad." According to him, it was apparent that "something terrible had happened" even before she told him what that was.

Mr. Tuttle also let me know that he "knew something was wrong" the weekend before, when he visited Ms. Stoddard in her dorm room on the morning of September 3, although on that occasion she didn't tell him anything about the night before.

IV. Interview of Joelle Pasha, Witness for the Complainant

Mrs. Pasha is a nurse at Carter University Hospital System in the ER department, where she is the nurse on call for sexual assault. Her interview corroborated Ms. Stoddard's version of what took place the night of September 9.

She added that she found Ms. Stoddard's behavior and demeanor to be consistent with that of a person who has recently experienced assault.

V. Interview of Ellen Harris, Witness for the Respondent

Ms. Harris is a third-year student and a friend of the respondent's. The night of September 2 she was with the complainant and the respondent in his dorm room.

Ms. Harris corroborated the respondent's description of what took place in the earlier hours of the evening, specifically that they were all drinking heavily. She was with the respondent until he returned to his room for the night and did not feel that his behavior was out of control or that he was behaving in any way out of the ordinary. She added that she knows the respondent quite well and does not view him to be a person capable of sexual assault. She told me that she was very surprised to learn of the allegations and that he seemed very upset telling her about them.

She does not know the complainant apart from that one evening they spent together on September 2.

Summary and Conclusion

The investigator finds the witnesses' statements credible. Both complainant and respondent agree on the facts of what took place on the nights of September 2 and September 9. Where they disagree is over whether Mr. Brand understood that Ms. Stoddard was not consenting to sex on either occasion. She argues that her "body language" made her lack of consent clear, whereas he argues that, in large part owing to inebriation, this was not true and that he believed her to be consenting.

The investigator is available to provide additional information or impressions at the request of the administrator.

September 25, 2017
The Office of the Dean of Students
Carter University
120 Campus Drive
Tyler Brand
CU Box 937
Via email

Dear Mr. Brand:

An investigation into allegations made against you under the university's sexual misconduct policy is now complete. Based on the findings of the external investigator, along with character letters submitted on your behalf and on behalf of the complainant, the administrator hereby makes the following findings:

Allegations

Allegation #1—Sexual Assault on September 2, 2017

Based on evidence presented, the administrator finds under a **clear and compelling** standard that you are **not responsible** for violating the university sexual misconduct policy as laid out in the Carter University Student Handbook. The reasoning on which this decision was made appears below.

Allegation #2—Sexual Assault on September 9, 2017

Based on evidence presented, the administrator finds under a **clear and compelling standard** that you are **not responsible** for violating the university sexual misconduct policy as laid out in the *Carter University Student Handbook*. The reasoning on which this decision was made also appears below.

Reasoning

As to Allegation #1, both parties conceded that excessive drinking clouded their memory of events, and so we are left to piece together the facts without the aid of their memories. Intoxication is not a defense to assault; it is, however, an obstacle to obtaining an accurate understanding of events, which this office is repeatedly frustrated by in cases such as this one.

This office uses the following evidence to infer what took place on September 2: A female witness on behalf of the respondent stated that just prior to the interaction in question between the parties, the respondent was behaving normally. The complainant's statement that she "kept going" and was "pulled in different directions," along with her behavior in continuing to interact with the respondent and agreeing to go out with him again, support the finding that he is not responsible.

As to Allegation #2, there is no evidence that Ms. Stoddard was under the influence of alcohol, and her testimony that she was not under the influence of alcohol is credible. Mr. Brand stated that he was intoxicated, however, "both times" and that he struggled to "remember specifics." Thus, Ms. Stoddard's version of the night's events is given more weight. Ms. Stoddard stated that she made "very clear" her lack of consent.

It is impossible for this office to determine precisely what took place, and thus a finding of assault is inappropriate at this time. However, the university's sexual misconduct policy requires an affirmative duty to respect others sexually:

Sexual respect for others

Sexual respect for others is broadly defined as a commitment to communicating and acting with respect for one's fellow students in regard to all sexual and sex- and gender-related activity. It does not include unwelcome conduct such as unsolicited commentary on one's sex or gender, inappropriate gestures or communication, or refusing to adhere to an individual's express wishes for bodily autonomy.

Mr. Brand is found to have violated the mandate of sexual respect.

Sanctions

The administrator's finding that the respondent violated the university's sexual misconduct policy will be met with the following sanctions:

- Mr. Brand is hereby placed on academic probation for the remainder of the school year.
- As a condition of remaining enrolled as a student at the university and as a term of his probationary status, Mr. Brand will immediately, within three days of the issuance of this decision, enter into supervised training on the university's sexual misconduct policy.
- As a condition of remaining enrolled as a student at the university and as a term of his probationary status, Mr. Brand will, within seven days of the issuance of this decision, enter into an alcohol-treatment program of his choosing, to be approved by the administrator and monitored by the administrator.

Mr. Brand, please take these sanctions seriously. If you are found responsible for a second violation of the sexual misconduct policy while you are enrolled as a student, you could face more extreme penalties, including possible expulsion.

Sincerely,
Sharon Maddox Arroyo
Dean of Student Conduct

PART II

Justice

Thursday, September 28

Please, please steal my phone

by the Irreverent Rooster

Ladies and Gents! Nonconforming and nonbinary individuals! People who despise gendered salutations and people who despise those people!

According to Monday's police log, a first-year Rooster's phone was stolen this week by a miscreant[a] on Science Row.

Upon reading this news, was my immediate reaction:

A. Oh, no!
B. How terrible.
C. Can that please happen to me?
D. All of the above.

If you answered (D), you probably have a perfect SAT score; congratulations, but that scores you no points here.

The correct answer is (C).

For the love of our founder, Reginald Purcell Carter,[b] someone please pry my phone from my clammy addict hands?

Let's consider the perks of being the victim of a phone theft, shall we? When your phone is stolen, in that brief period before your parent ships you a new one, you are spared the following:

1. Your first-year dorm's GroupMe messages.[c]
2. Campus news alerts about inclement weather that never comes.
3. Campus news alerts about inclement weather that has already passed.

4. Campus news alerts about mild weather that has no effect on anything about your day.
5. The despairing silence of the Sigma Chi guy you hooked up with last weekend.
6. Your high school boyfriend's Instagram.
7. His new girlfriend's Instagram.
8. She's not even that pretty.
9. Seriously, who's prettier, me or her?
10. Wait, I was making a weird face just now. Let me put on lip gloss.
11. How about now?
12. OK, last one: my parents' text that SURPRISE! they drove up to see me and want to meet for breakfast and, meanwhile, I was out so late last night that even KA had shut it down when I stumbled past rape central[d] soooooooooo . . . sure, Mom. I'm so happy to see you, too. And what do you mean I smell like Uncle Joe[e]?

But seriously, anyone want my phone for a minute? I'll pay you in dining dollars.

Glossary

a. MISCREANT: Anyone who does not attend Carter but dares to step foot onto campus for a reason other than serving us food or coffee—in this case, to snatch a phone.
b. REGINALD PURCELL CARTER: I made this up. Who is our founder for real? Someone with the last name Carter who, I am guessing, owned slaves?
c. YOUR FIRST-YEAR DORM'S GROUPME MESSAGES: No, I don't want to come to your play about a one-legged banana farmer that's "genre-bending." We weren't friends when we lived across the hall on South, and we definitely aren't now.
d. RAPE CENTRAL: The PiKa-ATO-KA axis.
e. UNCLE JOE: Family alcoholic.

Annie

So this was life.

I thought it would be better.

Even after it all: the burns, the scars—I had believed people to be decent. Expected goodness enough. Not outrageous goodness, not universal goodness. I did not expect to be let down so completely by everyone in my world before I even made it out of my teens. I did not expect to be gutted either, and then I was, but this, this was somehow, astonishingly worse. To be gutted was one thing. To be abandoned by the pack for it—that knocked the wind out of me.

As I reached the end of the decision letter, I found myself thinking back to first-year orientation, to when Dean Sharon had told us first-years that we were safe at Carter.

Welcome to Carter, she'd said. *You're part of the family now. This is a safe space for you to ask questions, to become who you truly are.*

At the time, I'd found it an odd thing to say. Of course, we were safe. Why wouldn't we be? Now I understood: she meant we weren't.

Then I found myself thinking of phrases that sounded almost cheesy in their simplicity but that felt so true they made my eyes grow hot. Like that the part of me that made me *me* had been stolen. That I had been hollowed.

I forwarded Matty the decision and then lay down on my bed and stared at the ceiling until he arrived, opening the door to my room and letting himself in. I rolled my head to face him, and the lack of surprise on his face just reiterated the cruelty of it all.

He took a seat on the edge of my bed. I sat up and said nothing, awed by the void that had welled up within me. In place of my soul, a great canyon had materialized, and this was interesting—I didn't care. I did not give two shits about it. Like a god surveying her vile, indifferent creation, I felt merely a weary disappointment.

"It's awful. But it's not just here," Matty said. "It's everywhere."

I didn't ask how he knew this. Matty, who hated socializing, who didn't even date because he claimed he was too busy, knew this, and I hadn't. His precocious knowledge no longer impressed me. It made me nauseous.

Everyone knew that Tyler would walk away unscathed, I realized: the nurse, the dean, Matty, Simone. Tyler himself probably knew.

I told Matty I wanted to be alone.

After he was gone, I reached for my headphones, plugged them into my phone, and turned the ringer on silent. I scrolled through my music until I found the *October Sky* soundtrack. I closed the blinds, slipped the earbuds into my ears, and crawled into bed.

THE CELLO IS not an instrument that one learns in order to hide in the back of the orchestra. If the violin is the leading lady and the timpani is the worthy foe, the cello is the noble suitor, the heart throbbing beneath the story. When I was a child, I'd dismissed the cello for the same reason I'd dismissed the violin: it was too popular.

But when I awoke the morning after I received the decision letter, which was also the last day of classes before fall break, there was only one thing on earth that interested me. I had once read that the cello is the sound of the human heart breaking. Was that why I couldn't think about anything else?

A bunch of us kept our instruments in the student center so we didn't have to haul them back and forth to our dorms. I texted my cellist friend, Abigail, asking if I could borrow hers, and she wrote back that she was already in Cancun, having left for break a day early, and that I could *have* her cello if I wanted, which I interpreted to mean she was already drunk.

Before the decision in my case I'd planned to take the bus home for fall break—it was only about a four-hour trip, and my mom or dad would pick me up in Atlanta. I'd bought a ticket but was relieved to see it was exchangeable. That evening, I texted my mom that, last minute, I would have to stay for rehearsal, a lie. She was clearly disappointed but didn't argue; my parents had a respect for my music bordering on insanity. They credited it with getting me into college and securing a scholarship that allowed me to attend a private university. Whereas my brother's illness and its expense had blindsided them, yanking the future out from under them, the bassoon had swept in to fix everything. I would see them in two weeks, anyway, for Parents' Weekend.

I found I still couldn't tell my parents, but I also couldn't pretend that everything was fine, and so I was avoiding them. They noticed. Over FaceTime, sitting so that they were both in frame, they begged me to reveal to them what was wrong, threatening to drive up to Carter. I told them I had been seeing a guy who turned out to be a jerk, leaving it that vague. This had seemed to satisfy my mother enough.

The music building was empty. As I passed the concert hall on my way to the practice rooms, I opened the door to peek inside. The room felt larger and more reverent than ever without a soul in it, hundreds of tan seats facing the clean, barren stage framed by grand velvet curtains.

"Hello!" I shouted. My voice echoed back to me. Why would I play in a practice room when I could play in the concert hall? I walked down the center aisle, my TOMS crunching on the gritty carpet, noisy in the broad silence. I climbed the stairs to the stage. Stacked in the wings were the folding chairs we used for performances. I set down Abigail's cello case, dragged out a chair, and flipped it open. I fetched a music stand from offstage, sat down, and pulled out the instrument.

I opened the sheet music to *October Sky*, which I'd swiped from Abigail's cubby. I didn't know how to make the notes, but at least I knew that each string *was* a note and that the fingers changed them, and I didn't plan to leave the music building until I figured out how to play the damn thing.

I'm not sure how Matty found me. I'd taught myself the first bar by ear and was playing it over and over, again and again, when I heard a distant door click shut. I swallowed, squinting into the shadows. The silhouette of a stranger materialized into Matty, coming toward me and taking a seat near the front of the house. I ignored him and resumed playing until my arm ached and trembled. I let it fall onto my thighs.

Matty spoke first.

"Want to get dinner?" he asked. His voice echoed through the cavernous hall. I didn't answer. He stood and walked down the few remaining feet of sloping aisle to the stage. He climbed it.

"Let's get dinner," he said, taking the cello and bow from my hands and placing them properly in their case like the expert in everything that he was.

I DIDN'T FEEL like seeing anyone, so we ordered Domino's. We sat on opposite ends of his sofa, waiting for it to arrive.

"You didn't go home so that you wouldn't have to tell your parents?" he asked gently.

"Something like that," I said.

"You don't ever plan to tell them?" he asked.

I shrugged. "I don't know why I would do that to them." Then I added, with a snarl, "Apparently, there's nothing to tell anyway because nothing happened. Wait, why aren't you in DC?"

His gaze drifted past me. "I might go up. Still undecided." So he'd stayed for me. "But back to your parents."

"They'll be here for Parents' Weekend. Maybe I'll tell them then," I said to end the conversation. How long had it been since I slept? "Do you mind if I lie down and close my eyes while we wait for the pizza?" He shook his head, and I tried to ignore how sadly he was looking at me.

I'D BEEN ASSIGNED a student advocate, my "source of support," as Simone had described herself to me. Simone was a third-year and spoke to me as if she were my kindergarten teacher, as if instead of being raped, I'd been assigned to her class, in which we'd be learning shapes and colors.

"Do you have any questions?" she asked in a voice that made me think *nothing bad has ever happened to you.*

"No," I said, desperate for her to leave my room. But after I wrote my testimony, she surprised me. In her same singsong voice, she asked me to redo it.

"Can you maybe rework this so that it's a bit more . . . assured? I think we really want no room for ambiguity."

So I had reworked it, this time by hand. I noticed my handwriting was different than usual, less careful; it was slanted and sloppy, with errant slips of the pen, as if I'd been writing quickly. It was more like my mother's than my own, as if overnight I'd begun to write like a grown-up. As soon as I thought it, I revolted against the idea that being assaulted had matured me in some way; if it was true, I resented it.

When I chose my character references (my orchestra conductor, Juan-Pablo; Matty; and my boss at the bookstore, Frank), Simone said sweetly, "Are you sure you don't have any professors you could ask?"

"Not any that know me. I was in big classes," I lied. I was too embarrassed to ask a professor. Juan-Pablo was on the faculty, but since he wasn't *my* professor and therefore wouldn't be grading me in anything, he felt more approachable. (As if being raped, which had touched everything in my life, could somehow even affect my GPA.) "A Title IX case," was all I'd said to him when I'd handed him the form.

So a perk of the case's being over was that I no longer had to talk to Simone.

But that was it. Other than that microscopic silver lining, the weeks after my case was decided were heavy, lonely, dreadful. I spent all day every day terrified of a run-in with Tyler. As I moved between classes, my job at the bookstore, and orchestra rehearsal, I left my headphones on, playing nothing, so that if we did cross paths, I could feign being on a call.

I didn't tell people. I told one, other than Matty—of my orchestra friends, my closest was Caroline, a tubist from Des Moines. I'd wondered before if we'd bonded solely because we were both small girls playing giant instruments. She loved video games, sci-fi novels, and coding club, all of which were foreign to me.

"You're *kidding*," she hollered over and over when I told her the story while walking home from rehearsal one evening. She was so loud that I stopped talking, which she didn't seem to notice. She'd told me a story about another friend of hers who was raped, and

I'd been left to express the appropriate horror and anger over a stranger's assault.

After that, telling people hadn't seemed worth the trouble.

Sometimes I noted, with interest, how abruptly my thought patterns had changed. Before, I would lie in bed at night swaddled in guilt. I had so much "on paper," as they say: good parents who loved me—parents who'd immediately accepted my brother when he came out; a kind and gentle sibling, even as a teenager, who looked up to me; a loan-free education at a prestigious school; my own room!; and, finally, a body I didn't feel the need to hide. I feared that perhaps I was unable to acknowledge my good fortune, unable to just accept it—I wanted more. Always more. To look better, to feel better, to be different, to accomplish more.

Now I wanted nothing. I cared about nothing.

And then there was this: I didn't understand how this new pain in me had been created.

It wasn't there, and then it was.

Did it not defy a law of physics? Wasn't energy supposed to be preserved?

The more I considered it, I couldn't shake the suspicion that Tyler had passed on pain to me he was supposed to feel for himself, leaving me to suffer it on his behalf.

I WENT TO the dean's office on a Friday afternoon in early October, almost two weeks after my case had been decided.

"Is Dean Sharon available?" I asked the woman behind the desk in the small waiting area outside her office, to which the door was open.

"I'm here! Come in!" the dean called from inside.

"Hi, Annie," she said as I entered. I remembered why I'd liked Dean Sharon from the start. She'd seemed down to earth, with a no-nonsense kind of energy that was nonetheless upbeat in the way a girls' volleyball coach might be portrayed on TV.

She was wearing a tailored gray suit and very little jewelry—a gold wedding band and, in her ears, gold studs shaped like leaves that peeked out from beneath her cropped hair.

"How are you doing?" she asked. *Doing* was how people asked when they assumed you weren't well. If they said "How are you?" without the *doing*, they were just treating you like everyone else.

"Not really okay," I said.

She nodded, as if she expected to hear this. "Are you still seeing a counselor?"

"No," I said, leaving out that I'd never gone to Student Mental Health after I'd been encouraged to, both by her and by Simone. "I feel like that's not the problem, though."

She furrowed her brow.

"I don't understand how he just got academic probation," I heard myself say. "I don't see how that has anything to do with rape."

"Annie," she spoke slowly, carefully. "Perhaps it would help to think of the academic probation as the more punitive piece, while the alcohol treatment is the more rehabilitative piece."

"But . . ." I forced myself to pause and take a deep breath to halt the quaking that had seized my voice. "I don't understand what alcohol treatment has to do with rape either."

She smiled at me sadly. "I know you're hurting. And I'm glad you came to see me. Would you reconsider going back to talk to someone in Mental Health? I don't know who you saw before, but it doesn't have to be the same person if he or she didn't suit you. We can expedite intake, get you in today. There are some very capable counselors over there. I'll personally make sure you get someone you feel you can trust."

It was kind, and so I began to cry. She stood, walked around her large desk and took a seat in the chair next to mine. She reached out to put one hand on my knee. She waited.

"Okay," I said after a minute.

"Okay," she said, lingering a moment longer before standing and giving my leg a final pat. "I'll call now. You can head straight over."

MY COUNSELOR, LORETTA ESPOSITO, Psy.D., was an Italian American woman who looked to be somewhere between the age of my mother and that of my grandmother. She wore a geometric print silk scarf and skinny jeans with black suede ankle boots, far more fashionable than my mother or grandmother would ever be. Her silver-streaked black hair was swooped into a messy bun, and in her lap rested a yellow legal pad and a glossy pen that looked expensive, the permanent kind you're gifted for a birthday in the second half of your life and then buy refills for.

"What brings you in?" she began.

I cut to the chase. I told her I'd been raped—the word I used—but didn't offer up details right away. I told her he'd been found guilty or, as the university put it, "responsible" for not "respecting me sexually," whatever that meant, but that he remained on campus. I told her what Dean Sharon had said about the punitive piece and the rehabilitative piece. Only then did I pause.

"How do you feel about that?" she asked. "What Dean Sharon said."

I considered it for a moment. "I feel like a piece is missing," I said. She nodded, not in a performative or condescending way but in a way that seemed to imply agreement. I felt the muscles in my torso release, my jaw loosen. "I feel like, if he raped someone, why should he even be allowed to stay here? You know?"

"Yes," she said. "That's what you *think*. How does it make you *feel*?"

My fingers began to tingle, and I noticed I was sitting on my hands. I pulled them out from under me and rested them on my lap.

"Let down. I feel so disappointed in this place."

As soon as I said it, I wanted to sleep. Words, words. Ever since reporting the rapes I'd been asked to come up with words. I was so damn tired of coming up with words. Wherever Tyler was, I doubted he was being made to be William Shakespeare.

"Annie," Loretta said, seeming to pick up on my sudden mood shift. "I am with you one hundred percent. And you know what I have to say about this case? Fuck. This."

I blinked. Were therapists, or as Dean Sharon referred to them, counselors, supposed to speak this way? A surge of something—vindication?—prickled through my body.

"You aren't just disappointed," she said, her accent thicker than I'd realized. "You're angry. Because *fuck. This.*"

Now I was the one nodding.

"Yeah," I said. "I am."

"And you should be." Loretta didn't break our gaze as she matched the rhythm of my nodding, her eyes wide, sparkling. She tapped her fancy pen against the yellow paper with a sharp thwack.

"None of this you brought on yourself. Do you understand that?"

Did I? I nodded, but it must not have been convincing enough.

"Repeat after me: None of this I brought on myself."

"None of this I brought on myself," I said.

"Again."

"None of this I brought on myself."

"Louder."

"None of this I brought on myself!" I obeyed her instruction three or four more times, until she had heard enough. Until I imagine she had heard, in my voice, a sliver of openness to the possibility.

Bea

MONDAY, SEPTEMBER 25

Wrapped in a towel, her shower cap still on, Bea sat at her desk and read the decision quickly. Her first reaction was that it seemed fair and relatively inconsequential for him—he wasn't suspended or expelled. He'd told his parents several days into the investigation, and while they'd insisted on bringing in a lawyer from Atlanta, he'd already been interviewed by the investigator by the time she arrived. The lawyer, a middle-aged woman always in hose and a tailored skirt suit, made a lot of loud noise about this, of course, along with everything else—the time line, the lack of evidence, the presence of alcohol. If there was a stink that could conceivably be made, this woman made it. Ultimately, though, the case seemed to have come down to his word against hers, and reading through the report, Bea found that she sympathized with the Title IX officer for having to decide whom to believe. There was no way of knowing for sure what had happened, since only Tyler and Annie had been there.

Bea had helped Tyler think about how to present Annie's behavior in a way that she could be viewed as unreliable. Bea hadn't seen this as unethical in any way—first, because there was a bias against him going in, something even she had felt. Someone needed to help correct for it. Plus, everything he'd said about Annie in his interview and testimony was, it seemed, true, or at least he believed it to be so. He and Bea had never hinted at the idea of fabricating facts to improve his case. Tyler had seemed genuinely convinced it was a misunderstanding, and, as far as Bea knew, it was.

Yet there was a small part of her, a part she tried to dismiss, a voice she told herself was the bias talking. This part of her believed Annie Stoddard and had wanted Tyler to pay.

When she was with Tyler, she found it easy to be on his side. In hearing more about his background, she'd found that she related to it more than she cared to think about: the solitary early years of childhood, when she would turn the decorative throw pillows of her mother's bed into friends, followed by the mixed bag of boarding school, where she missed her mother desperately but also was nurtured by the friendships she formed there. Spending time with Tyler and then in class or in discussion with Dr. Friedman, she'd felt at ease in her role.

The cognitive dissonance of it she had found challenging in private flashes—reading the full case report once a copy was provided to Tyler; noticing Annie was in her abnormal psych lecture, which she never had before; or opening the decision letter via email that morning alone, the light slicing through the window to cast a single orange cone across the room. *Am I on the wrong side?* she'd wondered briefly, fleetingly, in these moments.

How would her mother feel about what she was doing? She wasn't sure—her mother had been a Democrat and against capital punishment, and she had been concerned by the rate of incarceration of black men in America. But she also had heard her mother use the term *ambulance chaser* to describe the lawyers who sued her and her colleagues, and once, when Bea asked if she had any interest in their neighbor Anthony, who was *clearly* interested in her, Phaedra had said absolutely not, that she'd never date a prosecutor.

But how did she feel about defense attorneys? It had never come up.

More than leaving Bea sad, the mystery excited her, highlighting how uncharted this path was for her.

And still there, hovering not so far back in Bea's mind, was the correspondence that hadn't come—yet another day, day sixteen, in which Lester Bertrand had not written her back.

For how long would she wake, disappointed, to his silence? When would she accept that she was just never going to hear from him?

Seated at her desk, contemplating this question, she saw her phone light up. The screen read "Dr. F calling."

"Hello?" she answered.

"Bea, did you see the decision?"

"I did," she said.

"I wanted to let you know that I spoke with the Brands, and they sang your praises. They said Tyler had only wonderful things to say about you. Excellent job. You should be very proud. You triumphed over the qualms and hesitations you had in order to put your client's needs first. That exhibits real maturity and commitment. I'm very impressed."

Dr. Friedman knew the Brands? It shouldn't have been that surprising, Bea reasoned. Tyler had mentioned his parents were big donors to the school, and, of course, Dr. Friedman was always working to raise money for his program. They were clearly terrible parents based on what Tyler had shared about them, but there was no reason Dr. Friedman would know that side of them.

"Are you still planning on applying to the summer fellowship with me?" he was asking.

"Um, yeah, I think so?" She'd assumed she would, but between classes and C.U.N.T., she hadn't given it much thought.

"Applications are due at the end of October, and a decision will be made by the end of the semester," he said. "I think you should."

"Okay," she said, a smile creeping up her lips.

"But a warning. . . . It's not like other internships, not like the kind your peers will have. There won't be too many opportunities for fun nights on the town. I'm talking late nights most nights, Saturdays in the office. Calling it intense is an understatement. We have a number of capital defense matters on our docket. That means the stakes are literally life or death. The only friends you'll have time to see will be your coworkers. Social time will be a quick coffee or ice cream during which you'll continue discussing work."

He let out an easy laugh.

"I just remembered that Kyle, last summer's fellow—I think I've mentioned him to you?"

"You have," Bea said.

"The friend he was staying with for the summer called one afternoon to make sure he was alive after he'd spent three nights at the office. Literally slept on the floor."

"Man," Bea said, awed.

"That's an extreme example, but it gives you an idea of how, at the CJRI, we understand the gravity of our responsibility and take it seriously. This is why, Bea, I think you'd fit right in."

The longer he spoke, the more she wanted it. Not wanted. The feeling was sharper than that. Bea ached for what Dr. Friedman was describing, which was bigger than a job and more important than an internship. It was a shared purpose, a community in which she'd be welcomed as a critical member—like the Turtles but with a mission that mattered. What he'd described was a family.

When they hung up, Bea slipped on her shoes. It was time to close some doors.

Improv had ignited in her a craving for the unknown, for stepping out before she knew what she would say and dwelling there, in uncertainty. The more she did it, threw herself into that terrifying spotlight with no clue what she was going to do inside it, the more she wanted to do it again.

So Lester Bertrand wanted nothing to do with her. Fine. She

was done trying to be someone she wasn't, done with premed, done trying to salvage a relationship that had never existed in the first place with a father who hadn't bothered to make himself known. New Bea was an improviser—a good one—and a public defender in the making. She would apply for the summer fellowship; she would get it, and work late nights on cases with real stakes, and sleep on the office floor, and drink too much coffee with her new, impassioned comrades. She would help the improv team win nationals.

Two weeks earlier she'd told Tyler that she'd been fine without parents, that she'd survived, when she was trying to reassure him that he would be okay. In the moment before uttering those words, she hadn't been confident in them, but in speaking them they'd become truer, as if she'd brought the truth into being by stating it aloud.

Now she was, if not certain, at least resolved: If she had no parents to make proud; she would make herself proud.

The first step was to withdraw from physics. Bea dressed, packed her books for the day, and headed out. On her way to psych, she'd go by the academic advising building and pay a visit to her adviser, a tiny fellow with black plastic-rimmed glasses and a frantic nail-biting habit whom she'd met only once, the week that school started. That had been a box-checking kind of meeting, five minutes to confirm that she was, in fact, taking four courses and was enrolled. She figured there would be simple paperwork to complete, perhaps a justification needed. She was prepared to lie and say she was on the verge of a breakdown owing to stress if that was what it took.

But as the bus crawled to a stop before her and a herd of students hustled forward to board, she received a text from Early.

I GOT MUGGED!!!!!!!

WHEN BEA REACHED her dorm ten minutes later, she found Early and two cops facing each other in the hallway in front of their room. The cops, a thin woman in a bun, and a stocky man with a belly, were clutching walkie-talkies. Early stood, arms crossed, her eyes wide and shimmering. She was texting on her phone in its pink, glittery case. Bea noticed the screen was shattered.

"May I help you?" he said to Bea as she approached.

"She's my roommate," Early said.

He turned back to Early. "The clerk at the campus store called to report someone had come in using a stolen student ID. Kid tried to buy cigarettes with your card. Thought she couldn't see the photo when he swiped it but didn't realize your photo appears on the monitor when you run it." He shook his head like this was the apex of idiocy. "We apprehended him just a couple miles away." The other cop was tapping busily on a tablet. A loose cluster of girls from Bea's dorm had assembled at the far end of the hall and were openly gawking. Early was listening so earnestly that Bea had to look away. The girls at the end of the hallway tittered.

"Have you ever been the victim of a crime?" the male cop asked her.

"No," Early said gravely.

He pulled a card out of his back pocket. "Here's my card if anything comes to mind you'd like to discuss," he said. "We'll be in touch."

As the officers exited the dorm, the three girls who had been conspicuously observing the scene hurried over—Bea didn't know their names. She hadn't yet met any of them. Their worried expressions belied an unmistakable glee in their eyes.

"What happened?" one asked hopefully.

"She lost her wallet," Bea said, annoyed, opening the door and gesturing for Early to go in first.

Inside the room, Early started unloading to Bea. "There are

never any open bike slots in the main campus docks," she said, speaking with urgency. "So I was docking the bike in the row behind the computer science building—I didn't even know one was there until today—and I'd just gotten it clipped in. I was late to calc so I was hurrying up that hill right there between the science buildings and the woods, you know those?" Bea nodded even though she didn't. "And this kid stepped out, like, a teenager. He told me to give him my wallet. I almost told him that I don't have a wallet, just a phone case with my student ID in it, but then I realized that was super dumb and just handed him my whole phone in the case."

She stopped.

"Then what happened?" Bea said.

"He ran away! He didn't even look to see what was in it. He just said 'thanks' and ran away."

"He thanked you?" Bea asked, astonished.

"I thought that was kind of funny, too." Early spoke rapidly and was almost grinning. "I went to one of those blue phones? I know. I actually used one of those. I called. And campus police sent a car to pick me up and bring me back here."

"How'd you get your phone back?" Bea asked.

Early frowned.

"The policeman brought it to me," she said. "Shouldn't it go into evidence or something?"

Bea shrugged. "You'd think," she said. "Maybe this is trivial enough that they don't care." Realizing the comment had perhaps been insensitive, Bea asked, "Were you scared?"

"Um, *yeah*. I still have goose bumps." Early held up her arm.

A moment passed.

"Are you going to press charges?" Bea asked.

"What? They already arrested him," Early said, seeming to notice Bea's expression for the first time since Bea had arrived. "Why do you seem weird?"

"What do you mean?" Bea said.

"You're acting weird," Early said.

Bea tried to sound casual as she said, "I bet you could stop them from prosecuting that kid if you wanted."

"Why would I do that?" Early said, an edge seeping into her voice. Bea didn't respond, just let her gaze drift behind Early, to the window.

"Bea, I'm going to cooperate with the police. That kid mugged me."

"But you don't know what his life is like. I don't know, I'm just saying there may be a way you can keep it from happening. We could talk to Dr. Friedman."

Early moaned. "Dr. Friedman, what would he do, what would he think? You have this guy on this pedestal!" She hesitated, then added, almost whispering, "My brother says he dates his students."

"What?" Bea tried to hide her distress at hearing this. It wasn't true. It couldn't be. "No way."

"It's common knowledge," Early said in a tone that Bea could tell was meant to be nasty. "Isn't that gross?" Bea didn't answer. "He's so old. And he has a *wife*."

"I mean, I don't know. It's not like assault or harassment if it's consensual," Bea heard herself saying.

"Um, it's cheating."

"Maybe. Or maybe not. You don't know what his understanding is with his wife."

Early glared at her. "Bea, he's a professor. He's like forty-five. We're eighteen. He has *authority*."

"I'm nineteen," Bea said.

Early's expression softened into something resembling pity.

"Right," she said.

Stayja

"Since when did Victoria's Secret get so PG?" Nicole said. The two of them were at the mall, spending the morning before their shifts searching for lingerie because Nicole wanted to buy some "skanky shit" to wear for Chet.

"Since when do you wear stripper clothes?" Stayja asked.

"Since I get a bigger paycheck than you do," Nicole snapped back, rubbing it in Stayja's face for the umpteenth time that she'd been promoted. It had been a serendipitous accident as far as Stayja understood—some kid had come to the QuikMart and tried to use a stolen ID. All Nicole had done was call and report him, which rendered her noble or especially capable in Frank's eyes. He'd promptly transferred her over to the bookstore, where she now made fifty cents more per hour than her cousin.

"What exactly are you looking for, if this is too conservative?" Stayja asked.

"I'm keeping an open mind. I'll know it when I see it."

Nicole led them back into the main corridor of the mall.

"What's the occasion?" Stayja asked, smirking.

"We said 'I love you,'" Nicole said.

Stayja snorted.

Nicole swatted her arm. Her face crumbled, then hardened. "We're in love! Like it or not."

"How do you know?" Stayja asked.

"Because you just know."

"That's called oxytocin. It floods your brain when you have sex with someone and confuses you and makes you think you're in love."

"Why don't I fall in love with everyone I fuck, then?" Nicole said.

"That's what I'm asking," Stayja said. "What makes this time different?"

They entered Dillard's and walked to the escalator. Intimate apparel was on the second floor.

"I don't fucking know! Like, I want him to be happy more than I want me to be happy and shit." They rode for a moment in silence. "And I want to, you know."

"What?"

"Make myself better for him. Like, be, you know."

"What?"

Nicole rolled her eyes.

"You want to be what?" Stayja said.

"Honest and shit. Responsible."

Stayja didn't say anything. She was too stunned.

"What about you?" Nicole asked. "How's it going with that guy?"

"Fine," Stayja said, trying to leave out the question mark in her voice. Tyler had, two days earlier, gotten the decision in his case. It hadn't turned out well. He was now on academic probation and had been found guilty of sexual misconduct, which had devastated him—he'd told her it basically meant he wouldn't be able to get into law school.

As they approached the racks of undergarments, Stayja shrank away from Nicole, who marched directly up to the saleslady behind the counter.

"Where's your kinkiest stuff?" she asked.

"This way," the woman said without batting an eye.

Stayja hung back, fingering a satin nightgown and thinking about love.

For weeks now, she and Tyler had met up nightly. She'd shut down the café, drive Nicole home, then come back to campus to hang out with him. That girl bringing the rape case against him had destroyed him. He was anxious, terrified, not eating. They'd sit on his couch, and he'd lie in her lap while they watched shows or just talked. His parents were furious and giving him the silent treatment. Most of his friends, he'd told her, didn't know about the case, because he was too embarrassed to tell them. He felt alone, abandoned.

"What would I do without you, Stayja?" he said one night, wrapping his arms around her waist and squeezing as if he could physically stop her from leaving.

Often she returned home after midnight or one. She'd sleep until nine or ten, then clean the house or knock out errands before heading into her shift at two.

These evenings were becoming her favorite hours of every day. She felt needed, and not for the kinds of things she was accustomed to giving others: her money, rides home, her sense of responsibility. These demands from Nicole and even her mother tapped her out and left her tangled in guilt and resentment and languor.

Tyler wanted only her affection and attention, and these she was willing to give him in spades. In his presence she felt as if she had a bottomless well of care to draw from as long as he stayed close, and she could caress his hair and reassure him it would be okay. She felt full driving home on these nights, and she knew what it meant.

"Hey!" Nicole hollered, standing under the Fitting Rooms sign. "Are you coming?"

Stayja waited outside the fitting room door while, on the other side, Nicole yammered about running into the student whose card had been stolen. *You'd think she saved the girl's life*, Stayja thought.

". . . and so I gave her a free Godiva bar. I was like, *I* know because I'm the one who turned in the guy who took your stuff . . . you deserve this."

"Nicole, for the millionth time, you can't give away shit you're supposed to be selling," Stayja said.

"Oh, please. It was just Annie and me there. Annie doesn't care."

"Who?" Stayja asked, her stomach rolling.

"Annie. She's, like, a normal one."

Surely it was a coincidence.

"Well," Stayja said, "if you're not more careful this Annie is going to report you to Frank and you're going to be out of work. *Again*."

"Annie has other shit going on, dude. You have no idea. She was *raped* recently. By this guy who totally got off the hook."

"That sucks," Stayja said, her stomach now pitching like a boat in a storm. She pressed her arms into it and was relieved her cousin couldn't see her face.

When Tyler had told Stayja about the sexual assault allegation, it wasn't that Stayja assumed the girl was lying. She just believed him that there was a fair amount of gray to the situation. She'd seen him hammered, and she knew how drunk those Carter girls got. The girl may not have wanted whatever happened between them, but, ultimately, this Annie had surely had chances to bow out, opportunities she hadn't taken.

"Yeah, it does," Nicole said.

A long pause stretched out between them.

"What's taking so long?" Stayja finally asked. When Nicole didn't answer, she said, "Nicole! It can't be this hard to decide if you want to buy a thong or not." She leaned down to look under the stall. Nicole was standing still, her feet planted. So she was doing something on her phone.

"What's your boyfriend's name again?" Nicole asked from the other side of the door.

"He's not my boyfriend," Stayja said.

"What's his name?"

When Stayja didn't respond right away, the door flew open. Nicole clutched a black teddy to her chest, the right strap dangling off her shoulder. She held her phone in her other hand.

"I don't think you should keep seeing him," Nicole said, suddenly very serious. "I don't think he's a good guy."

"Oh please," Stayja said. "Get dressed."

"He's a rapist."

"She told you that, I know. But I heard a different version."

Nicole's mouth dropped open.

"God, I would have thought of all people that *you* would be feminist about this," she said.

Stayja was quiet, debating whether to even try to explain to her cousin what she was thinking, which was that the male body was its own unruly beast. It was biological. A matter of science. Guys couldn't even control when they got erections; *that* was how not in control they were, with all that testosterone surging through them. So if all the girl had said was yes—yes to kissing, to clothes off— and then suddenly her position became no? She couldn't be shocked when the male body—any male body—had trouble switching lanes.

"I think it was a misunderstanding," Stayja said. "It sounds like she waited really late to change her mind or something. I'm not saying she's a liar."

Nicole yelped in horror.

"Fuck that!" she squealed. Stayja was relieved they were the only ones in the fitting room. "I don't care if he's *inside* me, if I tell him to get out, he better get the fuck out."

"Are you done? Or can you finish up?" Stayja said, checking her phone out of habit, for anything—the time and to see if he'd texted.

"I'm serious. You have to break up with him," Nicole said.

"Oh?" Stayja asked, her voice rising. "Is Chet the married traffic lawyer the kind of upstanding citizen you would prefer for me?"

"At least Chet isn't a rapist," Nicole said.

"You know what? You can take the fucking bus home," Stayja said, storming out of the dressing room.

AS STAYJA WAS pulling into the driveway, she was only beginning to feel guilty for leaving Nicole at the mall (though Chet, the apparent love of her life, could pick her up if she didn't want to take the bus) when she spotted LA crossing the lawn between their houses, headed toward hers. He saw her at the same time and held up a letter in front of his face so that his eyes were hidden. It was a regular-sized envelope, white.

She parked and climbed out of the car.

"Look what accidentally came to my house instead of yours," he said, handing her a piece of mail.

It wasn't uncommon for them to get each other's mail. Many decades earlier, LA's property and Stayja's had been on the same lot, so they nearly shared an address: 319A and 319B.

She glanced at the return address and swallowed. The Internal Revenue Service.

"Maybe you got a big refund or something," he said.

"Fuck," she muttered. Whatever it was, she was sure it wasn't that. Correspondence from the government was never good.

She slid her thumb through the upper edge and unfolded the sheet of paper inside.

It was a bill. For $6,292, due by October 30th.

"Motherfucker," Stayja said, folding it back up.

"What is it? Let me see," LA said.

"No," she said, climbing back into her car.

"Where are you going?" he asked. "Can I come?"

She ignored him as she pulled the door shut and started the engine.

TWENTY MINUTES LATER, Stayja sat across from an adviser at H&R Block, distracted by the coral lipstick smeared across the woman's left front tooth as she half heard the worst possible news—that there was no basis on which to dispute the bill. Stayja was sure it had been a mistake, but according to this woman, when Stayja had started working at Carter, she'd taken too many allowances on her W-4. The woman had pulled out a sample form, pointing to "W-4" at the top of it as if Stayja were an idiot.

"See? W-4. You filled out one of these. And you should have put a 'one' here at the bottom," the woman said, "but you probably put a 'three' or something."

"It says to put one for yourself, another one if you are single, and another if you file as head of household. That's three."

"I know that's what it *says*," the woman said, "but that's not actually what you should have done." The woman's tone was politely superior, as if what she was telling Stayja were common sense and not arcane, bureaucratic nonsense. "Think of it this way," she continued. "You haven't paid any taxes. And even though your income is minimal, sweetie, everyone has to pay taxes."

"You're saying I'm not poor enough because my disabled

mother is not as expensive as five children?" Stayja said, her voice louder. The woman looked over at a couple sitting in a nearby cubicle and gave them an apologetic half grin. Stayja shoved her paystub across the woman's desk and pointed again at the deducted sums. "Again, please explain to me how you can say I paid zero taxes if in just *one week* I paid forty dollars in taxes?" she asked.

"That's not tax. It's Social Security and Medicare."

"Since when is that not taxes?"

"Ma'am, please keep your voice down. We have other customers in the facility."

"I am not trying to cause a scene," Stayja said. "I am just trying to understand what is going on. I added up the numbers just like they told me to. That number there plus that number there. And now you're telling me that the numbers don't actually mean what this sheet says they mean and, as a result, I have to pay the government six thousand dollars I don't have."

The woman sighed. "You didn't actually do everything correctly. You haven't filed your taxes in five years. *That's* why you have this bill. You owe penalties and fees. And your, you know, taxes."

"Why *now*?" Stayja asked. "If it's been five years."

The woman shook her head slowly.

"The government's slow to catch these things sometimes."

"Did I tell you I'm in school?" Stayja said. "I'm a student. I must qualify for some kind of credit."

The woman raised an eyebrow. "What school?"

"Wake Community College. Nursing program."

"At least half-time?"

"What does that mean?"

"Two classes or more per semester."

Stayja shut her eyes. "No."

When she opened them, the woman was shaking her head slowly, pity in her eyes. "I'm sorry," she said.

"Fine. I should have filed. Is there really nothing I can do at this point? Can we not reduce this at *all*?"

"Sweetheart, I wish I could help. But you gotta file and pay taxes if you work. Everyone does. And I hate to be the bearer of more bad news, but this bill is only from the federal government. Once the state eventually catches on, you're going to get a bill from them, too."

STAYJA LET THE espresso canister drop into the sink with a crash and then slammed the blender pitcher into it as well, ignoring the student buried in a book who started and glanced over at the noise. She felt the urge to break something, to throw the heavy aluminum ice scoop through the window of the café. She leaned onto her elbows on the counter and covered her face with her hands.

So there was no way she'd be able to resume classes in the spring. Or probably summer or even fall. This bill had just set her back *years*.

Stayja wasn't a spiritual person; she hadn't been raised to be. Donna's take that "I don't trust anyone who needs something to happen to *my* soul" had always sounded right to her.

But standing there in the café, that damn tax bill tormenting her from her bag in the cabinet, she found herself bidding someone, anyone, who might be listening for help.

I can't do it anymore. Please.

Very plainly, a word popped into her brain, as if someone had spoken it aloud.

Gibson.

After Tyler's suggestion that she apply for the medical linkage program, she'd spent several days half-entertaining the idea. She'd been flattered by it, but it seemed outrageous in many ways, un-conquerable, even the basics: the seventy-five-dollar application fee, never mind the cost of attendance. Moving.

Moving. She couldn't leave her mother, so even if she were to be admitted and figured out how to pay for it, Donna would have to come along. Donna did love the beach, though, and Gibson was on the coast. Still, Donna would never want to leave Adrienne. Then again, Donna and Adrienne weren't currently speaking.

Whenever she thought of a reason not to apply, it seemed to be followed by a conflicting consideration. Of course, she couldn't afford it—now less than ever. But if she became a doctor, she could pay back her student loans.

If you're going to take out a loan, take out one for nursing school.

But the nagging, the tugging at her.

Did she even have a shot at being admitted? There was no way she would be. Then again, she'd made all As in all of her science classes so far, and the program advertised itself as being open to students transitioning from two-year programs. As Tyler had pointed out, the first phase of the application process required only an essay and an unofficial transcript.

And there was this: that she'd never shaken that conversation she'd had with Tyler during one of their early nights together, in which he'd unwittingly implied that she was poor because she made the kind of decisions poor people make.

He hadn't meant it to come across that way, but was it true?

Annie

SATURDAY, OCTOBER 21—SUNDAY, OCTOBER 22

"I guess I just mean, what's the goal of therapy?" I was seated across from Loretta on a Thursday, the second of our two forty-five-minute sessions for the week. I'd decided to bring up the frequency of our sessions—what was the point?—not because I had any problem with meeting so often (since I was a student, it didn't cost anything, and because I had no interest in a social life, I had the time), but because I wasn't sure what I was supposed to be doing in it. I didn't know if I was doing therapy right. I'd just show up and talk.

Truthfully, I liked it. Loretta was the only person I could really talk to. I was finding it increasingly difficult to relate to Matty. I wondered if it had to do with his air, however subtle, of self-satisfaction at having been right about Tyler. It wasn't anything in particular that he said—it just wafted off him, leaving me to wonder if the whole thing had been my fault. Unlike Matty, I had failed to recognize Tyler's true nature when I should have. As for my other friends, there weren't really any I felt close enough to talk with about what had happened.

And so I talked to Loretta.

Still, I grew impatient, frustrated by the lack of concrete take-aways generated during our sessions. I brought this up—what was our goal in meeting so often? Like a good therapist, she threw it back at me—what did *I* think the goal was?

"I don't know," I said. "To 'get over' my rape?" I quoted the air with my fingers.

She smiled kindly. "I am guessing you know that's absurd and that's why you put air quotes around it like that."

I conceded this with a slight smile.

"The rape as a traumatic experience is a part of you now. It's something you will carry with you for the rest of your life. It may always make you sad. Or it may trigger new feelings as time goes on. Your relationship to it may evolve, just as relationships with people do. For now, I think the step is realizing this—there will be no 'getting over' it."

We sat listening to the air conditioner humming. I appreciated that Loretta—and it seemed only Loretta—said it the way she did, that she called it rape. She didn't say "what happened to you" like Caroline, or "the thing" like Matty, or "the assault" like Dean Sharon. Were people afraid that by calling it what it was, they'd somehow alert me to that fact? As if I didn't already know?

"How does that make you feel?" she asked after a long silence.

"Rage," I said.

THE PARENTS' WEEKEND CONCERT was the best we'd sounded since I'd joined orchestra at the beginning of my first year, and afterward I accepted the orange daffodils Matty's mom had brought for me and thanked her and his dad for coming to hear our performance.

"Matt told us your parents couldn't make it, and we're so sorry they weren't able to hear this incredible concert. Truly a treat," she said, lightly touching my arm. She smelled like perfume, which my own mom never wore. I'd wound up asking my parents not to come up, insisting on it by claiming that I was way too busy preparing for midterms to have time for them. To my surprise, especially after I hadn't gone home for fall break, they had agreed to respect my wishes.

"Where is Matty?" I asked her.

"He had to run out halfway through the concert for some deadline or story—you know how he is with the paper. We're heading back after we grab some lunch. Wonderful to see you, Annie. Have you lost weight?"

I resisted the temptation to make a joke—a perk of rape is a decrease in appetite! Then I realized Matty hadn't told his parents, and I was grateful.

"Annie!" a voice called. I turned to find Diana Yeager, Danny's mother, rushing toward me. Behind her was Danny, my former bassoon student, looking taller and with more pimples. I was surprised to see them both, since they had moved to Tennessee in July. "Hi!"

She hugged me and stepped aside so that Danny and I could embrace. He shyly leaned in for a side hug and then stepped back in a hurry. He was notably taller.

"We came down for the weekend. Danny is dying to go to Carter now because of you. Aren't you, Danny?"

He blushed and looked away as Matty's mother gave me a small wave and disappeared.

"Your former pupil is here!" Juan-Pablo said, approaching. "I hope you enjoyed the concert," he said to the Yeagers.

"Absolutely!" she said. "Annie was fantastic. Wasn't she, Danny?"

Danny mumbled a yes.

"I was telling her Danny is dying to come here now after hearing how much she loves it. Is college still treating you well, Annie? How is your year so far?"

"It's good," I said, aware of how high my voice had jumped in pitch.

"Diana, would you like to meet the vice provost?" Juan-Pablo said, placing an arm on her shoulder to escort her away.

Juan-Pablo, always protecting me without either of us having to spell out anything. It nearly made me tear up.

AS I HEADED back to my room, my long cotton orchestra dress did little to shield my shrunken body against the crisp late October wind. Upon entering the dorm, I recognized their legs first: my mother's red clogs and black ankle pants, my father's brown Clarks, and Matty's blue Vans. They were seated facing each other on opposite couches in the common room, their upper bodies hidden by both sides of the wall. My mother leaned forward at the sound of the door opening.

"Hey," I said, walking over. "You came."

"Sweetheart," said my mom, rising to put her arms around me, her face sunken with concern. "I hope it's okay."

"Of course it's okay," I said. Matty was staring at the floor.

"How was the concert?" my mom asked.

"Good. I mean, you could have come if you were going to be here anyway." I was surprised how normal I was acting, the most normal I'd acted in weeks. Maybe it was that I was still in performance mode. Or maybe I wanted to perform normalcy to spare them the pain I knew they'd feel if they knew the truth.

"I told them to come because I'm worried about you, Annie," said Matty feverishly. "I'm sorry if you think I betrayed you, but you sleep all the time. You seem depressed."

So this was how this was going to happen—an intervention in the common room of my dorm.

"We should go to my room," I said, turning. "I need to tell you something."

IT FELT AS if it took forever and no time. As soon as the words were out of my mouth, it was over, but at first no one said anything or moved. When they did speak, they asked questions I hated answering. Why didn't I tell them sooner? Had I needed a lawyer? Did I need one now? Why had the investigation been over so quickly? There was rehashing that I didn't feel in the mood for but endured. My dad and Matty both mostly stayed quiet, though I could tell how difficult my dad was finding the conversation by the way his chest was visibly expanding and contracting in his golf shirt. That, and the fact that his face had flushed burgundy.

"I am going to talk to the dean," he said, his jaw clenched. "This is unacceptable."

"Dad, please don't. Please." Outside my first-floor window, which was cracked open, a stream of parents and younger siblings passed in a frenzy of green-and-white Carter gear, coming from the football game, a swirl of foam "Number 1" hands, dinky pompoms, and camping equipment used for tailgating. "I don't want you to do that. I just want it to be over," I said.

His eyes darted around the room.

"I promise," I said as my voice cracked, "I am okay. I promise. I am twenty years old. I can handle it."

"I can't not say something," he said finally. "I can't." My mother was gripping her knees, a maze of purple pressing against the thin skin of her hands.

"Fine," I said, exhausted. "Say something."

"Oh, Annie," my mother said. "This is very hard. This is unimaginably hard." I wasn't sure whether she was speaking for herself or for me, and I didn't ask her to clarify.

WE SPENT THE next twenty-four hours of Parents' Weekend pretending things were normal while the fact that I'd been raped accompanied us like an annoying fifth person we collectively—and unsuccessfully—were attempting to ignore. Matty came along for all of it, which I presumed to be his self-imposed penance for summoning my parents. That afternoon, we went to see the *Eighteenth-Century European Women Painters* exhibit at the Carter art museum. My dad, an art history buff, rose out of his brooding long enough to lecture us on what he remembered about the painters, all of whom seemed to have been successful only because at some point Marie Antoinette recognized their talent, including Anne Vallayer-Coster, whose 1773 *Portrait of a Violinist* drew my mother's attention.

"Look, Annie, it's you."

The girl, expressionless, gazed down at a score in her lap. In her right hand, she gripped a violin in a way no one would ever hold that instrument.

The panel to the right of the painting read: *She draws us into the intimate world of the model: an inexpert violinist who has broken off her musical exercises and is lost in thought.*

"If the violin were a bassoon, I mean," she said.

Her comment made no sense, because I wasn't inexpert at the bassoon, so I didn't say anything back.

When Matty proposed going to the family-friendly show performed by the campus improv team, I was so grateful that I almost forgave him. A show meant we wouldn't have to make conversation.

Then, as we waited in the buzzing auditorium for it to start, two girls near us in the audience began loudly discussing the campus news item of the weekend—a student running on the Carter running trail had been groped by a stranger. The story had been especially hyped in the newspaper, given that it happened at the start of Parents' Weekend, and the administration was responding by promising swift and dramatic action—more blue emergency phones along the trail and throughout campus and even temporary security personnel to monitor the path. Dean Sharon had been quoted encouraging students to run in pairs. As I'd read the initial article, the irony of the college's response had been irritating enough that I'd set the paper aside and pushed the story out of my mind. Now my family sat, not speaking, as the students in the row in front of us made it impossible to avoid.

"Like, who *gropes*? What does *groping* get you? I mean, like, I get that it's basically just a power move, like toxic masculinity baby steps, but it just feels so *silly* almost."

"Maybe things only ended where they did because she got away," the other student said.

Suddenly, my mom was lunging toward me and her hands were cupping my ears.

"Mom!" I yelled, yanking her hands off my head.

"Don't listen!" she whispered.

"Mom!" I said again. "Stop it. God."

In my periphery I saw Matty cover his mouth to stifle a giggle, and as the lights dimmed and the applause rose to drown out the girls' voices, I did find I was relieved to have avoided hearing more. The room sank into darkness, and I closed my eyes. *Don't fall asleep, Annie*, I told myself. I was certain I'd start snoring.

But sleep was impossible. The stage lights flew on to deafening cheers as the team ran out onto the stage. I watched, half paying attention, half fighting my heavy eyelids.

During intermission, Matty whispered, "I'm sorry. I wasn't thinking when I suggested this show."

"What?" I asked, confused.

"You came to an improv show with *him*," he said.

That had been so different and so long ago. Once again, I had the sensation of being deeply misunderstood. Just as people thought the word *rape* might trigger me, Matty thought improv might as well? How? By making me remember what had happened to me? I thought about what happened to me constantly. I didn't need an improv show to remind me.

"Oh," I said. "Yeah, no worries."

On the walk back to my dorm, my mother surprised me by asking, "You didn't like it?"

"I did," I said. "Why?"

"You didn't laugh at all," she said.

"I didn't?" I asked.

"Maybe you did, and I didn't hear it," she said, turning away.

By the time we were having Sunday morning breakfast at Lloyd's, my dad's favorite diner because of the coffee you can serve yourself while you wait for a table, I was desperate for my parents to leave. Their sulking over *my* rape had become insufferable. I had nothing left with which to buoy my own spirit, never mind my parents'.

We said goodbye in the parking lot of the diner. As soon as their Volvo disappeared over the crest of Main Street, Matty and I spoke at the same time.

"I know you're mad at me," he said. Before I could answer, he said, "But I have an idea."

Bea

"College is treating you well!" The Birches' pilot, a bald, potbellied man named Steve, opened his arms for a hug. He took her bag and opened the hatch at the front of the plane to store it as Bea climbed the narrow stairs into Lorn's family's Gulfstream. It was the Wednesday afternoon of fall break, and she was bound for Connecticut, where she'd spend the next five days. Lorn's parents, Audrey and Barry, would be there, of course, and as a last-minute surprise, so would Lorn, even though it wasn't Vassar's fall break yet. She was going to miss two classes so they could spend a few days together.

"Music?" Steve asked as the plane began to roll down the tarmac.

"I'm okay with whatever you want," Bea said. It was the third time she'd ridden on their plane but the first time without at least one of them present, and she was still a bit in awe of the soft, plush seats and her own casual distance from the cockpit.

A text arrived from Audrey: SEE YOU SOON! TEXT ME WHEN YOU LAND

"Stevie Wonder it is, then," he said as soul music filled the small space.

She was surprised when they said they'd send the plane for her, but Audrey had explained that Steve was flying back north after dropping off a colleague of Barry's in Atlanta and could "swing by." As they took off, Bea swallowed hard to pop her ears, her thoughts returning to the afternoon. She'd received her physics mid-term grade: a D. When she saw it on the screen of her laptop, she was dumbfounded. She'd never made lower than a B+ in any course or on any test that she could remember. A D! It was appalling, terrible, thrilling.

After Early's mugging had preempted her visit to her adviser's office to drop Physics, she'd never actually gone to meet with him. To get a D—a *D!*—was humiliating, but she'd also discovered a kind of strange delight about it, a pleasure in realizing that her actions had consequences. Was this what it felt like to be a rebel, to fail at something and not attempt to salvage it?

Looking out over the sheet of white clouds beneath them in the sky, she remembered once seeing a cresting wave, frozen, during Christmas break in the Hamptons. The cold air had captured it at the moment of its peaking. It was white and frothy, full of movement but somehow also perfectly still.

The clouds outside the plane reminded her of that wave.

It was how Bea felt too, in a way. Sometimes she felt as if she were moving forward so fast she might be crashing. Other times she felt as if she weren't moving at all, stuck in the threads of something invisible.

THAT NIGHT, AUDREY made spaghetti squash with a lamb sausage ragù and a vegan version of the same for Lorn. The four of them—Lorn, her parents, and Bea—sat at the formal dining room table while Mila, their housekeeper, filled and refilled their water glasses on loop.

Lorn was trying to explain to her parents the term *hypebeast* in the context of describing her new career plan of launching a streetwear company.

"It's a word for someone who's fashion-obsessed," she said.

"In a good way or bad way?" Audrey asked.

"Bad," Lorn said, handing Bea her phone so she could scroll through Lorn's list of start-up concepts. At some point over the six weeks since they'd started college, her friend had decided that she was going to be a feminist entrepreneur. An ethical capitalist, making tons of money while affirming women. And their bodies.

subscription box of just red lipsticks
app for making (women) friends
app for making apps (for women)
app for picking a red lipstick

"And how about you, Bea?" Audrey asked, stabbing at her pile of yellow noodles. "I love living vicariously through you girls! Tell us everything."

Bea handed the phone back to Lorn, then held up a finger. When she finished chewing, she said, "I have . . . well, I *had*, it just ended . . . my first case as a student advocate."

"Moot court!" Barry bellowed from the far end of the table. "I was in moot court."

"No, Barry," Audrey said, annoyed. "It's a real case. I told you that in her program she represents her fellow students. I *told* you this."

"No way. I'd remember that."

"I did."

"A college freshman providing legal representation? Are you kidding?"

"I'm more like a support person. He had a lawyer," Bea said. With Barry, you often had to speak up loudly—or interrupt—to work in your point.

"What'd he do?" Lorn asked, her mouth full, her hand hovering in front of her face.

Bea hadn't yet told Lorn about Tyler's case. They'd only FaceTimed a couple of times since August, and she hadn't brought it up. She wasn't sure why.

"It was a sexual assault case," Bea said, a trace of fear in her voice.

"Oh, my," Audrey said, dabbing her face with a white cloth napkin. "That sounds challenging. Do you get to pick which side you support?"

Bea shook her head. "We're assigned students randomly," she said, swallowing a slice of sausage and deciding that it might be a good idea to shift the focus of discussion slightly. "There's this summer fellowship that I really want. I'll apply this month and find out by the end of the semester if I got it. It's with the CJRI."

"The who?" Barry asked, then suppressed a belch.

"Barry Birch!" Audrey scolded. "What is the CJ . . . ?"

"The Criminal Justice Reform Institute," Bea said. "It's a non-profit run by my professor."

"So you're still thinking you'll go into law, honey?" Audrey said. "That's lovely."

"My CTO's son just made partner at a firm in the city," Barry said. "Which one, hon? Cooley? No, Wachtell."

"Paul Weiss," Audrey said. Then to Bea she said, "That's a better one for someone like you than Wachtell. They do a lot of pro bono. We'll have to introduce you . . . maybe over Thanksgiving."

"She's in her first year of *college*, Mom," Lorn said.

"Never too early to be thinking about legal internships," Barry said.

"I'm planning to be a public defender," Bea said, her eyes locked on her plate.

The Birches were moderate Republicans, Romney Republicans. They gave generously to the Susan G. Komen Foundation and the

Ronald McDonald House. They attended their Methodist church every Sunday and loathed Donald Trump, but more because they found him crass than that they took issue with his politics. They'd voted for him still, of course, "out of obligation" because of taxes and because Hillary was "at least as corrupt." They prided themselves on having friends of all political shades. How true that actually was Bea didn't know, but what she did know was that public defense wasn't a profession they were likely to rally behind.

In the heated rise of the Black Lives Matter movement the spring of Bea and Lorn's ninth-grade year, Bea was spending July with the Birches. Prior to that summer, Bea had followed the stories privately, with horror, from her quiet second-floor guest room. Cops killing black people. Black kids. When the grand jury declined to indict the white cop who killed Michael Brown in Missouri, the four of them—Bea and the Birches—were gathered in their palatial beige living room, watching the evening news. They listened in silence to the prosecutor's announcement.

"Let this be a lesson in how the media works. It's a ratings game," Barry had said to them, then offered a lecture on how, by running stories about racist cops, media companies made tremendous money.

"Fine, but also, they are racist," Lorn had said.

"What does that *mean*, racist?" Barry said. "We need better words."

"It means we treat people differently based on what race they are," Lorn said, annoyed.

"Maybe," Barry said. "I think I'm more likely to treat people differently based on how old they are or how well dressed they are than what color they are!"

"So you're ageist *and* classist, congratulations."

Audrey had thrown Barry a warning glance and stolen a nervous peek at Bea and changed the channel, then the subject.

The conversation had left Bea frustrated—mostly with herself for not speaking up. Normally Bea didn't get as frustrated with the Birches as Lorn did. Bea actually found them quite likable, especially Barry, who was amusing and often entertaining. But was it really that hard for him to understand that you're treated differently based on race? Or did he just not want to know it? Was it that hard to understand that you can have both good cops and bad cops? And that racial bias could be subconscious? *And* that the media could be making money on sensational stories, *and* that all of it could be true at once?

She was in ninth grade and she'd already figured out that much.

But Bea said nothing. She was in their home. Besides, he hadn't been wrong to bring up class. They drifted around New England in the first-class cars of trains or in the backseats of Lincoln Town Cars with drivers whose names they didn't know and didn't learn, moving from one elegant marbled space to another. Fresh flowers were ever present, fish was always wild and often raw, and the odds were high that a tag on any given item contained the name of a brand with a storefront on Madison Avenue. She'd seen Barry apologize to a friend of Audrey's for ignoring her when he had assumed she was someone Audrey had hired for some sort of house task.

So he'd acknowledge his own class bias but refuse to own any understanding of American race dynamics.

In the intervening years she hadn't become any more vocal around the Birches when it came to her social and political opinion. She let Lorn be the provocateur daughter, the voice of the leftist youth.

Announcing her public defense aspirations, Bea saw that they hadn't expected this from her. For several seconds, everyone chewed in silence. Then Barry began to laugh.

"What's so funny?" Audrey asked.

"I'm sorry. It just took me by surprise."

Audrey set down her fork. "You're going to represent criminals?" she asked.

"Mom, everyone deserves representation!" Lorn snapped.

"Is it *that* surprising? I am in a program called Justice," Bea said with a tight laugh.

"Well, yes, but I'd assumed you were learning about both sides of justice." At once Audrey set down her fork and gasped. "Did you all hear? That man who abducted the little girl in Darien was just sentenced. Twenty years. *Twenty. Years.*"

"Do you know what she's talking about?" Lorn said to Bea.

Bea shook her head.

"Mom, we don't follow your local news."

"A five-year-old girl was abducted and murdered by this monster whom they had on tape confessing—on tape!—and yet his trial went on for, oh, how long, honey? Months."

"Couple months," Barry said, scraping his plate.

"He didn't even get life. He'll be out again, preying on some other child. I can't stomach it. I don't know why I'm bringing it up at dinner. Oh, because you're going into public defense."

Mila entered the room carrying a glass bowl of fresh fruit—sliced kiwi and blueberries and strawberries.

"Did the guy do it?" Lorn asked. It took Bea a moment to realize Lorn was speaking to her and referring to Tyler, not the Darien murderer.

"Um, I don't know," Bea said.

"What do you think?" Lorn asked.

Bea hesitated. "I don't think it matters," she said.

Audrey yelped.

"Jesus, Mom," Lorn said.

"Of course, it matters!" Audrey shrieked.

"Aud," Barry said. "Calm down."

Bea stood and set her napkin next to her plate as she'd been taught in the etiquette class she and Lorn had been forced to take in ninth grade. She didn't have to use the bathroom, but she figured that if she left, then by the time she returned Barry and Lorn would have placated Audrey.

But as she reached the corner of the open dining room into the hallway, Audrey hollered, crossly, "Where are you going?!"

Bea spun to face her.

"I don't care what you think!" she snapped before stomping out of sight.

AUDREY APOLOGIZED THAT NIGHT and again, more sincerely, the next morning, but it was clear to Bea that she remained troubled. Even Lorn, Bea could tell, was bothered by Bea's unwillingness to say she believed Tyler was innocent—she could tell because Lorn hadn't brought it up again.

They went shopping at the boutiques on Greenwich Avenue, and Audrey bought them both multiple semiformal dresses. Neither cared much for the ones they found, but Audrey was insistent, and they could tell it made her happy, so they walked out with three cocktail dresses each.

When it turned out that Barry had to head back to Atlanta on Friday rather than Saturday, Bea was relieved that the plane would be leaving earlier than planned.

As they soared quietly through the sky southbound, Barry looked up from his computer and said, out of the blue, "Proud of you, Bea."

"Seriously?" she said, shocked.

He laughed. "Is it that shocking?"

Then, because she'd always liked Barry and because she believed him and maybe because she needed to tell a parent figure, she said, "I'm making a D in physics." As she said it, she looked out the window. There were no clouds, only blue sky. She turned back.

"Maybe don't become an astronaut, then?" he said, breaking into a wide grin.

BACK AT CARTER, the confrontation with Audrey bothered her more as the days passed. She didn't know, of course, how her own mother would feel about what she was doing in supporting someone accused of assault, or in pursuing a career of defense work, but she knew her mother would have a more nuanced take on it than Lorn's mother had displayed. Audrey's knee-jerk reaction ("You're going to represent criminals?") had left Bea feeling lonelier than she'd felt in a long time. While she certainly hadn't made the decision to dive headfirst into her Justice course work in order to please Audrey—she still just thought of Audrey as Lorn's mom, not as her surrogate parent—Audrey's reaction had highlighted just how truly Bea was on her own.

Even Lorn didn't get it.

No one but Dr. Friedman and her C.U.N.T. teammates got her.

The more she did improv, the better she felt she got at it, and the better she got at it, the more she wanted to do it. The "and" was where Bea thrived. The addition of material, the piling on of the things that led to laughter—the absurd, the physically challenging, the silly. She steered away from the intellectual "ands" preferred by some of her teammates—the clever references, obscure and punny and heady. This wasn't a conscious decision, but more instinctive, a compulsion to delight herself. She was rewarded for it with laughs, sometimes cheers. Compliments specifically to her after shows: Bea, you're amazing. You're hilarious.

Her favorite part was the moment her eyes met her scene partner's, and both saw that neither knew what was going to happen next: *We're in this together—now what?*

As the end of October approached and regionals were only eight, then seven, then six weeks away, the energy in the group grew more electric, and Chris's stress level, which was normally low, became noticeably high. He insisted they add an extra weekly rehearsal, then instituted a lecture at the beginning of every rehearsal in which he reviewed "the fundamentals." He would read printouts from the Internet on what makes great improv and make them watch and discuss YouTube videos of other improvisers, as if they were a football team reviewing plays.

One afternoon, he was giving them a lecture on listening. The best improvisers in the world, he said, understood that listening was what makes good improv. As the others nodded along, Bea wondered—was she a good listener? She'd been listening her entire life—for clues to the foreign worlds around her as she started over again and again, in Boston after New York, then at Porter's, then at Carter. She'd never been the first one to speak up or raise her hand; in school, she waited to be called on, preferring to make her points in writing, in her papers. The glory of a point well made aloud in the classroom was never something that seduced her, which is one reason why the draw of improv was so unexpected. Part of the fun for her was the pleasure of the spotlight, the kind of attention that she'd never craved before, even in middle-school theater club, where she was fine to play small roles. She'd thought about it and decided the difference was that improv was not like making a smart point in class. Improv brought people joy. Including, as the hours she spent in improv rehearsal accumulated, friendships. AWGs—"Anonymous white guys"—had emerged as her nickname for her teammates, to keep them on their toes. It had been born when she'd had trouble remembering their names early on; it had taken her weeks to recall which one was Bart and which one was Todd. Only Russell and Chris had been memorable from the start.

"You all have anonymous white boy names," she'd said. Having never been around so many white boys in her life, she was amazed: they acted the same, talked the same, looked the same, and had the same names.

They had happily picked up AWG, too, referring to themselves by the term.

"How many AWGs are missing?" Chris would ask at the time rehearsal was scheduled to begin. "Two, plus Lez?"

The intimacy she felt with them stemmed largely from the freedom she derived from their collective determination to mine for the funny, which cultivated in Bea a kind of guarded honesty that allowed her to be more open about her life than she usually was for fear of being pitied. Free to turn her background and circumstances—dead mother, absent father—into humor, she found herself sharing memories she'd not thought about in years. One afternoon, she told them about how, in the handful of plays performed by her middle-school theater club, she was cast in the exotic roles: an Indian once, a gypsy fortune-teller once, the Spanish neighbor.

"What did the Spanish neighbor do in the play?" Todd had asked. "Besides make tapas, of course." They were never off, never stopped joking.

"I had to do a little dance," Bea said.

"Wait, was it a musical?" Chris asked.

"No, she just did a little dance whenever she entered the stage."

"That seems highly racist," Bart said.

Bea nodded cheerfully and performed it for them as well as she could remember, the cha-cha flamingo arms, the messy footwork.

"Bea," Chris said, "you must hate us. We're a bunch of assholes."

How could she say what she was thinking, that, yes, they were a bunch of AWGs—sometimes assholes, occasionally ignorant, and quite crass a lot of the time—but that she loved them? That she felt more seen by them than she ever had by anyone, even Lorn.

This included Lesley, the one other girl, but still Lesley herself Bea had not yet figured out. A third-year from the Bronx, she was fearless onstage, sassy offstage, and well versed in pop culture while also casually devoted to studying British literature. An English and Anthropology double major, she'd described her thesis (which she was getting a full year's head start on) to Bea as follows: structural and thematic parallels in *The Bachelor* and *Paradise Lost*. Lesley's worn, casual confidence was of a kind that Bea didn't see on girls at Carter. It was uniquely Lesley. It was almost as if she wasn't a girl.

Only once had Bea attempted to connect with Lesley one on one. It was the afternoon that Bea had noticed Bart tended to select characters with power over others in a scene: if they were teachers, he was the principal; if they were giraffes, he was a lion; if they were leprechauns, he was the leprechaun king.

"Bart always does this thing," she whispered to Lesley one afternoon during rehearsal as they watched Bart play a landlord. The joke in the scene was that a group of guys who lived in his building were smoking rosemary believing it to be weed. Unaware, they were pretending to be high in order to impress each other. Bart as the self-assigned landlord was informing them that they were going to be evicted unless they halted their illegal activity immediately, because the whole building smelled like drugs and Rosemary on the fourth floor was pregnant. She didn't need to be breathing in drug fumes, lest it affect her baby. He emphasized *baby*.

"Oh, I know," Lesley said. "The film references are never-ending. How many people our age who aren't film majors have actually seen *Rosemary's Baby*?" Bea didn't say that this hadn't been what she meant.

BY PARENTS' WEEKEND she'd almost forgotten about her difficult conversation with the Birches. She hadn't mentioned the weekend to them, worried that Audrey would want to come. Without that burden, she was excited to perform for her biggest crowd yet.

She was lacing up her sneakers for a run the morning of the show when Early rushed in, breathless, holding the campus paper.

"Did you hear?" Early asked, shoving it into Bea's hands. "My mugger got charged with assault. He was the groper! *Ugh*." She performed a gagging motion. "I was so fucking lucky."

"Wait, what?" Bea said, reading the headline: *Woods Groper Identified, Gets 60 Days*.

Bea skimmed the article. He was eighteen and was therefore charged as an adult. He'd serve sixty days' jail time for sexual battery and—because the student victim was young for a college student at only sixteen—he would be placed on the sex offender registry for at least ten years, up to thirty.

"Officer Andrews called me and left a message when I was in Comp Sci. He wanted to let me know that I may be needed to testify in the other victim's case. But it turned out he didn't need me. Officer Andrews was like, 'Ben pled,' as if I know who Ben is! I don't know his name just because he stole my phone, dude."

Ben, Bea thought. Hearing his name rattled her. A kid.

"The girl ID'd him in a lineup. Apparently he tried to take *her* wallet, and when she said no, he grabbed for her boobs. Also, did you see that she's only sixteen? And at Carter? She must be a genius."

"He's a kid, too," Bea said.

"Bea," Early said, crossing her arms. "He's eighteen. So, no, technically he isn't. He's a thief *and* a perv. You don't have to defend him right now."

Bea bent over to tie her second shoe and looked up at her roommate. "I'm just saying, witness identification is super unreliable, and now this kid is going to be on the sex offender registry until he's thirty. Or longer."

Early dropped her arms. They dangled as she studied Bea.

"Women don't lie about assault, remember? The suggestion that they do is antifeminist propaganda."

"I'm not saying I think she lied about being groped."

Early rested against the end of her bed as her chin began to quiver. "Bea, I was scared that day. It was *scary*. Do you get that?"

"I do!" Bea said, not sure she did.

"I didn't want to be afraid." Early wiped her eyes. "But you can't actually help your feelings. Even if you learn all the statistics in the world. They are what they are."

STARTING FROM THE trailhead nearest to her dorm, Bea would reach the fourth mile of her six-mile run just after she passed under the Bridge. Here was the stretch she found most challenging: 1.5 miles of dirt road tracing the soccer and baseball fields before dipping back into the woods for the last stint.

Usually, she slowed to a walk or at least a light jog, for a portion of it, but today she decided she was going to run the whole damn thing.

She sprang forward to the rhythm of her pop mix, each stride launching her closer to the glistening blue phone that she used as her carrot. Once she reached that phone, she was almost done. The phone grew larger, then was next to her, then behind her, until the stretch's elusive end point was finally in sight. She pumped her arms, hurling her body into a sprint for the homestretch, then veered left with the trail and back into the towering trees on all sides, where she scampered to a dusty halt and screamed. At once she was sailing through the air, skidding across the pebbly dirt.

From the ground, she yanked and twisted her head back to find, feet from where she landed—nothing. It wasn't a person, just a piece of dark clothing hung on a tree branch, at human height. She pushed herself up to sitting. Both of her knees were bloody, and her palms were scratched up.

She stood and tenderly brushed off her legs and hands.

So things were frightening sometimes.

Did it mean she was going to quit? No. Because sometimes things were hard and you were alone on your journey, but that didn't mean you whined about it and blamed someone else for it. Sometimes you could be scared, but you kept going forward anyway because you knew it was the right thing to do. Sometimes you had another mile to go.

Bea searched for and found the AirPod that had dropped from her ear in her fall. Then she turned her music back on, gritted her teeth, and started to run—even faster now, even harder.

Stayja

Over fall break Stayja had sent Tyler her admissions essay, asking for his thoughts. When he hadn't responded, she told herself it was because he was in St. John. He was probably partying on a beach somewhere. She wouldn't want to read someone's essay either if she was on vacation.

Then fall break ended, and the students all returned to campus, including him—he'd posted a photo on Instagram of prepackaged hard-boiled eggs from the airport with a caption about how gross airport food was. #butstarving.

She didn't officially follow him. She wasn't sure he'd want her to, so she stalked him in secret. Besides, she never posted anything herself anyway. She preferred being a quiet observer to an active user when it came to social media.

She'd sent him four texts total—one during break and three after—none of which he'd responded to. She knew what others would say it meant, but she refused to believe he was ghosting her suddenly after all they'd been through. It didn't make sense. The other photos he'd posted from St. John over the break—yes, they were of him with other girls, blondes like her and one whose resemblance to her was startling, in fact. But just because he was pictured with his arms around them in an outdoor, beachfront bar didn't mean he was hooking up with them. Right? Or even if he was, as much as it stung to think about that, it didn't mean that he no longer wanted Stayja in his life.

Meanwhile, there was the fucking IRS bill. She'd called the IRS after a late-night Google session had informed her that they'll let you pay off a bill on a payment plan, and she'd been on hold for over an hour when Frank came in and she'd had to hang up. She'd asked him for new W-4 paperwork, putting zero allowances this time. She had no idea how much that meant her paycheck would decrease going forward, just that it would. Of course, it would. She'd have six grand to pay off on a smaller paycheck.

Stayja rolled down the window and lit a cigarette, resisting the urge to check his Instagram for the third time in ten minutes.

Whenever her phone vibrated, her eyes flew up from whatever she was doing to find messages from, invariably, the same three people: bus broke down waiting for it to get fixed (her mother); coming (Nicole); how r u today beautiful? (LA).

Had Tyler stopped finding her teeth cute?

where r u, she texted Nicole. She was taking Nicole to get her license renewed. Chet had gotten her DUI purged from her record, which meant she could drive again—except that her license was about to expire. Now that Nicole was working at the bookstore, her hours fell earlier than Stayja's—she started at eleven and ended at seven. Once she had the license, she'd ride with LA to work, then drive herself home in Stayja's Corolla, and then return to pick up Stayja each evening at ten.

Finally Nicole appeared, jogging to the car, her bag bouncing on her shoulder.

"I hope this doesn't take forever," Stayja said.

"Oh, it will," Nicole said, rolling down her window and lighting up. "It's the DMV."

Her phone buzzed in her lap. She jumped and scrambled for it.

"Jesus!" Nicole said. "Can you focus on driving, please? Hand it over." Reluctantly, Stayja passed Nicole her phone.

"Dear Stayja," Nicole began to read. "There comes a time when a person must be honest about their feelings. I need you to know how I feel about you. . . ."

Stayja felt a blossoming in her chest—could it be? It was too good to be true—until Nicole continued, "I know you told me six months ago that you and I are never going to happen, but I am unable to go on without you."

Twice a year or so, LA professed his love for Stayja using vocabulary plucked straight out of Hallmark cards and TV westerns. Every time, he wrote the declaration from scratch, as if it weren't composed of the same canned phrases and syrupy words. He always seemed shocked when Stayja didn't reciprocate.

"This is from LA," Stayja said, rolling her eyes and trying to hide her disappointment from her cousin.

"Do you want me to keep going? It's about six more paragraphs long."

"No, please don't," Stayja said.

"Why don't you just tell him you're dating someone now? Then maybe he'll leave you alone."

Stayja shrugged.

"How's Chet?" she asked to change the subject.

"Leaving his wife!" Nicole said happily.

"Wow," Stayja said. "Doesn't he have a kid?"

"Yeah," Nicole said, ashing her cigarette as they pulled to a stop at a light.

"Are you going to, like, marry him? How old's the kid?"

"I don't know," Nicole said. "Maybe. He'd only have the kid some of the time. It's not like I would be the mom. The kid is, like, four or seven."

Stayja turned on her left blinker.

"You think you're ready to be a stepmom when you don't even know how old the kid is?" Stayja said and instantly regretted it. She had such a hard time holding her tongue when it came to Nicole. She'd resolve to be nicer, to be more accepting and less critical. She was aware of how often she came down hard on her cousin, and she knew it was annoying. But Nicole had an uncanny ability to push her buttons. It just happened.

Nicole turned to look out the window. Ignoring Stayja's comment, she said, "I don't need to take the car tonight. I'm staying on campus late. I'll get a ride or take a cab or something."

"Okay," Stayja said. She could tell Nicole wanted her to ask why, but she didn't want to give her cousin the satisfaction.

"I'm hanging out with Annie," Nicole finally said. "We're going to watch *Sex and the City*. She'd never even heard of it."

TWO MONTHS OF weekly transfusions, which Donna had learned to give herself at home, had breathed new life into her, the fresh blood reviving some of her old, pre-COPD energy. While only a fraction of the former Donna had returned, Stayja had been pleased to arrive home multiple nights in October to find that her mother had tackled household projects that previously she would have found overwhelming: rearranging the living room furniture, resewing the buttons on their coats, and even sponge painting the kitchen walls.

When Stayja asked where she got the paint, Donna had said, "Adrienne took me to Lowe's," as if their running errands together again, too, was no big deal. This was how Stayja learned that her mother and Adrienne had made up.

"Want to watch *Sex and the City*?" Stayja said later that night, sitting with Donna in the living room. They used LA's Netflix password.

"Sex and the what? Why would I want to watch that?" Donna said.

"It's a rite of passage, Mom," Stayja said. "And it's from your generation. I don't know how you missed it."

"Ha!" Donna said, munching on a bowl of canned peaches. "I passed through before there was such a thing as rites of passage. You know what my rite of passage was? *Frasier*. Now, that was some good television."

"We can watch *Frasier*," Stayja said. "I can't find *Sex and the City* on Netflix anyway."

"Great!" Donna said, standing. "I'm gonna make us some pop-corn."

Stayja cued up the show, then opened Instagram. From the kitchen came the sound of popcorn popping and the cozy smell of butter.

He hadn't posted any new photos.

She dropped her phone and sighed. Then she had an idea. She picked it back up and pulled up the photos he'd posted from fall break, the ones with blondes. They were tagged. She followed the tags to their accounts, searching for him in any pictures others had posted in public accounts. Finding nothing, she did the same thing with the girls pictured in earlier photos, then earlier, then earlier.

Donna returned, and they started the show, but Stayja kept digging.

Forty-five minutes in, at the start of their third episode, she found one. On the previous weekend, he was with a group of guys—two black, two white—all beaming at the camera.

Donna started cackling. "Did you see what Niles said to Daphne? You have to rewind. Rewind. You missed it."

"I'm okay," Stayja said.

"Rewind!" Donna commanded.

As Stayja sped the show backward, she wondered what Nicole and Annie were doing. If they were having fun. Of course, they were. Fun was Nicole's best skill.

AND, THEN, ONE night near the end of October, he was back.

She was at work when she saw his text. Come over after work?

She waited as long as possible before replying, then went with a casual if you want, but I can't stay late.

She spent her break hurrying to QuikMart to buy toothpaste and a toothbrush and a razor and shaving cream and then shaving her armpits and bikini line in the handicapped stall.

After work, she caught the door as another student was entering and followed him into the building. She found Tyler in his room, tanner, with sun-kissed hair, and ecstatic.

"Remember the party I told you about? The black and white party?"

It took her a moment. He sat at his desk, facing his monitor, typing.

"Come here." He leaned back so she could see his laptop screen on which a headline read: *Black and White Party Is Black and White Triumph, Just What Carter Needs.* Beneath it was a photo of a mass of students outside, all dressed, appropriately in black and white.

"Congratulations," she said. "That's great."

She remained standing as he began telling her about how it was the most highly attended event of the semester so far, excluding football games, and how he had gotten to meet his idol, some rapper. He'd danced on the stage. People came from all over, not just Carter students.

Then why hadn't he invited her?

"Hey, did you get my essay?" she said. Her application was due in just under two weeks.

He looked at her blankly.

"Remember that program you thought I should apply for? At Gibson? I texted you my essay. I thought maybe you would read it for me."

"No prob," he said. "I remember now. Sure thing."

"You could read it right now," she said. "It's just on my phone."

He hesitated, then turned back to his computer.

"Cool, while I read that, will you read this?" He clicked, and a document flew open on the screen. At the top of it was the photo she'd found—the one of him with the guys. "It's an op-ed I'm going to send in to the paper. It'd be good to get your take on it."

"Sure," she said, taking a seat at his desk as he took her phone and plopped down on his couch. As she started to read, she became aware that he was watching her. She turned.

"What?" she asked.

"I'm just nervous what you'll think."

She resumed reading. The article was about the party he'd thrown but also other things. How it was so important to promote diversity, given who was president. How divided the country was. He used the word "inclusion" a lot and "walking the talk."

"What would you say the theme is?" he asked.

"Um, it feels like it's sort of about a lot of things," she said.

"It's not about a lot of things. It's about unity."

"You asked my opinion. I'm just telling you."

"Did you read the whole thing?"

"Yes, and I don't know what President Trump has to do with the party you just threw." Her annoyance with him for ghosting her and not even apologizing for it was rearing its head.

He stared at her.

"Who did you vote for in the last election?" he asked, a dare in his voice.

"I didn't," she said. "I had to work."

"I mean, you could have voted absentee. Who *would* you have voted for?" he asked.

"Trump, probably," she said.

"Oh, my God," he said.

"What? I'm a Republican," she said, openly frustrated. "Don't be patronizing."

"You're a Republican?!" he exclaimed. "That doesn't make any sense!"

She shrugged and looked back at the computer screen, wishing she'd just fucking lied and told him the essay was fine.

"I'm sorry," he said. "I should have worded that differently." He paused, then in a controlled, careful tone, he said, as if he were an interviewer on public radio, "Why do you identify as Republican?"

"Because the government sucks. I'm sick of paying taxes and not getting shit for it."

Tyler was shaking his head. "You have the wrong guy. The government isn't your enemy. Conservative ideology does nothing for people like you."

Stayja glared at him, her pulse quickening. "That's really fucking condescending," she said.

"I'm sorry," he said. "I just mean, if you're skeptical about public benefits because you think they don't help you enough, well, conservative policies aren't going to help you either."

She let out a groan. She'd already had a long day—and she'd spent the end of her shift arguing with a student over whether she could make him an espresso even though she'd already cleaned the machine and shut down the register.

"Hey," he said, his tone softer. "Come here."

She didn't move.

"You look hot in that shirt," he said. "Do you maybe want to take it off?" He was grinning.

"I'm tired," she said. "I'm going to head home."

"Fine," he said. "I'll take mine off." He pulled his T-shirt over his head and tossed it into the mini basketball hoop hanging on the back of his door. Then he picked up her phone, which she'd set on the coffee table, and started taking selfies while flexing and puckering his lips.

Stayja found herself smiling. He walked over to the desk. He picked her up, just scooped her up like a baby—he was stronger than he looked. He took her to the bed and dropped her on it.

She wasn't in the mood, but she also wanted him back in her life. Yes, he was condescending and had disappeared without explanation, but it was things like this: his playfulness, his enthusiasm for life, his desire for her.

He was still her favorite person.

A FEW DAYS LATER, on Friday morning before her shift, Stayja and Nicole were weeding the short stretch of lawn between their houses. That is, weeding the *weed* that had resumed growing there, that once upon a time had been planted by Nicole. For months Donna had claimed she smelled pot whenever the wind blew from the direction of Adrienne and Nicole's house, and she and Stayja both assumed Nicole was smoking again, that it was just a matter of time before Adrienne caught her. When Stayja had brought it up to Nicole, her cousin was insistent that she'd been clean for months.

They discovered that Donna wasn't crazy and Nicole wasn't lying when Stayja noticed that the bush Nicole had grown there two years earlier and destroyed once her mother discovered it had revived itself in full, abundant glory, a veritable marijuana forest right there between the two houses.

The girls ripped out stalk after stalk and chucked them into a plastic garbage bag as Nicole conspicuously pocketed a small stack of leaves.

Stayja frowned.

"It's for Chet. He's never done it," Nicole said happily. She was taking the day off to go to a Carolina Hurricanes game with him. They'd invited Stayja, but she wasn't a hockey fan and preferred not to lose the money by calling out.

Stayja's phone, resting on the ground, lit up with a text from Tyler.

Emailed u notes on ur essay.

Stayja grabbed the phone and navigated to her in-box, vaguely aware that her cousin was pretending not to watch her out of her side eye.

This essay is way more about your mom than it is about you. I think you should make it more about your classes and stuff. What has interested you most about them? Why do you want to go into medicine? Can you handle the workload, the academic rigor of med school—that's what you're going to have to prove, coming from community college. I think you have to show that you're capable of the work required. An emotional story about your mother being sick misses the mark.

The grammar is also problematic. I don't have time to fix it all but a few spots: at the end of a sentence, it's "my mom and me"/"my family and me," not "my family and I." You aren't the subject. Also, you don't study hard, you study well. Hard isn't an adverb. And some of these sentences are sentence fragments. You need a subject and a verb to make it a sentence. Also, although this is kind of an archaic rule (and an ironic comment since I literally just violated it), I'd be wary of beginning so many sentences with "and." Basically you want to be more formal.

"What's wrong?" Nicole asked.

"Nothing," Stayja said.

Nicole lunged and snatched Stayja's phone before she could hide it.

"Don't!" Stayja cried, but Nicole was already reading his email.

"This is bullshit," she said. "Your essay made me cry." She tossed the phone back to her.

"Nicole!" How had she even known she'd written an essay?

Nicole shrugged. "I snooped. Kill me. I wanted to know what you were doing all the time on your phone. I thought you were texting him about me. But you were writing that essay that made me fucking cry. Ignore that asshole. Send it in."

Stayja gazed up at the cloudless sky, too disappointed by Tyler's reaction to be annoyed at her cousin.

"You know what you need?" Nicole gripped a handful of weed, made a show of rolling it between her hands, and lunged at Stayja, stuffing the wad of green under her nose and tackling her.

"Ganja!" Nicole yelled. "Ganja! Ganja!"

"Stop!" Stayja fought her off, laughing.

Annie

TUESDAY, OCTOBER 24

Student Mental Health had locations on both campuses, and Loretta's office happened to be on South, so every Tuesday and Thursday morning I boarded the bus and took the nine-minute ride down Campus Drive, under the Bridge, and up the hill to where the first-years lived.

Matty's idea had been for me to write an op-ed about my case, and how the school had handled it—without naming Tyler, of course. I'd drafted it that night, and it was already with the editor of the Opinions page. In the op-ed, I talked about how the decision had left me feeling: deserted. Riding to South Campus, I wondered what Loretta would think when I told her.

Why did I look out the window at the Bridge? Because I always did—I'd loved the Bridge since before I was a Carter student, since the first image I saw of it in the recruitment packet that arrived at my home. Exploding with color, it affected me the way a Keith Haring or Henri Matisse did, leaving me energized and always a little bit happier. So as the bus looped left, I turned out the window to catch the first sight of the Bridge.

I blinked. I thought I was hallucinating. But it didn't fade. It grew bigger, clearer.

Dazed, I lifted my phone to take a photo, and by the time we'd passed underneath the Bridge, I was struggling to text the blurry shot to Matty, my thumbs trembling.

So he'd done it to someone else, too. Somewhere out there was another girl or girls who understood what I was feeling. I was shocked but also surprised that I was so shocked; of course, there were more of me. Of course, he'd done it to others and would likely do it to more. Still, the whole experience had felt so isolating that it hadn't occurred to me I might not be the only one.

"Hey," I answered.

"What *the fuck* is that!" Matty said.

"I know," I said quietly. The handful of students on the bus hadn't noticed—they were occupied on their phones.

"You know anything about it?" he asked.

"What?" I said. "No!"

"I feel like maybe my article doesn't work now," I said.

"What? Why?" he said, panting. "Sorry, I'm sprinting. I want to get a good shot of the Bridge before they paint over it. You know they'll do that in three seconds. Hello?"

"I'm here," I said as the bus screeched to a stop. "Going into therapy. We can talk about it later." I wasn't sure why, but my article now felt silly. Anticlimactic.

"A LOT HAS happened," I said as I plopped down on Loretta's teal couch and adjusted the pillow behind my back.

I told her everything—my parents surprising me on campus, telling them about the rape, my dad insisting he was going to talk to the dean (but thankfully not having done it yet, as far as I knew). Then I told her about Matty's idea, about staying up late drafting the op-ed, and now, this morning, about Tyler's name on the Bridge. When I got to that part, her jaw dropped, as mine had.

"Wow," she said. "Wow, wow."

"It'll probably be down by the time I leave here," I said, echoing Matty. "But the thing is, I don't really want to publish my op-ed now."

She tilted her head.

"Why is that?"

I shrugged.

"Do you fear that people will think you're connected to the graffiti somehow?"

"No," I said without pause.

The suggestion was absurd. I would never do something like what this girl had done, whoever she was. Not because it was all that physically challenging. The Bridge was sparsely trafficked, so there wasn't a safety issue or anything. One needed only a can of spray paint and a step stool or a ladder if you wanted to paint high up. I'd participated when the orchestra had tagged it to advertise our spring concert.

Whoever she was, she had done it alone—bought the paint, climbed a ladder, wrote those words. She was remarkable to me for her bravery, her boldness, and I ached to know more. What had happened to her? Had the university failed her as well? Something must have occurred to provoke an act of such desperation. I wanted to know her, and I wanted to be more like her.

My article felt inconsequential, a flimsy attempt at retribution, in light of this bloodred indictment.

"I'm not afraid I'll be linked to it," I said. I was afraid because I knew I wouldn't be, and what did that mean?

ON THE SHUTTLE BACK, I texted Matty.

Let's just sit on it till the Bridge thing passes.

As the bus barreled forward, I checked in, as Loretta had encouraged me to do, with my emotions.

There was confusion and sadness. Both of those were familiar now.

There was anxiety. Also no stranger.

But, newly, there was a hint of relief. Yes, that was there—I felt some relief, the kind you feel at the end of the flu, when you can get out of bed again, when you take your first shower and have your first real meal. He'd been exposed.

Even after they erased it, my fellow students, the ones who had something to fear, would be wary of him now. Talk of things like this spread. Cloistered as Carter was, compartmentalized into Greek and non-Greek, branching further into enclaves based on how you saw things and how you looked and how much you really wanted to drink on an average Friday night, a common thread pierced through the labels and social stratification: no one wanted to be raped.

When Matty had pitched the op-ed to me, I'd said that I wished there were some place I could simply warn other girls about Tyler. An online forum or something.

"The sororities have blacklists," he said, but I wasn't in a sorority. "There used to be this forum where you could post it." He described an anonymous discussion board online that got taken down after people turned nasty and started posting bigoted stuff and threats against Jewish students. "You know. What always happens with those things. At some point, they turn on us Jews." Matty's mom was Jewish.

So I'd accepted that there wasn't a way for me to warn people about Tyler, but now it had happened. His outing on the Bridge—this was what I'd wanted.

And yet it wasn't enough. What about the university's role? Its confusing decision that left me scratching my head and jumping every time I turned a corner and spotted a flash of blond hair in the distance?

I really think we should go ahead and run the op-ed, Matty wrote back.

No, I texted back. Let's wait.

We approached the Bridge headed north, and as we passed underneath, I turned. It was still there, the truth, scrawled furiously. I understood her fury. I got it.

Thursday, October 26

A Serious-Ish [a] Column on Free Speech

by the Irreverent Rooster

It's me, your most irreverent of roosters. In case you're living on another planet, sh*% has gone down this week, some real sh$&, some serious sh}¥. Namely: someone has been accused of rape—by name—on the Bridge.

I'm not going to repeat the person's name here because, believe it or not, I am an adult with a sense of ethics and an ability to draw boundaries. I know. It astonishes even me, frankly.

But that doesn't mean I'm above finding the situation utterly fascinating. Because isn't the whole point of the Bridge free speech? Is that not how it's described in the glossy brochure that arrived at all of our homes when we were in high school?

And yet, free speech has its limits. Hate speech, as we know—the Carter Bridge being no stranger to old-school racism or homophobia—isn't "tolerated"[b] here. I would imagine that neither is slander.

But I just asked my friend who's a 1L at the law school, and he says it's not slander if it's true. If he's correct (Tony, I'm not saying I'm doubting you, but you are just in your first year, dude), maybe there's not really a justification why this isn't okay.

This is the first time in this rooster's memory that a personal attack has been wielded.

Listen, obviously it will have disappeared by the time you read this.

But is this the beginning of a new era? Will more students take to voicing personal grievances against each other on our hallowed monument to free speech, leading to its demise, like YikYak?[c]

Reasons I would *not* be all that disappointed if that happened:

1. All implosions are interesting.
2. The Bridge is ugly. I said it. It's ugly.
3. No one actually writes anything interesting on it.
4. It's primarily ad space for a cappella groups, and since 90 percent of the student body is in an a cappella group, word of mouth has that covered.
5. Maybe they could turn it into an art space. No ads allowed. You can paint, but it has to be beautiful!

That last item introduced a new idea here at the end of the column. Sorry, my writing 101 prof, Dr. Perez. You taught me better. And this column doesn't even have a conclusion.

Here's a stab at a thesis statement: Might this be the beginning of the end of the Bridge?

Glossary

a. SERIOUS-ISH: Just kidding. Nothing I do is serious.
b. TOLERATED: Hahahahahahahahaha, of course, it is.
c. YIKYAK: Before the time of some of you young'uns. It was an anonymous online forum that got so nasty it imploded, proving that people at their core, including Carter students, are terrible.

Guest Op-Ed
Friday, October 27
by Gloria Leopold, Professor of English

The recent instance of defamation on "the Bridge" has incited extensive debate among friends, colleagues, and my students over the question of due process and related notions. The truth is that considerations of equality have been absent from university protocol around sexual assault for some time now.

I have been teaching at this university for nineteen years. I have witnessed the rise of contemporary identity politics and its resurgence as a different beast. I have grieved the sacrifice of consciousness and community in favor of knee-jerk political correctness and thoughtless individualism in feminism.

There is a natural tension that emerges when young people coming of age discover their sexual identity. There is collision, conflict, discord. Under Title IX, this learning curve is now treated by universities as male-on-female terrorism, a view that at its heart is, simply, the same old sexism dressed up in the latest style. Under this view, women are passive; men are actors. Women lack the ability to communicate consent by any means other than the most childish, the most direct, while men are assumed capable of reading between the lines of all interaction, virtual PhDs of social behavior. The underlying principle is the infantilization of the female and the elevation of the male to near superpower status.

Meanwhile, the administration and Title IX office are cast as the knights in shining armor, armed with policies and procedures to protect the impotent female.

The tale of the woman in peril and the savior who swoops in to save her is all too familiar in the course of human history. And yet somehow it has become the prevailing feminist narrative on American college campuses in 2017.

The trend is antithetical to intellectualism, to feminism, and to the intellectual foundation of collegiate life. A dynamic that bestows all agency on the male does not further the feminist cause. It diminishes it.

Comments:

BB2022: Honestly, I don't even know what counts as sexual assault on this campus. Did we learn that?

Bulldog3sixty: It was a skit at orientation. Remember the puppets? Lol

BB2022: Oh God those puppets lulz whyyyyy

R.P. 2009: Insightful, but you overlook an important point here: money. The Title IX industrial complex. It's been ballooning since 2011, when the Department of Education's Office of Civil Rights (OCR) expanded its definition of gender discrimination to include "sexual misconduct," everything from assault to harassment to a so-called hostile environment. Universities don't want to be targeted by OCR for investigations because those are expensive to defend against. They also don't want to be sued. It's a giant financial mess.

If I were cynical I'd say that every case is a cost-benefit analysis. It all comes down to money.

At least now the standard is a bit better than it was under Obama.

SmokingGun69: No one seems to be pointing out the obvious. The Brands have donated far more than any lawsuit will cost to defend.

FredPreekIII: Not money. The problem is booze. Why can't we talk about that?

Guest Op-Ed
Monday, October 30
by Annie Stoddard, Second-year

Yesterday morning I woke up to an email from my best friend.

"Now?" was all it said.

You see, prior to the incident on the Bridge last week (read about here if you haven't—for the record, I had nothing to do with it), I had been planning to write an op-ed on the topic of sexual assault on campus. In fact, I'd already written it and submitted it to the *Chronicle*.

But I decided to pull it after learning of what had been written on the Bridge, because I wasn't sure how what I had to say related to the conversation that would emerge in the wake of the Bridge incident.

Now I feel differently.

I have followed the discussion in the pages of the *Chronicle* over the past week, and I have noted that while it has been a rich discussion (this is Carter, after all), there's still a voice missing, a voice that I believe needs to be heard.

Mine.

The case I brought against my rapist has been almost as traumatic as the rape itself. Contrary to Professor Leopold's op-ed, I find that people are unwilling to consider that a guy, my rapist, could possibly understand any communication that wasn't verbal. Talk about infantilizing—that's some major coddling. Meanwhile, in a self-contradicting decision letter finding that he'd committed "sexual misconduct," he was essentially given a slap on the wrist. Don't half side with me, then not bother protecting me.

Did I tell him to stop? Everyone asks. Did I say no *verbally*?

Listen, women. You will get this: It was clear to me what was going to happen, regardless of whether I literally said "no" or "stop." You don't plead when it's clear that pleading isn't going to work; the whole experience becomes more dehumanizing than it already is.

Despite my reporting the rape and doing all I could to follow proper procedures, the administration has done nothing to ensure that this doesn't happen again to me or to anyone else. He is still here on campus. And so am I.

Two months ago, I was a student with some good stuff going for her: a psych major, a bassoonist, and an older sister. Now I am a rape victim.

I assure you, that is not a status anyone wishes on herself.

My fear, my flashbacks, and my constant ruminations (should I have worn something different?) consume the portion of my brain that used to think about other things, like my music, my classes, and my goals. Being raped has colonized a whole district of my brain. And while I hate the person who did this to me, a person I fear and dread seeing every day—that part? I hate even more.

If I want to leave you with one idea, it's this: You don't speak when you know no one's listening. You don't fight back when you know you're going to lose.

#MeToo

Comments:

nasseravid: I heard from a reliable source that she accused him of doing it twice. If that's true, I think the fact that there are even two times to speak of says it all. Why would you go out a second time with a guy who raped you? Because he didn't.

RRniner: what's wrong with her legs?

HamBam: real brave to bully a disabled person. you're a real man.

nasseravid: how is she disabled? That's just a skin disease lol it's not like she's handicapped.

nasseravid: Who ISN'T disabled now according to the libs????
SCOPE CREEP

. . . and 71 more

Bea

"What a fantastic opportunity for you to observe and reflect on the language people use to talk about justice, particularly given your initial reservations about taking on the case."

Dr. Friedman sat cross-legged facing Bea in the sitting room area of his hotel suite at the Carter Boathouse, the only hotel on campus, where he held weekly one-on-one meetings with the Justice students. He and Bea were discussing the Bridge incident. Since his case had concluded, she was no longer Tyler's advocate, but Dr. Friedman was constantly pushing for what he called "radical real-world reflection." That's what, he believed, would lead to radical justice.

"Get out there and learn from what you see and hear. Don't just trust what professors and books tell you. Draw your own conclusions. Set aside this week's reading assignment if you need. Write your reaction paper on this."

"Okay," she said.

"What is it?" he asked.

"It's just that the application for the fellowship is due in two weeks, and I have to submit the academic paper as a writing sample, and I didn't like my one on distributive justice or the one on the plea bargain state. Do you think I could write one about this that's . . . rigorous enough, I guess?"

He smiled. "Bea, your qualifications for the fellowship are very clear. Don't worry." He winked. "Now go out there and listen. Ask yourself hard questions. Get gritty."

BEA REREAD THE op-eds, letters, and dozens of online comments that had been published. She followed the various threads of argument and considered their merits. There was discussion about the reasons why someone would "out" their rapist in this way. There was discussion about university hypocrisy and censorship. Around the country, people were posting #MeToo on social media, and the phenomenon bled onto campus. Someone made stickers, and girls walked around with them on their shirts: #MeToo. But the one thing everyone seemed to agree on at first was that painting TYLER BRAND = RAPIST!! on the Bridge wasn't okay.

Then, on social media, girls everywhere—the news had traveled beyond Carter—began to come to the defense of the mystery victim. (Bea stayed quiet about knowing who'd done it. She found herself impressed with Annie. She hadn't thought the girl had it in her.)

Clearly, people argued, given the multiple exclamation points, this person was acting in a fit of rage. Could we really blame #mysterygirl for losing her cool and taking it to the one place she knew she could speak up and be heard? The place lauded as a safe haven of speech? #Mysterygirl was being held to an impossible standard of human behavior. So she lashed out! She was human!

#Weareallmysterygirl began to trend.

"This is how it always is with women, isn't it? We take it, and take it, and take it, and when we finally snap, WE'RE out of line. Gaslighting on cue," one tweet read.

Another: "Once again, a man's reputation matters more than the substance of the claim."

And finally: "We must remember that whoever this is, she was likely raped. Let's consider that before we all jump to judgment of her."

On a cold Monday night in early November, the black ice on the roads causing the buses to creep cautiously between campuses, Bea made her way to a meeting room in the student center. A sign that read "Sexual Assault Panel" hung from a hook on the door. She entered and took a seat. The room was chilly and utilitarian—taupe carpet, symmetrical rows of metal chairs, fluorescent bars of light.

Her phone dinged, startling her. She never turned her phone off vibrate and must have by accident. She fetched it from her bag. The text was from her lab partner.

When are you going to make up the lab??

Without responding, she quickly silenced it as someone took the seat next to her. Within a few minutes, at eight, the scheduled start time for the panel, half of the chairs in the room were loosely occupied. The moderator, a third-year with lavender hair who introduced himself as head of the Student Relations Committee, announced that the student government had issued a resolution urging the administration to review its policies on sexual assault reporting and investigation. The room erupted into applause, and Bea clapped along.

Then he introduced the panelists—a Gender Studies professor, a cop from campus police, the president of Sigma Chi, and Annie. Bea noticed on the placard placed in front of Annie that her last name was misspelled: "Annie Stodard," it read, with one D.

"I'd like to turn the floor over to you, Linda," the moderator said.

"Thank you, Kai," said the professor, facing the audience. "In our Gender and the College Experience class this fall, which Kai is in"—they exchanged smiles—"we have been talking about power. Institutional responses to sexual assault really tee up questions of power. I'm happy to be here as a part of what I hope will be an ongoing conversation with the larger campus community. Not just in here." She lifted her hands and pointed both downward, pumping them. "But out *there*." She flipped her palms so that her hands were pointing outward.

"Rory—you look as if you want to say something?" Kai said.

"Sure," the Sigma Chi guy said. "I just want to second what, uh, Linda said. I am really happy to be here and just, you know, proud that we're tackling this topic. So thank you all for coming. I think *you* all deserve a round of applause just for being here." With that, he began to clap, and a handful of people joined in.

So far, Bea thought, there had been a lot of clapping and not much said. She could imagine Dr. Friedman becoming impatient with the lack of substance from the get-go.

"Annie," Kai said. "Would you be willing to start us off? We'd love to hear from you about your experience with the administration on campus. Anything you're comfortable sharing."

"Well, I guess I think . . ." Annie paused. To Bea, she seemed very nervous. "I think this panel is an example of what's wrong."

She paused again. The room was quiet apart from a few low murmurs.

"Who are we talking to?" She gestured to the rows of chairs. "These people aren't the problem. The people who really need to talk about rape are frat guys. I think the frats need to be held accountable."

When she said "rape," Bea sensed a shift in the room's energy.

"Annie," said Linda in a practiced gentle tone, "you're so right about the importance of including a broad spectrum of people in the conversation. That is what I was getting at a moment ago. I do, however, want us to be careful not to essentialize who is 'doing' what or who 'needs' what. The language we use is powerful, and categorizing people into buckets can obscure the real issue."

The Sigma Chi panelist leaned forward to speak, his large elbows resting on the table, which creaked under his weight. "Don't misunderstand what I'm about to say here, but I think the reason for this panel is honesty. And so I have to be honest and say I think this issue is more complicated than that."

"How so?" Kai asked brightly.

"All right. If your buddy confesses to you that something happened that he doesn't feel comfortable about—maybe that he doesn't even remember that well because he was drinking and whatnot—and he's confiding in you, your job is to give him advice and so forth, but I don't know if it's fair to say that your job is to report him. That's unrealistic. And I think we aren't gonna change things until we can acknowledge that that's a hard situation to be in as a friend."

In the audience, though they were silent, people were nodding thoughtfully.

"Thank you, Rory," Kai said. A hand two rows in front of Bea shot up.

"My question is for Linda. Are you saying that guys can be victims, too? Or are you saying that we shouldn't use gendered language when talking about sexual assault at all? Those seem like different points."

"I'm saying a bit of both, really." Linda the professor drifted into a lecture as Bea thought about what the fraternity president had said. Everyone had just moved on, but it seemed like a really important point. He'd said that guys weren't going to report their friends. But if people weren't accountable to their friends and their friends were the only people around, who could change anything?

"Officer Hal," said Kai when the professor stopped talking. "We haven't heard from you yet."

Officer Hal cleared his throat. "You okay, miss?" he asked quietly, looking at Annie. It was nearly a whisper, but thanks to the small mic in front of his face, they all heard it.

"Not really," she said softly, but, amplified, her words filled the room. Then, as if she were summoning strength from someplace else, she said, "You know, the worst part of this entire process has been stuff like this. When I got the decision letter in my case, it talked about how maybe the fact that I actually had confidence in my looks for the first time made me crazy. That was included in the report. As if that's okay to even suggest. And here, how do I feel right now? I'm being treated like the crazy one just for saying what I think."

Bea stopped breathing.

"You aren't crazy, Annie," Linda hurriedly said. "You aren't."

"We believe you, Annie," Kai said. "You're here because we believe you and respect you and want to hear from you."

The applause that followed was different from the earlier clapping. This applause had heart behind it. People began to yell, "We believe you!" Bea only clapped a few times as a pit began to take shape in her gut.

"Thank you," Annie said quietly.

Then Officer Hal said, "My turn then. I'm honored to be here." Bea found his friendly demeanor and southern accent disarming. "I guess I'll, uh, use this opportunity to say that you can always come to us with anything. We're here for you. And we just ask that you do your part, too, like reporting suspicious behavior and taking standard precautions. We have key cards for a reason. Don't let just anybody follow you into your dorm from off the street. Once people are in the dorms, it's harder for us to protect you."

As he spoke, Bea stood quietly and hurried out.

ON HER WAY to the shuttle stop, Bea knew at once what she needed: alcohol. Who did she know who could get alcohol?

Chris.

You around? she texted him. Within minutes she was standing over his mini fridge holding up two shot glasses she'd spotted on top of it.

"Really? Shots on a Thursday at"—he checked the time—"eight thirty?"

"Sure," she said. "Why not?"

He poured the vodka, she counted down, and they took one shot, then another.

To her relief, Chris was happy to decide what came next. They sat side by side on his futon as he pulled up video after video of his favorite comedy sketches on YouTube. An hour in, she felt tipsy enough to lean into him.

He gently pressed a hand against her shoulder, not letting her come closer.

"What's going on?" he asked. "Are you okay?"

She nodded.

"Are you sure? Because I feel like you're not okay."

Her gaze fell on the corner of his room, where a cluster of dust bunnies had gathered, quivering under gusts from the furnace.

"Do you want to talk about it?" he asked.

She shook her head.

"Can I guess?"

She shrugged.

"Did someone die?"

She took a deep breath.

"You know the feeling when you think someone you respect would be disappointed in you if they knew what you were doing?"

"Of course," he said.

His response encouraged her to go on.

"I was the support person for this guy who got accused of rape, and I sort of, like, gave him ideas for things he should say to attack her character. And he did it. And she read the things he said because they were in the case report, and I heard her on a panel tonight talk about how they made her feel. And now . . . I guess now I feel like a giant asshole."

"Why'd you do it?" he asked.

She shrugged.

"Because I was his advocate. I was supposed to do everything I could to help."

He thought about it.

"Then maybe whomever you're thinking of wouldn't be disappointed in you, if you were just doing your job."

"Can we keep watching?" she said, pulling her knees up.

"Sure," he said and turned up the volume.

SHE LEFT JUST before midnight. Despite the cold, she decided to walk the mile to South Campus, putting in her AirPods and searching her library for Whitney Houston. She tapped on "I Wanna Dance with Somebody" and walked rapidly, her breath clouding in the thin winter air. Chris had run out of vodka two hours earlier, and she'd since sobered up, opening up a channel for the weight she'd felt during the panel to pool again.

Several minutes into her walk, the song changed, and Bea scrambled to a stop, searching for her phone at the bottom of her bag. "Run to You" had started up. This was not acceptable. Her fingers found her wallet, her keys, a tampon, a tube of ChapStick but not her phone as Whitney cooed the first few lines of the song. When her hand finally closed around the phone, it was too late. She sat down on the curb and let the song continue to fill her ears.

In 2009, Bea was ten, and Whitney had just come out with a new album and was promoting it on *Good Morning America*. Bea and her mother went to Central Park, two long blocks and six short ones from their house, to hear the legend debut her new album. Just before singing the opening to the title track, "Run to You," Whitney had devoted it to her own mother, who was in the crowd.

"That's my mother, y'all!" she yelled. Everyone cheered. Then she said, hoarsely, "I'm gonna try to do this." *Of course, she could do this*, Bea remembered thinking. She was Whitney Houston.

Then she sang, and as they listened, Bea looked up to see her mother crying. She'd never seen Phaedra cry until then and wouldn't again. Not one other time. On their walk back to their apartment on Lexington Avenue after the concert, Bea asked why.

"Because she's so broken," she said. "Her voice is destroyed."

Bea remembered being confused. She hadn't heard that at all.

Three years later, Whitney died. Bea and her mom watched the funeral on TV. Her mother didn't cry. Four years after that, after her mother's funeral, Bea found the video of that performance on YouTube, the one they'd seen together in the park.

Watching it in the wake of Phaedra's death, it was so obvious what her mother had meant. It had been a mystery to her as a child, but somewhere between nine and sixteen, somewhere between having a mother and losing her, Bea had learned to hear brokenness.

Bag in her lap, Bea sat on the curb in the darkness and listened to the flawless recording of the song she and her mother had once heard live, gravelly and cracked.

"Am I making a mistake, Mom?" Bea whispered. "Am I the bad guy?"

21

Stayja

Stayja's car wouldn't start.

"Motherfucker," she said, turning the key a fourth time, a fifth time. Her shift started in ten minutes. She'd been letting it run on fumes. She told herself that it was because the Citgo where gas was cheapest was ten minutes out of the way, that it was too easy to push it off another day, then another. In truth, every time she got out her debit card to pay for anything she thought of that IRS bill, tucked away in her bedside table, burning a hole through the wood. It was due in six days.

She couldn't pay it off right now, and she'd rather not think about it. So in a drawer it lived until she could figure something out.

"Hey," a voice said. "What's wrong?"

LA opened the driver's-side door and gestured for her to get out and hand him the keys.

"Why aren't you at work?" she asked.

"I'm sick," he said, then faked a cough. "You and Nicole both," Stayja said. He climbed in and tried to start the engine just as she'd been doing.

"Brilliant strategy," she said. "Why didn't I think of that?"

"When was the last time you filled it up?" he asked.

Stayja groaned. The gas light had been on for days. "I don't remember."

"You mean you don't remember as in two days ago or you don't remember as in two weeks ago?"

"I don't remember," Stayja said again, checking her watch. "Dammit."

LA climbed out of the car. "Come on," he said. "I'll drop you off and then come back and take a look. It's probably the fuel pump."

On the ride to Carter, he kept stealing glances at her.

"What?" she asked.

"You never responded to my text," he said.

"I don't want to date you, still," she said.

"I figured," he said, sounding less surprised and more disappointed. At least that was progress?

"But I want to talk to you about something else. You've seemed down lately," he said.

"I'm fine," she said.

"Anything you want to talk about?"

"No," she said.

"Because you can talk to me about anything," he said.

"I'm fine, LA."

"Is it that douche bag?" he asked.

She didn't answer.

"I could tell he was a douche bag. It's the hair. He has douche bag hair."

He turned onto campus and then, instead of going straight toward the student center, took a right.

"Where are you going?" Stayja asked.

"I want to show you something, in case you haven't seen it yet."

"LA, I don't have time. My shift is starting *right now*."

"This'll take three seconds. Trust me, it's worth it. You'll be glad."

Before she could protest further, she saw what he was talking about—ahead of them, spray-painted on the Bridge in bright red, TYLER BRAND = RAPIST!!

"Oh my God," she said.

"You're welcome," he said. "Motherfucker messes with you, motherfucker messes with me."

"*You* did this?" Stayja yelled. "What the fuck, LA!"

"You bet I did!" he said.

He'd taken a detour to show her the Bridge and had made a U-turn to take her back to campus, to work. As they passed under it again, she moaned. *Why?* Why did this have to happen? Tyler knew that she was friends with LA. There were probably cameras all over. LA would be found out, and Tyler would trace it to her. He would think she had something to do with it.

"You don't even know him!"

"I know what Nicole told me. And I know he hurt you. That's all I need to know."

She wondered if she should text him? Surely, he already knew—it was almost 2 p.m. But why hadn't someone painted over it yet?

"What are you doing?" LA asked, pulling to a stop in front of the café.

"Telling him about it," Stayja said, climbing out.

"Why?!"

"Because he needs to know so he can take care of it." She slammed the door as LA rolled down the window and yelled, just before speeding away angrily, "You're welcome!"

Before she went inside, she thought she'd just quickly lap around the lot to see if his car was there. In a spot midway between the café and his dorm, she spotted it, white and glistening in the noonday glare. He hadn't yet replied to her text. She was turning to go when she detected, on the driver's side, a profile barely visible behind the tinted glass.

She approached and knocked on the window. He rolled it down a few inches. She could tell by the look on his face that he knew about the Bridge.

"Hop in," he mumbled.

"I just texted you," she said as she opened the passenger-side door and climbed inside. "I just saw the Bridge." It was warm in the car—the heat had been running awhile.

"Why would she do this to me?" he said, his elbows on the steering wheel and his palms on his head. "This is a nightmare."

"Yeah. It's pretty fucking bad," Stayja agreed. "Is someone going to paint over it?"

"They better," he said. "If they don't want to get sued."

"Good," she said, feeling a little better.

"She's taken this too far. The only option she's left us is to sue her. Not that she has any money."

"Sue her?" Stayja asked, trying to disguise the fear in her voice. "For what?"

"She can't just ruin my life because she regrets a drunken blow job."

Stayja turned away. Outside the window, a tour group of at least fifteen parents and teenagers was being led by a tour guide into the Rooster.

"I have to go," she said. "I'm already late." She gave his knee a squeeze. "I'm sorry this happened."

"Me too," he said.

"It'll be okay," she said just before she closed the door.

"You don't know that," he said.

AFTER MAKING WHAT felt like an endless list of drinks for the tour group, Stayja hurried back outside to call Nicole.

"Are you okay?" Nicole answered. It was rare that Stayja would call and not text. In the background, Stayja could hear the sounds of a boisterous crowd. So Nicole and Chet were already at the hockey game.

"What did you tell LA about Tyler? Did you tell him about the thing with Annie?"

Obviously, Stayja knew that she had, but she wanted her cousin to admit it.

"What is 'the thing' with Tyler and Annie? That he raped her, you mean?" Nicole was not even trying to keep her voice low. So Chet knew as well. Everyone in their lives thought Stayja was dating a rapist. "Probably. I don't remember. Why?"

"Because he's lost his fucking mind is why," Stayja said and then told her cousin about the Bridge and LA's stupid machismo about it and about Tyler's saying he was going to sue whoever did it.

As Stayja spoke, Nicole was quiet—Stayja could hear only the faint sounds of cheering nearby and the announcer calling plays.

"You don't think they have a camera on that thing do you?" Nicole said when Stayja had finished.

"I think it doesn't matter whether they do or not. I have to turn him in. Or persuade him to turn himself in."

"Stayja! No! Why would you do that?"

"Because they're going to find out either way! These people have a lot of money. They're huge donors to the school. He's poked a bear, Nicole."

Nicole was quiet again.

"Well?" Stayja said.

"I'm here."

"What do you think?" Stayja couldn't remember the last time she'd asked for Nicole's advice. Probably never, but this felt bigger than what she could handle alone.

"He'll lose his job. Don't do that to him, Stayja. Don't."

"I'm saying they'll find out."

"But you don't *know* that."

A longer pause passed between them. Stayja half wondered if Chet was listening in and half didn't care.

"Tyler will be fine," Nicole said. She sounded assured, confident. "Guys like Tyler are always fine."

Then Stayja heard Chet's voice say, "That took forever, but here's your soda."

"Don't do it. I'm telling you," Nicole pled, quieter now. "You'll regret it."

"I have to go," Stayja said.

BY SIX, TYLER had let her know by text that it had been painted over. He'd said his parents were working with the university to investigate who'd done it and that there would be repercussions.

Like what? she responded and was waiting for his response when a male voice interrupted her thoughts.

"Doing anything fun for Halloween?" She looked up.

Eric Gourdazi had gained weight in the month or two since she'd last seen him. His jawline was softer, and he was wearing glasses now. Otherwise, he was as handsome as he'd always been. A familiar flutter passed through her rib cage.

"Halloween is my favorite holiday," he said as if he'd prepared. "Know why?"

"No," she said.

"The pictures of babies in costumes. I'm a sucker for a baby in a costume."

"That's nice," she said. What on earth was going on?

"Do you remember," he said, "that I said something kind of crappy earlier this fall? I know this sounds dumb, but I've wanted to apologize for it ever since. I decided I wouldn't come back here until I did."

Eric Gourdazi had been thinking about her for months?

"Uh," she said, "I don't remember. What do you mean?"

"I said that this girl would know better than you if tuna salad had gone bad. And I just wanted to say . . . I saw your face, and I think you misunderstood what I meant. You looked like you thought I meant . . . See, that girl is obsessed with tuna. She eats it constantly, in class and stuff—it stinks up the whole room. And then she tried to make me smell it. And then she made *you* smell it. So I said to her that she probably knew better than you if the tuna smelled bad because she eats it all the damn time, but I could tell after I'd said it, based on your face, that I'd offended you. And I realized you maybe—correct me if I'm wrong, but maybe—thought I was saying that you, like, wouldn't be able to tell if tuna is bad or something. And I just . . . I wasn't saying that. And now I'm in a program where I need to apologize for the things I've done. So I'm just here to apologize."

So Eric Gourdazi was an addict in recovery. Huh.

"Hey, no hard feelings. I appreciate it. What can I get you?" she said.

Appearing relieved, Eric said, "Regular coffee, please." As she filled the paper cup, she thought about how, months earlier, she would have craved that interaction. She still had a chance. She could turn around and indulge him, flirt back, inform him that she also found tuna fucking gross, that she respected him for entering recovery, that she wished him well.

But she didn't want to be with Eric. She wanted to be with Tyler.

She handed him his coffee with a polite smile, and as he walked away, she texted Tyler.

I'm coming by after work. I have to talk to you.

"I DON'T UNDERSTAND," Tyler said, standing by his window, holding a beer he'd just cracked open. "Why would he do that?"

Stayja shrugged.

"He's an idiot."

"That's not a reason, though," he said. "Why?"

"Because he's jealous? He probably thought it was funny in a way."

"It's not fucking funny."

"*I* know that."

"Why did he even know about my case?" he asked suspiciously.

"My cousin told him."

"Who's your cousin?" He threw his hands in the air, exasperated, as if there were too many pieces of the story to follow.

"She works with Annie. At the bookstore."

He sighed and took a long swig. "So your cousin thinks I'm a rapist is what you're saying." He sat down at his desk.

"My cousin doesn't know you. It doesn't matter what she thinks."

After a moment he said, "So that's a yes."

She didn't respond.

"You have to turn him in," he said.

She didn't expect this from him. She was hoping he'd tell her the opposite—that it didn't matter, because it wasn't Annie, and so the whole thing could just fade into the past.

"He'll lose his job," she said.

"As he should," Tyler said, taking another long sip.

She studied a faint brown stain on his gray rug, then looked back up at him.

"People think it's true," he said, desperation in his eyes. "Please. Just call campus police." He grabbed his phone to pull up the number.

Annie

On a windy Tuesday night in November, I shivered as I made my way to the main quad to attend a "survivors' vigil." I'd been invited to speak by a senior who directed what I learned was called the Sexual Assault Prevention Network—an organization I'd never heard of. "Vigil" made me think of what you do when people die or go missing, but I'd accepted.

It was scheduled to start at 9 p.m., and we'd all been instructed to wear yellow. I dressed in a yellow T-shirt and a pair of jeans—my lower body's uniform again after the online pummeling that I'd been dealt in the wake of my op-ed.

I wasn't a newbie to Internet culture. I knew it was a bad idea to read the comments on my article. But an hour and a half after it was published online, I had anyway.

I was ugly.

I didn't understand the legal process.

I deserved it.

How was I smart enough to get into Carter?

My legs were diseased.

What was wrong with my legs?

Among the harsh realities crystallizing for me in the wake of my rape, coming into focus like a Magic Eye image, was the fact that my legs still branded me. I'd known that lasers can only do so much, but I'd believed that they were enough improved to constitute an afterthought rather than a focal point.

For some commenters, my scars made them want to protect me. For others, it made them want to attack. For me, of course, it made me wonder if the whole thing was a kind of karmic payback for getting the surgery. I'd been vain, and this was my punishment. Because there was no question that if I hadn't gotten the surgery, I wouldn't have been hit on by Tyler Brand. I don't mean because I wouldn't have been attractive enough (although I did feel sure of that). I mean because I also wouldn't have *felt* attractive enough to talk to him in the first place. And so it had begun to feel like a kind of cosmic penalty: I had wanted too much, hoped for too much. If not Tyler, it'd have been something or someone else. I'd dreamt too big, when in truth I was Annie Stoddard, made for the middle: middle class, middle looks, middle expectations. I had reached beyond my tier, past the natural order of things. Like that game at Chuck E. Cheese's with the critter heads that pop up solely to be slammed by a mallet, I'd dared to make myself visible.

"I told you this was going to happen," Matty had said over lunch after I'd read some of the comments aloud to him. "The Internet was basically invented *to* harass women. You realize that, right?" Then he'd begun frantically tapping on his phone, loving nothing more than to prove a point no one was contesting. "'As a student at Harvard,'" he'd read, "'Mark Zuckerberg was disciplined after he brought down the university's server because of the high level of traffic to his early version of Facebook, *which ranked girls.* He built the site in 2003 to allow visitors to view side-by-side photos of fellow students *and vote who was hotter.*' Then it says he used their photos without their permission. See? The origin of social media was violating women's privacy to make them feel bad. You're just the next generation."

As the letters poured in to the *Chronicle* and the conversation ballooned on Twitter, I'd followed, hooked on the anger it lit in me. With each letter and each comment, I felt more like a pawn, everyone grabbing at me, spinning me into whatever they needed in order to craft their particular argument. They changed facts; they changed the story; they talked about me in the abstract. I felt present in so little of it.

So at the beginning of November, when I was invited to speak on a sexual assault panel, I'd accepted, eager for an opportunity to reenter the conversation. But it was a disaster. I couldn't keep my cool, I broke out in tears at least once, and I left feeling more misunderstood than before.

Later, Linda, the gender studies professor on the panel, had called to check on me.

"It wasn't right to ask you to be on a panel so soon after your assault," she'd said. "That was our failing, and we apologize." As if the problem were asking me to speak, rather than treating me like an alien when I did.

Now, with a couple of weeks to recover, I hoped this vigil would be what the panel wasn't. I wanted to feel heard.

As the senior who'd asked me to speak welcomed the forty or so of us in attendance, mostly girls, I couldn't help but feel that the gathering did have a funereal quality. We faced her, poised solemnly in front of the bronze statue of Carter's founder whose name no one ever remembered, arms crossed and hands tucked, shoulders hunched against the cold. We had all lit candles, but as survivor after survivor spoke, tearfully recounting boozy late nights in the dorms and meetings with sleazy professors turned hostile, gusts of wind kept blowing out our candle flames. A skinny, pale boy had taken on the task of reigniting them. He darted about with his lighter, hunkering over smoky candle after smoky candle.

I felt strangely out of place, but I also understood that this was providing catharsis for many of the people around me. I listened while mentally rehearsing my speech about the administration and campus policy so I could get home and go to bed.

When a male second-year in green pants and a banana yellow polo peeking out of a navy wool jacket climbed the short platform and began to talk about the importance of sexual partners' mutually agreeing on what constitutes consent, my pulse quickened.

"We can all do ourselves a favor by not assuming that our understanding of how consent is expressed is the same as our partners'. Sexual respect starts with good communication."

He finished, stepped down from the dais to tepid applause, and it was my turn.

"And now," the senior who'd invited me to speak said, "to close the night, here is Annie Stoddard."

The notes for my speech were on my phone in my bag, but I didn't retrieve it. I scanned the crowd for the boy who'd just spoken and spotted him on the fringes of the crowd holding hands and chatting with a pretty brown-haired girl.

"Dan?" He didn't look up. "Excuse me, the Dan who just spoke?" He lifted his head, surprised. "I really don't buy that you guys are that confused."

Then I stepped off the platform and made my way across the grass in the direction of my dorm. It had been a short run, but my activism days, I knew, were over.

LATER THAT WEEK I had stationed myself in a practice room for the afternoon, setting my laptop on top of a stack of books on the piano bench so I could play eye to eye with my YouTube instructor, Celia "Learn the Cello in One Month" Solofa. Her program was free and consisted of thirty thirty-minute lessons, seven of which I'd blown through, and my goal was to finish the full course within a week, by the time I went back to Pineville for Thanksgiving.

I had just taken a break to grab a Snickers from the third-floor vending machine. I made my way back downstairs to my second-floor practice room. At the bottom of the stairs, a tall Asian guy was standing in the hallway in front of my practice room, facing my direction. He looked pleased to see me.

"Annie?" he said. "I'm Henry. I recognize you from the orchestra. You're the bassoonist, right?"

"Yeah," I said, not recognizing him. "You're in orchestra?" I tried to place his face.

"This is my first semester here. I hope to join you guys in the spring."

Henry, I learned, was a third-year who had transferred from Georgetown to Carter. He was a bassist.

So many transfers, I thought. Who knew so many people just picked up halfway through college and tried an entirely new school?

But then he said he'd wanted to be closer to his family owing to personal issues on which he didn't elaborate.

"I heard you in there. Switching from reed to string?"

"That's embarrassing," I said. "I'm bad."

"Can I see your hand?" he asked. I lifted my palm, faceup.

There, on the top of my left index finger, was a bulbous round blister, a perfect purple sphere.

"You're doing too much too quickly," he said, running his thumb along the pads of my fingers in a studious, clinical way. My stomach jolted in a good way. His fingers were long and bony, like him—stealing a look at his body, I noticed that his shoulders fell at sharp angles, and he had that tall, skinny guy slump. "You need to take a day off here and there, especially if you're going to play for so many hours."

"Okay," I said. "Thanks."

"Can I come in?"

"Sure," I said, as he followed me into the practice room.

"Show me how you're holding it," he said. I sat and positioned myself around Abigail's cello.

"May I?" He bent over and adjusted the height of the pin sticking out of the base of the cello. He stood. "Much better. The end pin was too extended for you. That will lead to tension, which will affect your playing. And your back!"

I could instantly tell a difference in my posture. "Thank you," I said.

"Playing music isn't supposed to be work," he said. "It's supposed to be fun. That's why we call it playing."

I groaned. He did, too, and took my right hand.

"Loosen," he said, and carefully—it wasn't threatening, somehow—he laced his fingers through mine. He gently jostled them until they went limp, then dropped my hand onto the top of the bow. "Loose around the bow. No one wants to see any pinkies sticking up in the air."

He stood back. "Last thing," he said. "When you play the bassoon, you look sure of yourself." So he'd not only seen me, he'd watched me. I wasn't sure whether to be creeped out or flattered. "When you play the cello, you look like a little girl who doesn't know what she's doing."

"Because I don't," I said.

"Pretend. Act like you're first cellist in the New York Philharmonic."

I laughed. He didn't. He waited.

I inched to the front of my chair, sat up straight, and fudged my way through the bars I'd spent the previous two hours learning. It was a performance rife with mistakes, but when I finished, he burst into applause.

"So much better!" he exclaimed. "You faked it till you maked it!" He winked to let me know he'd made the error on purpose. "I'll keep teaching you on one condition." He stood, and my stomach flipped. "You teach me bassoon," he said.

"Deal," I said, relieved.

HENRY AND I began to meet daily. First we'd focus on my cello playing and next on his bassoon playing.

"What's your Myers-Briggs?" I asked the third afternoon of our lessons.

"INFP," he said. "You?"

"INFJ," I said. So we were both introverts. That made sense. I found it strange that he had no real friends yet, though I guess he could probably say the same about me. Anyway, he'd only been at Carter a couple of months and spent a fair amount of time at his parents' home forty-five minutes away.

I wasn't sure if transfers ever joined fraternities or sororities, but regardless he had no interest in Greek life, which he didn't explain derisively, just matter-of-factly. He was opinionated without coming across as dogmatic, open-minded without giving the air of a pushover, confident without seeming arrogant. I kept waiting for him to disappoint me, and he kept not.

He also really liked me. That much he made clear—texting in the morning to ask how I'd slept and at the end of the day to say that he hoped work or rehearsal or studying had gone well. While I was definitely attracted to him and excited by how intrigued I was by him, I couldn't shake my suspicion that he didn't know what had happened to me. That he'd somehow missed it by being away from campus so much. If that was the case, it felt sort of as if he didn't know me at all.

I had not thought of myself as being defined by my rape, even after coming out about it publicly. But meeting and getting to know Henry brought into relief how much I now understood myself in terms of it. As Thanksgiving break approached, I began to feel as if I was lying to him, pretending to be someone I wasn't.

When I learned that the person who wrote TYLER BRAND = RAPIST!! on the Bridge was a landscaper whose photo I recognized as a friend of my bookstore friend, my rage, which had dissipated somewhat with the distraction of getting to know Henry, returned in full. Nicole had already told me that her cousin had been hooking up with Tyler and seemed sad, and she wasn't sure what exactly had happened between them.

Now it was clear. The only explanation for it was that Tyler had raped Nicole's cousin, too. Her friend, in trying to expose him, had lost his job.

"Could she bring a claim against him on campus as a nonstudent?" I asked Matty after I learned the news. "Or just go to the Cartersboro police?"

"Not sure," he said in his tone that meant he knew the answer but was preoccupied with something else.

The whole story left me outraged and reliving my own experience in the weeks afterward but unable to discuss it with Henry.

The night before Thanksgiving break, we walked back from orchestra rehearsal together—he'd begun rehearsing with us for the spring—and when we reached my room, he stepped just inside the doorway.

"I got you this to read over the holiday," he said, pulling out of his bag a hardcover book in a shiny sleeve: *Mozart: The Music, the Man, the Myths*. "I don't know if you like biographies, but I thought this one was good."

I took it. "Thanks," I said. "That was really sweet."

"Can I kiss you?" he asked, not timidly. We kissed for a minute, his hands on my arms, then my waist, squeezing. It unearthed an acute desire in me to invite him in, but the fear that I was somehow misleading him stopped me. Would it scare him off? Would he find me frightening? Or might he inexplicably find himself less attracted to me, my appeal abruptly receding in light of my status as a damaged person?

I pulled away.

"Have a great break," I said. "I hope you enjoy the time with your mom."

"Thanks," he said, then added, "I'm already looking forward to seeing you when you get back."

I couldn't let it end with that, not on that line.

"I think over break, you should look me up," I said. "In the *Chronicle* online. There's some stuff that happened earlier this fall that I think you should know about."

I could tell by his expression that I'd been right. He had no idea.

Bea

FRIDAY, NOVEMBER 17

"It didn't feel gritty. It felt like everyone was talking, but no one was saying anything."

Bea was back in Dr. Friedman's suite, meeting with him during the hour before class.

"It's complex, in other words?" he said, munching on a baby carrot.

"Not just that," she said. She'd decided she needed to talk to Dr. Friedman about her concerns. She'd found herself unable to write her paper reflecting on her "takeaways" from Tyler's case. Everything she wrote she deleted because it sounded false on one hand or insubordinate on the other. "I mean . . . did you hear about this man in Connecticut, that he abducted and killed this little girl?"

Dr. Friedman shook his head

"He didn't get life, so he'll be out at some point. And then my roommate was mugged by this kid who is serving time now for groping a student. He's poor and black and will be on the sex offender registry for up to thirty years. That was just for groping. And meanwhile, like, with Tyler, I guess what I'm wondering now is . . . what if he *did* rape her?"

"What *if*?" Dr. Friedman asked.

"It makes me wonder how what we're doing is good."

"Why is that?"

"Because he's here still. Around. Free to do it to someone else. Whoever that guy painted the Bridge for—I mean, was that person raped because of people like me?" She couldn't say "us."

He pulled a small pouch of almonds from his pocket, tore it open, and offered her one. She shook her head. He tossed a few into his mouth.

"Ever heard of carb cycling?" he said, chewing.

"No," she said. She was beginning to think he was obsessed with weight loss.

"You've heard of cutting out carbs to lose weight, though, right?" She nodded.

"And that works for people, right? Cutting carbs. Why?"

"Because carbs are calories."

"Exactly. Carb cycling just means going back and forth. Eating carbs one day, not eating them the next. Would you believe it if I told you that it's *more* efficient for weight loss than cutting carbs completely? How can that be?"

She shrugged. "Maybe the body's metabolism is kicked off by having carbs sometimes," she said. "And then burns more fat? I don't know."

"See! There you go, you don't need me." He finished the bag of almonds.

"But wait," she said when she realized he thought he'd sufficiently answered her question. "You're saying it's *better* that some guilty people go free?"

He ignored her question.

"Carb cycling isn't only good for weight loss. It's been shown to have far-reaching health benefits, from insulin regulation to improvements for chronic headache sufferers. Gut problems. Stress. Particularly for women." He dipped his head toward her as he said "women."

"It makes no sense, and yet it does. Because the body is a complex system of checks and balances and feedback loops, of which carbs are one small part. Caloric intake may seem counterproductive in the short term, but in the long term it isn't. You can't assess an entire picture by looking at one small piece of it.

"Similarly, we know that providing representation increases fairness across the system. That's proven. So you have some guilty players. Does that mean you're going to fault the entire enterprise? Consider stock market growth if you prefer that analogy. Sometimes the market falls. But overall, over time, it rises."

"Yeah. . . ."

"And those who understand this, what's the last thing they do when the market is low?"

"Take their money out?"

"Bingo."

Bea wasn't as reassured as she wished she were by his analogies. She saw the parallels he was making clearly enough. But still, they felt off somehow, missing the heart of the thing that was nagging at her.

"It just doesn't feel like two ideas," she said. "It feels like two hundred."

And then he did it, he pulled his Dr. Friedman magic.

Unfazed, he said, "I think when you get the chance to work off a college campus you're going to find more clarity of heart. You'll come up against some nasty stuff, some real heavyweights on the other side—prosecutors more callous than seems possible, judges who don't bother trying to see the humanity in your client. I think things will be clearer to you, ironically. You'll know what you stand for. Does that make sense?"

It made a ton of sense.

"Like that kid, the one who you said is serving time for groping someone. How would you feel representing him? Even if he did do it, I mean."

She didn't have to think about it. "I'd have no qualms."

"Why?"

"Because he's a kid. Because I don't think jail is what he needs. And because I think . . ."

"There you go," he interrupted. "That's what I mean. It's different out there. It'll feel different."

AS BEA MADE her way back home to shower and change for her show that night—their last before regionals—her optimism about the Justice program began to seep back in, her spirit awakening again. Perhaps he was right—she just needed to be off campus. Here, nothing felt real. People were living a pretend life and talking about it as if anything was consequential. "Academic probation" was a penalty, as if that *meant* anything. A panel to discuss sexual assault, as if anything would come out of that. Student government resolutions—what were those even? Did they carry any force?

She scrolled through her email on her phone, deleting the unimportant ones that had come in since she'd last checked—an invitation to a first-year holiday party in the dining hall, a student affairs reminder that some campus offices, including student health, would be closed over Thanksgiving, and one from her adviser, Dr. Toast, asking her to schedule her meeting with him. She didn't have time right now for Dr. Toast. Besides, she was skeptical that the socially awkward man named after bread had anything to offer her by way of actual advising. Delete.

She boarded the bus, her mind returning to her conversation with Dr. Friedman. Once she was working, come June, she'd encounter real stakes. Real people facing real problems, not Carter bubble problems.

Her phone shook: a blocked number.

Could it be Lester Bertrand?

But no, it was Barry, calling from his office.

"Had a thought," he said, launching instantly into the reason for his call. "It was Audrey's idea. Hope you're not offended. Before you take that summer fellowship with the crim law guy, we thought you just might want to talk with Dan Johnson's son Taylor at Paul Weiss. They do a loooot of pro bono. You might be into it."

"Thanks, Barry," she said. "But it's too late. I already got the fellowship."

Was it even a lie at this point?

"Aw, then, congratulations, kiddo!" he said. "Hope it's all you want it to be."

"AN EMOTION COUPLED with a mode of transportation that makes you feel that way."

Chris stood at the front of the stage at the top of the Turtles' last show before Thanksgiving, which Bea would spend on campus. It was in the South Campus black box theater and was standing room only. People were gathered at both entrances, holding their coats in front of them, shifting their weight, willing to forgo a seat to watch the team perform.

Bea listened as students yelled out various combinations of feelings and vehicles.

Sad plane! Jealous sports car! Angry subway!

"Anxious bicycle!" Chris announced, jogging back into line.

Here was the thing about Justice: its beauty was all theoretical for Bea. The stories Dr. Friedman told that left her hungry for more, eager to experience the daily grind and noble sacrifice for herself—these were what fed her devotion to it. Apart from her brief experience working with Tyler Brand and the bittersweet taste that had left behind, *her* participation was all yet to occur, future-bound. Justice offered her a vision of her one-day self. By summer, she hoped and expected, but future still. Justice Bea was inchoate. In the blueprint stage. Bea in the making.

Improv Bea was the Bea of the here and now. In improv, there was only this moment, this breath, this sentence uttered; it was visceral and instant and bolted to the present. Improv began with a step forward and ended with a step back, existing exclusively in between. It was an invitation to react and react and react again and walk away, leaving all of her reactions behind. She didn't have to carry anything forward with her.

Even delivering the monologue had become an experience Bea happily threw herself into. Since that first night she'd stepped out to offer one, she'd done so again a handful of times and found that she relished the warm spotlight illuminating her, the sea of curious eyes cast upward.

Bea stepped forward and gazed out into the dark rows of faces.

"First of all, we call them 'bikes' now, not 'bicycles,'" she said. A titter rippled through the audience. "Bicycles make me think of training wheels, unicycles, and those giant-wheeled bikes white men used to ride while wearing bow ties."

"Penny farthings!" a voice yelled from behind her. Bart.

"Sure," she said. "Those."

"And anxious makes me think of the disparate application of justice."

Some chuckles preceded a cry of "Nerd!"

"Yeah, I'm a nerd. I know." She continued, "Because if you grope someone in the woods around here and you're not a student, you get sentenced to three years and the university decides to install a hundred new blue phones all over the place. But if you, you know, do something similar or worse . . . 'sexual misconduct' or whatever they call it . . . and you *are* a student, you get an extra thousand points in dining dollars and a parade thrown in your honor."

The laughs were loud and affirming, and the show began.

A spin class of unicycles prided itself on this unique feature until the members were informed that all spin classes are, technically, unicycle classes, being that the stationary bikes contain one wheel.

A criminal case hinged on whether someone was a belligerent beggar or a mild-mannered mugger.

The sex offender registry won best float in a float competition.

As they packed up to go, Chris approached Bea.

"Hey," he said. "Can I talk to you for a minute?"

"Oh, sure," Bea said, worried he was going to say something about the two of them. Since the night she'd gotten drunk at his place, she'd declined his invites to hang out again. The truth was that she'd developed a crush on Russell, the Brit.

But he didn't want to talk about their relationship.

"Ready for Virginia?" he said. Regionals were at UVA in two weeks.

"Hope so," she said. "Why?"

"I want you to do the monologue there." She widened her eyes at him. "I know. It's not in the spirit of improv to assign it. So I'm not assigning it. I'm just saying that I want you to, okay? Step out."

She was flattered. "Okay."

He smiled and lifted his hand for a high five.

That night, for the first time in weeks, she signed into Facebook, curious what her maybe-father who'd never answered her message was doing. There it was, the introductory note she'd sent. She clicked it open to find a "read" receipt, dated the week she'd sent it. So he'd gotten it and read it. He just hadn't wanted to respond.

Stayja

LA had been arrested by town police within an hour after Stayja called campus police, and by the end of the day he'd been fired. He'd spent two nights in jail for defacement of public property before his arraignment and come home to no job to await his trial.

"It really broke him that you did that to him," Nicole said one morning as they took turns mowing the grass. LA usually mowed their small lawn for them, but he'd stopped after Stayja turned him in. His Netflix password was no longer working either.

"You destroyed him," Nicole said, taking off her gardening gloves, tossing them to Stayja and sitting down on the grass.

"It's not my fault he's an idiot," Stayja said, standing as she pulled on the soiled canvas gloves.

"He really thought if it came down to it, you'd be loyal to him. I mean he *is* family," said Nicole.

"He's not family just because he lives next door and once gave me a good deal on a car when he was getting a better one," Stayja said.

"He was making seventeen an hour there. He'll be lucky to find something that pays nine," Nicole said. "Chet is trying to get him a job with the property management company at his office."

"Might be hard now that he has a record," Stayja said.

Nicole shrugged. "Chet's well liked," she said.

Stayja reached down and yanked the mower to life, drowning out anything more Nicole could say. She was done with her cousin's attempts to guilt her. LA had brought his situation on himself. It wasn't her fault that he'd made a stupid decision.

EVERY YEAR IN mid-November, the four of them—joined by LA for the last two—would gather in Donna and Stayja's house for early Thanksgiving. Their annual tradition was a feast essentially designed to consolidate Adrienne's grief over her late husband's death into one holiday rather than forcing her to suffer through two: the anniversary of his death on November 12 followed by Thanksgiving on the last Thursday of the month.

In the early afternoon of November 15, before both girls had to head into work, they sat around the table.

"Why isn't LA coming?" Donna asked, removing the fifth place setting she'd laid out for him.

"He doesn't feel well," Stayja said, avoiding Nicole's eyes.

"I haven't seen him around lately," Donna thought aloud.

"He's looking for a new job," Nicole said pointedly.

"Oh? Didn't work out at Carter?" Donna said, distracted by the cranberry sauce she was shoveling onto a platter in the middle of the table. For Donna, job turnover was no big deal. But not for Adrienne.

"Wait, what happened?" Stayja's aunt asked.

"Ask Stayja," Nicole said.

Stayja turned to shoot daggers at her cousin.

"Nice necklace," Stayja said. Nicole was now sporting a razor thin, white gold chain, at the bottom of which hung a heart pendant full of tiny Swarovski crystals. Chet had given it to her for her birthday on November 2. Their mothers knew this, just as they knew about Chet—Donna and Adrienne liked to bug Nicole about when they were going to meet him—but they didn't know he was married.

The hush-hush nature of it all was the result of a sort of unspoken arms race between the cousins, as neither daughter wanted her mother to know her secret: for Stayja, that she was half-dating someone who'd been accused of rape and, for Nicole, that she was full-on dating a married man.

Donna set down her ladle. "What are you girls doing? What's going on?"

The cousins looked down at their empty plates.

"Whatever it is," Donna said, "work it out. Hear me? Work. It. Out. It's Thanksgiving, and family is what matters."

"Yes, ma'am," Stayja muttered.

"Nicole?" Donna said. "Okay?"

"Okay, okay," Nicole said.

"You think I'm kidding! Family comes first," Donna said, growing heated and breathless and plopping into her chair. "Everything else comes after. Boys. Jobs. School."

Nicole rolled her eyes.

"I saw that, missy. How do you think your mom and I managed to stay so close all of our lives? By putting boys before each other?"

"By getting into a fight every year and not speaking to each other for three months?" Nicole said.

A moment of tense silence passed. Then Stayja laughed. Adrienne joined in.

Donna's fury lasted several more seconds before a small smile broke through and she reached out, picked up a dinner roll, and chucked it at Nicole. It bounced off Nicole's forehead and onto the table. Without pause, Nicole grabbed it and took a bite, grinning.

FOR THE NEXT two weeks, Stayja did her best to take her mother's words to heart by forcing herself to get along with Nicole, and she could tell that Nicole was trying, too.

Still, all the small things about Nicole that had always bugged her continued to, leaving her irritated and resentful and fighting like mad to hold her tongue, just to keep the peace. The tax bill was still tucked away in her bedside table, unpaid and overdue, tormenting her with its impossible, crushing mandate, while Nicole's sudden influx of more money than she'd ever had before, coupled with the fact that Nicole herself had *no* living expenses or bills, had led her to indulge in things that made Stayja want to pull her skin off. Like microblading, which Stayja had never heard of until Nicole got it—eyebrows tattooed on your face. That cost a hundred dollars. Fake permanent lashes. (Stayja didn't know how much they had cost.) An eighty-nine-dollar pair of casual boots.

Had it never occurred to Nicole that, with her new income, maybe she could pay Stayja back for all the times Stayja had covered her ass?

But Stayja did her best to keep her resentment to herself, along with her condemnations of Chet for being a cheater. When Chet gave Nicole his old Apple TV and his HBO GO and Hulu passwords, the cousins were both elated. "This is so much better than Netflix!" Nicole exclaimed the night they started *Game of Thrones*.

Watching a movie on Stayja's couch after she got home from work became their nightly routine. Nicole invented a new game in which they'd take turns identifying an actor's "parents"—two celebrities whose faces, combined, resembled the actor or actress in question.

During *Legally Blonde*, Nicole said of Reese Witherspoon, "Carrie Underwood and Aaron Paul."

"Who?" Stayja said, pulling up Aaron Paul's IMDb page on her phone, then yelling, "I see it!"

Stayja would have to google at least one of the actors every time, but Nicole's mental stock of cinematic trivia was shockingly extensive.

For her turn, Stayja said of Selma Blair, "That girl from *Parks and Rec* with the brown hair and that hot Hispanic guy who won Ali Fedotowsky's season of *The Bachelorette*."

"You mean Aubrey Plaza and Roberto Martinez?" Nicole asked without pause.

"If only you could use your encyclopedic memory of useless facts for something productive," Stayja said. In truth, she was impressed with Nicole's ability to remember every name she ever came across, floored by it really.

Donna would occasionally join them on these nights even though she hated being in suspense. She would leave the room for the scary parts, puttering around in the kitchen, cleaning what was clean. Stayja and Nicole tried telling her the plot of the movie in advance, but that didn't help. Donna explained that it wasn't *her* not knowing that got to her, it was the *characters*' not knowing.

"It doesn't matter what *I* know. I can't stand watching them."

Mostly this amused Nicole and Stayja, who took bets on the number of minutes before Donna invented an excuse to leave the room.

"I need to go to the bathroom," she'd say, and they'd burst into laughter.

"It's not even scary yet!" Stayja would yell. "They're just eating hamburgers!"

"But I know they're not going to finish them!" Donna would holler from the bedroom, not even pretending to have been telling the truth.

THANKSGIVING ARRIVED, which meant all Carter eateries as well as the bookstore were closed for the holiday. Stayja and Nicole were both off work for four full days—a long weekend, the longest break Stayja had had in months.

Tyler had disappeared again after LA's arrest. Stayja didn't know whether it was because he was mad at her, busy, or something else, but she obsessively checked his Instagram over the holiday, hating herself for it but unable to stop. He was at his family's home in Houston. There were many photos of the family dog, Waldo, a Saint Bernard. Waldo in the park. Waldo on a chair. Waldo in a turkey sweater.

On Black Friday, she and Nicole went to the Carter art museum, which was still open and free to them as employees, where Nicole took photos of all the paintings and posted them online. They drove out to the outlet mall thirty minutes away, where Nicole bought Chet sunglasses for his birthday at the Sunglass Hut outlet, and Stayja chose not to ask how much they cost. They went food shopping at Sam's and ate all the samples, and Stayja bought a book of crossword puzzles, thinking of the bill in her bedroom as she handed the cashier a ten. She'd never done a crossword puzzle, but she wanted to be someone who did.

They didn't fight or talk about LA or Chet or Tyler. The only time Stayja snapped at Nicole was when Stayja accidentally cut off a guy in a gold truck, and, after he flipped them off, Nicole threw her upper body out of the window, cursing.

She missed Tyler.

Lying in bed the Saturday after Thanksgiving, she wondered if perhaps she was being too prideful in not asking him about the tax bill. He might have some insight into what she should do. More important, it gave her an excuse to text him again. Around midnight she caved.

I could really use your advice about something. I'm sure you're busy, but do you have a second later?

She fell asleep and awoke to the edges of her window glowing. She checked the time—it was sunrise. She quickly navigated to her messages. No reply.

That evening, Stayja and Nicole went to Stayja's favorite library branch, where Nicole read *Cosmo* while Stayja stocked up on new books. She searched the poetry section for anything by someone with the last name Brand and found nothing, but she did find several volumes that looked interesting. She pulled a handful off the shelf and added them to her pile to check out.

As they passed LA's house to pull into their own driveway on the way home, Nicole noticed that he hadn't put out his trash. Pickup was Monday morning, and LA always pulled out his barrels on Sunday afternoons—they knew this because he usually did theirs as well.

"Oh, we need to bring the barrels down," Stayja said. "I'll get them."

"Where are LA's?" Nicole wondered aloud.

"He just hasn't done them yet," Stayja said, bracing herself for a guilt trip.

"Do you think he's okay?" Nicole said. "That's unlike him."

"I don't know, Nicole," she said with a sigh. "And I don't care."

JUST AFTER NINE, Stayja was reading a book of poems titled *Likenesses* by someone named P. K. Fox and came upon one called "Turns Out We Underestimate the Sun:"

Even these days people
measure up light
in candles.
Candela: noun—
how many candles
does it take to
light your office?
350.
Outdoors, say, noon?
A thousand.
Ten thousand?
Ha! One hundred
thirty thousand.
Turns out we underestimate
the sun.
It's our pupils that fool us,
blocking what's too bright
for our wide-eyed souls.

The final lines felt personal, like a dare. She sat contemplating them when Nicole burst into her room.

"He's not fine," Nicole said, pacing.

"Huh?" Stayja said, sitting up and setting her book on her bedside table.

"I went over to check on LA. He's lost his mind. He's got no food in his house. He hasn't showered. He smells like a toilet. He smashed his TV. I don't even know how you do that. The thing is shattered."

"Jesus," Stayja said.

"He broke everything in his house. He broke his dishes. He broke his *window*. There's a goddamn hole in his wall. He would have broken his furniture if he could, I'm sure."

Stayja rubbed her eyes.

"He must have had a complete freak-out." Nicole sat on Stayja's bed, took in a loud inhale, and let it out slowly. "What do we do?"

"What do you mean what do we do?"

"He doesn't have anyone but us."

"Yes, he does. Ronald."

Nicole glowered.

"You mean the guy who just fired him? No, Stayja, that doesn't count."

"I'm sure they're still friends. It wasn't Ronald's decision to fire him."

"That's right," Nicole said, standing. "It was yours."

"Stop guilting me!" Stayja said, pounding her hand on her bedside table. "He lost his own job! I'm so fucking sick of being blamed for other people's mistakes. I'm sick of being associated with any of this bullshit. This isn't my fault, none of it. Stop making stupid decisions and then blaming them on me. All of you."

"What do *I* have to do with this?" Nicole said, crossing her arms, daring Stayja to say aloud what she meant.

"You're flouncing around spending money left and right, when I'm dealing with this!"

Stayja opened the drawer to her bedside table and reached in to pull out the tax bill. But it wasn't there. She gaped, confused.

"Wait, where is it?" she mumbled.

"I took it," Nicole said.

"What?" Stayja said.

"I took it," Nicole said again. "Why didn't you tell me about it, anyway?"

"Why would I tell *you* about it? It's not like you could do anything to help me."

Nicole laughed.

"That's funny," she said, "because that's exactly what I did. I gave it to Chet. He got us on a payment plan. So, yeah, you're welcome. Merry early fucking Christmas."

Stayja stared at Nicole, frowning.

"Hi? I just said something really nice I did for you?" Nicole said.

"I don't want Chet to know my business," Stayja said. "I don't trust him."

"Oh, my God!" Nicole put her hands on her head and resumed pacing to the window and back. "Unreal. You tell me to take responsibility and then get mad when I do it."

"Snooping in my stuff isn't taking responsibility," said Stayja. "Neither is passing it off to your married boyfriend to deal with."

Nicole pushed her hair out of her face and bit her lip.

"Chet isn't handling it, Stayja. *I* am. He got us on a payment plan. I've already made the first payment."

When Stayja didn't respond, Nicole said, "You know what you are? A walking double standard."

"All right," Stayja said nastily. "How is that?"

"You've decided LA is not worth your time because you're better than him. But that guy Tyler? He gets a pass. He's not better than you. And you're not better than the rest of us." When Stayja still didn't react, Nicole said, "While you're dumping the fuck-ups, why not dump me, too?"

"You're family," Stayja said. "I can't."

Nicole's chin began to tremble.

"You know what? I think you're jealous. Chet has made me a better person. I'm thriving, and you can't handle that." She stormed out, leaving Stayja sitting in the dark. The sun had gone down during their argument.

It was all so pathetic, Stayja thought, turning on the lamp and signing into Instagram.

She needed to get out of Cartersboro. She was made for more than this, for something greater than this.

I can handle the brightness, she thought.

Annie

My home in Pineville was single story, and, as a kid, I assumed this was because we weren't as rich as some of my classmates. I filed our lack of a staircase alongside other disparities, like the sweaters others received for Christmas labeled J.Crew versus mine labeled Old Navy. We still lived in that same wood-paneled, three-bedroom ranch house—my brother and I got our own rooms and shared a bathroom. But it was bright. My mother's only stipulation in finding a home, she told me once, was that it be well lit.

"You know me, a sucker for sun," she would say.

When I arrived home for Thanksgiving, I hadn't spoken to Cory in almost two months, apart from occasional text conversations about trivial stuff—TV, the Carter football team, our mother's annoying habit of "cleaning up" by pouring out your drink to wash your glass before you were finished. Only two years apart in school, we had spent our entire lives together—carpooling to school, hanging out with each other's friends. It had been the longest we'd ever gone without talking. With all that had happened, I hadn't thought much about him.

I could tell by the way he said hi to me from the living room couch that he was angry.

"Hey," I said as my dad rolled my suitcase to my room and my mother went to the garage pantry to dig up some brownie mix.

"Hi," he said, not looking away from his video game.

"Sorry we haven't talked much," I said. "Things got really weird this fall."

"What happened, anyway?" he asked. "I know something happened. But Mom and Dad won't tell me. They've been acting so fucking weird."

Cory didn't normally use the F word. It was a new thing. I wondered if he was doing it to impress me or if he was just that upset.

Of all that had been difficult about the fall, this was the worst—telling my little brother.

"In September I had a date with this guy from school. And he turned out to be a pretty bad guy."

"How so?" he mumbled, and I could tell that he knew.

"You know how," I said.

He set his remote on the couch next to him and looked at me.

"I want to kill him," he said.

"Me too," I said, thinking of Loretta telling me not to pretend I wasn't full of rage. "But I'm okay. I promise."

"Fuck that guy," Cory said loudly as my mom appeared in the adjoining kitchen holding a box of Betty Crocker.

"Cory!" she said. "Watch your language!" But we could tell she didn't mean it.

OVER BREAK, CORY and I finished off an entire pumpkin pie while bingeing *Queer Eye*. On Black Friday, I went to Dance Fit Aerobics at church with my mom and tried not to smile as a gaggle of gray-haired women in wind suits gyrated to eighties pop. And though I almost skipped the reunion dinner that night at Corona's Mexican Grill with my high school friends, in the end I had gone and had

had a much better time than I'd expected. Although I suspected some of them had heard, no one brought up what had happened to me.

And there was the cotton-ball pillow fight. Whenever I returned home from college, even if only for a few days, I'd colonize the bathroom, populating every surface, just as I had in high school, with my makeup, hairbrush, hair dryer and wand, nail supplies, and skincare products. Cory, meanwhile, had now had the bathroom all to himself for the first time in his life.

On the Sunday morning I was to return to Carter, I was sleeping in when my bedroom door was flung open, light flooded my vision, and something delicate and soft began hitting my face.

"Get your cotton balls out of my bathroom!" he yelled, pegging me with round after round until I was awake and throwing pillows at his head. We fought until we were breathless, and I was tickling him until he begged me to stop, because even though he was bigger than me, he was also more ticklish.

It felt so good to laugh that hard that, taking a shower later that morning, I kept going.

BACK IN MY room at Carter that evening, I was unpacking when my phone buzzed.

Can I come by and say hi? wrote Henry.

Hey Henry, I wrote back. Sure!

I hurried to the bathroom, where I brushed my teeth and washed my face, then reapplied my makeup and gathered my hair into a bun that I made look properly messy with three bobby pins. When I turned the corner headed back to my room, he was already at my door. He must have been waiting outside my dorm when he texted.

"Hi. I read everything," he said.

The load that had lifted back at home swooped down, and it occurred to me, standing there, that perhaps I could transfer, too. I could transfer to somewhere where I wasn't known for this heinous thing. Regardless of what Henry had to say about the fall, I could leave all of this, including him, behind. Start over, maybe in Indiana. Indiana sounded like a place with nice people.

"I wanted to say that you're the bravest person I know," he said. "But more important, I'm so good at the bassoon now. You will not even believe how good I am."

WITH EACH DAY, Henry made me feel more and more as if it was all going to be okay. Together, he and I were drawn to activities to which, pre-Henry, I'd have turned up my nose: putt-putt, a video arcade, the latest animated Pixar movie in 3-D. We did silly things, things that made me feel like a kid again. We drank a beer or two on occasion, but mostly our fun wasn't centered on alcohol, not in the conscious way it was by default for many people at college. But nor was our time spent moping in reaction to that social scene, the way Matty and Samantha and I had been our first year.

One afternoon, I was shelving new inventory at the bookstore when I received a text flagged "Urgent" from Matty (the only person I knew who ever actually used that function, which seemed superfluous, given that we all lived on our phones and responded to all texts immediately). His text was in all caps: CHECK INSTAGRAM NOW: ERIKA DIPATRI. He'd attached a screenshot of an Instagram post. Erika Dipatri, a student at the University of Arkansas, had posted a text image in loopy cursive—"Believe Survivors." The caption read:

Over fall break, while in St. John with my a cappella group, I was raped by someone I'd just met. He was there with a group of guys from Carter. I was very drunk so I don't remember his name, but he had this tattoo of different size squares. It took me weeks to share what happened, and when I did, fortunately I was believed. Many aren't. #believesurvivors #thesquaresIllneverforget #metoo

"WE OBVIOUSLY CAN'T make him show us his torso," Dean Sharon said.

"You don't have to make him. I'm telling you that he has it." Dean Sharon studied me sadly. I sat across from her in her office, holding my phone, the screenshot pulled up.

"Even if it's true," she said, "even if she was writing about him, it didn't happen here."

When I didn't respond, she said, "Listen Annie, I know you have reasons to be sympathetic to this woman's situation, but why are you here? What do you want to have come out of this meeting?"

She wasn't going to help me. She did not actually care if Tyler was raping people. Earlier in the fall I'd realized it, but in the interim I'd forgotten. I'd convinced myself that my expectations for a different outcome based on my word alone were unreasonable.

"I don't know why a known rapist gets to remain on campus," I said.

Dean Sharon stood and went to the window overlooking the quad. Peering out, she said, "People are fighting all kinds of battles on this campus, stuff you can't imagine." She turned back to me. "Do you know that there are students here who have no family? No one to go to when something happens to them. No one to visit during breaks. Then there are students who don't go home during breaks because it's not safe to be there. There are students who are completely alone in the world and students who have made it into this university in spite of all the odds stacked against them, and I don't just mean poverty. I mean no support system or luck or easy breaks. I mean fighting their way through schools without enough teachers to staff the classes, with addicts as parents, with siblings who raised them. You don't often hear from these students, but they're here. They're in Wiggins Library till three in the morning."

She came over and took a seat next to me in the other chair facing her desk, as she had the time before. Our knees touched.

"I am not playing down your situation. I get it. It's *shitty*." She said "shitty" as if it were the first time she'd ever uttered the word. "But you know what? The world is shitty. Do I wish we were better at preparing our students to enter it? I truly do.

"I wish I had better advice for you. But this is not the hill for you to die on, Annie. You are bigger than this. Your life is bigger than this. This is one sad, messed-up rich kid out of a hundred sad, messed-up rich kids. They don't know what they're doing, because they have never had to take responsibility for anything. And then they come here, and they have freedom and alcohol and dangerous ideas that they've absorbed from culture, the Internet, poor role models—and they do a bad thing. Or bad things.

"Say they get kicked out of Carter. What does that do? I'll tell you what it does. They go to the University of Mississippi, and they're the same person. They go to UNC, and they're the same person. Where was she a student again?"

"Arkansas," I said.

"They go there." She paused. "You must learn this sooner or later, so you might as well now. Some people aren't good. They won't ever be. The best thing you can do is learn to recognize them and do your damnedest to stay away."

"I'm not saying expel everyone who does something wrong," I said. "I'm saying expel the rapists."

She stood again, drifting back to the window. "Expulsion," she said, facing the quad, "isn't always an option. Not when people have paid exorbitant amounts of money to the university." She turned back to me. "I'm being very frank with you here, Annie, because I think you deserve honesty, and I don't want to patronize you by giving you any less."

"Do those people include women? Because we pay tuition, too," I said, wondering what my etiquette-conscious, southern mother would make of my insubordinate tone. Normally she'd not have approved, but maybe in this situation.

A look I couldn't identify crept across her face.

"You don't pay tuition," she said.

But we did—we paid a quarter of it. By that point my dad had spent over seventy weekends hunched over a Kaplan SAT tome at Starbucks, toiling the weekends of his life away with someone else's kids, not me or Cory, helping *them* get into college so that I could afford to go here.

I didn't bother telling her this.

I left Dean Sharon's office and headed back to my dorm, a fresh, simmering layer of outrage rising up within me. The temperature was dropping rapidly, and I hadn't worn a jacket. As I walked, shivering, it suddenly occurred to me what I'd been doing wrong.

I'd been trying to fight through the university, when I could simply go around it.

In which I not so humbly celebrate/reveal my identity

by the Irreverent Rooster

C.O.C.A![a] H.Y.H.Y![b] C.U.N.T.[c] has won the southeast regional improv championship!

What does that mean?

Your SAT reading comprehension skills are not required here. This means exactly what it sounds like: the roosters are the baddest, cleverest, funniest improv team in the region. A whole chunk of the country. Dozens of schools. Hundreds of improvisers. Millions of awkward hookups. Whatever. It's math.

Listen, I can say this without worry that I'm bragging, because I'm not one of them.[d]

I might be one of them.

Are you really that surprised?

Please imagine me clutching a metallic elfin statuette and weeping.

1. First, I'd like to thank Chris, our tireless leader, whose devotion to the team is astonishing and sometimes concerning. We will miss you next year.
2. Correct, I'm not a fourth-year.
3. If you're prelaw and actually care about my identity, this has just become a great LSAT warm-up. Grab a pencil!
4. Second, I'd like to thank you, readers, fellow students, for showing up to our shows night after night and laughing your faces off. Might I call you—this is going to be cheesy—our thirteenth member?

5. Awwwwwwww / what is happening?
6. Third, and finally, because rule-of-threes, I'd like to thank the Brand family, the alumni association, and the Carter Construction Committee[e] for continuing to provide endless delight and material with that one horrendous decision you made to adorn the new dorm with those god-awful Brandgoyles. Gargands. Bragoyles. First-year Bea Powers's monologue on the story, which set up our show, is 100 percent why we won.

Alas, exams start next week, which means this is my last column of the semester. I know. It's okay. You'll have the comfort puppies they bring into Wiggins Library from the puppy mill to make you feel happier while also guilty at your joy.

It's been fun, y'all.

xo—

L.E.S.L.E.Y.[f]

Glossary

a. C.O.C.A.: Obv come one, come all.
b. H.Y.H.Y.: Hear ye, hear ye.
c. C.U.N.T.: In case you don't live on this planet, our acronym-obsessed improvisers.
d. I'm not one of them: This is a lie.
e. Carter Construction Committee: I made this up but it's got to be close. Whoever builds stuff around here.
f. L.E.S.L.E.Y.—Wasn't quite ready to let go of the joke.

Bea

You tell yourself something isn't true, and then it happens to you.

There had been moments—quick flashes—when Bea had wondered if what Early had said about Dr. Friedman was true, if he was interested in college girls. At times she'd asked herself if it was why he had been so supportive of her from the beginning. But he never acted inappropriately, and eventually she'd stopped wondering. She was often in his hotel room with him, and nothing had ever gotten weird.

Then, one week before regionals, she was doing laundry when he called.

"Come to San Diego with me next weekend," he said as she folded her towel in thirds, the way her mother had taught her (because "everyone needs to be able to properly fold a bath towel"). The offer was casual, as if they were buddies on a road trip and he was suggesting a slightly ludicrous but not dangerous detour to see some special sight. He spoke as if he was confident she'd accept, as if there was no question. "There's a conference on sexual misconduct and Title IX that I think you'll find fascinating, given your recent work."

She set the towel down on her bed, unable to speak. Was he hitting on her? Or just inviting her to a conference?

"And my favorite restaurant in the world is there. It has amazing views of the water."

"I can't," she said rapidly. "I have an improv show." Because she didn't want to hurt his feelings or seem ungrateful by implying it was just *any* show, she added, "Regionals. In Virginia. I can't miss that."

"That's too bad," he said, professional and upbeat. "Well, good luck in the show. I'll let you know how the conference goes."

As she pulled the warm sheet over the corners of her mattress, she fluctuated between horror, confusion, and disbelief. Had he been hitting on her, or had he just wanted her to experience the conference? He'd mentioned her work, but then he'd also mentioned his favorite restaurant.

Should she go? Where would she stay? Certainly he hadn't expected she'd stay with him. Anyway, she couldn't miss regionals. She pushed it from her mind as she put away her clothes.

THE UVA AUDITORIUM was twice as large as the one at Carter.

"How many people do you think this place seats?" Bea said to Lesley during sound check, her voice sounding small and childlike in the vast space, the rows upon rows of empty, maroon chairs. "A thousand?"

"Fifteen hundred?" Lesley said.

At Carter, they performed for packed rooms of two hundred, maybe three hundred at the most, and those crowds felt enormous.

Three hours later, they stood in the wings, the fourth team of nine to perform. They had watched none of the first three groups, abiding by Chris's philosophy that to do so was bad luck. Good improv was fearless and playful, not competitive, and so they spent the first part of the show warming up backstage, goofing off, and generally stirring up their pool of collective effervescence in the hope that it would erupt at just the right moment.

When they received the five-minute warning, they circled up and placed their hands in the center, pin-wheel style. "C! U! N! T!" they chanted before jogging to the wings, which Sam—know-it-all Sam—unintentionally referred to as the "sidelines," inspiring a giggling frenzy. The UVA third-year manning the curtain had to shush them.

Then they were being introduced, and the light was blinding, and Chris was asking the audience for a favorite adjective. The students shouted words and more words, and then Chris was saying "bonkers." He swiveled to face the team and mouthed it again, making eye contact with Bea: *bonkers.*

Bea made her way to the front of the stage and stood at the mic that had been placed onstage temporarily for the monologist; tiny mics hanging from the ceiling would amplify the remainder of their Harold.

"So this crazy thing happened this fall at my school," she began, "involving some very rich donors and some gargoyles."

An hour later, they were going to nationals in January.

IN THE MEANTIME, there was school to finish. Back at Carter, Bea suffered through her three-hour physics exam and cringed only a little at the *D*-exam grade that arrived in her in-box two days later. She tried to focus on preparing for her other classes' final assessments: an exam and two papers. When yet another note arrived from Dr. Toast, asking her to swing by his office, she figured it had something to do with selecting courses for spring semester.

She stopped by his office on her way to meet Early at the gym and found him seated just like the last time she'd seen him, in the same glasses, with the same expression, possibly wearing the same clothes.

"Have a seat," he said and began chomping on a thumbnail. "It has been brought to my attention that you have made a D in your physics class. Is that correct?"

"Yeah," she said, sighing. "Unfortunately." So he was going to scold her? Since when did that happen? She thought college was about making mistakes and no one stopping you.

"Well, yes, it is. But I have some good news for you. The academic advising office has determined that you may retake Physics during the January term and as long as you make a C or higher, you can keep your scholarship and remain in the Justice program in the spring."

She blinked, confused.

"You realize you are in violation of the terms of your scholarship, correct?" he said.

"I thought I just had to maintain over a 3.0."

He reached for his computer monitor and pivoted it to face her. On the screen were several open windows. He hovered the cursor over one of them containing a block of fine text.

"A 3.0 *and* no individual course grade lower than a C."

She couldn't take physics in the January term. Nationals were in January—in Portland. And three days long. Plus travel days.

"Do you have the schedule?" she asked.

He happily handed her a sheet. "Already printed it for you. It's important to note that for all January term courses, perfect attendance is mandatory owing to their abbreviated nature. If you miss a class, you'll fall behind and will struggle to catch up. Obviously that's especially true for a course like physics, with a lab."

She scanned the course meeting dates. Five days a week: four hours on Monday, Wednesday, and Friday and seven hours Tuesday and Thursday. This included the week of nationals—in fact, the final exam was on the last day of the competition.

"I can't do this," she said, pushing the sheet toward him on his desk. "I have a conflict."

He appeared unable to process what she'd just said.

"I mean, you can't expect me to just be able to drop everything to do this, right?" she said. "On such short notice?" He continued to look at her blankly. She changed tactics. "Since when is it the policy that I can't make below a C? I only remember a 3.0."

He pointed to the monitor. "It's right—"

"No, I know it's right there, but I didn't *know* about it. Can't I take physics in the spring? I'll take it in the spring. I don't care. I just can't take it in the winter."

"I was not told that is an option."

"Why not?"

"I imagine because your scholarship funds for a full spring course load are dependent on whether you . . ."

"I don't need the scholarship. I don't care about the scholarship."

He looked rattled. "Well, it's not just the scholarship. It's also your status in the program."

She groaned. "But I didn't know."

"I suppose if you'd been able to make it to your midsemester check-ins we'd have had an opportunity to remind you of the policy." She tried not to roll her eyes, suspecting he felt pleased with himself for having worked in this small jab. "So should I enroll you for winter term physics or not?"

"Go ahead," she said, standing. She'd handle it on her own.

ARE YOU IN town yet? Can you talk?

Her text to Dr. Friedman was insistent, urgent, but she didn't care. It was urgent.

She paced back and forth in front of the academic advising building, delaying heading back to South Campus in case he was able to meet. It was Thursday, and she was pretty certain he usually landed by early afternoon.

Sure enough, within minutes he'd texted back.

Come on by. Room 209. Let yourself in.

As she huffed as fast as she could through the cold to the Carter Boathouse, her breath clouding before her, she found that she'd already begun to feel better. Dr. Friedman would take care of it. He was capable, he was powerful, and he'd been her cheerleader. It was as good as fixed.

She hurried into the hotel and took the elevator to the second floor. The door to Room 209 was cracked, held open by the metal security lock peeking through it.

She shoved the door open gently. "Hello?"

"Come in!" said a female voice. Veronique appeared, walking toward her, pulling the door open with the welcoming smile of a much older adult greeting Bea at a cocktail party at her home. "Lou is in the shower." Veronique went to the bar on which sat a six-pack of Perrier and a bowl of pita chips. She took a Perrier and held it out to Bea.

"I'm okay," Bea said as Veronique opened one for herself.

The *shower*?

After Dr. Friedman had issued his invitation to San Diego, Bea had decided that she'd read into it. That it had been innocuous. He'd just thought she'd enjoy the conference. Yes, he'd made the weird remark about his favorite restaurant and its view, but he did appreciate fine dining and ate well with his male students, too. But here was Veronique playing hostess in his hotel room while he took a shower, and now she was confused again.

Veronique plopped onto the suite's gold embroidered couch as Bea took the matching armchair.

"How was your play?" Veronique asked. It took Bea a moment to realize she meant improv.

"Good," she said. "We won. It was a competition, so . . ."

Veronique was nodding before Bea finished speaking.

"Cool, cool. The conference in San Diego was *incredible*. I wish you could have gone."

"Oh, you went?" Bea said, suddenly on alert.

"Mm hmm," Veronique said. "The work people are doing to bring due process protections into the Title IX aggrievement processes is so inspiring."

"Great," Bea said as a flush sounded from the bathroom.

"Like what?" Bea asked. How was she going to get Veronique out of the room? And why wasn't she making a move to leave on her own? If Veronique had shown up to a meeting with Dr. Friedman and Bea had been there, she certainly wouldn't assume she got to stay. That would be weird. As her classmate went on and on about the people she heard speak in California, Bea decided she would just have to ask her to leave. She certainly wasn't comfortable broaching the subject of her physics grade in front of another student in the program.

But then Veronique said, "I hope you're not upset about it."

"About the conference?" Bea said. "He asked me to go. I couldn't." She heard how petty it sounded, but she couldn't resist.

"No, the CJRI."

"What about it?" Bea asked, her breath catching in her chest. Surely Veronique didn't mean what Bea thought she meant. The water in the bathroom stopped.

"I just know that you also applied for the fellowship. Lou told me. He said it was a really difficult decision, actually. But I know you'll find something great. There are so many internships on publicinterestjobs.net. My roommate told me about . . ."

Bea had turned and was looking just past the entrance to the bedroom, where a bright orange suitcase lay open on the luggage rack. A pink makeup bag stained in tawny smears was splayed open. Glittery bronzer and a mascara-caked eyelash curler. A lacy garment that looked like a top of some sort.

She felt queasy.

"What's wrong?" Veronique asked, watching Bea realize whom the suitcase belonged to.

"I have to go," she said.

EVERYTHING, ALL OF their interactions—the hand on her back, the casual remarks about her intelligence and her potential, the mention of late summer nights at the office—all of it seemed menacing now.

Bea hurried back to South Campus and to her room, where she found Early in bow pose. When she saw Bea's face, she let go of her leg.

"What's wrong?" Early asked.

Bea filled her roommate in on everything. The physics grade and not being able to go to nationals. Veronique and her weird comments. The suitcase.

When she was nearly finished describing the contents of the suitcase, her phone started to rattle on her bed.

"He's calling," Bea said, looking down at it.

They both stared at the device until his name disappeared and "Missed Call" appeared on the screen, followed by "New voicemail."

Without saying anything, Bea pressed "Listen" and then "Speaker." She placed the phone between them on the rug.

"Bea." His voice was stricken—or performing stricken. She didn't know what was real anymore. "Listen, Veronique told me you're upset, and I understand. I didn't want you to get the news that way. I'd hoped to tell you myself. I'm sorry. But now that you know . . . It was only partially my choice. A whole committee of us decided. They were deciding between you and Veronique and wanted my opinion. Frankly, she'd made time to go to that conference this weekend. Not that there is anything wrong with you prioritizing your theater group"—*Improv*, she thought—" but I had to make a decision. And the fact that you had a competing obligation was the only way I could really rule out one of you. Was that fair? Maybe not, but we make the best decisions we can under the circumstances."

As he rattled on about how human beings can never know if their decisions are the right ones or wrong ones, she felt disgust swell in her gut. What had formerly dazzled her—his skilled arguing, his equivocating to dissipate tension, his mastery at sucking the life out of blame—these no longer charmed her. They felt toxic. They felt like lies. And she felt stupid.

Bea picked up her hefty physics book and threw it against the wall with all her might.

Early grabbed Bea's phone and pressed stop on the voicemail, halting Dr. Friedman midsentence.

"I feel crazy," Bea said.

"You're not," Early said, her eyes steely. "I promise."

Stayja

LATE NOVEMBER—EARLY DECEMBER

The week after Thanksgiving, Nicole and Stayja avoided each other as best they could. Both went straight to their own houses whenever they were home and were icy to each other when their paths did cross. The comment Nicole had made during their argument that had lingered, haunting her, was the suggestion that she was somehow *jealous* of Nicole and Chet. It was laughable. Stayja jealous of Nicole? If anything, Nicole had been jealous of Stayja their entire lives.

Nicole had also stopped swinging by to pick up the keys at the end of her bookstore shift at seven. *Good*, Stayja thought, *let her take the bus home or find another ride.*

One evening Stayja was having a cigarette during her break and saw LA's car idling near the student center. A few minutes later, Nicole climbed in, and they drove away.

Of course she's using LA as her chauffeur, Stayja thought. With Nicole there was always something in it for her. Behind seemingly generous acts was an angle, a potential gain she had her eye on. What that self-interest was when it came to the tax bill, Stayja wasn't sure. Maybe it was a move to get Stayja to like Chet more. She knew Nicole was looking for Stayja's approval of her relationship for some reason; that's why the two of them were always inviting Stayja along to things: dinner, games, shopping. (She'd never said yes to anything with the two of them and didn't plan to.)

That Nicole had actually taken on Stayja's tax bill was not something she ever would have seen coming. Stayja assumed that was no longer happening, given their fight. Even if they hadn't fought, Stayja was sure that at some point, whenever Nicole got bored or distracted or wanted a new pair of shoes or managed to get fired again, she'd stop making payments, leaving Stayja to deal with the fallout.

One morning in early December, she got a low balance alert on her checking account, and it pushed her growing anxiety about her debt over the edge. She googled the number for the IRS and called it. She was redirected several times to the proper department, then placed on hold. She sat there listening to light jazz for an hour when, finally, a human voice spoke.

"Internal Revenue Service. This is Fred."

Stayja closed her book and cleared her throat.

"I'm Stayja York. I'm currently on a payment plan for back taxes and just wanted to make sure my most recent payment went through."

"Hold, please," he said. The hold music resumed.

She set aside the British mystery she'd started and grabbed one of the poetry books she'd checked out but hadn't read yet, a collection by Jane Kenyon. She read a poem titled *The Suitor*. One line that caught her eye: *Suddenly I understand that I am happy.*

Had she ever been happy? In flashes, sure. Would it ever be more than that?

She sighed and reopened the novel. She'd started right after placing the phone call and was already sixty pages in. Outside, a door slammed in the direction of LA's house.

Stayja stood and went to the window. There were Nicole and LA, marching across his front yard, both crouched under heavy black trash bags. Nicole was in the lead with a bag slung over each shoulder. She made her way to the curb and dropped them, then turned as Stayja jumped away from the window.

Nicole, doing manual labor? Taking out LA's *trash*?

"Ms. York?"

"Yes," Stayja said.

"Your account is up to date. Your most recent payment of $198.23 was made yesterday and processed this morning at start of business."

"Thank you," she said. After she hung up, she slowly leaned forward to peer through the window again, but Nicole and LA were gone.

THE LAST WEEK of classes before finals each semester was always unpredictable—no one was on their regular schedule, everyone was frantic, and caffeine became a necessity at strange hours of the day. Stayja didn't find a moment to pause and catch her breath all afternoon, but by five, the onslaught had trickled down to nothing, and all was calm.

Alone in the café, she navigated to the Wake Community College registration page on her phone and logged in, then clicked on Spring Course Registration. If Nicole was seriously going to keep covering the IRS payments for the time being, Stayja might as well get back on her school schedule.

"Excuse me?" a voice said. She hadn't heard anyone come in.

Stayja looked up. Standing in front of her was Annie Stoddard.

"Hi," Annie said in a way that made Stayja want to run—as if she weren't just there to get a coffee.

"Hi," Stayja said, aware her tone wasn't neutral either.

"Would you mind chatting with me for a minute about something? Privately?"

Stayja scrambled for an excuse but couldn't come up with anything. The café remained empty apart from the two of them. There wasn't a person in sight. Fuck.

"I can't really step away," Stayja said.

Annie looked around and, turning back to Stayja, seemed to decide that the empty coffee shop was private enough.

"I know you also have a history with Tyler," she said. "I work with your cousin in the bookstore."

"I know you do," Stayja said. "What about it?"

"I just saw this today." Annie held out her phone. "A student at the University of Arkansas posted it." Stayja didn't move. She looked at the phone, then back up at Annie.

"What are you talking about?" Stayja said.

Withdrawing her arm, Annie suddenly appeared more nervous.

"I was thinking, maybe we could write a letter to the campus paper that we all sign or something. The three of us. I'm sure there are more."

"What are you talking about?" Stayja said again.

"Never mind," Annie said. "Nice to meet you." She turned and hurried back into the student center, walking all the way down the corridor and through the distant exit as Stayja watched.

So Annie Stoddard thought Stayja had been raped by Tyler. And she wanted her help in outing him.

What the fuck?

Fucking Nicole. This random girl was under the impression that Stayja was some kind of *victim*.

She needed to tell Tyler what was going on.

Stayja opened their text history. There, most recently, was the last one she'd sent from three weeks ago. It dangled at the bottom, unanswered:

I could really use your advice about something. I'm sure you're busy, but do you have a second later?

It had been hard enough to work up the courage to text him when she wanted to know what he thought she should do about the tax bill. The reminder that he'd never responded stung all over again.

Can u talk? she wrote. It's important. She hit SEND and waited.

AN HOUR PASSED with no word back.

As she stocked the dinner plates and ordered a fresh delivery of pastries for the morning, a new worry entered her mind—once she told him about Annie's plan, what could he do about it? Merely having a heads-up that she planned to sabotage his reputation wouldn't empower him to prevent it from happening. Annie didn't seem like someone who was going to respond well to threats. If anything, she could use something like that as ammo against him. But maybe there was a way that Stayja could help.

She grabbed her phone and opened her photos app. She scrolled back to the selfies he'd taken of himself a few weeks earlier—the ones she'd viewed a hundred-plus times—at work, at home, in the car, late at night. She picked her favorite, a shot of him topless, grinning, giving the camera a thumbs-up. She brightened it with a filter and uploaded it to Instagram, then tagged him and dashed off a caption:

This guy is one of a kind. A wonderful soul. His love for the world is contagious.

Then she posted it.

Now there was a story to counter whatever story Annie was about to broadcast to the world. And maybe it would bring him back to her.

Annie

Walking across the quad back to my room, bracing myself against the wind, I felt embarrassed, as if I'd just exposed a blind spot of my own in approaching that girl. Who was I to think she could get anything out of coming out publicly against Tyler Brand? She was probably terrified of him and his family. *I* was afraid of them, and I was a student, not a barista.

Back in my room, I took off my jacket, grabbed my computer, and fell down the rabbit hole of Erika Dipatri's social media. Between Instagram, Google, and Facebook—I couldn't find her on Snapchat—there were dozens of photos of her in bikinis, taking shots, and wearing halter tops on poorly lit dance floors. Since I'd been attacked for wearing a miniskirt one time, I expected this girl to have been engulfed by trolls, but when I looked back at her post, I found only positive comments. Maybe she was deleting the negative ones? I found myself jealous of the pure support in her feed, then ashamed of my jealousy.

It had been hours, and she still hadn't responded to the message I'd sent her.

After I'd exhausted Erika Dipatri's corner of the Internet, I searched for "Stasia." Despite my misspelling, she was easy enough to find, since I followed Nicole. *Stayja* had only ever posted three photos, the most recent of which was from two years earlier, of a sunset.

I looked around my room. I didn't know what to do with myself. A bad storm was rolling in—we kept receiving weather alerts about it. Matty was in his statistics final. Between the storm and exams, it seemed everyone had disappeared. The campus had the feeling of being shut down, and I felt smothered by the quiet.

I went to my bed, picked up my pillow, and buried my face in it. I screamed into it.

I put the pillow back on the bed, went to the mini fridge, got out a can of beer that had been in there forever, and took a sip.

I wanted to break something.

Maybe I should go exercise. Go to the gym, get on the elliptical or something.

"No!" I yelled, startling myself. *No!* I was sick of being responsible, sick of handling things well, of being mature and good and cooperative and understanding and compliant.

I threw the nearly full can of beer into my small metal trash can. It fizzed and sloshed and filled the room with its thick man smell. I grabbed a notebook and pen.

I'd tried it all: to move on, to accept that I'd never move on, to feel my feelings, to save others. Now that I'd passed through these stages, I found that on the other side of them there was only one thing left, a new desire: I wanted vengeance.

I wanted to hurt him in a way from which he would never recover. I wanted to scar him.

Seated on my bed, I started a list.

call/email law school admissions offices to ruin his prospects
    for next year
ruin all of his jobs forever by always calling/emailing
paint bridge again

The first idea wasn't scarring enough, the second required too much work over too long a period of time, and the third was too easily reversed. Plus, it had been done.

burn something

Yes. In fire there was permanence. But what? He'd actually *told* me that he didn't care about his stuff all that much. What was his phrasing? "Everything is replaceable." I'd died a little when he'd said that was why he left his door unlocked, and now I remembered how glad I'd been in that moment that Matty wasn't around to hear it. He'd never have stopped making fun of Tyler.

Then he'd shown me the one exception to his indifference. The dancers. His watercolors.

His paintings were irreplaceable, he'd said.

THE SKY WAS undulating yellow and gray as I made my way across the empty expanse of grass in my rain boots, armed with an umbrella and my waterproof jacket.

It was six o'clock, dinnertime, which I hoped meant he'd be out or leaving his room soon. If so, I'd go in and take the portfolio and then find a place to burn it that wouldn't draw attention, maybe one of the lots near the soccer fields that were usually empty or behind a dumpster somewhere. I just had to beat the rain.

I passed the entrance to his dorm and made my way around the corner of the building to the side where his window was last in the row of windows, the most distant on the first floor. If it was dark, I would go in.

It was glowing. Dammit.

But he would have to leave eventually.

I found a spot in a stairwell at ATO, the frat housed in the adjacent building. Being in an isolated spot in frat territory sparked a flicker of fear, but I sat down anyway. Everyone was hunkered down inside their dorms and would be until the storm passed. I was prepared to wait as long as it took.

Bea

MONDAY, DECEMBER 11
5:54 P.M.

Pull. Pull. Pull.

After leaving Veronique in Dr. Friedman's hotel room, Bea had gone straight to her room, where she'd changed and headed to the gym. She needed to sweat and not just a light jogging kind of sweat.

As she rowed, she thought about Dr. Friedman. He was gross. And disappointing. And maybe, all those times he'd complimented her, he'd only wanted to sleep with her.

She fumed, yanking at the arms of the machine. She loathed him.

After a half hour on the rower, her purple top soaked through, it occurred to Bea that while she loathed him personally, she still respected him professionally. Still furious, she almost chuckled. Conflicting ideas—what he'd taught her.

She wasn't going to miss nationals. If it meant she failed physics and got kicked out of the program, so be it. Maybe she didn't care.

But she did care. She wanted to remain in the program, very much so.

She climbed off the machine, wiped it down with the wipes from a small canister on the wall, and walked out into the cold sunlight, racking her brain for how she could somehow circumvent this ridiculous requirement that she retake physics before spring semester. She wasn't going to ask Dr. Friedman, of course—not now.

And then—she passed the gargoyles.

IT WAS A long shot. Tyler would have to agree to call his parents, who she knew terrified him. He'd have to ask them to do a favor on her behalf, someone whom they didn't know, someone whom *he* hardly knew. She hadn't spoken to him since his case was decided, but she knew he'd found her work helpful. Dr. Friedman had told her that he'd told his parents so.

She hadn't spent twelve years at elite schools without picking up on the power of money to make problems go away. From peers who got time and a half on exams, to the senator's daughter who never came to class and somehow was inducted into the Cum Laude Society for academic achievement, to Lorn's public drunkenness charge's disappearance from her record, Bea suspected that if anyone could pull a move to get an exception made to a policy—a very *minor* exception at that, for one otherwise above-average student—it was the Brand family.

SHE DECIDED THAT, rather than texting or emailing, she'd stop by to see if he was in his room. She told herself it was because she was close to his dorm, but in truth she didn't want to give him any opportunity to turn down or ignore her request.

The sky had blackened, and a carpet of clouds stirred ominously as she hurried from the gym to his building, damp in her workout sweats under her jacket. She made her way down the hallway, where she found his door ajar. She tapped and lightly pushed it.

He sat at his desk, his laptop open in front of a larger monitor. His eyes were threaded red, bloodshot.

"Look who it is," he said, venom in his voice.

"Hi," she said, hiding her alarm at his tone. "Sorry to just show up unannounced. I came to ask you a favor."

He sneered. She kept going anyway. Standing in the middle of the room in her workout clothes, she made her plea.

"Basically, I'm failing physics. Which . . . I don't care about. But what I do care about is that it means I'll lose my scholarship and my spot in the Justice program unless I retake physics. They're trying to tell me I have to retake it over winter session, but if I do that, then there's no way I can make it to the national improv championship in Portland at the end of January."

He'd become distracted, bending over to search the floor around his desk for something.

"I was thinking maybe you could ask your parents to make a call. Like, pull strings. It's a really small ask. I'll take physics in the spring. I don't care. I just can't take it this winter."

It had made so much sense in her head, but now that she was saying it aloud, it sounded foolish.

"Fucking unbelievable," he muttered. He'd stood and gone to his mini fridge. He opened and shut it.

"Would you please just do me this one favor?" she said with a sigh. "I helped you with your case, and I would really appreciate it if you helped me now."

"Why would my parents do anything for you when you embarrassed them publicly? Then your friend wrote about it?"

She didn't follow.

"There." He pointed to his coffee table, where a copy of the *Chronicle* lay. She'd stopped reading the paper after the series of op-eds on Tyler and his case had unnerved her. It was open to a column about her team. She picked it up and read as he watched her intently from his chair. It was silly, just as her monologue had been. She laughed.

"Oh, please. We weren't making fun of your family, and neither is Lesley. Everyone's just making fun of the school."

His face had grown vacant, as if he'd forgotten what they were discussing. He stood, stumbled to his closet door, reached into the pocket of a Carter jacket hanging there, and pulled out a set of keys.

"You're not going to drive, are you?"

"Yes, ma'am."

"You're drunk."

"I'm also out of booze."

"Give me the keys. I'll take you to the liquor store."

She stepped into his path, blocking the door. He squinted at her, amused, swaying. Then he held the keys in front of his face and dropped them. She lunged forward to catch them. He didn't move.

"You are so dumb," he said. "You have no idea."

For a long moment, they stared at each other. Then he said, "You think it's a coincidence that suddenly you can't go to nationals after you humiliate me and my family?"

"What?" Bea said. What was he talking about?

"It's not," he said with a smirk, enjoying her confusion.

But that didn't make any sense. She saw the grades policy, and she'd violated it. It wasn't as if the policy had changed overnight suddenly just to punish her.

"My physics grade is too low. That's my own fault," she said.

"But no one cared about it until today, did they? And do you know why that is?" He leaned in close, his hot, boozy breath in her face. "Because I *already* made a call. To my mom. Who called . . . that dude. The program dude."

"Dr. Friedman?"

"Whoever. She told him to shut you the fuck up." He stumbled over to the coffee table and sat on it. "Don't make fun of us," he mumbled again.

"Why would Dr. Friedman listen to your mother?" Bea asked, still clutching his keys.

He let out a drunken cackle. "Who do you think funds your program?" He was yelling now, leaning forward onto his knees, heckling her. "Not you! You don't fund your program, do you? You fucked with the wrong people, dude. People like you are only here because people like us *allow* it."

"People like me," she said, daring him. "Meaning what?"

"You know what I mean," he said, not backing down. "*Like. You.*" Then he swayed forward and caught himself. He sat up and rubbed his eyes, like a baby or a cartoon. When he brought them down, the whites were even redder than before. "My family doesn't pull strings. We are the strings."

She stood frozen as Tyler studied her.

"You're sad because you don't have a family," Tyler said, his tone suddenly softer. "I'm sad, too. I'm sad I'll never be good enough for mine." His eyes had grown vacant, and his gaze rested on the middle distance between them, on nothing. He sounded almost tender when he said, "You're not funnier than me. You're not better than me. We're the same."

Bea dropped his keys on the coffee table, and he flinched as they landed with a crack.

She walked out, her rage trailing behind her.

SHE PUSHED OPEN the door to find that the rain was coming down now in thick sheets. She pulled up the hood of her light wool coat and charged through it, not caring that she was getting soaked. She made her way past Tyler's dorm building, which seemed to go on forever, then darted into a covered stairwell to button up her coat.

"Hi."

She turned to see Annie Stoddard sitting on the steps.

"Hi," Bea said. She shook the water off her arms and took a seat next to Annie.

"This is gross," Annie said.

"Nasty," Bea said.

"I'm Annie," Annie said.

"I know," Bea said. "I'm Bea."

"You know because I'm rape famous?" Annie asked. Bea turned to see that she was smiling a little.

"Ha," Bea said. "No, because we were in abnormal psych together this semester."

"Ah," Annie said, looking ahead into the dark rain.

After a moment, Bea said, "Actually, that's not true. I was Tyler's student advocate."

"Oh," Annie said quietly.

"I told him to say that stuff about you. About your legs. And what you were wearing. And wanting his money."

Annie was staring at her rubber boots, picking at a loose strip of rubber along the edge of one of them.

"I'm really sorry," Bea said.

Annie turned to Bea. But before she could say anything, they heard the sound of a car trying to stop.

Stayja

Again, Stayja looked down at her phone. Still nothing. It was past six, when she usually took her evening break, but she'd been waiting to take it in case he wrote back and she could dash over to talk to him.

Maybe she just hadn't gotten an alert.

She opened the text thread again and reread her last two messages.

Oh no, she thought. How had she missed it before? Back to back like that, her texts made it seem like *she* needed help. "Fuck it," she said under her breath.

She had preferred to tell him about Annie's plan face to face, but she'd just do it over text.

-I just got approached by Annie. She is trying to out you in the newspaper. She is looking for other girls to sign her letter. I thought you'd want to know.

-What?? How do you know this?

-She came to the rooster to talk to me

-Why?

-I don't know.

-You don't know why your friend calls me a rapist on the

bridge. You don't know why Annie tries to get you to call me a
rapist in the paper. What aren't you telling me Stasia?
-It's Stayja.
-What are you after? Just fucking say it.
-I'm not after anything. I'm telling you what happened! That's
what I'm doing! Are you in your room? I'm coming over.

She took his lack of response as a yes. She grabbed her jacket and
rushed out the door. It was just beginning to sprinkle, but the wind
was already ferocious, ripping leaves from the trees and spiraling them
through the air. She pulled up the zipper as she jogged to his dorm.

She'd hoped someone would be at the door to let her in, but
there wasn't anybody in sight. She huddled against the wall, waiting.
A minute passed. Four minutes. The rain grew harder, toppling
over her like a wave crashing.

Her car, visible from the entrance to his building, was a better
place to wait. She hurried to it and threw herself into the driver's
side, letting in several buckets of water before slamming the door
behind her. She turned on the engine and flipped the heat to its
max setting as her phone buzzed.

-Why'd you fucking put me on Instagram?
-I did it to help you out. For your benefit. If you'll just talk to
me I'll explain.
-Fucking take it down.
-Can you just come let me in? I'll explain.
-Take it down!!! There's nothing to discuss. I don't want to be
in a photo on your Insta. I want nothing to do with you. Leave
me alone.

Stayja's phone rested on the steering wheel, and the rain pounded
against the windshield as the meaning of his words sank in.

He was ashamed of her.

He'd always been. It was why he'd never invited her to anything, any parties. Had never introduced her to any of his friends.

It was her teeth or her clothes or her grammar or the fact that she was a barista. Whatever it was—he thought she wasn't good enough.

Her whole body quivered despite the hot air blasting. She opened Instagram to delete the post and saw that there was already one comment on it. She clicked on it.

It was from *AStod2017*. It took her a moment to identify the profile.

Annie.

Annie had left a comment with no text, just a single tag—someone named Erika Dipatri.

Before Stayja tapped on the girl's name, she knew who she was. Sure enough—it led her to the account, where she promptly found the post Stayja had refused to read in Annie's presence.

It was a text-only photo. *Believe Survivors,* it read in a white, swirly font on a hot pink background. In the caption below the photo, the girl wrote about being assaulted over fall break in St. John. While she didn't mention Tyler by name, she did say that he was a student at Carter and described his tattoo.

The tattoo of the squares, featured in her own post, alongside his face.

Slowly, horribly, it dawned on Stayja that, in trying to stand up for him, she'd backed up the girl's story.

Her dismay was swiftly followed by a surge of hope—perhaps that was why he'd wanted so desperately for her to delete the post. Perhaps it wasn't the shame of being associated with her but that she'd unknowingly provided identifying information about him.

Then, an unwelcome thought: One person, Annie, having a

misunderstanding was one thing. But two? She didn't know what to believe, didn't know what was true. Staring into her phone screen, she found she couldn't delete the post. She couldn't.

STAYJA DIDN'T KNOW how long she sat. Long enough that she began to wonder if she was going to walk back in to find Frank there, ready to fire her. After his warning about pushing the lengths of her breaks earlier in the semester, she'd known he'd been watching her more closely.

As the rain pounded on the windshield, she reflected on all that had happened recently.

Perhaps she'd been unfair to Nicole, especially if it turned out Nicole was right about Tyler.

But if Nicole had been correct, why hadn't Stayja seen it before? Why had it taken a post by a stranger to make her suspicious of him?

But no, that wasn't quite right. He'd rejected her. That had also happened. She hadn't been willing even to *look* at the post before that.

Was Stayja so infatuated that she hadn't been able to see what was right in front of her?

But wait, no, she thought, *I didn't have bad experiences with Tyler.* It wasn't crazy behavior to trust someone who hadn't given you a reason not to trust him. She didn't even know Annie Stoddard. Why would she trust someone she'd never met over someone she knew?

The logic applied to Nicole as well: Nicole knew Annie, not Tyler, and so Nicole trusted Annie over Tyler.

And then Stayja had a sinking feeling, a startling realization that squeezed her insides: Nicole had never met Tyler because Stayja was embarrassed of her.

It had been devastating for Stayja to imagine that Tyler had felt this way about her. How must her cousin have felt?

She checked the time. 7:02. She'd been gone from the coffee shop an hour, and Nicole was just getting off.

Hey, you shouldn't wait for the bus in this, she wrote. If you don't have a ride, come take the car. I'm in the lot now.

oh thank christ coming, her cousin wrote back immediately.

I will do better, Stayja thought as she waited. *I'll be a better cousin and friend to Nicole.*

Within seconds Nicole appeared, fuzzy in Stayja's headlights. As she came closer, Stayja saw that Nicole was holding a plastic bag over her head in which she'd cut slits for eyes. She charged through the wind and rain, cutting diagonally across the lot.

Between them, halfway down the lot in the next row of cars, a pair of headlights sprang to life. Its beams swiveled back and forth before settling and growing wider, brighter, taking over Stayja's frame of sight. As the nose of an SUV came into view, she recognized it. Without stopping or slowing, he rolled down his window and began yelling at her, gesturing through the window, shouting words she couldn't hear.

Nicole, meanwhile, was advancing as fast as she could, the plastic over her head blocking her peripheral vision. As she stepped into the beams of the SUV, her leopard coat, jeans, and cherished brown boots were bathed in light.

Stayja called for Nicole to watch out, but the doors were shut, and Nicole couldn't hear her. She opened her door as the screeching of tires tore through the air. For an instant, his window still down, he was rigid, his profile clear enough for Stayja to watch as his face registered panic and determination. Then the dark pane was rising, and he was peeling out of the lot to the sound of Stayja's screams.

Article: Carter Employee Killed in Car Accident on Main Campus

By News Staff

December 12, 2017

At approximately 7:02 p.m. on Monday, December 11, twenty-one-year-old Nicole Rankin, a clerk at the Carter University Book Store hired in August of this year, was killed in the Student Center B lot when she was hit by a vehicle exiting the lot.

Police have not released any information regarding the death, which is under investigation.

Annie

DECEMBER–JANUARY

Are some people made for destruction? Do they move through the world like hurricanes, sweeping up perfectly good lives and smashing them to pieces?

We didn't see it happen, but we heard it. We heard his tires yowl as he braked; we heard his engine revving up; we heard Stayja.

My instinct was to stay away. Without knowing it had anything to do with Tyler, I was paralyzed. It was, I think, the sensation of having no more room in my body for any more trauma.

But reluctantly, with Bea in the lead, I went. I followed her following the sound of the screaming, and when I saw the body and registered who it was, I broke.

We'd only hung out once outside work, but at work she was my friend, irreverent and interesting in a different way than my classmates were. She reminded me a bit of people I'd gone to high school with—she would question authority without pause and could make anything a game. We spent hours rating the hotness of every customer in the bookstore at a given moment.

Suddenly all I had was room to feel.

I called 911. Bea watched as Stayja tried to resuscitate her, doing the motions of CPR without stopping, repeating them over and over and over until the ambulance arrived.

I wanted to help, but I didn't know how to do CPR. Bea looked pained by her helplessness as well.

As the minutes passed and I stood there powerless, I had the strange sensation that I was witnessing a person trying to turn back time. Stayja was thrusting her body at a miracle, desperate to reverse the clock. As if my cells were turning inside out, the molecular makeup of my being began to change.

I'm not saying it "put things in perspective"—that sounds trite and not quite right. I mean that if Tyler Brand had, in forcing his body upon my own, taught me to know *in my flesh* how heartless human beings can be, standing in the rain next to Nicole's cousin as she fought to give away her breath to Nicole brought me back into knowing how hard we can love.

When the EMT arrived and announced what we already knew, Stayja fell back onto her heels, placed her hands over her face, and rocked, choking on her sobs, retching, making sounds I'd never heard a person make. As if she were trying to both hold in the grief and purge it, as if the sadness that had come was both too much and not enough.

It felt almost sacred, the sound of her pain puncturing the night. The most raw stuff that we're made of.

We clean up grief, I know now. Mop it up and stick the dirty bucket in a corner, out of sight. When people ask, we offer polite half smiles and half-truths.

"It continues to be hard at times," we say. Or "It comes in waves."

But the night I watched Stayja, my first real experience observing human grief, there was nothing tidy about it. It was primal. Guttural.

I cried as quietly as I could where I stood, for her and for Nicole and because I was alive.

"DID YOU SEE what they did?" Matty said. "In Wiggins?" He passed his phone to me across the booth. It was the first week back after winter break, and he, Henry, and I were having breakfast at Lloyd's.

A photo of the library lobby showed a banner that read "We <3 Our Carter Family." I scrolled through more photos, these of easels surrounding the banner that held enormous headshots of Carter staff in uniform—dining, maintenance—captioned with facts about them: favorite hobby, favorite vacation destination, favorite book or movie.

The story of Nicole's death—inebriated Carter student recklessly kills an employee—had embodied Carter's evergreen, hot-button issues of alcohol abuse and staff-student relations. Carter had responded with the cringe-worthy display as some sort of effort to seem appreciative of staff. *See? We celebrate you! We don't want you to be killed while at work!*

"Jeez," I said and handed him his phone back, thinking again of Nicole. I'd been back to work only one afternoon since returning to campus, and it was strange being there without her. I hadn't realized I'd come to associate work with laughing because of her. There was no one to laugh with now.

"Did you know Annie's bad-assery made it on local news?" Henry said to Matty, shoveling cheese grits into his mouth. I'd decided to launch a project at Carter called Each Other's Backs, a community for people who'd experienced sexual assault. We would support each other through what Loretta called the "secondary and tertiary trauma" of being expected to go back to everything as usual in the wake of rape, to live life as if it hadn't happened.

"I do because I pitched the story," Matty said.

"You're like the Oprah of rape," Henry said cheerfully as Matty sipped his orange juice. We were fully dating now. We'd spent New Year's together at my parents' (they loved him) and were planning to try to be in the same city over the summer.

Matty pitched forward, coughing. "Please never say something like that again while I'm drinking."

"I'm proud of you," Henry said to me.

"We know," Matty said. "God, you've said it a million times. If you guys get any cuter, I literally can't be friends with you anymore. It's actually off-putting. And I don't mean in a way that I'm jealous of. I mean it's grating, asocial behavior."

"You're just sad to leave us," I said. Matty was only back in town to pack up his dorm room. He was going to spend the spring interning in Hong Kong with the *Financial Times*, and he'd scored a prestigious fellowship to study journalism in Paris in the fall.

"Leave some for me, please?" Matty said, slapping my hand as I finished off a full half of his blueberry pancake.

"I'm not the Oprah of rape," I said, "I just started a thing." Sometimes it was like Henry and Matty had forgotten. They hadn't known Nicole. But still, it was strange for me—to be the only one of the three of us who had and therefore the only one who thought about her.

"Did I tell you guys that before Nicole died, she sent in her cousin's application for med school?"

"Huh?" Matty said, flagging the waiter for more coffee. "You can just apply to med school for someone else? Didn't she have to take the MCAT?"

"This was a college-to-med-school program. She had me proofread the essay so she could apply for her."

"Why didn't the cousin apply herself?" Henry asked, jabbing his fork into a cube of pineapple.

"I think she got nervous or something. I don't know. I just thought it was sweet."

"Did she get in?" Matty said.

"I don't know," I said, picturing Stayja over Nicole's body, giving her breath.

Bea

"I have to take it in January or I get kicked out of my program. I don't have a choice," Bea said.

Bea and Chris faced each other at a small table by the window in a coffee shop off South Campus, two mugs of steaming tea between them. She'd invited him to meet her without telling him the reason. When she told him she wouldn't be going to nationals, he'd been far more upset than she'd expected. For ten minutes, he'd been peppering her with questions. Why? Why couldn't she just change it? Why was this even a thing?

"It's absolutely ridiculous," he said. "No. You aren't going to miss nationals."

She'd avoided telling him what Tyler had said to her a week earlier, the night of the accident. She wasn't sure why, except that in light of a young woman's death, it seemed like a petty thing to whine about.

But she hadn't expected this reaction from him, this much resistance.

"There's something else going on. This does not add up."

"Well, yes. Sort of," she finally said. And then she told him about the Brands' funding her program and how they'd felt attacked.

"So they clamped down, I guess. Maybe they don't care anymore. But no one else cares enough to reverse it. So here we are." He listened quietly. When she finished, he still said nothing.

"Don't piss off rich people is the lesson, I guess," she said, trying to smile. In the week since the horrible accident, Bea had felt numbed by it all, unable or unwilling to feel the devastation that she sensed lay under the surface.

"I don't accept this," Chris said. "We're going to do something about it."

"I don't know what you're going to do," Bea said. "It seems decided."

AND THEN, THAT night, they came—the feelings.

She'd agreed to accompany Early to hip-hop dance class at the gym and was tying on her sneakers—the first time she'd worn them since the night of the accident. She saw a flash of yellow and lifted the shoe. Stuck to the bottom of it was a scrap of caution tape.

"Ready?" Early asked from the door. "Bea?"

Bea crouched next to her bed, one shoe on and one shoe in her hand, weeping.

Early came over and put her arms around Bea from behind.

They stayed like that for a while. Eventually, Bea sat. Early did, too, still behind her, rubbing her back. Bea caught her breath. Her sobbing eased up.

Dr. Friedman. Tyler. The man she thought was her father. She'd been wrong about them all.

"Everyone is different than I thought," she said.

"I'm not," Early said. "I'm just as vain and superficial as you always suspected."

A small laugh escaped from Bea's throat.

SEVERAL HOURS LATER, it was almost midnight, and they lay in their beds, both quietly on their phones, when Early said, "Have you seen this?"

"What?" Bea asked. Early had a habit of asking a question like "have you seen this" without showing you what she was referring to or looking at.

"This petition for you."

"What?" Bea quickly climbed out of bed and joined Early on her bunk. Together they read through it:

Like improv? Like helping out your friends?

Save our beloved C.U.N.T. from the archaic and oppressive grades policy keeping everyone's favorite Bea, Bea Powers, from getting to go to nationals with us!

The petition went on to list one hundred—a hundred!—qualities of Bea's.

Don't like physics? Neither does Bea!

Do like ice cream? So does Bea!

The sheer length was astonishing. It went on for pages. It must have taken Chris all afternoon to write.

"It already has forty-seven signatures," Early said.

Bea's phone buzzed with a text from Chris.

We're on it, he wrote.

Just saw, she responded, then paused, unsure what else to write. She was touched. This must have taken you forever, she finally typed.

It wasn't just me. We all worked on it. Everyone sent in ten things about you. Except Bart. He sent in none because he's a Dick. So Russell wrote twenty.

Bea grinned.

Then: Why does my phone capitalize Dick?

Then: Other people may be rich, but we have what they don't.

What's that? she wrote back. A sense of humor?

People like us, wrote Chris.

"I'm sending it to all of my classes on GroupMe," Early said. "I wish I could sign it twice! Maybe I can."

By the time they turned off the light, the petition had over three hundred signatures. Bea stayed awake deep into the night, her eyes open wide in the darkness, feeling full in spite of everything.

THE NEXT MORNING her final paper was due for Justice, and they'd been directed to hand it in to Dr. Friedman personally. She had not seen or talked to him since he left her the voicemail about the fellowship.

Waiting for the printer to spit out the pages, she reread its final lines on her screen.

In sum, no one wants to lose power. People hold lofty principles of justice close to heart, but when those principles come up against their own lifestyle or status, most people aren't willing to sacrifice so someone else can have a chance. Radical justice, I have learned this semester, isn't all that radical. Because if the arc of the moral universe bends toward justice, even radical justice bends back toward the money.

She'd changed her topic last minute and written it in a heated frenzy.

Stapling the pages together, she felt apprehensive and exhilarated about seeing him face to face. Likely, it would be anticlimactic. He'd say something to try to win her over again, and she'd politely respond. Her paper, she felt, said all she needed to say.

She was putting on her coat to leave when a new email flashed on her screen and caught her eye. At the sight of his name, she gasped. She sat. No, she wasn't imagining it.

She hesitated. Did she really want to read whatever he had to say? Was she ready?

She was.

Dear Bea,

I'm sorry it's taken me so long to write.

I needed time to figure out what to say, what your mother would want me to say.

When you were born, the plan was for both of us to be involved in your life. Neither of us was interested in marriage (to each other), but we both wanted very much to be your parent.

Then I got offered a job in Michigan. This was what changed everything.

If I took it, were we really going to shuttle you back and forth between Boston and Ann Arbor? At first, yes.

But your mother, as you know, was the daughter of divorced parents, and she felt this would be deeply painful for you—having to say goodbye to a parent every other week or month or year. Missing one of us whenever you were with the other.

Your childhood, she believed, would be defined by absence and longing in one direction or the other. This would be the case no matter how smothered in love you were. And this, she felt—and convinced me—would as likely as not be *more* traumatic than the burden of an abstract, faceless absence. That is, of simply never knowing me.

I am not saying it was her decision. It was a mutual one. We agreed.

Was this the right decision?

Do we ever know how to answer that question when it comes to walking away from love?

Your mother actually reached out to me before she died. Strange, I know, given that her passing was so sudden, and I've often wondered about the timing of her correspondence. She emailed me to say that if anything ever happened to her, I had her blessing to contact you.

I didn't reach out, though, because I wasn't sure it was something you would want. Losing a mother is hard enough. I didn't want to add to that the fraught emotional load of a father suddenly emerging and announcing he's known about you all along. (I will say, and I hope you understand, I have not watched you all along. I have not observed your life. This was a selfish decision on my part. If I wasn't going to be involved, it was going to be a clean break. I wasn't going to do that to myself.)

When I heard from you a couple of months ago, I confess that I panicked a bit. My wife knew about you and Phaedra, but only the most basic outline of the story. We hadn't spoken of you or your mother in over nine years, since before we married. Even your mother's death three years ago—I'd kept that from her. I didn't see a reason to bring up something that might be hard for her.

So I put off telling her I'd heard from you because, well, I was afraid. How it would impact our family, our marriage. I was afraid she'd not allow me to write you back. I was afraid she'd make me choose.

Fortunately, this fear was unfounded. That is not the person I married. The other afternoon, at my son Roland's (he's seven now) robot-a-thon (they build robots), there was a long stretch of time during which we were killing time waiting for the kids to finish their projects. I couldn't make excuses any longer. In the corner of a hotel ballroom filled with parents, I told her about your note.

My wife's name is Zuzia. People call her Zuz (like "zuj"). She is eager to meet you, as am I.

This letter is a very long way of saying hello, nice to meet you, and I'm sorry. I hope you will forgive the delay in responding.

We will be celebrating Christmas at our home here in Ann Arbor this year, just the three of us. Do you have holiday plans, and, if not, would you like to join us?

Warmly,
Les Bertrand

Ann Arbor, she thought, was on the way to Portland.

Stayja

DECEMBER AND JANUARY

"The period of shock we all go through is grace," Stayja had read the one and only time she googled "how to recover after someone dies."

For her there was no period of shock—life did not grant her that grace. She knew instantly what had happened. She watched it. She could not undo it. She could not fix it. And it was much, much worse than any feeling, experience, or tragedy she'd ever imagined.

You have your list of things that can happen. Her mom could die. Her aunt. Nicole might do something stupid and wind up in prison. But she never expected to be holding her cousin in her arms as she died, and she never expected that experiencing such a thing would turn life on its head, yanking her out of one universe and into another. This new one didn't contain Nicole, but it didn't contain Stayja either. She might as well be named Jane or Claudia, or, shit, just let people spell it the way they've always wanted to: Stasia.

The stages of grief Stayja encountered were not the kind she'd studied in her Psych class. In the place of denial and anger and bargaining, her grief was physical and paradoxical and impulsive. She developed a flaky red rash on her arms and calves. She lost weight, but her face looked so bloated that Donna kept insisting she must be having an allergic reaction. She became overtaken by an urge to dye her hair pink and spent three hours one night searching the Internet for the best at-home hair dyes.

The only perk of not being the person she was before was that the things she'd cared about before no longer mattered to her.

Maybe that was her grace.

THE FUNERAL WAS dumb. The minister hadn't known Nicole but acted like he did, using words to describe her that didn't come close to the truth. As if anyone who'd known Nicole at all thought she was a "sweet soul."

Chet showed up, destroyed. He couldn't stop telling Stayja how much he had loved her cousin, how she had been everything to him that a woman could be.

"I don't know how I'll go on without her," he said tearfully, so full of heart that Stayja wasn't even tempted to mention his wife.

Adrienne hosted a gathering at her house after the funeral, which Chet attended, whimpering the entire time. LA showed up and thanked Chet for sharing his HBO GO password, which caused Chet to snap out of his mourning just long enough to appear nervous. Then he and LA began discussing possible lawsuits that Nicole's family could bring against the Brands.

"Can you guys not talk about that *right* this second?" Stayja asked after overhearing "wrongful death" and "damages." Chet resumed crying and reminding them how much he'd loved her, and LA told her he'd gotten a job as a manager at Home Depot.

Tyler was being charged with involuntary manslaughter, and his parents had hired some lawyer from DC with a specialty in white-collar defense. The lawyer must have been good, because according to the local paper, Tyler had been released on bail, was finishing up school, and would be graduating with his class. Walking across the goddamn stage and everything.

Meanwhile, Nicole was dead.

A week passed, then another. Stayja hadn't bothered going back to work, and Donna hadn't bothered her about it. Frank hadn't explicitly said she was fired, but she didn't care either way.

It was so devastatingly quiet without Nicole around.

One day in early January, Stayja received a letter from Gibson College informing her that she'd succeeded through the first round of the application cycle and had been invited to interview for the premed track. She was to submit references immediately.

Thank you for applying, and congratulations on making it this far. Following this stage, approximately 80 percent of our interviewees are offered placement in the class.

Even after all that had happened, her first thought was that Tyler had applied for her. It was only after she'd called and requested a copy of her application and recognized the handwriting on the pdf that was emailed back to her that she realized it had been Nicole. Nicole's last gesture of love toward Stayja, and Stayja hadn't even considered it possible that she could have done such a thing.

That evening at dusk, wearing her jacket and scarf and wrapped in a knit throw blanket, Stayja carried a kitchen chair into the yard, eager to get out of the house. In the side yard between their houses, the one she and Nicole had cleared of weed, she sat, looking up. She watched a bright fluff of cloud change from white to yellow to silver to orange to pink, then suddenly go gray and opaque. Dead. The sun hadn't set yet, but it was no longer shining on the cloud, and without it the cloud just looked like a regular rain cloud. The sun's reflection had been the only reason it had looked anything close to brilliant.

That's it, she thought. *I am that cloud. And Nicole was the sun.*

Dear Nicole,

Remember the time when I was ten and you were eight, and we walked out on that frozen lake by Grandma's? More like a pond than a lake. We were by ourselves, and you kept going farther and farther out. I ran back and kept calling you to stop, come back. You kept looking back at me and just laughing. Fucking laughing and laughing. Cracking up at how scared I was. You were having the best time, and I was terrified you were going to crack the ice and fall in.

Sometimes I feel like our whole lives have been a version of that day.

What I never told you, and maybe never really admitted to myself, was that I didn't know how to be like that. I didn't understand how you did it. How you acted so free when we had so much stacked against us.

Do you remember what you said after your settlement money got snatched up by the state? After that stupid snafu with your mom's account? You made a joke. You said, "Well, I can probably find someone else to grab my ass and then fire me."

It was twenty thousand dollars, Nicole.

I think I yelled at you or rolled my eyes. I'm not sure I yelled, but I'm positive I rolled my eyes. I'm also sure I made a show of acting annoyed by your flippant attitude, making sure you knew that I knew the burden of it would fall on me somehow.

But you know what I've realized? You never once asked me for help. You accepted it. But you never asked for it—that was all me.

When you told me you were paying my tax bill, I didn't know what to do. That wasn't how we worked.

Now I look back and see that it was probably, I don't know, sort of threatening maybe. If you were going to start taking care of shit, not only your own shit but mine too, *and* you were the free spirit, where the fuck did that leave me?

I acted embarrassed of you. I'm sorry. I wanted to be more than poor and was scared I wasn't.

You already knew you were.

Stayja

JUST BEFORE NOON on a Saturday in mid-January, Stayja and Donna lay on the couch and in the recliner, respectively, watching *Frasier* when there was a knock at the door. Was it already time for a gas meter reading? Annoyed, Stayja shuffled over in the same gray sweatpants and T-shirt she'd worn for three days. Her socks—Nicole's old ones—were dirty and too big but kept her feet warm. They'd been keeping the heat off at night to save money.

The woman at the door was rich. That was all that really registered when Stayja opened it and saw her there—that she was not the kind of person who showed up in the neighborhood.

"Stayja?" the woman said, pronouncing her name correctly. "May I come in?"

"Who are you?" Stayja asked.

"Kitty Brand," she said. So this was Tyler's mother. "I was hoping to speak with you and your mother."

Stayja expected to feel rage, but she still hadn't actually felt anything since Nicole's memorial service, and she found that this remained the case.

"Come in," she said.

Mrs. Brand followed Stayja inside.

"Mom, this is Tyler's mom," Stayja said. "She wants to talk to us about something." It occurred to Stayja that her old self would have been self-conscious of the stained tan carpet and wood paneling of their house, its low ceilings, and the kitschy objects Donna kept on every surface: ceramic angels and glass gnomes and dusty unlit candles. But now she couldn't bring herself to care.

Donna slowly reached for the remote and turned off the television. Stayja sat back down on the sofa. Mrs. Brand remained standing.

"Your sister preferred not to speak with me. She sent me here to talk to you all instead. I want you to know that we feel absolutely terrible about what happened, and we want to make it better for you however we can."

Donna grunted.

"I know we can't compensate you for your niece's death, but if there is a way to ease some of the burden, we are happy to. We don't feel that it's necessary to involve the courts, because we aren't going to fight you on this. We're good people. And we have the means to help you. So why wouldn't we?"

She seemed to ask this as if she wanted one of them to respond. They didn't. She focused her attention on Stayja.

"For example, Tyler tells me that you are in nursing school. Perhaps we could defray some of the costs."

A light rapping sound drew Stayja's attention. On the windowsill, a squirrel tapped at an acorn. She watched it.

Stayja had questions. If this woman went around cleaning up Tyler's messes, why hadn't she done something sooner? Here she was trying to make things better, but Nicole was already dead.

"You're a poet?" Stayja said.

Mrs. Brand looked surprised.

"I know a lot about your family," Stayja said.

"I see. Well, you have to understand, Tyler isn't always truthful. He gets by on his charm, really. I'm constantly surprised by what he can talk his way out of. He has a knack for bending facts to get what he wants."

"No fucking way," Stayja said sarcastically.

"Not to make excuses, but he's been this way since Max, his dog, died. Max was his lab until he was eleven. Liver cancer. We had no choice but to put him down. Tyler was furious we didn't try chemo. Things changed after that. Truth became a fuzzy thing with him."

Was she suggesting that Tyler's losing his dog explained why he raped people? Why he drove drunk? Why he killed Nicole?

Donna cleared her throat, a signal to Stayja to get back to the offer: *Take the money.*

"So you're not a poet then," Stayja said.

"Oh, I am. I didn't mean he lied about that."

"I tried to find your poems," Stayja said. "I couldn't."

"I write under my maiden name. And my first and middle initials— P. K. Fox." Reading Stayja's stunned expression as confusion, she explained, "Kitty is short for Kathryn, my middle name."

Stayja stared, her arms tingling. What kind of awful coincidence, what cosmic joke—she tried to swallow and couldn't.

She studied the woman. Her white-blonde hair was wild and curly, like her son's, but tamed with product. Her face, smooth for a woman her age, contained other just noticeable traces of plastic surgery—a slight lift at her lips' corners and eyes, an upturned quality to the whole thing. She wore a tailored, fuchsia A-line dress with a thin gold belt. This was not how Stayja had pictured P. K. Fox.

She certainly hadn't pictured her being related to Tyler.

The Brands had ruined her life and also changed her. The Brands were terrible and also the reason she was going to be a doctor. The reason she wanted to stare down the brightest light she could find on earth and not look away.

"Listen, again, I am absolutely not trying to make excuses for my son. But he has had a very difficult fall. I don't know if you know this, but he was falsely accused of sexual assault, and it almost destroyed him. . . . He's not his best self right now. It's just terrible that his poor decision making had to lead to something this tragic."

Falsely accused. As Mrs. Brand spoke, it suddenly struck Stayja that if *she'd* struggled to reconcile Tyler's behavior with who she wanted him to be, what must it be like to be his mom?

She almost pitied her.

"So, we can pay for nursing school?" Mrs. Brand said, reaching into her purse and pulling out a checkbook. "I can write you a check."

What would Nicole do?

"I'm not going to nursing school," Stayja said. Her gaze had drifted to Mrs. Brand's shoes. They were the shade of milky coffee made of what looked like alligator skin, shiny cells of leather.

"You shouldn't make that kind of decision right now, teacup," Donna said to Stayja, her voice taking on a worried urgency.

Stayja, making eye contact with Mrs. Brand, ignored her mother.

"You can pay for medical school."

Epilogue:
Annie

Each Other's Backs became my thing, the project of my college days. Outside of class and orchestra, it was what I spent my time thinking about. I worked with students at other schools to start chapters on their campuses. An Art major named Emma and I came up with a T-shirt design, and within a few years it was worn by thousands of students across the country annually on September 9. My last year at Carter, we incorporated and became a nonprofit. We spread to high schools. I was proud. Through this community, I made friends, found a purpose, and eventually my version of peace.

And yet.

As I look back on my time at Carter—in particular, that fall—I find the phrasing of how it changed me elusive: "Nothing happened to Tyler Brand, but I found my version of peace," Or "I found my version of peace, but nothing happened to Tyler Brand"—with the "but" as ellipsis, as coda.

. . . but I never saw the world in the same way again.

. . . but I still don't understand how injustice is accepted and shrugged off.

. . . but will I ever be free of rage?

The summer after we started dating, Henry and I broke up. We stayed friends, of course. He's Henry. Two years later, after graduating, Matty and I moved to New York, where we shared an apartment in Brooklyn. He got a fact-checking job at the *Daily News*, and I worked in communications at a nonprofit focused on childhood hunger. We afforded our rent by tutoring English on the side, both of us. I learned to squeeze breakfast and lunch out of a single three-dollar bagel. At night we shared seven-dollar bottles of Malbec and binged shows on his laptop, and in the morning we took the R train to our respective stops in Manhattan.

Three years after graduating, I heard from Bea, who was moving to the city to get her master's in Public Health. She said we should have coffee. I wrote back saying I'd love to but never followed up when she asked me to pick the day.

As for Tyler, I heard that he'd been paralyzed in a ski accident in Colorado but didn't confirm it or bother trying. I also heard he was in law school in Houston. Whether that time of my life, and what took place between us, still ripples through him the way it ripples through me is a question I can't answer.

Because that's the thing about these stories—where the "but" falls for the Tyler Brands of the world. Does it sneak into their thoughts, reminding them of who they are or at least of who they once were?

One morning, a few months after we'd moved into our apartment, Matty was running late, so I left without him.

As I swiped my card and passed through the turnstile at the station, I spotted him ahead of me on the platform. He'd beat me.

"Where were you?" he asked. "I thought I'd catch up."

I explained that when we weren't together, I took a different route—down Second Street to Fourth Avenue instead of down Third. It was longer, if only by a little, and it wasn't until I said it that I realized why: I'd once spotted an old college face, a PiKa, on Third.

I didn't say that last part to Matty.

"Why?" he asked. I shrugged as the sound of the R train rumbling into the station drowned out our conversation, preventing me from having to answer. We entered the car, which was near empty for once, and took seats next to each other, sitting close as the train hurtled through the underground tunnels and into the mornings lying ahead of us.

Acknowledgments

This book sold the day I had my first baby. It was surreal and thrilling. I didn't know how to raise a new baby or write a book while raising a new baby. Suddenly life was full of glorious unknowns.

Reader, I will spoil the ending: I wrote the book, and the baby now walks (and sings!). I wrote it in large part by leaning on others. Thank you to my incredible editor, Emily Griffin, and my phenomenal agent, Claire Anderson-Wheeler. Thank you also to my husband, Lucas Richter, my mom, Clista Adkins; and my angels, Rachel Fischer and Rachael Fowler, for lovingly caring for Finn in 2018 while I wrote.

I'm so grateful to my writing community and to my friends who supported this book's genesis in one way or another: Lucas Schaefer, Chandler Phillips, Emily Stirba, Naomi Shatz, Tamara Giwa, Haley Hoffman, Rachel Abramowitz, Kate Tellers, Stephen Ruddy, Gregg Lachow, Sarah Stone, Joselin Linder, Jorge Novoa, Nicole Solomon, Alex DiFrancesco, Jess Mannion, Joanne Solomon, TJ Wells, Gabra Zackman, Katie Beth Ongena, Jack Thomas, Tony Brown, Melissa Feldman, Simone Policano, Christian Probst, Carly Stern, and Niev Mooney.

Finally, to the women of All of the Above at Duke—all the generations of you—I hope you keep owning and sharing each other's stories for years to come.

Loved *Privilege*?

Read on here for an extract of Mary's
novel *When You Read This*.

For four years, Iris Massey worked side by side with PR
maven Smith Simonyi, helping clients perfect their brands.
But Iris has died, taken by terminal illness at only thirty-three.

Adrift without his friend and colleague, Smith is surprised
to discover that in her last six months, Iris created a blog
filled with sharp and often funny musings on the end of a
life not quite fulfilled. She also made one final request: for
Smith to get her posts published as a book. With the help of
his charmingly eager, if overbearingly forthright, new intern
Carl, Smith tackles the task of fulfilling Iris's last wish.

Before he can do so, though, he must get the approval
of Iris's big sister Jade, an haute cuisine chef who's been
knocked sideways by her loss. Each carrying their own
baggage, Smith and Jade end up on a collision course
with their own unresolved pasts and with each other.

SIMONYI BRAND MANAGEMENT
96 Morton Street, 9th Floor
New York, NY 10014

June 18

Dear Mr. Simonyi:

I came upon your company on the Stanford University Employers Forum, on which your firm is listed as a place where Stanford students have had positive internship experiences previously. Grace Wang ('16) wrote that she had a wonderful summer working with you and your colleague Iris. While "wonderful" is rather nebulous and uninformative, her point is well made. I see that you have not posted a fall internship opening, but I am writing to express my interest in interning for you come September.

I am a rising fourth-year with a deep and abiding commitment to public relations and communications work since the wee age of three and a half, at which time I launched my first promotional campaign for a line of children's toys created by my father, Carl Van Snyder Jr. My contribution consisted of conspicuously playing with the toys (which later became the award-winning ToddleGenius™ line) while at day care, in line with my father's at-home demonstrations. ;)

Since that time, I have established a proven track record of promotional success after promotional success. I am the youngest ever member of my fraternity to be elected social chair, and as such, I organized the Palo Alto chapter of the Race Against Alzheimer's this past spring, raising over $100,000 for the organization Don't Forget Us. I am also a Krav Maga black belt, nationally ranked chess player (12–15 age group), and founder of the online magazine *SHAVED*, devoted to topics of personal hygiene and masculinity's fluctuating contours.

I would be thrilled to join Simonyi Brand Management in New York City as a fall intern and am available to begin as early as August 24. Also, I would not require a salary, as this Urban Internship Semester must be in exchange for credit hours only.

My résumé is attached. In an attempt to be thorough, I have declined to be brief. Please let me know if you have a page limit, and I will do my best to trim it down to one (though the font size, of course, may have to decrease, which I'm aware can be a challenge to more mature eyes).

Sincerely,
Carl Van Snyder III

If you want to find out you're dying from a bot, I have a rec-
ommendation: Dr. Hsu at New York Presbyterian delivers death
warrants with the empathy of a salamander.

I should have expected nothing less, given that two weeks
ago, he informed me that a CT scan showed lesions on my lungs
by saying "This does not necessarily mean you have cancer."

I explained to Dr. Hsu that telling someone they don't necessarily have cancer is only good news if they already think they
have cancer. For those of us who believe ourselves to be healthy,
the correct phrasing is, "I have some bad news."

He thanked me for the suggestion.

Here's how it happened today. I arrived at the office around
8:30 as usual, before my boss as usual. I was reading news online. NASA reports that 25 million Americans have stockpiled
guns in preparation for doomsday. A man has spent $100,000 on
operations to become a real-life Ken doll. My phone buzzed, and
like that, I have lung cancer.

Dr. Hsu explained that not only are the lesions on my lungs
indicative of cancer, but they also mean that I will probably be
dying soon. He mentioned chemo, trying it, seeing what happens. But my cancer is special. It isn't referred to in stages like
other cancers. It only comes in two varieties: limited and extensive. Mine is the bad kind.

"I want to be honest with you. The prognosis is not good," he
said. I thanked him for his honesty, because that's what you do
when someone bothers to point out they're being honest.

"Death is a fact for us all," he went on, "but yours will most likely come in six months or sooner," like the end of my existence is a gestating baby, or the love of my life. Half a year. Twenty-four weeks. Before summer.

The call was short, just long enough for us to plan for me to go in Wednesday. At some point in the conversation my boss walked in, and I noticed my 98-cent deli coffee had tipped over. The puddle dripped off the desk onto the floor. "WE ARE HERE TO SERVE YOU," the paper cup promised, sideways.

As I told Smith that I have six months to live, I laughed, like it's a joke. Is it?

He hugged me. I can't remember if I hugged back. He smelled like the Ralph Lauren cologne I once bought for Daniel but then gave to him instead, after some fight Daniel and I had, of the dozens or hundreds. *Do you tell ex-fiancés you are dying?* The question flitted through my mind as a matter of etiquette, one my mother would have an answer to. Somewhere, on a shelf in Virginia, there probably is a well-worn book with a paragraph on what courtesy ex-lovers owe one another with regard to announcements of terminal illness.

For Smith's benefit—he looked like he might have a heart attack—I kept talking, explaining the series of increasingly ominous events that led to this morning. First came the chest pains, then the CT scan, the results of which were delayed because of Christmas. Then the biopsy. It felt like someone else was talking about me. The actual Iris had fled. She's already gone.

He asked how long "this" has been going on. I know now that by "this" he was referring to the tests—to my discovery of the disease rather than to the disease, itself. But I misunderstood.

"Who knows?" I said.

I realized on the train home he meant the tests. He meant: *Why didn't you tell me?*

I didn't tell him, of course, because when you tell people things, they treat them as real, and then you have to decide. I had been hoping for the best. I have always been an optimist.

Neither of us knew what one does after being diagnosed with cancer that will probably kill you. Certainly not resume business as usual. So I came back to my apartment, which I'm now regretting. Maybe I'll go back to work. At least then he'd stop texting to ask if I'm okay being alone.

Is that what people do? Avoid being alone with their new cancer? I could call Jade, but I'm sure she's in the kitchen with her cell tucked away in a closet. Using my triannual call to my mom to tell her I have cancer just seems cruel. And I'm not in the mood for the baby mamas (my friends from my early twenties who had babies in our early thirties and then ceased to be capable of talking about anything but their children, so we've drifted. Plus, our friend Sabine, who was the glue keeping us together, moved to California).

Frankly, I'm surprised this site made it to fruition. A year or so ago the founders came to the firm looking for branding assistance in exchange for equity in their "graphic storytelling platform start-up." Todd and . . . Chad? Ethan? According to Ethan/Todd/Chad, both people with terminal illnesses and stay-at-home moms were itching to blog in triangles, arrows, and colorful bar graphs. They had a colorful binder of demographic research on target niches, and Smith had been intrigued, initially (I wasn't—they were both the same shade of too-tan and talked about the future like it was a lottery they'd rigged). They had originally called it a d-log (drawing log, like "vlog"), but that didn't go over well in focus groups. Throughout the presentation,

Smith and I both fought to suppress our laughter. For days afterward, he and I came up with who else might like to make a d-log: geriatric clowns! Racist poets! Disgruntled ghosts!

Now, here I am, a data point come to life. Bravo, Chad. I have a heads-up, a full six-month lead. I get to sit with my impending death over coffee so we can make plans.

Things you don't think about dying, until it's happening: I will break my lease.

I was an assistant while I saved to open a bakery, which never happened. I wanted a family, too, but so much for that. I got skinny then fat then skinny again. I smoked then quit.

She was an admin who got skinny then fat then skinny then died.

Here's the thing I need to figure out. This whole time I thought my real life hadn't started yet. Turns out that was my life. I have six months or so to make that okay, somehow.

COMMENTS (10):

DyingToBlogTeam: Welcome! We see you've already begun sharing. Remember that commenting on other users' Exit Posts will bring more visitors to your own page. Dying to Blog is a community of members facing the same challenge, and we want you to get your Maximum Departure Value™ out of it!

BonnieD: hi I'm Bonnie. I like your blog. u have to use more graphics tho because this is a graphics site and posts that get on the Popular page are never ones like yours. no offense but it looks like a word document. but i stumbled on you and like u so i will follow u anyway.

IrisMassey: Thanks, Bonnie. Do you have a blog on the site?

BonnieD: no. my mom used to be on it.

BonnieD: hers was really good but it moved to the afterlife page.

BonnieD: they have to move them otherwise u'd just have a bunch of corpse blogs and that would be depressing lol

IrisMassey: I'm sorry.

BonnieD: it happens

IrisMassey: Thanks for the tip.

Jan10101010101: buy Viagra buy romaine penis large buy not here thank u for your excellent content

EIGHT MONTHS LATER

Friday, August 28 | Simonyi Brand Management

---

from: smith@simonyi.com
to: rosylady101@yahoo.com
date: Fri, Aug 28 at 10:55 AM
subject: Vandalism of your posters

Dear Rosita,

I got your message. I understand your concern, especially after, as you note, we spent so much time perfecting the subway ad, and I remain grateful for your patience and gracious spirit during the photo shoot—agreed, he wasn't the most professional photographer around (apologies again for the fingernail clipping on-site), and I know you weren't thrilled to learn that I plucked him off of Craigslist, but that says nothing of how much I value you both as a client and as my dentist.

Remember that a year ago, no one knew who you were, because no one knew Paula Abdul had a ghastly mouth as a child. But then we all learned, thanks to that intrepid *Post* reporter, that you built Paula's mouth chair-side. You *made* Paula. It is a phenomenal feat, and one for which I'm glad you're finally receiving the recognition you deserve. Since the news broke, we have done an outstanding job (if I say so myself) harnessing your initial publicity to develop a personal brand. The interviews, the book deal, the additional celeb endorsements. Now that the book's coming out, and our campaign targeting commuters in the region has finally launched, I need to warn you about something:

fame comes at a price. You will have haters. It is inevitable. My clients don't read the comments, don't read the blogs, don't read the tabloids. And in your case, they don't pay attention to a little graffiti on a few subway ads.

We knew (or at least I did, and perhaps should have made more clear) when we decided to place the posters in New York subway stations that they would be vandalized. If you spend much time riding New York City transit, you will notice that no advertisement is immune from the occasional mustache or profane smear. These interactions with the ads, I would suggest, aren't something to bemoan. On the contrary, they enhance the likelihood of people noticing and remembering your smoldering, shimmering grin! Rosita de Santiago, DDS!

This is the time to welcome attention in any form.

You reference with loathing the estimable Dr. Zizmor, New York City's first medical professional to take to in-motion, 2-D campaigning on the trains. Sure, his posters about getting rid of pimples rendered him the target of ridicule. He also now owns a yacht and three houses on two different coasts.

Relatively speaking, I think T-E-E-F-S neatly penned across your five front incisors is fairly innocuous.

Warmly,

Smith S. Simonyi

President

Simonyi Brand Management

Newport Community
Learning & Libraries